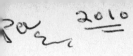

THE OLD MAN AND THE BOY

Grenadine Etching

The Honey Badger

Poor No More

Something of Value

The Old Man's Boy Grows Older

The Old Man
and the Boy

ROBERT RUARK

illustrated with line drawings

BY WALTER DOWER

A Holt Paperback
Henry Holt and Company
New York

Holt Paperbacks
Henry Holt and Company, LLC
Publishers since 1866
175 Fifth Avenue
New York, New York 10010
www.henryholt.com

A Holt Paperback® and 𝖍𝖕® are registered trademarks
of Henry Holt and Company, LLC.

Library of Congress Catalog Card Number: 57-10425

ISBN-13: 978-0-8050-2669-6
ISBN-10: 0-8050-2669-X

Henry Holt books are available for special promotions and
premiums. For details contact: Director, Special Markets.

Originally published in hardcover in 1957 by
Holt, Rinehart and Winston

First Holt Paperbacks Edition 1993

Printed in the United States of America

23   25   24

This book is for the memory of

my grandfathers, Captain Edward Hall Adkins and Hanson

Kelly Ruark; for my father, Robert Chester Ruark, Sr.;

and for all the honorary uncles, black and white,

who took me to raise

AUTHOR'S NOTE

Anybody who reads this book is bound to realize
that I had a real fine time as a kid.

R.R.

Contents

THE OLD MAN AND THE BOY

1

It Takes a Gentleman to Approach
Another Gentleman

The Old Man knows pretty near close to everything. And
mostly he ain't painful with it. What I mean is that he went to
Africa once when he was a kid, and he shot a tiger or two out
in India, or so he says, and he was in a whole mess of wars here
and yonder. But he can still tell you why the quail sleep at
night in a tight circle or why the turkeys always fly uphill.

The Old Man ain't much to look at on the hoof. He's got
big ears that flap out and a scrubby mustache with light yellow
tobacco stains on it. He smokes a crook-stem pipe and he shoots
an old pump gun that looks about as battered as he does. His
pants wrinkle and he spits pretty straight in the way people
used to spit when most grown men chewed Apple tobacco.

The thing I like best about the Old Man is that he's willing to talk about what he knows, and he never talks down to a kid, which is me, who wants to know things. When you are as old as the Old Man, you know a lot of things that you forgot you ever knew, because they've been a part of you so long. You forget that a young'un hasn't had as hard a start on the world as you did, and you don't bother to spread the information around. You forget that other people might be curious about what you already knew and forgot.

Like the other day when we called the dogs and the Old Man and I went out into the woods to see if there were any quail around. Turned out there were some quail around. Pete, who is the pointer, whirled around like he was crazy, and then he stuck his tail straight up in the air and settled down in a corner of the peafield as if he planned to spend the winter.

"I ain't shooting much these days," the Old Man said. "You'd better do it for me. Take my gun, and walk in past Pete now. Walk gentle, kick up the birds without making the dog nervous, and let's us see can you get one bird. Don't worry about the second bird. Just concentrate on the first one. You got to kill the first one before you can shoot the second one. It's what we call a rule of thumb. Suppose you try it to see if it works."

I walked in past Pete, and the birds came up like rockets on the Fourth, and I did what most people do at first. I shot at all of them, all at the same time. I fired both barrels and nothing dropped. At all.

I looked at the Old Man, and he looked back at me, kind of sorrowful. He shook his head, reached for his pipe, and made a great to-do about tamping down the tobacco and lighting it with a kitchen match.

"Son," he said, "I missed a lot of birds in my time, and I will miss some more if I shoot at enough of them. But there is one thing I know that you might as well learn now. Nobody can kill the whole covey—not even if they shoot the birds on the ground running down a row in a cornfield. You got to shoot them one at a time."

The Old Man said we ought to give the dogs a little more

time, because the birds wouldn't be moving as singles the very moment they hit and they left most of their body scent up in the air, anyhow; so why didn't we sit while he smoked his pipe and then we would go put up the singles. The Old Man said he didn't know what I would be when I grew up, and didn't care a lot, but he said I might as well learn to respect quail, if only for practice in the respect of people.

This little bobwhite, the Old Man told me, was a gentleman, and you had to approach him as gentleman to gentleman. You had to cherish him and look after him and make him very important in his own right, because there weren't many of him around and he was worthy of respectful shooting. The way you handled quail sort of kicked back on you.

Figure it this way, the Old Man said. A covey of quail is a member of your family. You treat it right, and it stays there with you for all the years you live. It works in and around your garden, and it eats the bugs and it whistles every evening and cheers you up. It keeps your dogs happy, because they've got something to play with; and when you shoot it you shoot it just so many, and then you don't shoot it any more that year, because you got to leave some seed birds to breed you a new covey for next year. There ain't nothing as nice as taking the gun down off the hook and calling up the dogs and going out to look for a covey of quail you got a real good chance to find, the Old Man said. The little fellow doesn't weigh but about five ounces, but every ounce of him is pure class. He's smart as a whip, and every time you go up against him you're proving something about yourself.

I never knew a man that hunted quail that didn't come out of it a little politer by comparison, the Old Man said. Associating with gentlemen can't hurt you. If you intend to hunt quail, you have to keep remembering things—like, well, like you can't shoot rabbits in front of the dog, or you'll take his mind off the quail.

And then you have to worry about the dogs some, too. A dog that won't backstand a point—"honor it" is the word—a dog that won't concede to another dog is a useless dog, and you might as well shoot him. One of the troubles with the world is that everybody is crowding and pushing and shoving, and if your dog hasn't got any manners he hasn't got any real right to be a dog.

The same way with a dog that chases rabbits. If he's a hound, let him go chase rabbits. But a setter dog or a pointer dog hasn't got any right to indulge himself in chasing rabbits. It is what the people in Washington call a nonessential luxury. A dog or a man has got to do what he has got to do to earn his keep, and he has got to do it right.

The Old Man smiled and sucked at his pipe. "I mind well a little setter bitch named Lou," he said. "Belonged to an old friend of mine named Joe Hesketh. She was about as dumb a bitch as ever I saw in the field. But she was loyal. She was real loyal. She was a backstanding kind of bitch.

"Joe's real bird-finding dog was a big old Gordon setter who was as black as your hat. He was named Jet. He looked like a charred stump when he pointed a bird. He was as stanch as a stump and as black as a stump. So Lou spent her whole life pointing stumps. You would walk through the broom grass in the savannas, and there was poor old Lou, froze solid on a burnt stump. There wasn't much Lou could do except backstand, but that was the backstandingest bitch I ever saw. She made a career out of it and never got to hate it. Her eyes failed her finally, and she got killed. She backstood a fireplug in the middle of a busy street, and she wouldn't break her point for an automobile that was coming along in a hurry."

The Old Man smiled some more, in the gentle, evil way he had, and made a new essay for himself.

"Fellow can learn a lot about living from watching dogs," he said. "Like about snakes and terrapins. The best bird dog in the world will point a terrapin, and he will point a snake. But he won't back off from a terrapin. He will point a snake and walk backward away from it. This is what the dog would call a public service. But when a good bird dog points a rabbit, he cocks his ears peculiar and looks over his shoulder at you with a real guilty look, like he was stealing an apple from the fruit-stand, and you know he expects a licking. He knows. He knows it just as he knows it when he gets himself all roused up and runs through a covey of birds. Or when he hard-mouths a dead bird when he knows it's wrong. Never underestimate a dog. If he's got sense enough to be bred from a family with a nose and a sense of decency, any mistake you let him make is *your* fault."

The Old Man said that he had kind of gotten off the subject of quail, which is a way he has of explaining that even an old man can get wrought up, and then he came back to the original subject. He said that any man with brains would never change a covey of quail from the original acre that they loved to live in.

The quail is a member of the family, the Old Man said again. He expects to get fed, like any other member of the family. So you plant him some field peas or some ground peas or some lespedeza or something, and you leave it there for him to eat. You plant it close to a place he can fly to hide in. A bobwhite is pretty well set in his habits. He will walk off from where he roosted, but he likes to fly home. It is a damned shame, the Old Man said, that the human race wouldn't take a tip from this.

But there is a stupid thing about quail like there is about people, the Old Man said. He won't let well enough alone. He starts a war and puts himself out of business just like we do, which is why we have wars and famines and even game laws, which I am basically in favor of, because they keep people and birds careful. If you don't lay the law of sound economics on a quail bird, he will start fights in the family and inbreed himself, and eventually he will kill himself off. The cock birds fight and the hen birds cannibalize the eggs, and all of a sudden where you had birds there ain't any.

This is no good for anybody, including the birds, the bugs, and you. Not to mention the dogs. So you shoot 'em down to a reasonable minimum each year. Let's say there is a covey of twenty. You shoot 'em down to half. The foxes will get some and wild tame-cats will get some more, and of the two clutches they try to hatch that year the weather will get one. But if you cherish 'em enough and don't get greedy, you can keep them in the back yard forever.

Just before I met your grandmother, the Old Man said, I dug into a place down South and I was interested in dogs. I lived there thirty years, and I trained all the dogs that I owned on the same covey of birds in the same back yard. While I trained the dogs I trained some young'uns, too.

This used to be called *laissez faire* by the French. I trained the birds to stay close to the house. I trained the dogs to be polite to the birds in the nesting season. I trained the children to be polite to the dogs while the dogs were being polite to the birds. I never shot over these birds more than three times a year, and I never shot more than three out of the covey at once. And I never shot the covey down to less than 50 per cent. And I planted the food for them all the time, the Old Man said. They were guests in the house, so to speak.

There's a lot I could tell you about birds, the Old Man said, but I find I'm talking too much lately. If you can remember to take your time and never shoot at the whole covey, if you can remember to keep them fed right, and if you can remember to make your dogs respect the birds—well, hell, the Old Man said, what I just delivered was a sermon about respect. I might say that it will cover most situations, whether it's bobwhite, dogs, or people.

"This ain't a very expensive gun," the Old Man said. "It's not a handmade gun, and it hasn't got any fancy engraving on it. But it'll shoot where you hold her, and if you hold her true she'll kill what you're aiming at. Some day when you go to work and get rich, you can take a trip to England and buy yourself a set of matched doubles, or you can get a special job built in this country with a lot of gold birds dogs on it. But for you to learn to shoot with, this is all the gun you need right now."

It was maybe the most beautiful gun a boy ever had, especially if he was only eight years old at the time and the Old Man had decided he could be trusted with a dangerous firearm. A little 20-gauge, it was only a twenty-dollar gun, but twenty dollars was a lot of money in those days and you could buy an awful lot with it.

The Old Man stuffed his pipe and stuck it under his mustache, and sort of cocked his big stick-out ears at me, like a setter dog looking at a rabbit he ain't supposed to recognize socially.

"In a minute," he said, "I aim to whistle up the dogs and let you use this thing the best way you can. But before we go out to the woods I want to tell you one thing: you have got my reputation in your hands right now. Your mother thinks I'm a damned old idiot to give a shirt-tail boy a gun that is just about as tall as the boy is. I told her I'd be personally responsible for you and the gun and the way you use it. I told her that any time a boy is ready to learn about guns is the time he's ready, no matter how young he is, and you can't start too young to learn how to be careful. What you got in your hands is a dangerous weapon. It can kill you, or kill me, or kill a dog. You always got to remember that when the gun is loaded it makes a potential killer out of the man that's handling it. Don't you ever forget it."

I said I wouldn't forget it. I never did forget it.

The Old Man put on his hat and whistled for Frank and Sandy. We walked out back of the house where the tame covey was. It was a nice November day, with the sun warm and the breeze not too stiff, and still some gold and red left in the leaves. We came to a fence, a low barbed-wire fence, and I climbed it, holding the gun high up with one hand and gripping the fence post with the other. I was halfway over when the barbed wire sort of caught in the crotch of my pants and the Old Man hollered.

"Whoa!" the Old Man said. "Now, ain't you a silly sight, stuck on a bob-wire fence with a gun waving around in the breeze and one foot in the air and the other foot on a piece of limber wire?"

"I guess I am, at that," I said.

"I'm going to be pretty naggy at you for a while," the Old Man said. "When you do it wrong, I'm going to call you. I know you haven't loaded the gun yet, and that no matter what happens nobody is going to get shot because you decide to climb a fence with a gun in your hand. But if you make a habit out of it, some day you'll climb one with the loads in the gun and your foot'll slip and the trigger'll catch in the bob-wire and the gun'll go off and shoot you or me or somebody else, and then it'll be too late to be sorry.

"There's a lot of fences around woods and fields," he said. "You'll be crossing fences for the rest of your life. You might as well start now to do it right. When you climb a fence, you lay the gun on the ground, under the fence, with the safety on, ten foot away from where you intend to cross the fence. You got the muzzle sticking in the opposite direction from where you're going. After you've crossed the fence you go back and pick up the gun, and look at it to see if the safety is still on. You make a habit of this, too. It don't cost nothing to look once in a while and see if the safety's on."

We walked on for a spell until we hit the corner of the cornfield. Old Sandy, the lemon-and-white setter, was sailing around with his nose in the air, taking the outside edge, and Frank, who was pretty old and slow, was making some serious game with his nose on the ground. In a minute Sandy got a message and went off at a dead gallop. He pulled up in full stride and froze by a clump of gallberry bushes. Frank picked up a little speed on the trail and headed up to Sandy. He raised his head once and saw Sandy on the point and stood him stiff and pretty. Maybe you've seen prettier pictures. I haven't.

"Can I really shoot it now?" I said.

"Load her up," the Old Man said. "Then walk in, and when the birds get up pick out one and shoot him."

I loaded and walked up to the dogs and slipped off the safety catch. It made a little click that you could hardly hear. But the Old Man heard it.

"Whoa," he said. "Give me the gun."

I was mystified and my feelings were hurt, because it was *my* gun. The Old Man had given it to me, and now he was taking it away from me. He switched his pipe to the outboard corner of his mustache and walked in behind the dogs. He wasn't looking at the ground where the birds were. He was looking straight ahead of him, with the gun held across his body at a 45-degree angle. The birds got up, and the Old Man jumped the gun up. As it came up his thumb flicked the safety off and the gun came smooth up under his chin and he seemed to fire the second it got there. About twenty-five yards out a bird dropped in a shower of feathers.

"Fetch," the Old Man said, unloading the other shell.

"Why'd you take the gun away from me?" I yelled. I was mad as a wet hen. "Dammit, it's my gun. It ain't your gun."

"You ain't old enough to cuss yet," the Old Man said. "Cussing is a prerogative for adults. You got to earn the right to cuss, like you got to earn the right to do most things. Cussing is for emphasis. When every other word is a swear word it just gets to be dull and don't mean anything any more. I'll tell you why I took the gun away from you. You'll never forget it, will you?"

"You bet I won't forget it," I said, still mad and about to cry.

"I told you I was going to nag you some, if only to satisfy your mother. This is part of the course. You'll never walk into a covey of birds or anything else any more without remembering the day I took your new gun away from you."

"I don't even know why you took it," I said. "What'd I do wrong then?"

"Safety catch," he said. "No reason in the world for a man to go blundering around with the catch off his gun. You don't know the birds are going to get up where the dog says they are. Maybe they're running on you. So the dog breaks point and

you stumble along behind him and fall in a hole or trip over a
rock and the gun goes off—blooey."

"You got to take it off some time if you're planning to shoot
something," I said.

"Habit is a wonderful thing," the Old Man said. "It's just
as easy to form good ones as it is to make bad ones. Once they're
made, they stick. There's no earthly use of slipping the safety
off a gun until you're figuring to shoot it. There's plenty of time
to slip it off while she's coming to your shoulder after the birds
are up. Shooting a shotgun is all reflexes, anyhow.

"The way you shoot it is simply this: You carry her across
your body, pointing away from the man you're shooting with.
You look straight ahead. When the birds get up, you look at
a bird. Then your reflexes work. The gun comes up under your
eye, and while it's coming up your thumb slips the safety and
your finger goes to the trigger, and when your eye's on the bird
and your finger's on the trigger the gun just goes off and the
bird drops. It is every bit as simple as that if you start at it
right. Try it a few times and snap her dry at a pine cone or
something."

I threw the gun up and snapped. The gun went off with a
horrid roar and scared me so bad I dropped it on the ground.

"Uh huh," the Old Man said sarcastically. "I thought you
might have enough savvy to check the breech and see if she was
loaded before you dry-fired her. If you had, you'd have seen that
I slipped that shell back when you weren't looking. You mighta
shot me or one of the dogs, just taking things for granted."

That ended the first lesson. I'm a lot older now, of course,
but I never forgot the Old Man taking the gun away and then
palming that shell and slipping it back in the gun to teach me
caution. All the words in the world wouldn't have equaled the
object lesson he taught me just by those two or three things.
And he said another thing as we went back to the house: "The
older you get, the carefuller you'll be. When you're as old as I
am, you'll be so scared of a firearm that every young man you

know will call you a damned old maid. But damned old maids don't shoot the heads off their friends in duck blinds or fire blind into a bush where a deer walked in and then go pick up their best buddy with a hole in his chest."

We went back to the house and up to the Old Man's room. He stirred up the fire and reached into a closet and brought out a bottle of old corn liquor. He poured himself half a glassful and sipped at it. He smacked his lips.

"Long as we're on the subject," he said, "when you get bigger, I suppose you'll start to smoke and drink this stuff. Most people do. You might remember that nobody ever got hurt with a gun if he saved his drinking for the fireside after the day's hunt was over, with the guns cleaned and in a rack or in a case. I notice you ain't broken your gun yet, let alone clean it, and it's standing in a corner for a child to get ahold of or a dog to knock over. I suggest you clean her now. That way you know there aren't any shells left in her. That way she don't rust. And since you have to break her to clean her, you might as well put her in her case."

Maybe you think the Old Man was cranky, because I did then, but I don't any more. I've seen just about everything happen with a gun. One fellow I know used to stand like Dan'l Boone with his hands crossed on the muzzle of his shotgun, and one day something mysterious happened and the gun went off and now he hasn't got any hands any more, which makes it inconvenient for him.

I've seen drunks messing with "unloaded" guns and the guns go off in the house, sobering everybody up. An automatic went crazy on me in a duck blind one day and fired every shot in its magazine. Habit had the gun pointed away from the other fellow, or I'd of shot his head off with a gun that was leaping like a crazy fire hose. I saw a man shoot his foot nearly off with a rifle he thought he'd ejected all the cartridges out of. I saw another man on a deer hunt fire into a bush a buck went into and make a widow out of his best friend's wife.

The Old Man nagged at me and hacked at me for about three years. One time I forgot and climbed a fence with a loaded gun, and he took a stick to me.

"You ain't too big to be beat," he said, "if you ain't adult enough to remember what I told you about guns and fences. This'll hurt your feelings, even if it don't hurt your hide."

When I was eleven, the Old Man stole my little 20-gauge from me. He grinned sort of evilly and announced that he was an Indian giver in the best and strongest sense. I was puzzled, but not very, because the Old Man was a curious cuss and a kind of devious mover. I went back to my bedroom later, and on the bed was a 16-gauge double with a leather case that had my name on it. There were engravings of quail and dogs in silver on the sides and my name on the silver butt plate.

The Old Man was taking a drink for his nervous stomach when I busted into his room with the new gun clutched in my hands. He grinned over the glass.

"That there's your graduation present," he said. "It's been three years since we started this business, and you ain't shot me, you, or the dogs. I figure it's safe to turn you loose now. But I'll take that one away from you if you get too big for your britches and start waving it around careless."

I'm big enough to cuss now, and I've seen a lot of silly damned fools misusing guns and scaring the daylights out of careful people. But they never had the Old Man for a tutor. Some people ain't as lucky as other people.

2

A Walk in the Woods

It was the kind of day when a walk seems necessary, and the Old Man and I just sort of fell into step and started out for the woods without much plan or purpose. It's nice to just walk if you aren't going any place in particular or in a hurry, and we weren't particular or in a hurry. We weren't looking for anything special, either.

"It's a real funny thing," the Old Man said as we traced the river around to where you either have to swim or cut across high in the sandy hills. "A man can spend his life with his eyes open and never see a dingdong thing. Most people just stumble through this foolish business called life, bright-eyed and bushy-tailed, but when the old boy upstairs whacks you with the scythe you ain't seen anything much. I thought we'd spend some part of this summer getting you accustomed to seeing things instead of just registering them and forgetting them, like a damn camera."

We heard some chittering high in a tree and stepped quietly around it on the pine needles. Two squirrels were chasing each other happily back and forth on the branches, disregarding the strangers at the foot of the tree.

"Whoa," the Old Man said. "Let me read you a little lecture on love and its evil effects on things in general. That's a girl squirrel and a boy squirrel up there. They are squirrels in love, for this is the time of year for it. Look at 'em cavort. In the fall when the leaves come off, one would be flattened on the oppo-site side of the tree and t'other would already have departed for other countries.

"But not now. Love has come to the squirrel kingdom, and they don't care anything about anything but whatever a squirrel thinks about when he's in love. I'm not going to shoot 'em, but you could bag the pair with a slingshot and they wouldn't know what hit 'em. This is known as losing your head over a lady, which is fatal whether you're a squirrel or a boy."

"Yessir," I said.

When the Old Man has an attack of philosophy coming on, all you can do is hold still and listen. This was one of the philosophical days. We sat down quietly and observed the squirrels at play.

The Old Man fired up his pipe and ran his fingers over his tobacco-stained mustache. Squirrels, he said, were always a puzzle to him. Some were red and some were gray, and some were cat squirrels and the big black-and-gray ones were fox squirrels, as big as a tabby cat and with teeth like a beaver.

"I try to figure out what God had in mind," he said, "when He made all the different kind of things, and I can't for the life of me decide why He made so many different kinds of squirrels. It seems to me that if you were just going to make squirrels you'd cut 'em all to the same mold and forget the whole busi-ness. But He made a lot of little people and big people and people of all sorts of colors and languages; so I guess He just had to balance off with squirrels. With everything you see it's the same. All kinds of sharks. All kinds of deer and quail and rabbits and people. Puzzles me some. Look there!"

He jerked his gnarled thumb up to where the squirrels were playing and a new boy came on the scene. He was a dirty off-white cat squirrel, an albino. He leaped down on the limb, his bushy tail waving, and almost immediately the fun stopped. Three squirrels—the male and female and another male—took out after the white squirrel. They snarled in a squirrelly fashion, and the big male bit him. He let out a loud *chirr* and took off through the tree tops, all three of the other squirrels chasing him and sort of growling.

"Never saw that before," the Old Man remarked casually. "Seen a lot of strange color variations in a lot of animals, but never saw an albino squirrel before. But did you notice how all three of the other ones lit out after him? You know why?"

"No, sir," I said.

"It was because he was different," the Old Man answered. "The Lord played a trick on him and made him white, when all the other squirrels you know are red, gray, or black. He's a curiosity in the squirrel world. All the other squirrels look at him and say to each other, 'What's this, a white squirrel? Must be a foreigner.' And then they light out after him. Must be tough, being a white squirrel. Every squirrel's hand against him. I suppose after he's run away enough, if somebody don't kill him, he'll wish he was born an alligator or a turtle or something, instead of a squirrel with bad luck enough to be born a strange color."

I was beginning to get tired of squirrels. I wanted a little more action and a little less philosophy.

"Let's go get the car," I said, "and go on over to Caswell and spend the night in the shack. The moon's about right for the turtles to be laying, isn't it?"

"I surmise so," the Old Man said. "I think that's a very good idea. Sea turtles can be very interesting, especially when the moon is nigh full and the old girl comes up to bury her eggs in the sand. You never saw that, did you?"

"No, sir," I said. "You always said you were going to take me on a turtle hunt, but you never did. Can we go now?"

"Sure," the Old Man said. "Let's go crank up the Liz."

We had a little shack over on Caswell, which is a big island. Not much of a shack. Just a one-roomer made out of rough boards and tar paper, but it had a sloppy kind of makeshift kitchen built off the big room and enough space above the big room to sleep a whole squad of people if they didn't mind roughing it under the eaves. It was right on the beach, and the waves lapped up to the front door. I loved going over there, whether it was fishing or poaching the squirrels that lived on the Government part or just hearing the ocean. Lots of times I'd seen the big herringbone tracks the turtles made when they came up to lay, but I never was lucky enough to see one of the turtles laying.

Lots of people don't like turtle eggs, because there's no way you can cook them long enough to get the whites to solidify and they wind up kind of gooey. But I like 'em. The way you eat 'em is to boil them about five minutes until the yolk gets hard, and then you pinch off the top of the leathery skin, shove a little butter and pepper and salt on top, and then squeeze the bottom. That's where the dimple is, the dimple you can't ever iron out of the egg. It tastes remarkable fine that way if you don't think too hard about the white.

Once in a while the Old Man had fetched home a mess from somebody who had caught a turtle in the process of laying them, and he educated me into not being afraid to eat things that ain't quite as pretty as steak or cake. He said he didn't have any patience whatsoever with people who wouldn't eat oysters or snails or suchlike truck just because they were a little off the beaten track.

We drove over slow to Caswell and stirred up a pretty simple dinner, and while the Old Man was messing around with the kerosene stove I peeled off my pants and took a swim. The Old

Man had the finishing touches on the food when I came out of the ocean, and was muttering to himself. He was muttering about how men were always better cooks than women, because they didn't fuss about it and were content to cook a couple of things and not go around fretting about six or seven courses. As usual, it was ham and eggs. The Old Man says that when God made hens and pigs He could have quit right there, because ham, eggs, and hominy are all a man needs to sustain life.

We ate and went out in front of the little shack to watch the moon rise, and pretty soon up she came out of the ocean. The Old Man said he reckoned that it wasn't Venus who came out of the ocean at all, for the Greeks to look at, but it was probably one drunk Greek watching the moon rise and he got it all mixed up with women.

"And I might as well educate you right now," the Old Man remarked. "Don't ever let me hear you calling her the Venus de Milo. Her name was Aphrodite, and she came from the Greek island of Melos. Venus is Roman and Milo is in Italy, and the word *de* is French. It's remarkable how much inaccuracy can come down through the ages."

The moon was tilting a little higher before the Old Man finished with a lecture on the Greeks and the Romans and historians in general, and was starting on the Egyptians and the pyramids when we decided to go look for a turtle. I was barefoot, walking in the firm, grainy, cold, wet sand down close to where the waves were lapping, and the night was so bright that you could have read a book. I didn't mention this to the Old Man, because he would probably have sent me off to find a book, just to see if I was exaggerating.

There's something pretty wonderful about a beach in the nighttime, with nobody around to make a lot of noises, and the gulls crying quiet, and the waves lapping soft and contented on the shore. I walked along looking for turtle tracks, and I got to thinking sort of like the Old Man. When God made water and mountains, I thought, He sure knew what He was doing.

We only walked about a mile when we came on some fresh turtle tracks. The flipper marks were still crumbly on the sand, and there were no other marks leading back down to the ocean. We followed the tracks—as easy as following a tractor—and came to where the dunes started, where the sea oats quit growing, and there she was. She was durn near as big as the dining room table.

She had dug a deep hole and had let down a sort of tube for the eggs to fall out of. The hole was dug big at the bottom and little at the top. She had it about half-filled with the eggs, which were dropping out of her at a rate of about six a minute. She had a big curved nose that made her look like an old parrot, and her half-filmed-over eyes were full of tears. I don't know why a turtle weeps when she lays her eggs, unless it's because it hurts. But she cries like a wife who's mad at her husband and wants to make a point of it.

Turtles are real peculiar critters. The male, they say, is a lot smaller than the female, and he never, ever comes out of the ocean. He lives there and they breed there, and when the mama's ready to lay her eggs she comes out of the sea, crawls painfully up the beach, and digs herself a hole. Then she drops those eggs out of a tube, and when she's through she covers up the hole and toddles off back into the sea. The sun warms the eggs and hatches them, and when the little turtles bust out of the leathery shells they head straight for the water. I'd think that even a turtle would want to hang around and see what her kids looked like, but evidently they're not curious.

While Aphrodite (I named her this, to show the Old Man I hadn't forgotten his lecture) was weeping and laying her eggs I looked her over. She was about six feet long and four feet wide in the shell, and she had busted barnacles on her as big as soup plates. And a lot of moss, like an old piling that's been in the water a long time. I asked the Old Man how old he figured she was, and he said he didn't know, but from the look of her she was older than Grandma.

She finally finished her chores and covered up the hole,

swinging her flippers like a bulldozer shoving earth, and when she had it tamped down she headed for the sea.

"Ride her," the Old Man said, "like that other mythological character that rode the bull out to sea and never come home."

I rode her. I climbed on her back and she wobbled down to the water. I stayed on her back until she started to swim and to head for deep water. Then I went back and we dug open the hole and counted the eggs. There was 137, a little bigger than big walnuts and each one with the same little dimple.

"We'll just take a couple of dozen," the Old Man said. "Leave the rest to hatch into turtles. Would be a shame to make the old girl do all that work for nothing. We'll have 'em for breakfast tomorrow, and try to come back when the little ones hatch, but cuss me if I know how long it takes for a turtle to get itself borned."

We walked home slow in the moonlight, with my cap full of new turtle eggs and nobody talking. When we went to bed, with the surf booming and the gulls screaming and the moon still high, I fell asleep thinking that I could have stayed home and gone to the movies, and I was awful glad I hadn't.

3

A Duck Looks Different
to Another Duck

It was one of those November weeks when the skies were about the color of putty and the wind bored holes in you, and even down South there was a little feeling of snow in the air. The clouds were very low and the gray river was chopping straight up and down. One night after supper the Old Man checked his barometer and said it was dropping some.

"I guess you don't know much about ducks," he said. "Tomorrow looks like it's going to be real nasty. Some sleet and mebbe a little snow flurry. Stiff north wind and a choppy river. They'll be flying, and they'll be flying low. Maybe we better get up early and break you in on ducks, now you're a quail expert."

The Old Man grinned at me and I grinned back. I was a very

chesty young fellow since yesterday afternoon. It was the first time I had ever got a limit on quail. It had been one of those wet days with the birds holding good for the dogs and the singles scattering just right in the broom grass. I was shooting the new 16-gauge double the Old Man had given me and taking my time. I got two sets of doubles on the covey rises and only missed with both barrels once. When I shot the fifteenth bird, even the dogs looked pleased, but they didn't look as pleased as I did.

"Just because you know about this quail business now," the Old Man said, "don't go thinking that the same thing applies to ducks. Quail are reflexes, like I told you. There isn't time to do any figuring. But ducks are ballistics."

"What's a ballistic?" I asked him.

The Old Man had a lot of big words he liked to spring with no explanation, just waiting for me to ask him. He said curiosity was necessary to intelligence, and that curiosity never killed the cat. The cat died from stupidity, he said, or mebbe an overdose of mice.

"A ballistic," he said, "is sort of hard to explain. Let's see can I. Suppose you take the speed of a bird and the angle of flight and the speed of wind and the direction of the wind and the height of the bird and the size of the shot pattern and the speed of the shot or the strength of the powder, and then you grind them all up in one mill and the right answer comes out. Maybe that ain't the book definition, but it's my definition. I can explain it easier to you after you've missed a few ducks."

We got up the next morning away before dawn, and it was so cold your breath was standing out in front of you and your ears felt like they'd drop off if anybody touched 'em. Getting out of that warm bed and into ice-cold long drawers and into your pants and your ice-cold hip boots was torture.

When I got downstairs, the Old Man was in the kitchen. He had a fire going in the stove—one of those old, big, square wood burners that lit up rosy when she really got to jumping, and warmed up the room like a furnace. The Old Man had his pipe going, and he was busting some eggs into the skillet over pieces of bread that were already sizzling in bacon fat. He had some strips of fried bacon laid out on a tin plate, and the coffee-pot was talking on the back of the stove.

"Ain't nothing quite as cold as a cold duck hunter," he said, "unless maybe it's a cold, *hungry* duck hunter. You can build a fire in your belly with some hot vittles that'll spread all through you and keep your insides warm even if your ears and hands are cold. I allus say if a man eats a big breakfast he don't have to worry about dinner. Come and git it."

The Old Man laid out the eggs on the fried bread, with the yolks broken and soaked down into and bubbling up from the bread, which wasn't crunchy like toast but was part of the egg and the bacon grease, and he put the bacon strips across the eggs and poured the coffee. We ate about six eggs apiece, and I don't know of anything that tastes as good as eggs cooked that way when it's cold as sin outside but warm inside the room. They don't make that kind of coffee any more, either, coffee percolated in a tin percolator until it's got some body to it and you can smell it all over the house.

After we finished, the Old Man went over to the crockery cookie jar, winked at me, and stole about two dozen of Miss Lottie's yesterday's baking off the top, picked up two apples and two oranges, and made a little package of them. He took down a thermos jug and poured the rest of the coffee in it, and filled a quart milk bottle with water from the pump on the back porch. He put on his mackinaw and his old wool cap with the ear flaps and reached for his pump gun and announced that we were ready to go duckin'.

We walked down through the cold night, with the stars still bright when you could see them through the racing clouds and the little bit of moon just starting to die, down through the dead streets to the river. The roosters were just beginning to crow and the dogs beginning to stir and bark without much heart in it. It was cold down by the river, cold and black.

We went to where the Old Man kept the skiff, and he sent me

up to the bow and then untied her painter and kicked her off the bank. He said he would row her; it kept his circulation up. He said I could row her back when we came home in the sunshine, if there was any to come home in. The breeze was stiff on my back as the Old Man rowed the skiff along, her nose bouncing on the little waves and sending spray up on my neck, the spray standing like dewdrops on the stiff, hairy wool of my mackinaw. But I was warm inside me from the breakfast, just like he said I'd be.

I looked at the back of the Old Man's neck as he hunched his shoulders over the oars, and I could see his big ears standing out from the side of his head and the pipe stuck out of the corner of his mouth and the ends of his mustache blowing in the morning wind. He rowed about two miles, and then he ooched the boat around a corner of marsh grass and rested his oars. "Hand me the push pole," he said as he shipped his oars and stood up.

I reached him the push pole, which I had helped him whittle out of a piece of the toughest hickory I ever laid a barlow knife to. It was just a little limber, and you couldn't break it even if you were strong enough to bend it in a half-circle. We had sanded her down until even the bumps were smooth as glass, with not a splinter to come off in your hand.

The Old Man stood facing me in the back of the skiff, and he shoved her along until we came up into a little, shallow, sweet-water pond, with lily pads on it and all sorts of curious snaky-looking roots growing down into the black mucky bottom, where the push pole roiled up the water and made muddy puffs. The skiff sort of bubbled along on the surface. She was flat-bottomed and didn't draw much, and she just slid along. We went all the way across the pond to a little headland where the grass grew five or six foot high.

"This is as good as any," the Old Man said.

He got out, with his hip boots pulled high and hooked onto his belt with string. He braced his feet and pushed the skiff, with me in it, all the way into the grass. The grass finally jammed her bow, and he wedged her stern in with an oar, the blade sunk down deep into the ooze. "Throw me the decoys," he said.

I threw him the decoys. We didn't have more than a dozen. The Old Man had whittled them out of cork, sitting on the back steps by the fig tree and whittling very carefully. Then he had got some paints and painted them. They didn't look very much like ducks to me. I told him so. He was pretty short when he answered me.

"They look like ducks to a duck," he said. "Trouble with most people is that they always think about everything selfish. You ain't going duck hunting to shoot you. You're going to shoot ducks. From up in the sky these things will look like ducks to a duck."

The Old Man waded out, with decoys strung all over him, hanging from his hands and over his shoulders by the strings with the lead weights on the ends. He started throwing the ducks out sort of haphazard, about twenty-five yards from where I was, with one out there by itself, two or three together in one clump, a couple here and a couple there. All together they made a little half-circle around the point of grass. The wind was blowing from behind us, I noticed, and the decoys were bobbing and dancing on the water, with the wind mostly in their faces.

"Bend them reeds down over the boat so's to cover most of it from the sky," he shouted at me. "Leave us a couple of peep-holes to see through without raising up. I'll be through directly."

I cramped the reeds down so that when I was sitting down you couldn't see there was a boat or a boy in the grass, and made a couple of holes in the front and sat back. The Old Man was wading back now, and it was just coming a little light. The stars were gone, and the clouds had gathered and were very low. The wind had picked up considerable. It seemed to be getting colder.

You could hear the soft brush of the wings in the dark sky,

and occasionally a whistle as some teal passed low, chuckling. A hen mallard quarreled at a passing flock from her feeding place in a mudhole in the marsh, and the drake answered her from away high up in the sky. The rush of the wings was all around us now, and occasionally you could see a small flash of black against the lighter sky. You could hear splashes in the marsh, too, as the mallards began to sit down like motorboats in the pools where the water was shallow.

"How long before——" I started to say to the Old Man, and he cut me off.

"Might's well learn not to talk too much in a duck blind," he said. "Maybe it don't make any difference, but it takes your mind off watching. And four-fifths of shooting ducks is watching. *Shhh.* Sun's beginning to come a little now. It'll be shooting light in a minute. When you start to shoot, do it your way."

There is something about waiting just before dawn in a duck blind that makes you forget everything but the slow passage of time. Seemed to me like it never was going to get light enough to shoot. The whole sky was full of noise, and you could see the long strings of ducks, flying away high, it seemed like, but not very high because you could hear the whistle of their wings. Out on the water the decoys were bumping and rocking and making little noises in the water. One seemed to be standing on its head. Another was looking under its wing. In the half-light they looked an awful lot like ducks now. If I was a duck, I would think they were ducks too, I said to myself.

I forgot it was cold. I was looking through my peephole, trying to see ducks. The red-winged blackbirds had started to sing all over the marsh, and the bitterns began to croak and the marsh hens to rattle and the bullfrogs to growl and the ducks everywhere to quack. There was a hiss in front of us, and a swarm of teal dipped and passed low over the water, to get away, long gone. It was very light now, not even very gray any more, and a little more pink was showing on the horizon.

"You can shoot now," the Old Man said, "whenever you see anything to shoot."

I loaded up my 16-gauge with No. 6's and shoved her nose away from the Old Man, pointing the barrel over the stern. The clouds were dropping even more, and the strings of ducks had lowered in their flight until you could hear the wing beats very plainly. You could see the flicker of light on white bellies as one string wheeled over us.

"Pintails," the Old Man said. "Big ones."

In a minute he reached over and clamped my shoulder with his big, knotted hand. He nodded his head and looked straight ahead. "Mallards," he said. "Coming this way."

I looked and looked and I couldn't see anything, but in a few seconds I made out a string of dots. How he knew what they were or which way they were coming I couldn't say, but they kept getting bigger. They got closer and closer and I tensed up and half-raised my gun, but the Old Man said, "No," just as they wheeled around us and passed to the left. "They'll be back," he said, and began to gurgle and chuckle softly, like mallards do in the mud puddle in the back yard. Then he nodded to the right, and I could see the birds pass. The Old Man now began to cackle like his life depended on it. *"Gack-gack-chuckle-gurgle-gack,"* he was saying around his pipe.

The birds swung and came in to us fast. There were about twenty, with a big greenhead out in front. They set their wings, put on brakes, and, coming low over the water, dropped their feet at the outer edge of the decoys.

"Now," the Old Man said, and I lurched to my feet, bringing the gun up under my chin, with my eyes never off the big greenhead that was coming in for a landing.

As he saw me he turned and went straight up. I covered him and pulled, and he kept going. I pulled again, and he still kept going. I turned to the Old Man, shaking, pale, and sick.

"There'll always be more," the Old Man said.

I was baffled out of my mind and sick to my stomach when the big duck went off and took the other ducks with him. Those big mallards had come roaring into the decoys as though they planned to live there all their lives. The drake was as big as a goose, and so close you could make out all the gray and blue and green and yellow of him. You could see even the close-barred markings on his sides and the blue feathers on his wings, he was that close.

Once again I was wanting to cry, because I felt as if I had let the Old Man down, but then I figured I was a pretty big boy now and big boys that cry generally get their guns taken away from them; so I played it tough.

"Okay," I said. "Okay. I did it wrong again. I missed him clean and I ain't glad, but I musta done something wrong, and you might as well tell me what it was. What was it?"

The Old Man grinned, very happy. He took a lot of time lighting the big redheaded match and shielding it from the breeze as he cupped his hand around the pipe. The Old Man had times when he enjoyed cruelty.

"You did it all right," he told me. "You missed that big duck as clean as a whistle. The reason you missed him was ballistics. You remember yesterday we were talking about ballistics?"

"Yessir," I said. "But I remember that you weren't too sure about ballistics, either. Gimme some more ballistics."

All this time I was thinking: *Damn ballistics! I missed that duck, that duck as big as a turkey, as big as a house, and I don't know why. So now I get a lecture from the Old Man.*

The Old Man snickered a little more. "I think I got this ballistics drawed down to where you can understand it. I got it what they call reduced to its component parts.

"Let's say you are watering the lawn. Your Cousin Roy runs through the back yard and you got the hose in your hand and all of a sudden you would like to wet down your Cousin Roy. He could probably use a bath, but let's don't get personal.

"If the kid is running against the wind and you got a hose in your hand and you want to wet him, you got to do several different things. One, you are pointing the hose. Two, you are figuring the wind. Three, you are figuring how fast is Roy running.

"So you know that a hose will squirt only so far before it bends backward in the wind. You know that Roy can run only so fast. So if you're as smart as I think you are, you point the hose somewhere ahead of Roy, let the wind take the water stream backward, and then let Roy and the stream collide at a point you've already figured out.

"That's duck shooting. That's ballistics. Shot go from a gun like water out of a hose. The duck comes on like Roy is running. The shot goes one way, like the water goes one way. The ducks go one way, like Roy goes one way. And the wind adjusts the relationship between Roy and the water, between the shot and the ducks. Because shot always string out like water from a hose."

The Old Man settled back with that any-questions look. I had one to throw at him. "Sure, that's fine, this hose and Cousin Roy business. But the one I missed a minute ago was coming down fast and going up fast. Gimme one of them ballistics on this, that rule of thumb you're always talking about."

"It's really a shame," the Old Man said. "I hate to spoil you so early, but there was once aponst a time when I shot ducks down in Louisiana with a Cajun guide, and he told me a very wise thing. I will tell you now. When a duck is coming down, you aim at his tail. When a duck is coming up, you aim at his nose. When he is doing either one of those things but crosswise, lead him. Lead him twice as far as you think you need to lead him. That won't be far enough, but you'll probably hit him in the tail and slow him down, anyhow."

"How far is a lead, a real good lead on a duck?" I asked him. "Golly, I mean how can you make a rule out of it?"

"A lead is as far as you can swing a gun ahead of the bird," the Old Man answered. "You'll never be able to lead one far enough, because you can't pull the gun that far ahead of him in the time you've got to do it. There are all sorts of ducks that fly all sorts of speeds. Teal go off on a level line faster than most of the others. But under certain circumstances a mallard will be faster than a teal. Bluebill coming in low give you a bigger ballistic, because they look faster than they are and mostly you are shooting down at them, which means you'll shoot over 'em unless you're careful. Hell," the Old Man said, "I can't tell you how to do it. You just got to miss enough to make you automatic. And there will always be enough for you to miss. Like now. Get down, boy! We got pintails in the breeze!"

The pins came in like pins almost always come in, which is fast and undecided and not wishing to tarry unless somebody asks them. The Old Man asked them, using his pleading pintail voice this time. They swirled in a big circle and slanted low, and then they shot up in a hard, smooth skid from the water they didn't want much of anyhow. I was standing straight up in the boat when they zoomed, and when I shot I was bending backward. The pintail I was pointing at hit the water about the same time I did, because the discharge of the gun sent me tail over tip into the mucky water, mashing the reeds and back-tilting the boat. The Old Man seemed pleased at both results.

"If you can retrieve yourself," he said, "I'll go out and pick up a fine drake that you must have killed by accident. Very fine bird, the pintail. He doesn't cheat, which is more than you can say of some people. He won't eat fish on you, like a mallard will, or even like a canvasback will. And he's the best-looking duck in the business, unless you like 'em loud-colored like the French ducks, the big greenheads."

I climbed, dripping, back into the boat, scraped off some of the awful-smelling ooze, and watched the Old Man retrieve my first duck. Did you look at your first duck, or your first pheasant, real close? Ever see a bull pintail at close range?

Maybe this wasn't a very special pintail, but the gray on him was like a fine herringbone suit, and his belly was white, and the crest on his head was still ruffled. His open eye was white-rimmed, and his head was dull red-golden brown, and his tail was sharp as a dart. He was as big as a mallard and would taste just as sweet, because he was an honest duck that wouldn't cheat on you and go gormandize himself on fish.

And he was *my* pintail, my first duck, my first big duck. Sometime later I might shoot a goose or a wild turkey or almost anything, but this was my first real big duck. I hated to think that he would stiffen up and his glossy feathers would get soggy and his fine open eyes would glaze. A man's first duck is an adventure.

I still didn't know how I had shot him, except that whatever I did sent me backward, overboard. I swore I would try to do better. In the meantime I would admire my pintail. The Old Man stopped my reverie in full bloom.

"If you ain't so caught up in your own importance," he whispered, "you might be interested in the fact that there's a hull passel of mallards about to decoy in your front yard. Maybe you better figger it out for yourself."

I came out of the fog, and there among the decoys were a double dozen mallards, in the water already, two drakes out ahead, swimming into the blind, some brown-flecked hens behind, already chuckling happily and standing on their heads. Some more drakes and some more hens behind them settled down into the decoys as if they'd found friends and relatives with money. I looked at the old boy. He broke a rule and talked.

"There's three or four in line," he said. "If you were hungry, you could loose off at the lot and fill up the boat. But if you're wondering how good you can shoot, I'd recommend that you stand up and holler, 'Shoo!' and see how good you can do. It's up to you, bud."

It seemed that the Old Man was looking very intently at me, and I decided I'd better stand up and holler, "Shoo!" Which is what I did. The two drakes went out of the water in a vertical climb, and I never saw at all what the rest did. My eyes were full of mallard drakes.

I pointed the gun at the first drake's nose, as the Old Man had said. Then I pushed her ahead a couple of feet and pulled on the trigger, and the first drake came down like a sack of meal. The other one had got up high enough and had squared off and was heading for elsewhere. I led him as far as I could and pulled again, and down he came like another sack, and all of a sudden there were two big green-headed, blue-winged, yellow-billed and yellow-footed, curled-tail mallard drakes floating belly up on the pond. And they belonged to me.

"Easy, ain't it?" the Old Man said. "Once you know how, I mean."

"I think it's pretty simple," I agreed. "You make it awful easy the way you say it."

"I wouldn't get awful cocky about it, if I were you," the Old Man warned. "Not just because you got three ducks in the boat and they're all good big ducks. You'll miss a lot of ducks before you get as old as I am. You'll very likely miss some ducks today."

The Old Man was right. Some more pins came in a little later and decoyed to the Old Man's pretty-please talk as tame as bluebills. I made the same shot I had killed the mallards with, and as far as I know I never pulled a feather. Some teal came in and squished down in the decoys, and I led one a mile and he dropped like a rock. I led another the same mile, and he went on to Mexico.

There were a lot of ducks around in those days, and not much of a limit to worry about. The weather got better as the morning wore on. The clouds massed low and solid, keeping the ducks down. The open water was rough and the ducks were looking for the still-water ponds.

I burned powder until my arm was black on the muscle, but I could have shot a 10-gauge off my nose that day and never noticed the difference. The Old Man didn't coach me too much. He would just nod when I killed a hard one and shake his head when I missed an easy one. He didn't shoot anything flying. I had a lot of cripples, and he shot their heads off with his creaky old pump gun. Every time he turned a cripple over he looked sort of sad and disapproving, as if a man shouldn't go around crippling ducks because of the cost of gunpowder.

Along toward the end of the morning, when the ducks stopped about nine-thirty, as they usually do, I figured I had a pretty good grasp on the Old Man's idea of ballistics. At least I knew one thing for sure: you can't aim at it and hit it unless it's coming straight at you or going straight away, and this never really happens. A duck coming is either dipping down or slanting up, and a duck going is always heading up a little. You got to aim at where you think it'll be when the shot gets there.

It began to snow a little at ten, when the Old Man counted the ducks in the boat and said, "That's enough. We got more than we can eat at the house and give to the neighbors. Let's save some for next week, or maybe next fall."

We sat there in the marsh, with the marsh smell coming strong on the breeze and the soft flakes of snow falling, drinking what was left of the coffee and eating the apples and Miss Lottie's cookies we had stolen out of the crock. The red-winged blackbirds had shut up, and there was only an occasional string of ducks flying low under the solid clouds. It was getting colder all the time.

"We had a pretty good morning," the Old Man said. "I thought you did pretty good for an amateur. I guess you feel like celebrating some; so I suggest you row the boat home. It'll calm you down."

4

Fish Keep a Fellow
Out of Trouble

The summertime had come, as it comes swiftly in the South, with the trees heavy with summer smells and all the roses blooming in Miss Lottie's garden, and the magnolia all busted out in those great, heavy waxen blossoms that turn brown if you touch them.

The Old Man was watching us play a game of two o'cat one day, and when we wound it up he called me to one side and said he reckoned it was about time for us to go fishing. It was just a question, he said, of what kind of fishing we wanted to do.

"This is the summertime," the Old Man said. "This is not a time for heavy fishing. In the summertime you don't belong to work too hard. My idea of summertime fishing is to take a pole and a length of line and sit by a fresh-water crick and catch a black bass, or else to get in the rowboat and go find one of those big holes full of speckled trout and use a hand line on them. The whole purpose of summer fishing," the Old Man said, "is not to worry about catching fish, but to just get out of the house and set and think a little. Also, the womenfolk are very bad-tempered in the summer. The less you hang around the premises the less trouble you're apt to get in."

I said let's us row out to the channel and find us a trout hole and throw a hand line over and let the day take care of itself. The Old Man said he thought that was a fine idea, but that even summer fishing took some preparation. He dug in his pocket, and found a dime, and flipped it at me.

"You go on down to the shrimp house and buy us a dime's worth," he said, "and mind they're fresh and little. Wait for one of the boats to come in, and get them while they're still kicking. No!" he said. "On second thought, give me the dime back. We'll go catch our own. You might as well learn how to use a cast net now as any other time. It's almost as much fun as fishing, if you do it right."

I went into the kitchen to snitch the makings for some lunch and to fill the water jug, and the Old Man crawled under the house where he kept his tents and some spare boats and a side-saddle Miss Lottie used to ride, when people still rode horses sidesaddle. He came out swearing, with a crick in his back and the cast net, carefully rolled, in his hand. The Old Man had made the net himself, knotting each line in the net to form a fine, thin web, and carefully spacing each leaden sinker that hung from the hem of the net. It was a work of art. As I recall, it took him all winter, although, of course, some of the time he was working on a miniature full-rigged ship, which used up a lot more of his time when he wasn't hunting or playing the fiddle.

We walked down to the water, the Old Man carrying the net slung over his shoulder and a couple of hand lines wrapped neatly around two pieces of wood, notched at each end, with the hook bit deep into the wood and the sinker hanging free.

I had the lunch box and the water bottle and a fishing-tackle box full of extra hooks and sinkers and leaders. The Old Man was very particular about the extras. He always said that a fisherman who lost his hook might as well not be there at all unless he had another hook, and that a hunter who didn't carry some sort of spare gun was wasting his time in the woods.

The boat was hauled up high and dry on the beach with her oars under her. We flipped her over, and I walked, barefoot, of course, backward into the water, where we hauled her free and set her to bobbing in the little glittery summer wavelets. We stowed the stuff under one of the wharfs, and the Old Man took a push pole and shoved her over to the corner of the marsh, where you could smell the mud, very salty and foul, but where the little schools of mullet and shrimp were making extra wrinkles in the water. The Old Man shipped his push pole and reached for the cast net. He shook it until it hung free, like a lead-weighted skirt, and then swished it very carefully through the water to make it wet and free-running, so as not to snarl.

In case you don't know about a cast net, it's a thing like a big circular skirt, which fans out at the bottom. It has drawstrings on the bottom that come up through its narrow horn-rimmed neck. It lands flat on the water, and the lead weights carry it swiftly to the bottom. A simple twitch closes the wide bottom and makes it into a net bag, with whatever's inside trapped safe and sound. You have to use it in shallow water, of course, because it's not much good at over four or five feet deep, but throwing it is an art—I found out—and it's a deadly way of collecting your small bait with a minimum of trouble.

The Old Man stood up and flipped out his net, like a bull-fighter flipping his cape. He put one of the lead sinkers on the bottom in his mouth. Holding the drawstring in his left hand, he stretched his right hand to grab another piece of the hem, and steadied the whole three-cornered arrangement—right hand, mouth in the middle—with the left hand grabbing the outer left-hand edge of the net's hem. He carried his left hand behind him, taking that part of the net's skirt with him, crossed his right hand past his chest, and threw. The net swirled out, lovely and graceful, opening to its full diameter like a great round butterfly. It settled at full extension on the water, covering a small school of bucking shrimp. It sank, carrying the shrimp down with it, and the Old Man's left hand twitched the draw-string. Then he began to haul in the net.

The lead-weighted bottom, tucked in now from the stress of the drawstring, made a secure trap for the shrimp. As the water poured out of the net you could see the tiny little grayish-yellow shrimp fighting and kicking inside. The Old Man dumped the weighted part on the deck of the boat. He released the draw, encircled the horn ring with thumb and forefinger, and shook the net gently. Its closed bottom opened. The shrimp, a hundred or more, leaped and kicked and quivered on the deck. The Old Man scooped them up by handfuls and dropped them in a bucket of salt water.

"Now you try it," he said. " 'Tain't as easy as it looks. You got to make the net swirl out like a lady's dancing skirt when you throw her, and if you ain't careful that sinker in your mouth will pull out a couple of front teeth. Also, there's a knack to when you haul taut on the drawstring. You got to give her a chance to settle over the shrimp, but not too long, or they'll get out from under the bottom. Give her a whirl."

I spent most of the morning with that net. I hurt my teeth with the sinker. I snarled it and fouled it and twitched it too soon and didn't twitch it fast enough, or forgot to lead the swimming schools of shrimp and little mullet I was practicing on. Finally I got to where I could throw her and make her swirl, and eventually I caught a couple of pounds of shrimp and some little three-inch mullet. A lot later on I was going to have a mess of fun with that net, fishing the shallows and catching sizable fish that had come in close to feed on the bait. But this morning I just about pulled my arms out of the sockets before the Old Man said that was enough, and let's have some lunch and then go fish the ebb tide.

We rowed out a mile or so to where the water made an eddy around some rocks, and the Old Man dropped the anchor overside and let out all the slack in the line. The boat yawed around and hung in a clear place, with rapid-running water on both sides of her, and we started to unwind the fishing lines, letting them flow downstream to get the kinks dampened out. Then we hauled them back in, hand over hand, making a neat wet coil on the deck of the boat. The Old Man reached into the shrimp pot and chose a lusty kicker and threaded him on the hook, gently circling the shrimp's spine with the barb. He tossed him over the side, and I did the same with mine.

We caught fish that day. We caught big sea trout, weakfish, that had come in through the inlets, fellows going up as high as three and four pounds—big, beautiful, speckled salt-water trout with mean chins and anger at the hooks in their mouths. We caught blackfish and croakers with a grunt like an unhappy pig. We even caught some small sharks and an occasional big perch. We caught fish until our hands were chapped and cut and tired from hauling them in.

Summertime is an overrated time, I think today, full of sunburn and poison ivy and expensive vacations. But for a boy like me, at that time, summertime was a time of almost unbearable happiness. School was out, of course, and we had a song that went: "No more school, no more books, no more teachers' cross-eyed looks." Summertime was when I went to stay with the Old Man, and got loose from my ma and my pa. Summertime was June-bug time and firefly time, each tiny fly blinking his parking light on and off.

If you are a very small boy, being close to water makes the summer a marvelous thing. There is something of the kiss of the sun on dancing little waves, fresh salt breeze in your face and sun on your head, the taste of salt fresh on your lips. It was like that this day when the Old Man taught me to use the cast net and all the fish were hungry for the little gray shrimp we had caught at the edges of the steaming marshes.

The sun was low when the Old Man announced that we

had had enough and put me to the task of rowing us back to port. My face was fiery from the sun and there was salt in my pores and my hands hurt on the hard handles of the oars, but I bent my back with a right good will and listened to the Old Man, who was talking now, more or less to himself.

"The thing about fishing," the Old Man said, "is not how many fish you catch or what kind of fish. I, for one, think that making a hardheaded profession out of fishing is a waste of time, because a fish is only a fish, and when you make a lot of work out of him you lose the whole point of him.

"A fish, which you can't see, deep down in the water, is a kind of symbol of peace on earth, good will to yourself. Fishing gives a man some time to think. It gives him some time to collect his thoughts and rearrange them kind of neat, in an orderly fashion.

"Once the bait is on the hook and the boat anchored, there's nothing to interfere with thinking except an occasional bite, and even an idiot with reflexes can haul in a fish without inter-rupting his train of thought. This isn't true, I hasten to add, of sport fishing, game fishing, because that calls for a great deal of concentration and some skill and an awful lot of work.

"I mean that, for a rest cure for your head, you got to go fishing like we just been fishing, a holiday from yourself and all the things a man gets mixed up in. Setting out here in this boat, your ma can't get at you and your grandma can't get at you. There ain't any telephone or postal service or radio or automobiles. There ain't anything but just you and the fish, and these kind of fish are all fools. So you put a shrimp on the hook and throw it out, and if one bites you haul it in, and if one doesn't you've still had a mighty fine day in the open where it's quiet and only the sea gulls are noisy.

"Once in a while," the Old Man said, "a fellow wants to get away from everything that's complicated, and fishing is really the only way I know of to do it. Later on we'll do some serious fishing, which is work, but I don't think you ought to do it in the summertime. One of the reasons people drop dead is from doing serious things in the summertime.

"Look at us, for example," the Old Man said. "We have had us a fine day away from the women. We haven't bothered each other with a lot of problems. You learned how to throw a cast net, and this afternoon we caught a mighty pretty mess of fish. So we go home now, with all the wrinkles smoothed out of us, hungry, tired, and ready for dinner and bed. The women can't be mad at us because we weren't underfoot all day, and on top of it here are enough fish to feed the whole block. In a way we are heroes, just because we had sense enough to loaf all day without people watching us.

"One thing you will learn," the Old Man said, talking at me, "is that you must never be lazy in front of anybody. Loafing is fine, but energetic people get mad at you if you take it easy in front of them. That's one of the troubles with women. They got a dynamo in them, and they run on energy. It pure riles a woman to see a man having any fun that doesn't involve work. That's why fishing was invented, really. It takes you away from the view of industrious people. Lazy men make the best fishermen, and they usually amount to something in the end, because they have time enough to unclutter their brains and get down to the real flat basics.

"I do not admire people who are industrious all the time. They're like people who swat at gnats and miss the mosquitoes. They are always so damn busy running here and yonder on fool's errands that they never have time to settle down and cerebrate a little. Lean a little harder on them oars, boy. I'm getting powerful peckish."

We came back to the beach, and we hauled up the boat and cached the oars under her and collected the oarlocks and pulled the fish in from the string that let them swim behind us. Then we walked up the hill to the house, tired and sunburnt and rested.

When we got there, Miss Lottie was on the front porch,

agitating because we were a little late to supper, and there was some sort of telephone call from my ma that I would have had to answer if I'd been there, but now it was all settled because I wasn't there to answer it. We had some early supper —not very much, because in those days you ate heavy in the middle of the day, and supper was mostly ham and eggs and hominy and biscuits and coffee and maybe a piece of cake. I was yawning before I was through. Then the Old Man pointed to the back yard.

"Go clean those fish, son," he said. "I'm too old and tired to do it, and you might as well learn that a man who catches fish or shoots game has got to make it fit to eat before he sleeps. Otherwise it's all a waste and a sin to take it if you can't use it."

I near about went to sleep, squatting under the fig tree and cleaning those fish. I never saw so many fish. Seems to me we had caught all the fish there were. But finally they were all gutted and scaled and trimmed and washed down in salty water and stuck off in the icebox. I was sort of staggering off to bed when the Old Man hollered at me again.

"Go wash," he said. "I can smell you from here, and you smell like a consarned fish market. Miss Lottie'll raise hell if you fish up her nice clean sheets, and then we'll never be able to go fishing any more."

I went and washed and fell dead in the bed. One of the last thoughts I had was that the Old Man was right when he said that our kind of fishing wasn't work. But he meant that for *him*. He didn't mean it for me. I never worked harder in my life, but it was worth it next morning at breakfast when old Galena, the cook, brought in those trout.

5

September Song

When the autumn came to our coast, just a little ahead of the quail-shooting season, when all the summer visitors went away from Wrightsville Beach and the gray-shingled little beach houses had their windows tacked shut against the northern gales, when the skies got as gray as the shingles and a wood fire was nice at night and all the little shops closed for the long, unprofitable off season—that was when the Old Man and I got into big business with each other.

"It makes a wonderful balance of nature," the Old Man would say, eying the woodpile speculatively, which made me know all of a sudden that he was going to suggest an ax and a small boy to wield it. "When the dodlimbed tourists leave, the bluefish cannot be very far behind. There was a book along those lines, I recall, called *If Winter Comes* or some such. Except I think the writer was reading more spring than bluefish into the script."

As I remember the Old Man, he never said anything at all that you couldn't walk away from three ways and still find a fresh idea in it. I got to where I could listen to him with only one ear, separating the meat from the philosophy, and it wasn't until a lot of years later when I grew up to be a man that I found I remembered more philosophy than meat.

"It is now Labor Day," the Old Man said. "Never quite understood why they call it that, since nobody works on the week end before the Monday they named it after. But on Tuesday the boys will all be gone, and the men will be left. And the bluefish, having watched carefully from Topsail, will come in to commune with the men. Bluefish do not like summer tourists. They like people who admire nor'easters and don't mind a little rain and a squall or so.

"The first thing we will do about bluefish," the Old Man continued, "is to catch a mess of them easy, so you can learn to appreciate the other way. It's too early for them to be inshore, in the sloughs, so we will go trolling for bluefish like the rich people do, and let the boat kill them. I got a connection in the Coast Guard. We will go to Southport and leave early in the morning with Cap'n Willis."

We went on the cutter, and we went out past Caswell, out from Southport, around Frying Pan Shoals. The driver of the boat—he had to be named Midyette, because nearly all Coast Guarders come from Okracoke Island, near Hatteras, and they're all named Midyette down there—tooled the little craft so close to the edge of the shoals you could touch sand with your left hand and see ten fathom of water to your right.

The water was as clear and cool blue as in Bermuda, and the sand as white. The bell buoy was just a little bit behind you, making mournful sounds, and the lightship was over there, as lonesome as the men who lived on her. The gulls wheeled and screamed, and the gannets prowled the water looking for small bait, and off from the sand shoals you could see the big red living shoals of menhaden—pogies, we called them—that the fishing fleet preyed on to make fish-scrap fertilizer.

Here was where the mackerel (we always called them Spanish mackerel) lived, and the kingfish or horse mackerel lived. And here was where the bluefish and the sea trout came into the shallows for the small mullet and the shrimp that swarmed off the rim of the shoals.

"This is silly fishing," the Old Man said. "Don't take any sense or skill at all. All you need is a rod and some line and a hook and piece of bone to make the hook look like a minnow. Heave her over, and the bluefish fight each other for the right to take it. The speed of the boat half-kills the fish, so it is just a matter of hauling them in. Try it and see for yourself."

He handed me a light bass rod, and I flipped the bone minnow over the stern. The line hadn't paid out twenty yards when there was a strike and the rod bent double. It was pretty tough reeling, what with the boat going one way and the fish trying to go another, but I hauled him in. It was a nice bluefish, about two pounds, steely blue in the sun, with his jaw mean-looking and pugnacious and his teeth sharp. He was the first of a hundred, some smaller, which we threw back, and some bigger. One was a four-pounder.

Later on we hooked into a school of mackerel—big, stream-lined, speckly fellows that have a chin like a barracuda—and it was the same story. When we finished about 10:00 A.M., we had a boat full of fish—blues, mackerel, a few bonito, and a couple of big kingfish. We had enough fish to feed the whole Coast Guard station and half of the town. Like the Old Man said, it wasn't much sport after the first dozen. But there wasn't anything wrong with them in the skillet or on the little makeshift barbecue the Old Man rigged in front of the shack.

I feel real sorry for people who never had a chance at broiled bluefish or mackerel when the fish is so fresh you have to kill him before you clean him. Some say that blues and mackerel are too fat and oily, but there are some people who don't like snails or oysters and think carrots are just dandy. The way the Old Man cooked them, they tasted better than any fish has a right to taste. He just laid them on the grill over the hot coals and left them until you could see the skin blistering and cracking and turning gold and black, with the white showing through and the grease sizzling steadily onto the coals. When he finally took them off, he had to do it with a flapjack turner; they were so tender they just fell apart. He bathed them in about half a pound of butter per fish, poured vinegar over them, and then dusted them with black pepper. I ate about four pounds of fish before I quit.

Later on in the fall, after the first steady northers had begun to cut sloughs into the beaches and it was getting chilly in the afternoons, he announced one day after lunch that it was time to *really* go fishin'.

"We'll go to Corncake," he said. "I got a hunch the puppy drum are hungry and are in those sloughs stuffin' themselves on sand fleas. This is my kind of fishin'. It ain't murder—it's *fishin'*."

He dug out two big surf rods from under the house and got a big tackle box from his bedroom. We went down to the water front and bought some salt mullet—big ones, thickly crusted with salt—and set out. We took our time. The Old Man said it was no use fishing or hunting any time except real early in the morning or late in the afternoon, because even a fish or a jack rabbit had too much sense to bustle around in the heat of the day.

It was a gray, mean day, with the spume flying and the gulls moaning low and complaining. Along about 5:00 P.M. it was chilly enough for a sweater, and the water was cold on my bare legs. The Old Man spent the first hour trying to teach me to cast, with no bait on my hook. It looked so easy, the way he did it. It looked impossible, the way I did it. He would take the rod, wade out to over his knobby old knees, bring the rod back over his shoulder, with about four feet of line running free. Then he would bring the rod up and over in one single smooth motion, with a whip on the end of the cast. The line would sing through the reel, and the heavy, pyramid-shaped sinker would go whistling out to sea for maybe forty or fifty yards and fall with a plunk right where he was aiming in the slough. Then he'd reel in, very slowly, just enough to keep his line always taut.

When I did it I either threw the sinker into the water at my feet, or jammed the reel and threw the sinker away entirely, or had a backlash right in the middle of the cast. We spent most of the early afternoon unsnarling the reel or putting iodine on the fingers I cut and knocked and line-burned. But I expect young fellows learn pretty fast to do things with their hands, and by dusk I was still clumsy but getting the line out far enough to where at least some fish were. Then the Old Man took his sawbacked ripping knife and showed me how to cut the salt mullet in strips, slicing the inch-and-a-half strips diagonally across the fish. Next he showed me how to work the hook through the strips, weaving it back and forth until the mullet was firm and only the tip of the barb showed. The reason, he said, that we used the mullet instead of fresh bait or shrimps was that the salt had toughened the skin and she'd stay on the hook in rough surf, whereas the other stuff would work off every cast.

The Old Man used a long leader made out of wire, and he hooked two leaders, two hooks, and two baits onto each line. He grinned to himself, humming quietly as he fixed the tackle. His square hands with the broken, stubby fingers and with the old man's brown liver spots on the backs looked clumsy, but they weren't. Anything he handled, from a knife to a gun to a fiddle, was handled so swift and well that it looked easy.

It was growing dark when I stepped out into the icy gray water and cast. The line went out pretty well, the baits whirling through the air, and settled into a slough with a satisfactory chunk. I began to wind her up, to get the belly out of the line, when two bolts of lightning struck. The line screamed out of the reel, and I burned some more fingers before I could get the drag on. It was like being tied fast to two horses, each with his own idea about where he was headed. It seemed that whatever was on that line was going to pull me right into the ocean. But then I began to walk slowly backward, cranking a little bit, keeping the tension on the rod by holding the tip high, the reel close to my belly, and the rod jammed under my arm.

I finally backed up to where the dunes started and the sea oats grew, and I could see the fish coming out of the water, flopping and fighting even on the silver sands. They looked big, like live logs on the beach. I started toward them now, reeling in the slack, and went down to where they lay on the sand. They were both big bluefish, three or four pounds each. I felt like I had just played four quarters of football.

I played out pretty quick, because the rod and reel were heavy and every time I cast—when I didn't backlash—two big bluefish tied into me as soon as the sinker settled. It was taking me fifteen to twenty minutes to land the ones I landed. The ones I lost didn't take so long, and I lost a good deal more than I beached.

By black dark I was cold and wet and sore all over. My hands were cut and full of burning salt, and my back ached like a dissatisfied tooth. But I had caught maybe a dozen big blues, and once a ten-pound puppy drum with the big black spot on his silver backside.

After a while I built a fire out of some driftwood, and sat down to chew on some raw mullet—which tasted delicious— and to watch the Old Man work. The moon rose, about full, and it was like something I had never seen or imagined. The Old Man would wade out and cast into the slough. He would back up, and suddenly he would strike his rod, which would bend double. He would then begin that slow and dignified backward march up the beach, fighting the fish. I was fascinated, watching what eventually emerged from the dark seas onto the moonlit sands.

He fished until midnight. Once he hooked into two drum,

and not puppies. One weighed twenty-two pounds, and the other twenty. He was nearly an hour getting them ashore, and when they finally slid up on the sand they looked as big as a couple of Coast Guard surfboats. He never took a line out of the sea without two fish on it. They were starving, I guess, because he never quit until he was exhausted, and they were still striking two at a time the second the bait hit. The Old Man has been dead a long time now, but I'll never forget the way he looked in the moonlight, horsing two channel bass onto the beach, with the birds screaming and the wind high.

"This," the Old Man said as we headed home with the car full of fish, "is what fishing can be like, where you earn your fish and don't kill him with a boat. I'd rather have two mad bluefish on the same line in a cold ocean than catch all the sailfish and marlin ever made. The only thing I know of that's better is a frisky Atlantic salmon in a cold Canadian stream, on about six ounces of fly rod. I hope you get a chance to try it some day when you're bigger."

I did get a chance when I got bigger, and it was twenty-eight pounds of salmon, and he worked me an hour and a half. But he never gave me what I got out of those first two bluefish in an angry autumn sea.

Now the summer was completely gone, and all the memories of the summer. The time of year I liked better than any other had started. You could tell in so many ways that the summer was finished—your legs didn't sweat the crease out of your Sunday pants any more, and there was just a little nip in the evening air. The dogs that had been listless and shedding hair in the sticky heat got into condition again without being dosed, and began to look hopefully at the tin Liz, like maybe a ride was indicated.

The milky smell of summer was all gone out of the air, and had been replaced by the smell of leaves burning and the tart odor of the last of the grapes. You could feel your blood sparkling inside you, no longer heavy with the summer lethargy. A hot breakfast—pancakes and sausage and eggs busted and mixed into the grits—tasted just fine. The leaves were beginning to crinkle a little on the edges, and the first norther that brought the marsh hens flapping up from flooded marshes had already come and gone. A few ducks—teal, mostly—were beginning to drop in.

I don't know if you remember clearly the unspoken promise of excitement that early autumn brings, just before frost comes to grizzle the grasses in the early morning; before the chinquapins are ripe in their burry shells, before the persimmons lose the alum taste that twists your mouth. It's sort of like the twenty-third of December—Christmas isn't quite here, but it's close enough to ruin your sleep.

This was the time when we went fishing seriously on the week ends—fishing in the cold gray sea that always carried a chop except in the long, smooth sloughs; fishing in the inlets, and fishing off a long pier that went away out into the ocean. It was called Kure's Pier, if I remember right, and it cost something, ten cents or two bits, to fish off it. I used to see a couple of hundred fishermen casting off the pier, and there was so much fishing courtesy around in those days that when a man hung into a real big channel bass all the fishermen on his side would reel in and let him work his fish to the shore.

But by and large there weren't many big ones snagged off Kure's Pier. The stuff ran little—two-pound blues and an occasional sea trout, the odd puppy drum and a whole lot of whiting, which we called Virginia mullet. The Old Man and I didn't crave company very much; we went farther down the coast from Carolina Beach past Kure's to old Fort Fisher, where the big guns used to be aimed against the Civil War blockade runners.

Down there we had the peculiar kind of solitude the Old Man loved and which I loved then, without ever knowing why we loved it. Oh, but that was a scary, desolate beach, the offset currents cutting great sloughs where the big fish lay. The silver-sandy beach came down from steep dunes as high as mountains, with just a fringe of sea oats. There weren't any houses as far as you could see. The bush was warped and gnarled by the winds that never stopped, the myrtle and the cedars and the little hunchbacked oaks twisted and tortured and ever buffeted. The thin screech of the wind was always there, and the water was cold. The rafts of sea ducks looked gloomy, and the birds always screamed louder there than on any other beach I can remember. The general air of age was heightened by the fact that you were always stumbling over an old cannon ball or a rusty saber, and the ghosts flew thick at nightfall.

We used to stop off at Kure's Pier once in a while, just to swap lies with fishing friends. We were an odd bunch, I'm forced to admit. The one I liked best was Chris—Chris Rongotis, or some such name as that—a flat-necked Greek who owned a café, naturally, in town. Chris lived to fish. The restaurant was strictly side-bar. Chris always had a joke for me, or a slab of "oppla pie" or "peenoppla pie" or "strumberry tsortcake" he'd fetched from the restaurant, and a thermos of the hottest coffee in the world. He would tell me what it was like back in Greece, and I learned three bars of the Greek national anthem. Chris just about died laughing at my Greek accent.

There were also a doctor and a dentist and a World War hero with most of himself shot loose. There were a Portygee and a Frenchman and a big blowsy old woman who wore pants and hip boots and cussed worse than anybody I ever heard when she lost a fish. I reckon it was my first real taste of the international set—except none of these internationals could have bribed their way into a parlor. The Portygee even wore big gold earrings and shaved every other Fourth of July.

If you snapped a rod or threw your last leader or ran plumb out of cut bait, somebody would come along and lend you a hand without appearing to be doing you a favor.

What I'm trying to do is tell you how nice it was in the fall, in late October and early November, when the big blues ran close ashore to feed off the minnows and the sand fleas.

Looking back, I can't think of any real big fish we caught, or any lives we saved, or anything poetic or fancy. But this I do remember—an infection I caught which, if the good Lord is willing, I never aim to get cured of. That is the feeling of wonderful contentment a man can have on a lonesome beach that is chilling itself up for winter, sort of practice-swinging to get ready for the bitter cold that's coming.

We had a little weathered gray shingle-and-clapboard cottage rented for the fall fishing. It stuck up on a high bluff just between Carolina and Kure's Beach. If you stepped too spry off the front piazza, you would tumble right down onto the brown mossed-over rocks, which weren't so much rocks as case-hardened sand. There was a rough board step—more of a ladder, actually—that you had to climb up from the beach, about fifty yards straight up.

It wasn't very grand, I must say. It had a toilet and a ramshackle stove and a bedroom and a sitting room and a fireplace. The fireplace was what made it. This fireplace drew so hard that it dang near carried the logs straight up the "chimbley." That was how I pronounced "chimney" until I was about grown, and I still think "chimbley."

This place was home, castle, sanctuary. I mind it so clear, coming in off that beach in the black night. The surf would be booming spooky and sullen, sometimes wild and angry and spume-tossing when the wind freshened. Your feet in the heavy black rubber boots sank down into the squishy sand, and you had to pull them out with a conscious effort as you walked up from the firm, moist sand at the water's edge and slogged through the deep, loose sand to the first steep rise of bluff. You would naturally be carrying a heavy surf rod and a heavy reel and a tackle box, and were generally dragging a string of fish that started out about the size of anchovies and wound up weighing more than a marlin before you got 'em home.

There would be an ache all through your shoulders from casting that heavy line with the four-ounce sinker and the big slab of cut mullet. There would be an ache in the back of your legs from wading in and then walking backward to reel in the fish. There would be cramps in your cold, salt-water-wrinkled red fingers, and your nose would be pink and running. If anybody had snapped you on the ear, the ear would have fallen off. Your feet were just plain frozen inside those clammy rubber boots, and you were salty and sandy from stem to stern.

Somehow you wrestled your gear and yourself up the steep steps in the dark, and the door would open when you moved the wooden latch. The first fellow in lit the lamps, old smoky kerosene lamps, and there wasn't any quarrel about who fixed the fire. Among the Old Man's assorted rules was one unbreakable: you never left the house unless the dishes were washed, dried, and stacked, the beds made, the floor swept and—this above all—a correct fire laid and ready for the long, yellow-shafted, red-headed kitchen match to touch it into flaring life. The Old Man said you couldn't set too much store by a fire; that a fire was all that separated man from beast, if you came right down to it. I believe him. I'd rather live in the yard than in a house that didn't have an open fireplace.

One of the chores I never minded was being the vice-president in charge of the fire detail. I loved to straggle off in the mornings, with the sun still warm and bright before the afternoon winds and clouds chilled the beach, just perusing around for firewood. We had wonderful firewood—sad and twisted old logs, dull silver-gray from salt, big scantlings and pieces of wrecked boats, and stuff like that, all bone-dry and wind-seasoned. The salt or something caused it to burn slow and steady with a blue flame like alcohol burns, and the smell was salt and sand and sea grapes and fire, together. All you needed under it was a few tight-crumpled, greasy old newspapers that the bait had been wrapped in and a lightwood knot or two, and when you nudged her with the match she went up like Chicago when the old lady's cow kicked over the lantern.

With that fire roaring you could cut out one of the lamps, because the fire made that wonderful flickering light which will ruin your eyes if you try to read by it but which, I believe, was responsible for making a President of Honest Abe. You backed up to her and warmed the seat of your pants, with your boots still on, and then turned and baked a little cold out of your chapped, wrinkled hands. Only then did you sit down and haul off the Old Man's boots, with one of his feet seized between your legs and the other in your chest, and then he helped you prize your boots off the same way.

It's funny the things you remember, isn't it? I remember a pair of ankle slippers made out of sheepskin, with the curly wool inside. I would set 'em to toast by the fire as soon as I came through the door. When I popped my bare feet into 'em, they were scorching and felt like a hot bath, a cup of coffee, and a pony for Christmas. Then some hot water on my hands, to wash off the salt and the greasy fish and the dirt. Now I started out to do the supper.

The Old Man said that in deference to his advanced years he had to take a little drink of his nerve tonic, and the least a boy could do would be to lay the table and set up the supper. I liked that, too—the Old Man sitting sprawled in a rocker in front of the fire, his feet spread whopperjawed out toward the flames, puffing on his pipe and taking a little snort and talking kind of lazy about what all had happened that day. Shucks, getting supper wasn't any trouble at all.

You just started the coffee in the tin percolator and got the butter out of the food safe and sliced off a few rounds of bread and dug up the marmalade or the jelly. We had an iron grill that we slid into the fireplace as soon as she began to coal down into nice rosy embers, and it didn't take a minute to lay the halves of yesterday's bluefish or sea trout onto the grill. About the time the fish started to crumble and fall down through the grill I'd stick a skillet full of scrambled eggs over the fire, and in about two shakes dinner was served.

Full as ticks, we'd sit and talk over the second cup of coffee, and then the Old Man would bank the fire and blow out the lamp. We'd reel off to bed, dead from fatigue and food and fire.

These trips were only on week ends, of course, because there was that business about education, which meant I was bespoken five days a week. But from Friday afternoon until Monday morning early, when the Old Man dragged me out of bed before light in order to check my fingernails and cowlick for respectability, I was a mighty happy boy.

And it's funny, as I was saying earlier, but I can't remember the fish. All I remember very clear are Chris the Greek and the cussing lady in the hip boots and the Portygee with the earrings. And how the Old Man's face looked with the fire bright against it, making it cherry red on one side and shadowed black on the other, and how the wind sounded, thrashing on the stout gray shingles that kept us safe inside from storm. I haven't lit a fire from that day to this without seeing, and even smelling a little bit, the presence of beard and bourbon and tobacco and salt air and fish and fire that went to make up the Old Man. I guess that's why some people call me a firebug.

6

Mister Howard Was a Real Gent

The week before Thanksgiving that year, one of the Old Man's best buddies came down from Maryland to spend a piece with the family, and I liked him a whole lot right from the start. Probably it was because he looked like the Old Man—ragged mustache, smoked a pipe, built sort of solid, and he treated me like I was grown up too. He was interested in 'most everything I was doing, and he admired my shotgun, and he told me a whole lot about the dogs and horses he had up on his big farm outside of Baltimore.

He and the Old Man had been friends for a whole lot of years, they had been all over the world, and they were always sitting out on the front porch, smoking and laughing quiet together over some devilment they'd been up to before I was born. I noticed they always shut up pretty quick when Miss

Lottie, who was my grandma, showed up on the scene. Sometimes, when they'd come back from walking down by the river, I could smell a little ripe aroma around them that smelled an awful lot like the stuff that the Old Man kept in his room to keep the chills off him. The Old Man's friend was named Mister Howard.

They were planning to pack up the dogs and guns and a tent and go off on a camping trip for a whole week, 'way into the woods behind Allen's Creek, about fifteen miles from town. They talked about it for days, fussing around with cooking gear, and going to the store to pick up this and that, and laying out clothes. They never said a word to me; they acted as if I wasn't there at all. I was very good all the time. I never spoke at the table unless I was spoken to, and I never asked for more than I ate, and I kept pretty clean and neat, for me. My tongue was hanging out, like a thirsty hound dog's. One day I couldn't stand it any longer.

"I want to go too," I said. "You promised last summer you'd take me camping if I behaved myself and quit stealing your cigars and didn't get drowned and——"

"What do you think, Ned?" Mister Howard asked the Old Man. "Think we could use him around the camp, to do the chores and go for water and such as that?"

"I dunno," the Old Man said. "He'd probably be an awful nuisance. Probably get lost and we'd have to go look for him, or shoot one of us thinking we were a deer, or get sick or bust a leg or something. He's always breaking something. Man can't read his paper around here for the sound of snapping bones."

"Oh, hell, Ned," Mister Howard said, "let's take him. Maybe we can teach him a couple of things. We can always get Tom or Pete to run him back in the flivver, if he don't behave."

"Well," the Old Man said, grinning, "I'd sort of planned to fetch him along all along, but I was waiting to see how long it'd take him to ask."

We crowded a lot of stuff into that old tin Liz. Mister How-

ard and the Old Man and me and two bird dogs and two hound
dogs and a sort of fice dog who was death on squirrels and a big
springer spaniel who was death on ducks. Then there were
Tom and Pete, two kind of half-Indian backwoods boys who
divided their year into four parts. They fished in the summer
and hunted in the fall. They made corn liquor in the winter
and drank it up in the spring. They were big, dark, lean men,
very quiet and strong. Both of them always wore hip boots,
in the town and in the woods, on the water or in their own back
yards. Both of them worked for the Old Man when the fishing season was on and the pogies were running in big, red, fat-
backed schools. They knew just about everything about dogs
and woods and water and game that I wanted to know.

The back seat was full of dogs and people and cooking
stuff and guns. There were a couple of tents strapped on top
of the Liz, a big one and a small one. That old tin can sounded
like a boiler factory when we ran over the bumps in the corduroy clay road. I didn't say anything as we rode along. I was
much too excited; and anyhow, I figured they might decide
to send me back home.

It took us a couple of hours of bumping through the long,
yellow savanna-land hills before we came up to a big pond,
about five hundred yards from a swamp, or branch, with a clear
creek running through it. We drove the flivver up under a
group of three big water oaks and parked her. The Old Man
had camped there lots before, he said. There was a cleared-
out space of clean ground about fifty yards square between
the trees and the branch. And there was a small fireplace, or
what had been a small fireplace, of big stones. They were
scattered around now, all over the place. A flock of tin cans
and some old bottles and such had been tossed off in the bush.

"Damned tourists," the Old Man muttered, unloading some
tin pots and pans from the back of the car. "Come in here to a
man's best place and leave it looking like a hogwallow. You, son,
go pick up those cans and bury them some place out of my
sight. Then come back here and help with the tents."

By the time I finished collecting the mess and burying it, the men had the tents laid out flat on the ground, the flaps fronting south, because there was a pretty stiff northerly wind working, and facing in the direction of the pond. Tom crawled under the canvas with one pole and a rope, and Pete lifted the front end with another pole and the other end of the rope. Mister Howard was behind with the end of Tom's rope and a peg and a maul. The Old Man was at the front with the end of Pete's rope and another stake and maul. The boys in the tent gave a heave, set the posts, and the two old men hauled taut on the ropes and took a couple of turns around the pegs.

The tent hung there like a blanket on a clothesline until Tom and Pete scuttled out and pegged her out stiff and taut from the sides. They pounded the pegs deep into the dirt, so that the lines around the notches were clean into the earth. It was a simple tent, just a canvas V with flaps fore and aft, but enough to keep the wet out. The other one went up the same way.

We didn't have any bedrolls in those days, or cots either. The Old Man gave me a hatchet and sent me off to chop the branches of the longleaf pine saplings that grew all around— big green needles a foot and a half long. While I was gone he cut eight pine stakes off an old stump, getting a two-foot stake every time he slivered off the stump, and then he cut four long oak saplings. He hammered the stakes into the ground inside the tent until he had a wide rectangle about six by eight feet. Then he split the tops of the stakes. He wedged two saplings into the stakes lengthwise, jamming them with the flat of the ax, and then he jammed two shorter saplings into the others, crosswise. He took four short lengths of heavy fishing cord and tied the saplings to the stakes, at each of the four corners, until he had a framework, six inches off the ground.

"Gimme those pine boughs," he said to me, "and go fetch more until I tell you to stop."

The Old Man took the fresh-cut pine branches, the resin

still oozing stickily off the bright yellow slashes, and started shingling them, butt to the ground. He overlapped the needles like shingles on a house, always with the leaf end up and the branch end down to the ground. It took him about fifteen minutes, but when he finished he had a six-by-eight mattress of the spicy-smelling pine boughs. Then he took a length of canvas tarpaulin and arranged it neatly over the top. There were little grommet holes in each of the four corners, and he pegged the canvas tight over the tops of the saplings that confined the pine boughs. When he was through, you could hit it with your hand and it was springy but firm.

"That's a better mattress than your grandma's got," the Old Man said, grinning over his shoulder as he hit the last lick with the ax. "All it needs is one blanket under you and one over you. You're off the ground, and dry as a bone, with pine needles to smell while you dream. It's just big enough for two men and a boy. The boy gets to sleep in the middle, and he better not thrash around and snore."

By the time he was through and I had spread the blankets, Tom and Pete had made themselves a bed in the other tent, just the same way. The whole operation didn't take half an hour from stopping the car until both tents and beds were ready.

While we were building the beds Mister Howard had strung a line between a couple of trees and had tied a loop in the long leash of each dog, running the loop around the rope between the trees and jamming it with a square knot. The dogs had plenty of room to move in, but not enough to tangle up with each other, and not enough to start to fight when they got fed. They had just room enough between each dog to be sociable and growl at each other without starting a big rumpus. Pretty soon they quit growling and lay down quietly.

We had two big canvas water bags tied to the front of the flivver, and the Old Man gestured at them. "Boys have to handle the water detail in a man's camp," he said. "Go on down to the branch and fill 'em up at that little spillway. Don't roil up the water. Just stretch the necks and let the water run into the bags."

I walked down through the short yellow grass and the sparkleberry bushes to the branch, where you could hear the stream making little chuckling noises as it burbled over the rocks in its sandy bed. It was clear, brown water, and smelled a little like the crushed ferns and the wet brown leaves around it and in it. When I got back, I could hear the sound of axes off in a scrub-oak thicket, where Tom and Pete had gone to gather wood. Mister Howard was sorting out the guns, and the Old Man was puttering around with the stones where the fire marks were. He didn't look up.

"Take the hatchet and go chop me some kindling off that lighterd-knot stump," he said. "Cut 'em small, and try not to hit a knot and chop off a foot. Won't need much, 'bout an armful."

When I got back with kindling, Tom and Pete were coming out of the scrub-oak thicket with huge, heaping armfuls of old dead branches and little logs as big as your leg. They stacked them neatly at a respectable distance from where the Old Man had just about finished his oven. It wasn't much of an oven—just three sides of stones, with one end open and a few stones at intervals in the middle. I dumped the kindling down by him, and he scruffed up an old newspaper and rigged the fat pine on top, in a little sharp-pointed tepee over the crumpled paper.

He put some small sticks of scrubby oak crisscross over the fat pine, and then laid four small logs, their ends pointing in to each other until they made a cross, over the stones and over the little wigwam of kindling he had erected. Then he touched a match to the paper, and it went up in a poof. The blaze licked into the resiny lightwood, which roared and crackled into flame, soaring in yellow spurts up to the other, stouter kindling and running eager tongues around the lips of the logs.

In five minutes it was roaring, reflecting bright red against the stones.

The Old Man got up and kicked his feet out to get the cramp out of his knees. It was just on late dusk. The sun had gone down, red over the hill, and the night chill was coming. You could see the fog rising in snaking wreaths out of the branch. The frogs were beginning to talk, and the night birds were stirring down at the edge of the swamp. A whippoorwill tuned up.

" 'Bout time we had a little snort, Howard," the Old Man said. "It's going to be chilly. Pete! Fetch the jug!"

Pete ducked into his tent and came out with a half-gallon jug of brown corn liquor. Tom produced four tin cups from the nest of cooking utensils at the foot of the tree on which they had hung the water bags, and each man poured a half-measure of the whisky into his cup. I reckoned there must have been at least half a pint in each cup. Tom got one of the water bags and tipped it into the whisky until each man said, "Whoa." They drank and sighed. The Old Man cocked an eye at me and said, "This is for when you're bigger."

They had another drink before the fire had burned down to coal, with either Tom or Pete getting up to push the burning ends of the logs closer together. When they had a solid bed of coal glowing in the center of the stones, the Old Man heaved himself up and busied himself with a frying pan and some paper packages. He stuck a coffee pot off to one side, laid out five tin plates, dribbled coffee into the pot, hollered for me to fetch some water to pour into the pot, started carving up a loaf of bread, and slapped some big thick slices of ham into the frying pan.

When the ham was done, he put the slices, one by one, into the tin plates, which had warmed through from the fire, and laid slices of bread into the bubbling ham grease. Then he broke egg after egg onto the bread, stirred the whole mess into a thick bread-egg-and-ham-grease omelet, chopped the omelet into sections, and plumped each section onto a slice of ham. He poured the steaming coffee into cups, jerked his thumb at a can of condensed milk and a paper bag of sugar, and announced that dinner was served.

He had to cook the same mess three more times and refill the coffee pot before we quit eating. It was black dark, with no moon, when we lay back in front of the fire. The owls were talking over the whippoorwills, and the frogs were making an awful fuss.

The Old Man gestured at me. "Take the dirty dishes and the pans down to the branch and wash 'em," he said. "Do it now, before the grease sets. You won't need soap. Use sand. Better take a flashlight, and look out for snakes."

I was scared to go down there by myself, through that long stretch of grass and trees leading to the swamp, but I would have died before admitting it. The trees made all sorts of funny ghostly figures, and the noises were louder. When I got back, Mister Howard was feeding the dogs and the Old Man had pushed more logs on the fire.

"You better go to bed, son," the Old Man said. "Turn in in the middle. We'll be up early in the morning, and maybe get us a turkey."

I pulled off my shoes and crawled under the blanket. I heard the owl hoot again and the low mutter from the men, giant black shapes sitting before the fire. The pine-needle mattress smelled wonderful under me, and the blankets were warm. The fire pushed its heat into the tent, and I was as full of food as a tick. Just before I died I figured that tomorrow had to be heaven.

It was awful cold when the Old Man hit me a lick in the ribs with his elbow and said, "Get up, boy, and fix that fire." The stars were still up, frosty in the sky, and a wind was whistling round the corners of the tent. You could see the fire flicker just a mite against the black background of the swamp. Mister

Howard was still snoring on his side of the pine-needle-canvas bed, and I remember that his mustache was riffling, like marsh grass in the wind. Over in Tom and Pete's tent you could hear two breeds of snores. One was squeaky, and the other sounded like a bull caught in a bob-wire fence. I crawled out from under the covers, shivering, and jumped into my hunting boots, which were stiff and very cold. Everything else I owned I'd slept in.

The fire was pretty feeble. It had simmered down into gray ash, which was swirling loosely in the morning breeze. There was just a little red eye blinking underneath the fine talcumy ashes. After kicking some of the ashes aside with my boot, I put a couple of lightwood knots on top of the little chunk of glowing coal, and then I dragged some live-oak logs over the top of the lightwood and waited for her to catch. She caught, and the tiny teeth of flame opened wide to eat the oak. In five minutes I had a blaze going, and I was practically in it. It was mean cold that morning.

When the Old Man saw the fire dancing, he woke up Mister Howard and reached for his pipe first and his boots next. Then he reached for the bottle and poured himself a dram in a tin cup. He shuddered some when the dram went down.

"I heartily disapprove of drinking in the morning," he said. "Except some mornings. It takes a man past sixty to know whether he can handle his liquor good enough to take a nip in the morning. Howard?"

"I'm past sixty too," Mister Howard said. "Pass the jug."

Tom and Pete were coming out of the other tent, digging their knuckles into sleepy eyes. Pete went down to the branch and fetched a bucket of water, and everybody washed their faces out of the bucket. Then Pete went to the fire and slapped some ham into the pan and some eggs into the skillet, set some bread to toasting, and put the coffee pot on. Breakfast didn't take long. We had things to do that day.

After the second cup of coffee—I can still taste that coffee, with the condensed milk sweet and curdled on the top and the coffee itself tasting of branch water and wood smoke—we got up and started sorting out the guns.

"This is a buckshot day," the Old Man said, squinting down the barrel of his pump gun. "I think we better get us a deer today. Need meat in the camp, and maybe we can blood the boy. Tom, Pete, you all drive the branch. Howard, we'll put the boy on a stand where a buck is apt to amble by, and then you and I will kind of drift around according to where the noise seems headed. One, t'other of us ought to get a buck. This crick is populous with deer."

The Old Man paused to light his pipe, and then he turned around and pointed the stem at me.

"You, boy," he said. "By this time you know a lot about guns, but you don't know a lot about guns and deer together. Many a man loses his wits when he sees a big ol' buck bust out of the bushes with a rockin' chair on his head. Trained hunters shoot each other. They get overexcited and just bang away into the bushes. *Mind* what I say. A deer ain't a deer unless it's got horns on its head and you can see all of it at once. We don't shoot does and we don't shoot spike bucks and we don't shoot each other. There ain't no sense to shootin' a doe or a young'un. One buck can service hundreds of does, and one doe will breed you a mess of deer. If you shoot a young'un, you haven't got much meat, and no horns at all, and you've kept him from breedin' to make more deer for you to shoot. If you shoot a man, they'll likely hang you, and if the man is me I will be awful gol-damned annoyed and come back to ha'nt you. You mind that gun, and don't pull a trigger until you can see what it is and *where* it is. *Mind,* I say."

Tom and Pete picked up their pump guns and loaded them. They pushed the load lever down so there'd be no shell in the chamber, but only in the magazine. The Old Man looked at my little gun and said, "Don't bother to load it until you get on the stand. You ain't likely to see anything to shoot for an hour or so."

Tom and Pete went over to where we had the dogs tethered

on a line strung between two trees, and he unleashed the two hounds, Bell and Blue. Bell was black-and-tan and all hound. Blue was a kind of a sort of dog. He had some plain hound, some Walker hound, and some bulldog and a little beagle and a smidgen of pointer in him. He was ticked blue and brown and black and yellow and white. He looked as if somebody spilled the eggs on the checkered tablecloth. But he was a mighty dandy deer dog, or so they said. Old Sam Watts, across the street, used to say there wasn't no use trying to tell Blue anything, because Blue had done forgot more than you knew and just got annoyed when you tried to tell him his business.

Tom snapped a short lead on Blue, and Pete snapped another one on Bell. They shouldered their guns and headed up the branch, against the wind. We let 'em walk, while the Old Man and Mister Howard puttered around, like old people and most women will. Drives a boy crazy. What I wanted to do was go and shoot myself a deer. *Now.*

After about ten minutes the Old Man picked up his gun and said, "Let's go." We walked about half a mile down the swamp's edge. The light had come now, lemon-colored, and the fox squirrels were beginning to chase each other through the gum trees. We spied one old possum in a persimmon tree, hunched into a ball and making out like nobody knew he was there. We heard a turkey gobble away over yonder somewheres, and we could hear the doves beginning to moan—*oooh—oohoo —ooooh.*

All the little birds started to squeak and chirp and twitter at each other. The dew was staunchly stiff on the grass and on the sparkleberry and gallberry bushes. It was still cold, but getting warmer, and breakfast had settled down real sturdy in my stomach. Rabbits jumped out from under our feet. We stepped smack onto a covey of quail just working its way out of the swamp, and they like to have scared me to death when they busted up under our feet. There was a lot going on in that swamp that morning.

We turned into the branch finally, and came up to a track that the Old Man said was a deer run. He looked around and spied a stump off to one side, hidden by a tangle of dead brush. From the stump you could see clear for about fifty yards in a sort of accidental arena.

"Go sit on that stump, boy," the Old Man said. "You'll hear the dogs after a while, and if a deer comes down this branch he'll probably bust out there, where that trail comes into the open, because there ain't any other way he can cross it without leaving the swamp. Don't let the dogs fool you into not paying attention. When you hear 'em a mile away, the chances are that deer will be right in your lap. Sometimes they travel as much as two miles ahead of the dogs, just slipping along, not running; just slipping and sneaking on their little old quiet toes. And stay still. A deer'll run right over you if you stay still and the smell is away from him. But if you wink an eye, he can see it two hundred yards off, and will go the other way."

I sat down on the stump. The Old Man and Mister Howard went off, and I could hear them chatting quietly as they disappeared. I looked all around me. Nothing much was going on now, except a couple of he-squirrels were having a whale of a fight over my head, racing across branches and snarling squirrel cuss words at each other. A chickadee was standing on its head in a bush and making chickadee noises. A redheaded woodpecker was trying to cut a live-oak trunk in half with his bill. A rain crow—a kind of cuckoo, it is—was making dismal noises off behind me in the swamp, and a big old yellowhammer was swooping and dipping from tree to tree.

There were some robins hopping around on a patch of burnt ground, making conversation with each other. Crows were cawing, and two doves looped in to sit in a tree and chuckle at each other. A towhee was scratching and making more noise than a herd of turkeys, and some catbirds were meowing in the low bush while a big, sassy old mocker was imitating them kind of sarcastically. Anybody who says woods are quiet is crazy. You learn how to listen. The Tower of Babel was a study period alongside of woods in the early morning.

It is wonderful to smell the morning. Anybody who's been around the woods knows that morning smells one way, high noon another, dusk still another, and night most different of all, if only because the skunks smell louder at night. Morning smells fresh and flowery and little-breezy, and dewy and spanking new. Noon smells hot and a little dusty and sort of sleepy, when the breeze has died and the heads begin to droop and anything with any sense goes off into the shade to take a nap. Dusk smells scary. It is getting colder and everybody is going home tired for the day, and you can smell the turpentine scars on the trees and the burnt-off ground and the bruised ferns and the rising wind. You can hear the folding-up, I'm-finished-for-the-day sounds all around, including the colored boys whistling to prove they ain't scared when they drive the cows home. And in the night you can smell the fire and the warm blankets and the coffee a-boil, and you can even smell the stars. I know that sounds silly, but on a cool, clear, frosty night the stars have a smell, or so it seems when you are young and acutely conscious of everything bigger than a chigger.

This was as nice a smelling morning as I can remember. It smelled like it was going to work into a real fine-smelling day. The sun was up pretty high now and was beginning to warm the world. The dew was starting to dry, because the grass wasn't clear wet any more but just had little drops on top, like a kid with a runny nose. I sat on the stump for about a half-hour, and then I heard the dogs start, a mile or more down the swamp. Bell picked up the trail first, and she sounded as if church had opened for business. Then Blue came in behind her, loud as an organ, their two voices blending—fading sometimes, getting stronger, changing direction always.

Maybe you never heard a hound in the woods on a frosty fall morning, with the breeze light, the sun heating up in the sky, and the "aweful" expectancy that something big was going to happen to you. There aren't many things like it. When the baying gets closer and closer and still closer to you, you feel as if maybe you're going to explode if something doesn't happen quick. And when the direction changes and the dogs begin to fade, you feel so sick you want to throw up.

But Bell and Blue held the scent firmly now, and the belling was clear and steady. The deer was moving steady and straight, not trying to circle and fool the dogs, but honestly running. And the noise was coming straight down the branch, with me on the other end of it.

The dogs had come so close that you could hear them panting between their bays, and once or twice one of them quit sounding and broke into a yip-yap of barks. I thought I could hear a little tippety-tappety noise ahead of them, in between the belling and the barking, like mice running through paper or a rabbit hopping through dry leaves. I kept my eyes pinned onto where the deer path opened into the clearing. The dogs were so close that I could hear them crash.

All of a sudden there was a flash of brown and two does, flop-eared, with two half-grown fawns skipped out of the brush, stopped dead in front of me, looked me smack in the face, and then gave a tremendous leap that carried them halfway across the clearing. They bounced again, white tails carried high, and disappeared into the branch behind me. As I turned to watch them go there was another crash ahead and the buck tore through the clearing like a race horse. He wasn't jumping. This boy was running like the wind, with his horns laid back against his spine and his ears pinned by the breeze he was making. The dogs were right behind him. He had held back to tease the dogs into letting his family get a start, and now that they were out of the way he was pouring on the coal and heading for home.

I had a gun with me and the gun was loaded. I suppose it would have fired if the thought had occurred to me to pull the trigger. The thought never occurred. I just watched that big buck deer run, with my mouth open and my eyes popped out of my head.

The dogs tore out of the bush behind the buck, baying out their brains and covering the ground in leaps. Old Blue looked at me as he flashed past and curled his lip. He looked as if he were saying, "This is man's work, and what is a boy doing here, spoiling my labor?" Then he dived into the bush behind the buck.

I sat there on the stump and began to shake and tremble. About five minutes later there was one shot, a quarter-mile down the swamp. I sat on the stump. In about half an hour Tom and Pete came up to my clearing.

"What happened to the buck?" Pete said. "Didn't he come past here? I thought I was going to run him right over you."

"He came past, all right," I said, feeling sick-mean, "but I never shot. I never even thought about it until he was gone. I reckon you all ain't ever going to take me along any more." My lip was shaking and now I *was* about to cry.

Tom walked over and hit me on top of the head with the flat of his hand. "Happens to everybody," he said. "Grown men and boys, both, they all get buck fever. Got to do it once before you get over it. Forget it. I seen Pete here shoot five times at a buck big as a horse last year, and missed him with all five."

There were some footsteps in the branch where the deer had disappeared, and in a minute Mister Howard and the Old Man came out, with the dogs leashed and panting.

"Missed him clean," the Old Man said cheerfully. "Had one whack at him no farther'n thirty yards and missed him slick as a whistle. That's the way it is, but there's always tomorrow. Let's us go shoot some squirrels for the pot, and we'll rest the dogs and try again this evenin'. You *see* him, boy?"

"I *saw* him," I said. "And I ain't ever going to *forget* him."

We went back to camp and tied up the hounds. We unleashed the fice dog, Jackie, the little sort of yellow fox terrier kind of nothing dog with prick ears and a sharp fox's face and a thick tail that curved up over his back. I was going with Pete to shoot some squirrels while the old gentlemen policed up the camp, rested, took a couple of drinks, and started to prepare lunch. It was pretty late in the morning for squirrel hunting, but this swamp wasn't hunted much. While I had been on the deer stand that morning the swamp was alive with them—mostly big fox squirrels, huge old fellers with a lot of black on their gray-and-white hides.

"See you don't get squirrel fever," the Old Man hollered over his shoulder as Pete and I went down to the swamp. "Else we'll all starve to death. I'm about fresh out of ham and eggs."

"Don't pay no 'tention to him, son," Pete told me. "He's a great kidder."

"Hell with him," I said. "He missed the deer, didn't he? At least *I* didn't miss him."

"That's right," Pete agreed genially. "You got to shoot at 'em to miss 'em."

I looked quick and sharp at Pete. He didn't seem to be teasing me. A cigarette was hanging off the corner of his lip, and his lean, brown, Injun-looking face was completely straight. Then we heard Jackie, yip-yapping in a querulous bark, as if somebody had just insulted him by calling him a dog.

"Jackie done treed hisself a squirrel," Pete said. "Advantage of a dog like Jackie is that when the squirrels all come down to the ground to feed, ol' Jackie rousts 'em up and makes 'em head for the trees. Then he makes so much noise he keeps the squirrel interested while we go up and wallop away at him. Takes two men to hunt squirrels this way. Jackie barks. I go around to the other side of the tree. Squirrel sees me and moves. That's when you shoot him, when he slides around on your side. Gimme your gun."

"Why?" I asked. "What'll I use to shoot the——"

"*Mine*," Pete answered. "You ain't going to stand there and tell me you're gonna use a shotgun on a squirrel? Anybody can hit a pore little squirrel with a shotgun. Besides, shotgun shells cost a nickel apiece."

I noticed Pete's gun for the first time. He had left his pump gun in camp and had a little bolt-action .22. He took my shotgun from me and handed me the .22 and a handful of cartridges.

" 'Nother thing you ought to know," Pete said as we walked up to the tree, a big blue gum under which Jackie seemed to be going mad, "is that when you're hunting for the pot you don't belong to make much more noise with guns than is necessary. You go booming off a shotgun, blim-blam, and you spook ever'-thing in the neighborhood. A .22 don't make no more noise than a stick crackin', and agin the wind you can't hear it more'n a hundred yards or thereabouts. Best meat gun in the world, a straight-shootin' .22, because it don't make no noise and don't spoil the meat. Look up yonder, on the fourth fork. There's your dinner. A big ol' fox squirrel, near-about black all over."

The squirrel was pasted to the side of the tree. Pete walked around, and the squirrel moved with him. When Pete was on the other side, making quite a lot of noise, the squirrel shifted back around to my side. He was peeping at Pete, but his shoulders and back and hind legs were on my side. I raised the little .22 and plugged him between the shoulders. He came down like a sack of rocks. Jackie made a dash for him, grabbed him by the back, shook him once and broke his spine, and sort of spit him out on the ground. The squirrel was dang near as big as Jackie.

Pete and I hunted squirrels for an hour or so, and altogether we shot ten. Pete said that was enough for five people for a couple of meals, and there wasn't no sense to shootin' if the meat had to spoil. "We'll have us some venison by tomorrow, anyways," he said. "One of us is bound to git one. You shot real nice with that little bitty gun," he said. "She'll go where you hold her, won't she?"

I felt pretty good when we went into camp and the Old Man, Mister Howard, and Tom looked up inquiringly. Pete and I started dragging fox squirrels out of our hunting coats, and the ten of them made quite a sizable pile.

"Who shot the squirrels?" the Old Man asked genially. "The dog?"

"Sure," Pete grinned. "Dog's so good we've taught him to shoot, too. We jest set down on a log, give Jackie the gun, and

sent him off into the branch on his lonesome. We're planning
to teach him to skin 'em and cook 'em, right after lunch. This is
the best dog I ever see. Got more sense than people."

"Got more sense than *some* people," the Old Man grunted.
"Come and git it, boy, and after lunch you and Jackie can skin
the squirrels."

The lunch was a lunch I loved then and still love, which is
why I'm never going to be called one of those epicures. This
was a country hunting lunch, Carolina style. We had Vienna
sausages and sardines, rat cheese, gingersnaps and dill pickles
and oysterettes and canned salmon, all cold except the coffee
that went with it, and that was hot enough to scald clean down
to your shoes. It sounds horrible, but I don't know anything
that tastes so good together as Vienna sausages and sardines and
rat cheese and gingersnaps. Especially if you've been up since
before dawn and walked ten miles in the fresh air.

After lunch we stretched out in the shade and took a little
nap. Along about two I woke up, and so did Pete and Tom,
and the three of us started to skin the squirrels. It's not much
trouble, if you know how. Pete and I skinned 'em and Tom
cleaned and dressed 'em. I'd pick up a squirrel by the head, and
Pete would take his hind feet. We'd stretch him tight, and Pete
would slit him down the stomach and along the legs as far as the
feet. Then he'd shuck him like an ear of corn, pulling the hide
toward the head until it hung over his head like a cape and the
squirrel was naked. Then he'd just chop off the head, skin and
all, and toss the carcass to Tom.

Tom made a particular point about cutting the little castor
glands. Squirrel with the musk glands out is as tasty as any
meat I know, but unless you take out those glands an old he-
squirrel is as musky as a billy goat, and tastes like a billy goat
smells. Tom cut up the carcasses and washed them clean, and I
proceeded to bury the heads, hides, and guts.

The whole job didn't take forty-five minutes with the three
of us working. We put the pieces of clean red meat in a covered

pot, and then woke up the Old Man and Mister Howard. We were going deer hunting again.

The dogs had rested too; they had had half a can of salmon each and about three hours' snooze. It was beginning to cool off when Tom and Pete put Blue and Bell on walking leashes and we struck off for another part of the swamp, which made a Y from the main swamp and had a lot of water in it. It was a cool swamp, and Tom and Pete figured that the deer would be lying up there from the heat of the day, and about ready to start stirring out to feed a little around dusk.

I was in the process of trying to think about just how long forever was when the hounds started to holler real close. They seemed to be coming straight down the crick off to my right, and the crick's banks were very open and clear, apart from some sparkleberry and gallberry bushes. The *whoo-whooing* got louder and louder. The dogs started to growl and bark, just letting off a *woo-woo* once in a while, and I could hear a steady swishing in the bushes.

Then I could see what made the swishing. It was a buck, a big one. He was running steadily and seriously through the low bush. He had horns—my Lord, but did he have horns! It looked to me like he had a dead tree lashed to his head. I slipped off the safety catch and didn't move. The buck came straight at me, the dogs going crazy behind him.

The buck came down the water's edge, and when he got to about fifty yards I stood up and threw the gun up to my face. He kept coming and I let him come. At about twenty-five yards he suddenly saw me, snorted, and leaped to his left as if somebody had unsnapped a spring in him. I forgot he was a deer. I shot at him as you'd lead a duck or a quail on a quartering shot—plenty of lead ahead of his shoulder.

I pulled the trigger—for some odd reason shooting the choke barrel—right in the middle of a spring that had him six feet off the ground and must have been wound up to send him twenty yards, into the bush and out of my life. The gun said *boom!*

but I didn't hear it. The gun kicked but I didn't feel it. All I saw was that this monster came down out of the sky like I'd shot me an airplane. He came down flat, turning completely over and landing on his back, and he never wiggled.

The dogs came up ferociously and started to grab him, but they had sense and knew he didn't need any extra grabbing. I'd grabbed him real good, with about three ounces of No. 1 buck-shot in a choke barrel. I had busted his shoulder and busted his neck and dead-centered his heart. I had let him get so close that you could practically pick the wads out of his shoulder. This was *my* buck. Nobody else had shot at him. Nobody else had seen him but me. Nobody had advised or helped. This monster was mine.

And monster was right. He was huge, they told me later, for a Carolina whitetail. He had fourteen points on his rack, and must have weighed nearly 150 pounds undressed. He was beautiful gold on his top and dazzling white on his under-neath, and his little black hoofs were clean. The circular tufts of hair on his legs, where the scent glands are, were bright russet and stiff and spiky. His horns were as clean as if they'd been scrubbed with a wire brush, gnarled and evenly forked and the color of planking on a good boat that's just been holy-stoned to where the decks sparkle.

I had him all to myself as he lay there in the aromatic, crushed ferns—all by myself, like a boy alone in a big cathedral of oaks and cypress in a vast swamp where the doves made sobbing sounds and the late birds walked and talked in the sparkleberry bush. The dogs came up and lay down. Old Blue laid his muzzle on the big buck's back. Bell came over and licked my face and wagged her tail, like she was saying, "You did real good, boy." Then she lay down and put her face right on the deer's rump.

This was our deer, and no damn bear or anything else was go-ing to take it away from us. We were a team, all right, me and Bell and Blue.

I couldn't know then that I was going to grow up and shoot

elephants and lions and rhinos and things. All I knew then was that I was the richest boy in the world as I sat there in the crushed ferns and stroked the silky hide of my first buck deer, patting his horns and smelling how sweet he smelled and admiring how pretty he looked. I cried a little bit inside about how lovely he was and how I felt about him. I guess that was just reaction, like being sick twenty-five years later when I shot my first African buffalo.

I was still patting him and patting the dogs when Tom and Pete came up one way and the Old Man and Mister Howard came up from another way. What a wonderful thing it was. when you are a kid, to have four huge, grown men—everything is bigger when you are a boy—come roaring up out of the woods to see you sitting by your first big triumph. "Smug" is a word I learned a lot later. Smug was modest for what I felt then.

"Well," the Old Man said, trying not to grin.

"Well," Mister Howard said.

"Boy done shot hisself a horse with horns," Pete said, as proud for me as if I had just learned how to make bootleg liquor.

"Shot him pretty good, too," Tom said. "Deer musta been standing still, boy musta been asleep, woke up, and shot him in self-defense."

"Was not, either," I started off to say, and then saw that all four men were laughing.

They had already checked the sharp scars where the buck had jumped, and they knew I had shot him on the fly. Then Pete turned the buck over and cut open his belly. He tore out the paunch and ripped it open. It was full of green stuff and awful smelly gunk. All four men let out a whoop and grabbed me. Pete held the paunch and the other men stuck my head right into—blood, guts, green gunk, and all. It smelled worse than anything I ever smelled. I was bloody and full of partly digested deer fodder from my head to my belt.

"That," the Old Man said as I swabbed the awful mess off me and dived away to stick my head in the crick, "makes you a grown man. You have been blooded, boy, and any time you miss a deer from now on we cut off your shirt tail. It's a very good buck, son," he said softly, "one of which you can be very, very proud."

Tom and Pete cut a long sapling, made slits in the deer's legs behind the cartilage of his knees, stuck the sapling through the slits, and slung the deer up on their backs. They were sweating him through the swamp when suddenly the Old Man turned to Mister Howard and said, "Howard, if you feel up to it, we might just as well go get *our* deer and lug him into camp. He ain't but a quarter-mile over yonder, and I don't want the wildcats working on him in that tree."

"What deer?" I demanded. "You didn't shoot this afternoon, and you missed the one you——"

The Old Man grinned and made a show of lighting his pipe. "I didn't miss him, son," he said. "I just didn't want to give you an inferiority complex on your first deer. If you hadn't of shot this one—and he's a lot better'n mine—I was just going to leave him in the tree and say nothing about him at all. Shame to waste a deer; but it's a shame to waste a boy, too."

I reckon that's when I quit being a man. I just opened my mouth and bawled. Nobody laughed at me, either.

7

Somebody Else's Turkey Tastes Better

It was pushing on for Christmas when my grandma, Miss Lottie, pursed her mouth one day after she finished pouring the coffee, and remarked that if there were any menfolk in the house worth the powder and shot to blow them to perdition they would bestir themselves and go find a couple of wild turkeys that were dumber than they were. "The price of meat," Miss Lottie said, "has gone up something terrible, and I do not propose to pay ten cents a pound for turkey. You either shoot it or you don't eat it this year."

The Old Man cut his eyes at me over the coffee cup and allowed that he would finish his coffee on the piazza, because he wanted to smoke his pipe, and Miss Lottie had some definite ideas about smoking in the house. Unless she did it herself. She had the asthma and smoked Cubeb cigarettes for her chest troubles. I broke in on Cubebs at a very early age.

"The way of a man with a woman is hard," the Old Man said when he was settled down in his rocker and had fired up the Prince Albert. "I reckon there's just nothing for us to do but leave her bed and board for a spell. It's a tough life, son, and you might as well recognize it early. Here we just got back from a hard week in the woods, up every morning before dawn, do-ing our own cooking, walking all day long, freezing on stumps waiting for deer to come by, and now we got to go back to the same place we left and do it all over again. My, *my*. Women are so unreasonable. If I had of suggested even mildly that maybe you and me ought to go turkey hunting, she would of found sixty different reasons to keep us home."

The Old Man knocked the dottle out of his pipe and walked laboriously upstairs. He came down five minutes later with a peculiar-looking flute thing made out of cedar and a stick of chalk in his hand. He rubbed the chalk on the cedar and moved some sliding parts, and the most lonesome piece of hen-turkey clucking I ever heard came out of it. Then he did something else to the calling apparatus, and a ferocious gobble emerged. The Old Man stuck the turkey caller in his pocket and pulled out his watch.

"I'd say four minutes, maybe five," he said softly, and when I asked him what and why, he just nodded and said to wait.

I had a dollar watch of my own, and I pulled it out to see what he was waiting for. In exactly four and one-half minutes Tom and Pete came roaring down the street, taking giant strides in their hip boots.

"Well," the Old Man said, "I was pretty near right. I estimated between four and five minutes, and you split the difference with me. I reckon you're both gettin' old. There was a time you would of been here in two minutes flat when I I sounded off on a turkey call."

Tom and Pete grinned. "We're ready to go now if you are, Ned," they said. "Lend us the boy and the flivver, and we'll be ripe to leave in an hour. Ain't nothing to do but th'ow in the tent and the guns and the food and the blankets and the shells."

"Get her ready," the Old Man said. "We can make the place by dark if we hurry, and be up in the morning. When Miss Lottie demands turkeys, I hate mightily to disappoint her."

All through this double-talky stuff I was not saying a word, because nobody had come right out to say whether I was invited or not. I was thinking of myself as a real professional about now, after having recently shot me a deer, but I knew you couldn't crowd the Old Man any and, for all I knew, he and Pete and Tom and Grandma were all in some sort of plot or other to torture me. Wouldn't be the first time it happened, either.

I helped Tom and Pete load all the duffel into the flivver, and Pete drove her up in front of the house. I just stood there and didn't say anything, looking kind of wistful like Oliver Twist asking for another helping of gruel.

"Well, boy," the Old Man said, "I see everything in this Liz but your gun. Who's going to shoot the turkeys if you don't rustle upstairs and get that 16-gauge?"

I rustled.

Tom and Pete were in the front seat and the Old Man and I were jammed into the back of the Liz. We didn't head up the main road, but went up the River Road, a back road. The Old Man addressed the back of Tom's head.

"It would seem to me," he said to nobody in particular, "that a wild thing is God's property. A turkey or a deer is born, and he ain't got any way of knowing whether he belongs to a rich man or a poor man. But a rich man will come along and buy up a great passel of land, and then go off to New York or to Paris, France, and leave the land there all by itself. Gradually the word spreads around amongst the wild critters that this here is heaven on earth, a kind of pie-in-the-sky operation for everybody. The rich man, like the feller that owns these Magnolia Acres, is off playing Willie-off-the-pickle-boat in his yacht somewhere, and what is happening? Nobody is shooting over his ground, but all the birds and animals for miles around are hived up there. The cock birds are fighting the other cock birds, and the deer are fighting the deer, and inbreeding is going on, and the first thing you know diseases will start, and then we'll have an epidemic of blacktongue or screwworm or galloping pip, and all the crittes'll die off or get inbred or something and do nobody no good in the meantime.

"Now," the Old Man said, "I'm a law-abiding man, first, last, and always. If this Willie-off-the-pickle-boat would ask me to caretake his property, I would be pleased to keep his game shot down to a reasonable balance; but as long as I ain't got a yacht and don't live in the French Riveera, there ain't much chance of him asking me. Mind, I wouldn't set foot on his property for a pretty, because it plainly says 'Posted' every whipstitch. But he don't own the other side of the road. That he don't. That's public ground. And I was just thinking that if a turkey was dumb enough to cross that road we might shoot him legal-like, since we all have hunting licenses. If this offends anybody's sense of morals, ethics, or legal tendencies, now's the time to speak up."

I could see the neckskin stretch on Tom and Pete when they grinned. The chances were pretty good that no Christmas or New Year's ever passed without a houseful of wild turkey, and I reckoned that the three had had themselves a dead-sure cinch for more years than I was born. But this was the first crack I'd had at looking at it.

We drove on for an hour or more and finally came up to the millionaire's place, which was highly fenced off on one side of the road and every tenth tree had a big "No Hunting" sign on it. We turned off a little washboarded clay road in the other direction, drove about half a mile, and came to a campsite that looked exactly like the last one I saw that the Old Man had anything to do with. He left a trade-mark on all his camps. They looked like he'd manicured them before he left. I *know;* I manicured the last one until all that was left was a neat pile of stones for the cook-fire. Everything else was either burned up or buried.

We made a swift camp, had a swift meal, built some swift beds, and went swiftly off to sleep. I hadn't even turned over good before Pete was shaking me. The moon was still high and the stars still very bright. It was four o'clock in the morning, an awful hour for anybody to get up. It was cold as Christmas in Canada. We had a cup of coffee and that was all.

"All I ask of you, young man," the Old Man said, "is to just follow me and Pete and Tom, do what we do, keep your mouth shut, try not to step on no dry sticks, sit when we sit, and when I punch you on the arm you shoot. You will know what to shoot at."

We headed off through the black woods, stepping carefully along an old deer path, Tom first, Pete second, then the Old Man, and finally me. We walked about a quarter of a mile, until we came to a little glade about a thousand yards from the main road. It had bush all around it. At the far end, away from the road, it had a suspicious-looking hump of bush that didn't look quite like the other bush. Pete and Tom and the Old Man disappeared in it. I followed. It was quite a comfortable blind, broad enough to hold four shooters, with little slits cut for the eyes to see out of and big enough to poke a gun out of. It was still dark, and my Lord, but it was cold, sitting shivering on the slick brown pine needles.

The Old Man whispered, "As soon as it comes gray light you're going to see some turkeys. They may fly in, light in trees, look around, and then come down. They don't do it so much in the morning, but I never trust a turkey. He's smarter than you are most all the time. Likely they'll walk. If it's a little flock, there'll be a gobbler and mebbe three, four, five hens. If it's a big flock, there'll be more'n one gobbler and a whole passel of hens. I want you to shoot whatever's biggest that's closest to you, when I punch you, and not before. Take a bead on his head and try to think that you're shooting a robin. No point shooting him in the white meat when his head is right there and plenty target. This one is for your grandma. Now be quiet and watch."

It came on dawn and the Old Man got out his turkey call. He fiddled with it in the gray half-light, and then he sounded off like he was the sole owner of a turkey farm. He chuckled seductively, like a hen turkey hunting a boy friend. He gobbled like a boy friend hunting a hen turkey. Then he shut himself up and never struck another note. Later he told me that the point in turkey calling was not to overdo it. If there was a turkey around that was coming to call, he'd come.

A lot of years later I sat in leopard blinds, and that was tense. But it wasn't as tense as waiting out a turkey. The turkeys never flew in. They crept in like wraiths, as fog sweeps into narrow alleys. First they weren't there, and then they were there, looking as big as cows. They came out of a little avenue in single file. The first ones were hens. Then there were some yearling gobblers. Then more hens, and finally the Chief.

They fanned out, feeding gently toward us. I suspect now that Tom and Pete had kept that clearing ankle-deep in corn against the annual T-day, but baiting was legal in those days, and anyhow they could have been eating pine mast. I didn't care, one way or the other. I was watching that gobbler, the Chief. He spread his tail like a vast fan and let out a gobble that sounded like "The Bells of St. Mary's." He gazed arrogantly around him and dared any turkey in the neighborhood to flap so much as a wattle at one of his wives and he, personally, the Chief, would tear him limb from wing. He hustled his gang along, coming straight at the blind; Pete told me later there were sixteen or seventeen turkeys in the family. I dunno. All I saw was the head man, his wattles red in the early dawn, his purplish breast as big as a feather bed, his bronze-and-black coming out in the emerging light. I never will see a moa, but this thing was bigger than any ostrich.

Finally he strutted down the center of his family, cursing quietly to himself in Turkish, and hauled up about thirty yards from the blind like a general surveying his troops. Then he let out a gobble fit to wake the millionaire in Paris, France, and stretched his neck to heaven, saying he would take on any angels that were flying around loose that morning too. That's when the Old Man punched me on the arm.

I hid his head with the front sight of the little sixteen and hauled down. When I hauled down, Tom, Pete, and the Old Man hauled down. I only hauled once. They hauled twice, but what happened in that grassy little pine glade I'm not apt to forget. My man, the Chief, was down, with his head shot off, but he was roaring around with his wings like he was a windmill gone crazy. So were exactly six other turkeys. Seven wild turkeys doing a death dance in a quiet forest glade before sunup make any pictures I ever saw of the poor souls in hell look like a quiet pastoral.

Everybody seemed to be whooping and running, including two turkeys which got up and headed for the brush, but which caught loads of No. 2 shot in their trousers and decided to stay. But for confusion I've never seen anything like it, now, then, or ever, even the one day when I was a grown man and got mixed up with nine lions. Seemed to me the whole danged countryside had turned into turkey.

What happened was that, when I assassinated the Chief, Tom and Pete and the Old Man had also picked targets and whanged off at them, killing them real dead. Then they threw the other barrel into the flock as it took off, and scored again. Like I said, only two were wounded enough to run.

I expect that set some sort of record. My victim—that turned out to be tougher than whit leather—weighed nineteen pounds, which I understand now is a lot of turkey. We had two other toms over ten pounds, and the hens were all a nice six, seven, eight pounds of plump eating.

I mean we were a sight to see when the Liz drew up in front of the house and Miss Lottie came out with that all-right-where-is-it look on her face. We slung 'em out one at a time, and even Miss Lottie couldn't keep her face straight in front of seven big new wild turkeys. We had turkey those holidays until I wished I'd never seen one. The Old Man didn't have much to say about the feat. Sometime between Christmas and New Year's he got me off to one side and muttered a parable at me.

"The trouble," he said, "with people and turkeys is not knowing which side of the road to stay on in face of temptation."

One of the great things I remember about the grown-ups who raised me was that when Christmas came around they never gave me anything I needed. By "needed" I mean to say I knew a kid next door who was always getting something worthy, like a new pair of shoes or a school suit, which may be practical and fine economy, but I never saw any romance in a roof on a house. A house belongs to have a roof, and is not supposed to get one for Christmas. When a boy gets a school suit or a new pair of shoes, they aren't a gift. They're a roof on a house.

Fair times or foul, what I got for Chistmas and birthdays was a luxury, even if it was only a pocketknife worth fifty cents. Most of the time it was considerably more, because that was before the Big Depression, and everybody had some money to spend on fun. By "everybody" I suppose I mean my own family, because the early Christmases started out with air guns and bicycles and such, and wound up with hunting boots and knives and scout axes and punching bags and shotguns. I reckon the most memorable of them all was the one when I got a blue Iver Johnson bicycle *and* a shotgun.

It was a lot of fun prowling the ten-cent stores to buy notable gifts for the grown-ups, and it was a lot of fun waiting for Santa Claus to bring you something you'd been hammering at the family about for six months, but the real fun didn't start until afterward, around the New Year's, when you were still free from school and could really concentrate on using the loot you'd found under the tree.

Christmas itself was pretty well cluttered up with grown

people—visiting aunts and cousins and stuff, largely city people come slumming to the country—and a fellow was expected to hang around with a clean face and a decent air of raising until they all cleared out and let you revert to dirty fingernails and your normal lack of hair comb. Then was when the pure fun started.

The holiday season was pretty special for me. As soon as school let out, about the twentieth, I took off for the little town where the Old Man lived, and I didn't get back to my own city until the day before school started again. For better than two weeks I lived a life like I imagine it might have been in the old English-squire days, when they hung the halls with holly and it took three men and a boy to haul in the Yule log.

I don't remember any pigs stuffed whole, with apples in their mouths, but I do know that certain expeditions had to be made by the Old Man and his willing assistant, which was your ob't sv't, and these expeditions lasted right on through the holidays.

First, there was the oyster business. Holiday time was oyster time, because there were plenty of R's in the months, and the oysters were fine and firm and fat, as big as cucumbers, with their gray-and-white shells the color of a pintail duck and the big deep-cut wrinkles running down to the scalloped edges. Maybe there isn't much romance to an oyster unless you find a pearl in one. To me oysters even without pearls are romantic.

The Old Man and I used to go out in the skiff, with the tongs, on a cold gray day when the ducks were scudding low and sitting cosy around corners of the marsh. We would take the guns, of course, because there would always be some fool duck that would wait too long to take off, and whichever one of us wasn't poling or rowing the skiff would grab a shotgun off the gunwale and haul him down. Once I saw a little animal with a head like a rat swimming, and the Old Man said, "Shoot him!" and it was a big boar mink. We skinned him out and stretched him and salted him, and the man in town gave me two dollars for his hide.

But you would go out over the wind-stirred gray waters,

with your nose and ears bitten red by the cold, and finally come to the oyster beds. You would take the tongs and grapple along until you tied into a likely clump, and up they'd come, muddy, and you would swish the full-loaded tongs back and forth in the water until most of the mud washed off, so as not to muck up the boat too much. When you had half a boatload, you poled her back, and by this time I would have had the knife out and a couple of dozen opened.

It was very simple to open those oysters. You just took the heavy back of the knife blade and crushed the thin serrated edges of the oyster, stuck the point of the knife in close to the muscle, gave your wrist a little twist, and bong, there was your oyster, lying salty and clean on the shell and still dribbling cold briny water. That water was chilly enough to numb you. While I have eaten a lot of oysters since, with a lot of contrived sauces, I don't remember any oyster tasting as good as one of those big ones that came streaming straight up out of the mud.

Getting oysters was one of the expeditions. The Christmas-tree expedition was another. They tell me people buy Christmas trees now. We scouted a cedar tree for a year in advance. It had to be just the right size and shape and hard enough to get at so that nobody else was apt to swipe it out from under your nose. Mostly, the whole family—Ma, Pa, the Old Man, the grandmas, and the dogs—all piled into the car and went to get the tree. It was a special event.

You couldn't go very early, because the tree had to endure until after New Year's. So we went about two days before Christmas; and if I had spotted the tree, I usually tried to locate it deep in a big swamp or away off in a gallberry bay so that I'd have an excuse to take a gun in case a squirrel or a deer attacked me.

The mistletoe and holly procurement was my special province. Mistletoe had to be climbed after, if it was any good, and somehow I never went after any mistletoe that wasn't hung away up in the mizzen of a cypress as big as a California redwood. You would see the little white waxy kissing berries against the dark green leaves, parasiting happily up there in the clouds, and this was fine, because it was something a boy could do that a man couldn't do. I would take a knife in my teeth—of course in my teeth, because I was Mr. Israel Hands, straight out of *Treasure Island*—and I would shoot up the rigging like a monkey and cut the mistletoe and throw it down.

The holly berries were easy to get at, since they grew on a low bush, but somehow the sight of those glowing red berries against the dark fleshy green of the sharp-bristled leaves made your heart jump high. When you finally got all the stuff home and the women went to work with it, your house smelled just like a good woods camp from the smell of the cedar, and the clean, late-afternoon swampy smell of the holly, and the smoky spice coming from a big oak or hickory log with the resin-dripping lightwood kindling crackling under it.

Women are generally a bother to a boy or a man, but around the holiday season they sure earned their keep. Miss Lottie, my grandma, was a fair hand with a stove, and between the smell of what she was cooking, the smell of the evergreens, and the smell of the strange Yule specialties that you never saw at any other time of the year, the house literally trembled with odor.

Miss Lottie would have had a couple of big fruit cakes under way since along about September—cakes as big as mill wheels, full of dark green citron and fat raisins and candied cherries and juicy currants, and soaked in enough brandy to get you giddy on a slice of it. The fruit cake lasted forever, because the Old Man would slip in and sluice her down with a fresh dollop of brandy from time to time, and if you kept her shut up in a tin box she stayed moist until June.

We had the three kinds of cake around Christmas—the black fruit cake; another kind of cake they called Sally White, which was a blond cousin to the mahogany-dark one; and then pound cake, which was made out of angel's-down and vanilla icing that broke off in wonderful slabs.

For the holidays you had oranges, which never appeared at any other time, and whose oily hides added an extra pungency to the society of odors. You had the big brown-purplish Malaga grapes and fist-sized clusters of plump wrinkled raisins, sticky and sugar-sweet, as big as taw marbles. The Old Man used to pour a little brandy over the raisins too, and then set them alight, and the great game was to see who could dart a hand in and come out, unsinged, with a decent clump.

Then all the dishes were filled with nuts—English walnuts, shelled pecans, and the special treat, the greasy, plump white Brazil nuts we called niggertoes. Flanking the nut dishes were plates full of store-bought candies: little clover-leaf-shaped mints in various bright colors and stripedy hard candies with nasty soft centers that didn't taste very good but looked real pretty.

You cannot get through a holiday menu without devoting some tender thought to the ham. This was pig that needed no apple in its maw—very special pig. My household featured three kinds of ham. One was a hard country ham, as salty as the sea and deep red and tough-tender, which had been hanging in a smokehouse since Gabriel was an apprentice trumpeter. This was what you had fried in the morning, hot and salty with the grits. Then there was a corned ham, blond in color, that was stuck full of cloves. And finally there was that light pink one, a Smithfield, but not hard, because the slices curled up at the edges and crumpled at the corners and were streaked with rivers of soft white fat.

The smells of all this stuff mixed with the wild turkeys that were cooking slowly, being basted by old Galena, the cook, and the saddles of venison that somebody was dripping wine and jelly onto, and the wild ducks taking it easy in the bake pan with carrots and onions and slices of apple—and perhaps the quail frying for the breakfast meal, to help the ham along. There was a dessert the Old Man called raisin duff, an old English seagoing dish served with a hard sauce that had enough brandy in it to arouse the adverse attention of the Anti-Saloon League.

Each day of the holiday fetched a fresh excitement: testing the new gun, breaking in the new boots—the new soft boots that looked military but had the strap over the arch—and getting the feel of the new mackinaw with the wetproof game pocket. It all had a sort of electricity to it.

The men took extra time off and special hunts were arranged. If I minded my *p's* and *q's*, sometimes I would get asked to a deer drive or a coon hunt in the cold, frosty woods, or to go out with Tom or Pete to shoot some tame hogs run wild. There were quail to hunt and ducks to shoot and squirrels to tree, and every day of the holidays it was the same—wonderful.

You would come in half-dead and full-froze, and a blast of heat and the intermingled scent of food and festivity would smite you in the face. You went over and turned your tail to the fire, and you heated up your hands so that the hot water wouldn't torture them when you washed off the muck. Then you kicked off the new boots and put your tired feet in some sloppy slippers and crawled into a pair of softer pants and went to the table and ate dedicatedly until you had consumed more food than a battalion eats these days. You ate it all, and then came back for more. The butter-soggy hot biscuits, the size of quarters, were endless; the pickled artichokes and the watermelon preserves were only condiments. You dragged yourself up from the table by main force, but still had the foresight to grab a handful of raisins and a pocketful of candy in case you got a mite peckish in the night. Why I didn't founder myself I will never, never know.

The Old Man, as usual, tried to cram a little culture down me on top of the turkey and the sage dressing, but I don't think I really absorbed much. He hit me with *A Christmas Carol*, but got nowhere, because the Messrs. Scrooge and Cratchit and Tiny Tim were really not living in my league.

8

Old Dogs and Old Men Smell Bad

The Old Man cornered me one drizzly day after dinner—I mean the meal we ate in the middle of the day—and he said that he had an awful crick in his back and that he reckoned he was getting old and rheumaticky and that one of these days he was just going to say to hell with it and lay right down and die.

"There are two things got no place in this world," he said, "an old dog and an old man. They perform no useful function, and generally smell bad, too. It seems to me you ought to start branching out on your own hook, boy, because I have wet-nursed you long enough. My back aches and my feet hurt and I feel like a mess of quail, but I'm too feeble to go out in the wet and help you shoot 'em. It's about time you investigated the delicate art of making a dog behave himself in the woods. All you've ever done with the dogs is listen to me holler, 'Whoa!' and one of these days you will have to train dogs of your own. The best way to learn to train a dog is to let a dog that's smarter than you are train you."

It was late February, and it had been raining solidly for a week, and the rain was still coming down in spasms. A little weak sun filtered through every now and then, though; so the Old Man said he reckoned the birds were as tired of the weather as he was, and just might be out of the swamps for a breath of fresh air.

"You take Frank and Sandy," he said, "and turn 'em loose and watch 'em. The only order you got to give is to tell Sandy to hold when he tries to steal Frank's point, and he'll try to steal any covey point Frank makes. That dog is the biggest covey thief I ever knew. If he don't *whoa*, cut yourself a switch and wear him out. There are some dogs, like some people, who won't listen to reason and who respond only to a lick on the tail."

My ma took the Liz and dropped me and the animals out by a little crick named Jackie's Creek, and said she would pick us up at the bridge come sundown when she headed back from town. The dogs were raring to go. They'd been shut up for the last couple of weeks, and they craved action.

Sandy was a big lemon-and-white English setter with one red eye, and old Frank was a blue-ticked Llewellyn. They both had quality folks. As I remember, Frank had old Sir Sidney Mohawk for a grandpa. He wasn't flashy like Sandy, who thought anything under a mile was close hunting and who never had his nose on the ground in his life. He could stick that nose up in the air and wind a bird from here to Canada, if the wind was right and there was a bird in Canada.

Frank was a close hunter, and he believed that the ground was for smelling. On singles he was sure and sudden death, and if you gave him a little time no coveys were apt to escape him forever. When he froze, there were birds there. They were not over yonder; they were there, right under Frank's nose. If they ran, he ran with them, and they were still there, right under Frank's nose. He didn't point snakes and he didn't point terrapins and he didn't point rabbits. He pointed quail.

The dogs paid their respects, as dogs will, to all the trees, bushes, stumps, rocks, and footpaths that they encountered. As dogs will, they ran down the road as if they had lost a watch in it last week. Then they came back to the whistle and informed me that it was time to go to work. I waved the hand like I'd seen the Old Man do and swept it at a sad-looking cornfield. Frank looked at Sandy and Sandy looked at Frank and then they both looked at me rather wistfully. "No," they said. "This is ridiculous."

"Hie on," I ordered. "Dammit." I could cuss pretty good now when the Old Man wasn't around.

The dogs shrugged. Sandy took off and made a rectangular speed run around the edges of the field. Frank worked it diagonally one way, and then intersected himself and worked it diagonally the other way. Sandy finished his perimeter check and came back and sat down in front of me with his tongue hanging out and a slight sneer on his face. Frank showed up with the same sneer.

"All right," I said, "do it your own way. *Dammit.*"

The dogs looked at each other and commented briefly that the young'un was showing some signs of sense, however feeble. Sandy stuck his head into the air and tested. Frank, the vice-president, chewed a cocklebur out of his fetlocks. Then Sandy got The Word. He pointed his nose toward a high hummock of piney-wooded land, a little island in the sopping straw. There was a sawdust pile just behind it. Holding his nose in the air like a society lady making an entrance, he walked, not ran, with Frank ambling behind him, to the high hummock, disappeared into the gallberry bush, and his bell became silent. Frank stuck his head into the bushes, liked what he saw, turned around, more or less waved, and told me to hurry up, that we were in business.

In business we were. Sandy had been stricken stiff on the side of the little hill. He looked like he had been shot out of a cannon and then arrested in mid-speed. He was so taut forward that he was nearly off balance. The great plumed tail was as rigid as a rudder. Frank had gone back into the bushes and was backing, his head leaning lovingly against Sandy's flank and his tail wagging gently and indulgently. When I came up to Sandy's head, he jumped right into the middle of the covey. The birds got up and flattened out over the sawdust pile in a perfect fan. I missed with the first barrel, shooting too quick, but dropped a bird with the second.

Frank lolloped up the side of the sawdust pile where the bird was fluttering a little bit. He took him by the head, bit his neck, laid him down, dead now, and then picked him up gently, carrying him, cradled in his lower jaw, with just enough pressure from the upper teeth to hold him secure. He came up to me and reared up on my chest with his front feet. I opened the game pocket of my old canvas hunting coat, and he nuzzled his head inside and dropped the bird in the pocket. Then he got down, spat out some feathers, and said, "Let's go, bud."

Sandy heaved a sigh, and the dogs consulted briefly. Frank said that the biggest bunch of them went thataway, where the branch crooks out in a gentle curve with a lot of high broom straw in front of it, and they're likely to glide right and spread out in that straw because the swamp is too wet to roost in. Sandy said no; in his considered judgment they turned left, and would be in that pine thicket. Frank made an impatient movement and said very plainly, "Just who the hell is the single-bird expert around here, you yaller-spotted wind-sniffer? I say they went to the *right*." "Okay," Sandy said, "it's your dice. Let's go."

It occurred to me that maybe the birds went straight, but neither one of the dogs asked me.

Sandy consulted again with Frank and then flashed off, quartering swiftly around and taking up a noble stand at the edge of the swamp. Frank plowed into the high, yellow, soaking grasses, hit a trail, shook his hips like a shimmy dancer, and fell dead on his belly. I could hear Sandy's bell on the far side of the broom, and I hollered, "Whoa!" He *whoaed*.

The bird got up, just under Frank's nose, and I nailed him in a shower of feathers. "Fetch," I said. Frank looked annoyed. "Don't be ridiculous," he said, and whirled, dropping dead again. The little brown rocket soared. I turned him over, and Frank looked pleased. He worked on for another few feet and sagged again. Two birds, a hen and a cock, got up and, so help me, I got one with the right and one with the left. Frank looked around and grinned. "That's enough," he said. "Break the gun, son, because five's enough out of any covey."

I broke the gun. Frank sent a signal to Sandy to the effect that even an aristocrat could do a little work, and I heard Sandy's bell again. Presently he showed up with a bird in his mouth. He dropped it on the ground and sat down. Frank had gone after the double. He came back with both at once and carefully nuzzled them into my coat.

We crossed over the swamp, and I snapped the little 16-gauge back into working order. Old Frank meandered out ahead of me, sniffing the fringes of the swamp, and all of a sudden he hit a scent. He telegraphed Sandy. Sandy romped up to where Frank was spinning around in circles, his tail whipping back and forth. "All right, genius," Frank said to Sandy, "take over. They came out here, and the wind is blowing right up that snooty nose of yours. Go earn your corn bread."

Up went that head, which, as I remember it, was more beautiful than any statue, woman, or painting I ever saw later on, and over the hill he went. Frank looked around and beckoned to me, and we strolled over the hill together. About two hundred yards away was Sandy, pale as a ghost at the distance, carved into marble at the edge of a clump of scrub pines.

One bird ducked around a tree as I fired. Another dived over a branch as I fired. No meat. The dogs looked sorrowful. "This lad is strictly an in-and-outer," Frank said sadly. "One minute he's a firecracker, and another minute he's a bum. Maybe we better build up his confidence a little bit." Sandy just shrugged. "I can't do it *all*," he said, very plainly, and lay down to investigate something on his stomach.

According to the consensus, in which I was not included, the birds had gone through the swamp and out onto a slope on the side, but a slope that was still thickly wooded. We went into the swamp and, as we crossed, a single flushed wild on the edge. I banged at the blur, and a couple more got up. Nothing whatsoever dropped. You could barely see them through the branches. Frank considered briefly and then detoured me around the bird area. He stationed me up on the hill, and when I started to follow him down he said, "No, boy, for the love of Pete. I'm trying to make it easy for you."

I stood on the slope. Frank sent Sandy down into the swamp. He worked the slope down toward the swamp. Neither dog made any effort to point. They found birds and flushed them, and when they flushed they were clear targets in the open. A short while later I had four more birds in my pocket.

We worked back toward where I was to meet Ma. Sandy spied another sawdust heap and marched off toward it. This time the birds were in a three-foot copse of sparkleberry bushes. Murder. The dogs had given me so much confidence by now that I just sort of casually raised the gun and collected a double with as much assurance as if I'd been a meat hunter with a sawed-off. Sandy sat down to investigate his rear end, a portion of which seemed to have been mislaid. Frank went and got the birds and stowed them in my coat. He looked up and told me that for a dumb kid I followed orders pretty good, and now let's go home.

I looked longingly over to where the birds had pitched in a field of broom straw.

Both dogs said, "No, remember the limit. The Old Man wouldn't like it." I said okay, let's go find Ma. The dogs never made a move to hunt, although I knew of at least three more coveys in the land we passed. They just trotted along at heel.

When we got back, the Old Man seemed not to be so near

death as before, because I could detect a slight odor of the medicine he always used to ward off the chills. It came in charred kegs and was colored a mahogany red and was illegal at that time. He seemed real pleased when I spread the ten birds—six cocks and four hens—out in front of the fireplace.

"Learn anything?" he asked casually, puffing on the pipe.

"Yessir," I said. "One thing I know is that after the rains you got to hunt the high ground, because quail don't like to get their feet wet, and at this time of the year there ain't anything for them to eat in the fields, anyhow. The birds are in the woods, eating the mast and what's left of the berries. Also, they seem to like sawdust piles."

"I dunno why," he said, "but seems to me I never recollect a sawdust pile that didn't have a covey of bobwhite using near it. Maybe they like to dust in it, or maybe they eat sawdust instead of grit to keep 'em healthy. Learn anything else?"

"Yessir. I learned that late in the afternoon, especially when it's wet, birds don't want to roost in a swamp, but will either settle down on the near side or fly through and put down on the far side. Also, they don't fly so far late as they do early. Also, that there's no point in trying to shoot in a swamp when you can stand on the side and send the dogs in to flush for you."

"*Send* the dogs in?" the Old Man asked gently, crinkling his eyes.

"Well, the dogs went in," I said, sort of lamely, "And they wouldn't let me go in with 'em; so I stood on the side and shot four easy birds."

"Anything else?"

"Well, I found out I can shoot pretty good when I'm out by myself. You don't have to watch for the other fellow, and you can take chances on birds you wouldn't shoot at ordinarily, and somehow you pick up some confidence as you go along, because you're relaxed and you don't want to disappoint the dogs."

"That all?"

"Well, sir, one thing more. I reckon that there ain't nothing anybody can tell a good dog that the dog don't know better than the man. I reckon it's the dog's business to know his business."

The Old Man smiled a big, broad, tobacco-stained, mustachy smile. "I was kind of hoping to hear that, son," he said. "So few people ever learn it. You take a dog and you train him right, and then leave him alone and you got a good dog. The same thing applies to boys. Spoil a dog early, and no amount of hollering will cure him. That also applies to boys. Beat him when he's bad, early, and you don't have to take a stick to him later. Did you have to holler *whoa* at Sandy?"

"Just once."

"Did he *whoa?*"

"He *whoaed*."

The Old Man looked even more pleased. "Boy," he said, "I will tell you a very wise thing. If a man is really intelligent, there's practically nothing a good dog can't teach him. But a dumb man can't learn anything from a smart dog, while a dumb dog can occasionally learn something from a smart man. Remember that.

"And now," he said, and I knew what was coming, "go pick and gut the birds. Anything that's good enough to shoot is good enough to use, and the longer you put off cleaning a bird or a fish the harder the job is. Scat now, because I got a hankering for some quail with my grits. I don't believe I'm going to die tonight after all."

The winter had gone in a wild, cold flurry of nasty rain, and the sun was beginning to be a little more prevalent. It was too late to shoot and too early to fish, too hot for football and too cold for baseball. I had the adolescent nervous twitches. You know, when the house is too small and there doesn't seem to be anything around but school, with summer still too far off to be hopeful about. I reckon my behavior was not what the dictionary calls exemplary, unless it was a bad example.

The Old Man looked at me with some amusement. I was in

between engagements, so to speak, and he knew it. Maybe that's why he called me out to the back yard one day and showed me something. It was a pointer puppy, the saddest-looking pointer puppy I ever saw. It had feet as big as a grizzly bear's and one twisted ear, and was about half-dead from the mange, the hair gone off its hide and the skin wrinkled pink and ugly.

"This," the Old Man said, "is a damned fine bird dog. Pretty much in the rough, I'll admit, but a good dog nevertheless. I know about his parents. But he needs some work done on him, and the time to train a dog is in the spring, when you've got nothing better to do. The first thing we will do is get rid of this mange."

"Where'd you get him?" I asked. "I never saw such a homely critter."

"Don't let the looks fool you," the Old Man cautioned. "His blood is better'n yours. What happened was that the man that owns his mama had to go away for a spell, and he left the bitch with a share-crop farmer and the whole litter picked up the mange. Once we get this mange fixed, you will have yourself a dog. And now that you been pretty well trained by the old dogs, mebbe you'd better try your hand at training a puppy, so's you can learn some more about dogs, *from* dogs."

I grinned just a little bit, remembering the other day when Frank and Sandy gave me a kindergarten course.

"What do we do about this mange?" I asked him.

"Very simple," the Old Man said. "We go down to visit Gus McNeill at the filling station, and we beg some old used crankcase oil that he's got, from changing the oil in automobiles from winter to spring. Then we go see Doc Watson in the drugstore, and we buy a little sulphur off him. We mix the sulphur with the old crankcase oil and douse the puppy in it, and bimeby there won't be any mange."

The Old Man was right. We smeared the puppy with the mixture for a few days, and before long you could see the hair growing back, and it wasn't more than a month before he was haired out real nice and beginning to grow up to his feet. We named him Tom, for some reason or other, and I took over his education.

"A bird dog," the Old Man told me, "is trained in the back yard. There ain't no way in the world you can teach him to smell; so you don't have to bother about that. There ain't no way in the world you can teach him bird sense; so there ain't any use worrying about that. All you can teach this dog is a little discipline, so that he can use his talents to the best advantage. Like they're trying to teach you a little discipline in school. Whether you got brains enough to take advantage of it is strictly up to you."

"Where do you start?" I asked the Old Man.

"Well, there's all sorts of ways to train a dog and not break him. Don't you ever let me hear you use the word 'break.' You don't want a broken dog. You want to educate him, not crush him. A man who's got to break a dog don't deserve the dog. All you want to teach him is a little common sense and some politeness. The first thing you want to teach him is the difference between yes and no. We'll start with something basic, like food."

We only fed the dogs once a day; so they were pretty hungry. We fed 'em mostly table scraps and hard cold hominy and a lot of cold corn bread and turnip greens and fatback and now and then a can of salmon or some canned dog food, but not much. We fed them about five o'clock in the afternoon, and we always fed each dog out of his own tin pie plate, a few feet away from each other. I noticed neither Frank nor Sandy ever made a move at the dinner pail until the Old Man snapped his fingers and said, "Hie on." And right in the middle of the meal, if the Old Man said, "*Whoa!*" they quit eating. Old Frank was pretty cute. You could put a sliver of steak or some other tasty victual on his nose and he'd just sit there, and when you gave him the okay word he'd flip his head, toss the meat in the air, catch it, swallow it, and then sort of take a bow.

We trained the puppy very simple. We put his pan down, and when he lunged for the food I'd just grab him by the tail and say, "*Whoa!*" I would gentle him some and tell him he was a fine upstanding puppy, and then I would say, "Hie on" and let him go. It didn't take a week for him to get the message. He would head for his dinner, and I would say, "*Whoa*" and he'd *whoa*. He would turn his head and wait for the snapped fingers and the words, "Hie on," and then he would eat. In the middle of the meal I'd grab him by the tail again and say, "*Whoa*." He learned that one in about two days. When I said, "*Whoa*," even when he was swallowing, he would quit, haul back on his haunches, and wait the word again.

Like all puppies, he loved to go dashing after sticks or balls, and, like all puppies, he liked to run off with the stick or the ball and tease you with it. He was not what you'd call a natural-born retriever. He was a joker. The Old Man showed me how to lick that one, too. We bent a line on his collar and chucked out the stick, and when he picked it up and started off for the back forty the Old Man checked him in the middle of a leap with the rope and hollered, "Fetch!" Then he hauled him in so fast that he was sitting in front of us without his feet actually having touched the ground very often on the return trip. We added "Fetch" to his vocabulary in about three days. He quit thinking that this business of bringing things was a game. It was now a serious business.

"The thing about a dog," the Old Man said, "is that you got to teach him the difference between business and pleasure. And you got to keep reminding him of it. Like about rabbits. There never was a good bird dog that didn't like to chase rabbits. Rabbits are fun for him, where quail are just hard work. You can tell when a bird dog is pointing a rabbit, because he points all hunched up and with his ears cocked and his nose turned down kind of quizzical, and then he'll jump and look around at you like the village idiot that knows he's done something wrong but ain't quite sure what it is. The way to keep a dog from running rabbits is to discourage him early. We'll do this in the fall, before the bird season opens.

"In the meantime we will not let him run loose this summer, because a dog gets into a lot of bad habits in the summertime; and if you turn him loose to chase everything and anything, come autumn he has forgot what his real business is and ain't much good for anything in particular. I don't approve of chasing dogs except for a couple of things. One is running rabbits and the other is running up quail. A puppy is going to do both at first, out of natural high spirits and just plain puppy dam-foolishness. I wouldn't give you a nickel for a dog that wasn't jealous about another dog over the quail subject, but he's got to learn to control that jealousy, even if it drives him crazy. Else you got no dog. You just got a ham actor that can't be depended on."

We spent the spring teaching this pointer puppy Tom his back-yard manners, and we spent the summer insisting that he remember what we taught him in the spring. He learned "Heel," and he learned "Down," and he learned that the back of the car, not the front, was where he was supposed to jump into. He learned "Fetch" and "Go" and "Hie on" and "*Whoa*." He learned that a whistle was not a tin toy but had some pointed meaning, and that when you waved an arm one way it didn't mean that he was supposed to run the other way. All this time he never smelled a quail.

The summer passed and the leaves turned rosy-crisp. It was nearly time for the bird season to open, and here I had me a puppy, almost grown up to fit his feet, that was like one of those correspondence-course students who's learned it all by mail but hasn't had a chance to practice his theories. I didn't know whether I had an idiot or a genius, but at least his table manners were perfect.

One Sunday afternoon in early October the Old Man said, "All the young birds are big enough now not to mind a bit o' bother, and most of the snakes have gone to ground. Why don't we take the puppy out and see if he's got any sense at all?"

We took him out in the back section where there was a kind of tame covey of quail we could always locate, either in the broom straw or the grove or in the peafields, that the Old Man

had taught me to shoot on and had always schooled the dogs
on. We never shot it down under ten birds, and we always
planted plenty of food for 'em and left plenty of cover, so that
the birds stayed and stayed for all the years I can remember, sort
of like being in the family.

The first thing the puppy did was point a rabbit, jump him,
and chase him. He came back, his tongue hanging out, looking
triumphant. All the "*Whoas!*" I'd screamed hadn't made a
dent in his eardrums.

"Whip him," the Old Man said. "Whip him good. Wear
him out. And say, 'No!' "

I cut an Indian-arrow switch and beat him pretty good. The
next rabbit, he jumped at, ran a little ways after, and then
came back and lay on his back, all four feet in the air, and said,
more or less, "Beat me, boss." I beat him, but not very hard.
And that was the last of the rabbit trouble. He had learned
some early discipline in the back yard.

We steered him to where the quail had to be, and they
were there. It was a funny sight to see. He was like a potential
drunkard who had never tasted whisky before and had suddenly got the smell of it. He didn't know what he was smelling,
but he knew he liked it and he knew he had something to do
about it.

He approached very cautiously, cakewalking, and in the
great moment of indecision, the moment he didn't know himself what he was going to do and when every inclination was to
jump off and chase, he paid off his professors. He had a brief
argument with himself, and he won it. What he did was stick
his tail high in the air like a knobby flagstaff, and stiffen his
body into a crouch, and raise his right front paw, and aim his
nose right smack at where he thought something he'd never
seen and never smelled was. And he stayed there, in that position,
and he would be there now if I hadn't walked past him and
kicked up the birds and said, "*Whoa,*" when he started to chase
them, and he *whoaed* in mid-leap and watched them fly away.
He watched where they pitched and went over and pointed

five single birds, and never made a move to jump again. Maybe he was a miracle. I don't know.

But I do know that all the days he lived he never had another stick to his hide and rarely a command. He never ran another rabbit, and after the first "Whoa," when he was working with the old dogs, he never crowded a point. He would backstand until you needed a bulldozer to move him.

I took him out alone on the first day of the season, in another part of the country, with which he was entirely unfamiliar. He was less than nine months old. He went magically to the first covey, without fiddling, without fuss, without false-pointing. When he had it made, he made it, and lifted his fore-foot again to tell me about it. The birds rose, and I killed the first one and missed the second. He did not chase. "Fetch!" I said, and he sped straight to where he'd marked the bird—a bird whose feathers he had never tasted. He picked up the bird and brought it to me and laid it in my hand and spat out the feathers and said, "Well, boss, they went thataway," just like the old dogs did. And thataway was where they went, and where we went, and where the birds were, like he said.

I went home that day with a coatful of birds and a glowing progress report, but the Old Man wasn't the least bit impressed.

"I told you," he said, "that this mangy puppy had the right blood in him. When a dog or a person's got the right blood, all he needs is a couple of suggestions to use the blood right. I hope you turn out as well as the puppy, but, like I said, the puppy's bloodlines may be a little better than yours. At least, though, I didn't have to cure you of the mange."

9

All Colts Are Crazy in the Spring

We were living at a place called Wrightsville Sound that spring, a most fascinating spot to be young in. It had numberless attractions for a boy. As is so much of the coastal South, it was semitropic. There were vast forests of gnarled, craggy live-oak trees, which were hung with Spanish moss, and tall timberlands of longleaf pine.

The Sound itself led to two inlets on a beach two miles away, and the tides brought ocean fish into the Sound and kept the water clean. There were little back bays that were full of fish, and in the winter, ducks. The woods were chattery with squirrels, little gray fellows and the big black-and-silver fox squirrels. There were quail in the brushy flats, and some deer, and rabbits untold. The trees were full of the bright blue jays I never seem to see these days, and the little bluebirds that have also made themselves scarce.

Even the wild vegetation was exciting to a youngster. There were whole groves of wild plum, and the wild asparagus shot up in the spring, and there were blackberries growing wild by the millions. There were sparkleberries and pawpaws and chinquapins—the little brown sweet nuts like chestnuts—and wild artichokes. There was almost no day in the year when a boy couldn't go out on an expedition of his own and make an adventure of living off the country. A bellyache usually accompanied the experience, but at least a man felt free of his parents and the necessity of carrying a box lunch.

At this time I was almost completely a young Tarzan. There was no house that could hold me. I swung through the trees like an ape, and generally managed to bust something about once a month. I had a tree house built high in the branches of a wild cherry, and an interlocking series of caves that threatened to undermine the county. My progress in school was deplorable, because I was just marking time for that last bell to sound and let me loose into the bush. There was a convenient stream—we called it a crick—near the school, and we would slip off at recess and go swimming naked. One day the teacher surprised the lot of us, and nasty notes were written to parents. I didn't know then who I was, but it was a cross between Tom Sawyer, Huck Finn, Tarzan, Daniel Boone, Buffalo Bill, and all the heroes of Ernest Thompson Seton.

I contracted ground itch and poison ivy and various wounds from fish hooks. Jellyfish stung me in the water. I played hooky constantly and acquired magnificently bad report cards in the process. My mother caught me smoking secretly, and there was a loud flap about that. My companions were mostly fishermen, and my language was shocking. I was about to run away and join the Indians—somewhere, I don't know where—when one day the Old Man looked at me sort of sardonically with one eyebrow cocked and said, "Hey!"

"Yessir?" I said.

"It's about time you calmed down a little, young feller," he said. "You 'mind me of a young buck Apache with no warpath to play with. I know it's spring, and all colts go crazy in the spring, but you need some sort of project to quiet you down. I think I got the answer: a boat. There's something about a boat that is powerful soothing to springtime hysterics. If you'll pay a little more attention to clean ears and arithmetic, I'll help you build one this month, and when school's over you can learn a whole lot of new things about fish and water this summer. You can also learn a whole lot about yourself. Ain't nothing like a boat to teach a man the worth of quiet contemplation."

The business of building the boat took the rest of the spring. The Old Man was working very methodical. He collected a great pile of planks and some sawhorses and stuck them in the back yard. What he was aiming for was a twelve-foot flat-bottom skiff, broad in the beam, that wouldn't draw any water at all and could be controlled by a boy, but that had room in it for at least three people and some fishing or shooting gear. She had a locker under the stern sheets to keep fish or lunch in, and a bait locker. I reckon this was the cheapest piece of construction that ever went into a boat, because he got the wood for nothing from his friend in the sawmill, including the hickory that went into the oars that he whittled out himself and fined down with sandpaper until they were as smooth as glass. He fitted the strakes so close that, once we stuck her in the water and let her seams swell, she never leaked another drop.

The Old Man scorned a two-piece keel. He went out into the woods until he found a piece of hickory—dead but not decayed —with the right curve in it, and he built the boat around it. Apart from the nails and the anchor, there wasn't a piece of metal in her. He despised oarlocks, noisy, clumsy iron things that were always falling overboard or being stolen or that you had to always remember to carry home. He whittled out some limber thole pins that cradled an oar like a mother holds her baby and did about half the rowing for you. We named her the *Charlotte Morse* after two strong-minded women we were both afraid of, and cracked a Coca-Cola over her for launching purposes. The Old Man had a slightly more serious snort. He wasn't one to waste good whisky by pouring it over a boat.

If I ever get rich, I may buy me a boat of some sort, but it'll never have the adventures that the *Charlotte* had. They were never big adventures. I looked for buried treasure on Money Island with her, and got blistered by the sun, but never found the pieces-of-eight. I fell out of her and stuck her on sand bars and had to swim after her now and again when she slipped her moorings. I shot out of her and caught fish out of her and got lost in her and durn near drowned alongside her. But like I said, she gave me some quiet adventure that you don't get out of the comic books, because none of it was vicarious, which means, I think, getting your thrills out of what somebody else has already done better.

When I was out alone in that boat, I never had to worry about amusement. I was Captain Blood looking for pirates, or I was actually on Treasure Island, running from Long John Silver. I was Zane Grey catching marlin off New Zealand—wherever that was—or I was a section of the Spanish Armada or I was Hawkins or Drake. Occasionally I was Robinson Crusoe, marooned on a little island and looking for a Friday. I used to take those books with me and read 'em while pulled up for lunch on one of the thousands of little sandy islands, and they meant a lot more than they did on the Required List at the schoolhouse library, with some four-eyed schoolmarm standing over me.

But mostly I learned about how much fun a man can have amusing himself, and about how exciting solitude can be if you play it right. I would get up early in the morning, row her out to one of the sand bars, jab an oar deep in the sand, and make her fast. Then I would kick around in the ooze, feeling for clams with my feet and looking for soft-shell crabs. When I had a mess of clams, I would take the cast net and prowl the shallows for mullet and shrimp for bait, casting the net in a great circular spread that drove upward sharp slivers of water as she settled, with the shrimp and the mullet bucking and arching inside the cords.

In time I got to know, just by experimentation, where all the better holes were—where the big blackfish lived, where the weakfish hung out, where you couldn't catch anything but spiny-backed perch. Sometimes I would take the boat around into the channel and have fun with the skipjacks, the little channel bluefish, and then I would tie her up under the channel bridge by the barnacle-encrusted pilings and fish very quietly for sheepshead. There were those big stone crabs, too, and to catch one of the big black-and-yellow fellows, whose claws were all white meat and whose body was practically nonexistent, was a big event.

But the best of it was at night, when you rigged up a jack light, took her out on a low tide, and let her drift gently while you looked for the shadow of flounders in the flickering yellow glow. You used a three-pronged harpoon and nailed the flounder to the bottom, and he flopped mightily when you dragged him into the boat. I used to sell the flounders, if I had a good night, and made what to me was a power of money, sometimes as much as a whole dollar.

Some of the best part of going out in the boat was eating the lunch I'd caught myself, pulled up to another little sand bar or a palmetto island. I kept salt and pepper and a skillet in the locker, and there was always driftwood for a fire. It occurs to me now that I was dining then off the things people pay a lot for in restaurants—fresh clams and oysters and broiled soft crabs, the freshest fish in the world. Perhaps it was cooked crude, but I've never eaten better since.

It was maybe a three-mile pull at the end of the day, with your lips salty and burned from the glassy bounce of the sun off the water and your back sore and your bare feet shriveled from the salt water. That last half-mile pull seemed like it was never going to end, and it was a great temptation to just beach the boat and leave her dirty and full of mud and fish scales. But the

Old Man had caught me at that a few times, and the weight of his scorn at filthy fishing was too heavy for me to bear. I would wash her out and make her fast, and string the fish and shoulder the oars, and stagger home so tired that I could have cried. Nobody had to whip me to get me to bed. I was plain-out beat.

By the time that summer ended I think I must have known every inch of that Sound, every fish hole, every sand bar, every creek and cove. I knew the tricks of the tides around the inlets and the rate the water would drop, according to how the wind was blowing. It was all trial and error, cut feet, bruised fingers, mosquitoes and sandflies and sunburn.

By the end of the summer I was considerably calmed down. Like the Old Man said, there is nothing like being alone on the water in a boat of your own to learn the value of peace, quiet, and responsibility. I found out you didn't need companionship to amuse yourself; that there are actually times when you can have more fun without people. A boy alone on a big water is a very small thing.

I didn't ever tell the Old Man about the time I got caught in the rip and was swept out through the inlet into the sea, and had to let the boat go out more than a mile on the ocean before I could get loose from the tow and beat her back to the beach. I didn't tell anybody about the dead man I found—what was left of him—jammed into a little wedge of marsh. He'd been in the water a long time.

Didn't tell, either, about the rusty nail I had to cut out of my foot with a pocketknife I had cauterized in a fire. I remember that very clear, sawing and hacking at the underpart of my big toe, with the nail run clean up under the ball of my foot, the knife dull and me alternately crying and cussing. Told my mother I cut it on an oyster shell when I asked her for the iodine. I guess I was afraid they would keep me out of the boat, and the marsh hen season was coming along, with the big swollen tides of the September northers.

When the tides covered the marsh grasses so that only the tips showed, the big rails had no place to hide and would flap awkwardly up ahead of you, birds as big as woodcock, with soft deer eyes. You poled the boat then, and they flew so slow that you could leave the pole stuck in the ooze, grab a gun, and still knock down the bird. Or sometimes you moored the boat and got out of her, prowling the edges of the shore line, where the birds had come in from their flooded-out home in the marsh. They flushed skittering like snipe, and headed for water, and it was fine shooting.

Schooltime came again, and the weather got colder, and we hauled the boat up and put her on rollers for the winter. I went back to school feeling a little more like a man and a little less like a boy. I reckon the Old Man knew what he was talking about when he said there was nothing like a boat to smooth the kinks out of a kid. This must have shown on the report card a little bit, because for Christmas that year there was a little one-lunged outboard motor under the tree. The Old Man said he guessed I'd earned it.

10

Lazy Day—No Women

It was one of those special days in May, when there was a drowsy, almost-June feel to the softly stirring air. The little warblers were twittering away in yellow clouds in the molting fruit trees, and a catbird was meowing softly in a hedge. The sky was a pale washed-denim blue, and the sun shone down gold and warm but not hot. It was a day to sit, maybe, or perhaps a fishing day, but it was not a day to do anything that might rile up the blood.

The womenfolk were housecleaning, flapping sheets and dusting and sweeping and tormenting things, as women will, and the Old Man was nowhere to be seen. The Liz was sitting in the front yard, under the oak trees; so Himself couldn't have strayed far. In our town there were only so many places where he might be—the Cedar Bench, the pilot office, the poolroom, Uncle Jimmy's store, or Watson's drugstore.

I walked slowly down through the white oyster-shell street toward the water and took a slow sight on the Cedar Bench. It seemed to have a cluster of old gentlemen perched on it like crows, and amongst the old black coats, battered sea captain's caps, shapeless yellowed palmettos, and ratty old felts was the Old Man.

The Cedar Bench, I might say, was the exclusive property of the town's elder statesmen. It was a square wooden bench surrounding a wind-twisted, salt-silvered, ancient cedar. About equidistant from the pilothouse, the ship chandlery, and the shrimp dock with the shrimp houses, it wasn't too far from the fuel dock or the wharf where the pilot boat was moored, and the other docks where the pogie fleet tied up. The old Cedar Bench still hung together, but flimsylike, because it had been whittled at until parts of it were no wider than your hand. It had so much aimless knifework on it that the Old Man once remarked that if you sat long enough on enough sections of it your behind would eventually be engraved with the initials of everybody in town who was over fifty years old.

Nobody talked very much on the Cedar Bench, except around election time. It was a place of meditation. The Old Man was meditating real good when I arrived. He had his hat pulled down on top of his nose, like the pictures you sometimes see of Mr. Bernie Baruch sitting on a park bench. The Old Man's eyes were closed and his pipe had gone out. He had one knee cocked up, and his bony, brown-freckled hands were clasped around the knee. There was little sound except the scream of a sea gull, the hum of insects, and an occasional *splat* as one of the other elder statesmen ejected an amber stream of tobacco juice at an unwary butterfly. Some of those old boys could spit a curve against the wind and were deadly with the poolroom spittoon at ten paces.

I went and sat quietly down alongside the Old Man, and bimeby he opened first one eye, then the other. He kind of shook his head, as if to clear it. "Hello," he said. "What're you up to?"

"Nothin' very much," I said. "The womenfolk were cleaning house and it made me nervous."

"Makes me nervous too," he said, heaving himself to his feet. "I come down here for a rest—snuck out early when I heard the mops begin to swish and the buckets to rattle. Come on, let's walk down to the end of the dock so's we won't disturb these other gentlemen. It seems to be housecleaning day all over town."

We strolled down to the T-shaped end of the dock. The Old Man sat down creakily and leaned his back against a bollard, and I did the same. The gulls wheeled and curved and sailed on stiff wings, and the water was dimpled with the breeze, the sun striking tiny little sparks off the droplets.

The Old Man fetched up a gusty sigh and stuffed his pipe. "I reckon most folks would say we were just plain, cold-out, no-'count lazy," he remarked to one of the wheeling gulls. "It ain't necessarily so. Your grandma, if she ever saw fit to dirty her shoes on the water front, would take one look at the Bench and say something, with a sniff fore-and-aft of it, like: 'Look at those good-for-nothing loafers, so lazy that dead lice wouldn't drop off them, when they could be doing a hundred things we've been at them all winter to get done.' But, of course, that is women for you. It is the reason that, apart from having babies, no woman has ever done a first-class job of anything. They can't even cook as good as men. It's because they don't take the time to think. They're all like little old banty hens, scratching and pecking and looking around at every noise with a beady eye that's meant to be intelligent but ain't."

I had to laugh a little at that one. If you ever saw bantam hens, you'll remember that they're never still, always peering at their backs, looking for lice with their heads swiveled all the way round, or pecking at their chests or under their wings, or scratching, or flapping wings, or jumping up on something, and always cackling, either with indignation or in triumph when they've squeezed out another egg. Grandma—housecleaning, with a towel wrapped round her head, a dustcloth in one hand, and a feather duster in another—was just like a little-bitty old banty hen. She only paused to squawk.

"Now you take me," the Old Man said. "I'm not really lazy. A lazy man is a man who fiddles and fools around with a job he's supposed to be working at. I know a lot of do-less cusses like that. There is a difference between laziness and meditation, even meditation with the eyes closed. Just because I close my eyes and sit in the sun don't mean I'm triflin'.

"For instance," the Old Man continued, "today I am recovering from the rigors of the cold winter and the wet and windy spring. I am recovering from the past and storing up strength for the future. There ain't no telling what the next six months will bring that will call for full concentration and maximum effort. If I should git myself into some sort of big operation, such as inventing an airyoplane or running for Congress, it would be a shame to tackle it all wore out from last year's labors, and let some fresh, rested feller get the best of me."

I interrupted. "But you're a man grown," I said. (The Old Man didn't like anybody to refer to him as old, except himself.) "I ain't nothing but what Aunt Mae calls a shirt-tail boy. It seems to me that there is some sort of grown-up rule that rest is bad for boys, that they got to be doing something all the time. I never set down to whittle or snooze in the sun or fix a cast net that one of the women didn't come marching in with some chore for me to do, like going to the store or running over to Aunt Ada's for a cup of something or half a pound of something else."

"Unjust, unjust," the Old Man sighed. "Boys need more rest than grown-ups. Boys are busy growing bones and making meat to go on the bones, which is a full-time job in itself. Boys burn up more juice than grown-ups. Boys run a kind of a fever until they're past twenty-one years old. There seems to be some sort of deluded idea that boys were created to run errands for the old folks."

"Just like boys ain't supposed to like white meat." I was a little bitter. "Boys are supposed to like backs and wings and legs and the part that goes over the fence last. Grown-ups are supposed to like white meat. Boys are supposed to like to split kindling and clean fish and gut birds and go to the store and rake yards and cut grass. Speaking as boy to man, I would sure admire to say that the grown-up idea of what boys like is a sight different from what *boys* think boys like."

"True, too true," the Old Man said. "And unjust. But the grown-up's idea is that he's conditioning the boy for the toils and troubles of manhood."

"I'm going to be all wore out by the time I run into any toils and troubles of manhood," I said darkly. "I ain't got any time for what you call meditation, except when I'm hunting or fishing."

"I'd say you had enough time, then," the Old Man said tartly. "Seeing as how you manage to do one or t'other or both for about ten months a year, whenever you ain't in school. You never seem to be tired from rowing a boat ten miles or walking six hours in the rainy woods behind a bird dog."

"That ain't work," I said. "Work is doing what you don't like to do because somebody tells you to do it."

The Old Man ignored that for a bit. He chawed on his pipe stem and spat at a sea gull that flew too close. "Speaking of work," he said, "I am so rested up from this morning that I feel like a little honest toil wouldn't kill neither one of us. I'll make you a deal. You know that fishin' shack of ours took a powerful pounding this winter when we had them two hurricanes in a row. I figgered we'd build her back stronger this time. There's plenty of solid driftwood all up and down Caswell, big joists and logs and such as that. Now, if you was to stir yourself and walk—not run—up the street to your Uncle Jimmy's store and buy us a mess of provisions, such as sour pickles, johnnycake, a little fatback, some roofing nails, and some tenpenny nails, I might mosey over to the house and gather up the rest of the truck we need. We can spend the week end— The women are so busy getting everything antiseptic they'll never miss us."

That sounded like a fair-enough deal. I got up and stuck out a hand to the Old Man, hauled him creaking to his feet, and we walked off the dock. He headed home; I set a course for Uncle Jimmy's.

Now I could cheat and pretend that it happened to me, but it didn't. It happened to a little colored boy, and it was the standing joke around town. Most of Pa's family was pretty relaxed, but Uncle Jimmy was the champion relaxer of them all. He was relaxing when I got to the store, sitting on something on the porch, his hat over his eyes and his little fat hands folded on his little fat stomach.

"Hey, there," I said.

"Hey, there, son," he said. "You want something? Go roust it out and add it up on a paper sack and leave the sum on the counter." He closed his eyes to the bright sun. I snickered.

The story was that one day a little colored boy came to the store and found Uncle Jimmy in the same position.

"What can I do for you, son?" Uncle Jimmy kept his eyes closed.

"Papa sen' me say he need a poun' tenpenny nails, Mistah Jimmy. The back po'ch near 'bout fallin' down."

"You go look 'em, son," Uncle Jimmy said. "I think they're in the back of the store som'ers. Look som'ers around the pickle barrel and the overhalls."

The little colored boy disappeared and returned. "They ain't there, Mistah Jimmy."

"Well, son, try som'ers around the eatin' tobacco and the snuff and the two-for-a-penny cakes. You know, them pink ones with the coconut strings and the choc'late marshmellers."

The customer disappeared into the cool recess of the store, rummaged around, and reappeared. "I swear 'fo' Gawd and three 'sponsible witness, Mistah Jimmy, I done look high and I done look low, but I cain't fin' no tenpenny nails."

"You look 'round the yard goods and the bellywash and the

lickrish sticks? You look up high where we keep the Army shoes and the sardines?"

"Yassuh. I done look everywhere and I cain't fin' um."

Uncle Jimmy stirred, scratched his head, wrinkled his brow. "I know we got some," he said. "I ordered a mess from the hardware drummer last time he was around, and a whole shipment come in on the Willing But Slow the other day."

Uncle Jimmy let out a sudden guffaw and slapped his leg. "That's a joke on me, son," he wheezed. "Whilst we been talking about them nails, I been settin' on the nail keg this whole blessed time. Suppose, son," he said, closing his eyes again, "suppose you come back again *t'morrow*."

That's what they told on Uncle Jimmy, anyhow. They said he was the first man in the business to invent self-service, which became so popular later on. Except he didn't believe in a cash business. He sent out bills once every so often, when he thought about it, and when small boys came to pay the bills for their people he was always good for a sack of jawbreakers or one of those mammoth, sickly sweet soft drinks he called belly-wash. I knew where everything in the store was; so I made my purchases, scribbled down the total on a paper sack with a nubbin of a pencil, hooked a pink-striped peppermint, and went out into the sun. Uncle Jimmy grunted what was probably good-by and never opened his eyes.

By the time I walked most of the three long blocks home, the Old Man was in the Liz and heading in my direction. "Jump in," he said. "They're all cleaning like Old Ned upstairs and I give 'em the slip. Let's skedaddle. I left a farewell message pinned to the lamp shade in the parlor."

We bumped happily over the shell road and headed toward Caswell. As we came to the creek you could smell the pogie factory, and the odor of ripe fish meal was sweet to the nostrils, as was the hot smell of rotting marsh. The red-winged blackbirds rode the tops of the waving marsh grass, and away off a fish hawk was circling, looking for his dinner. The sun shone brighter, and the Old Man grinned. "How was Jimmy?"

"Just the same. All I got to do is look at him and I feel full of vinegar. I feel like work now."

"Me, too," the Old Man said. "But I wouldn't of felt like it if I hadn't of replenished myself this mornin'."

We pulled up to wait for the little ferry bridge to swing closed and let us over the creek. We weren't in no particular hurry to get there, and I noticed the Old Man had his hat tilted forward over his eyes again. His breath, or maybe the breeze, ruffled his mustache.

Today there's a lot of people who don't understand, when they see me sitting out in the yard in an easy chair, that I'm not really loafing. I'm doing what the Old Man said. I'm recovering from the past and storing up for the future.

11

Summertime, and the Livin'
Was Easy

June is a nice time of year, because school lets out and it hasn't got real hot yet. The mornings are fresh and dewy and everything is green and sweet-smelling, and generally the mosquitoes haven't started and the nights are still cool enough for covers. The nicest thing about June is that the awful memories of school are behind you, and September is so far away that it doesn't even count. The summertime belongs to boys. Grown-up folks might play around at the beaches and the country clubs and take vacations, but summer truly belongs to kids. It's sunburn time and ground-itch time and poison-ivy time. It's barefoot time and fishhooks-caught-in-your-ear time and baseball time and whippoorwill time and bullbats-swooping-low-in-the-dusk time.

Seems to me the summertime had so much good stuff in it that it should have been made illegal for most people. You had all sorts of wonderful things to give you the bellyache—peaches and pears and wild berries and tame berries, such as raspberries and strawberries, and the big purple plums and the yellow-and-rose plums, and the figs, and the big cool green watermelons or the tiger-striped ones that you took out of the cold water in the springhouse and ate by just shoving your face in and chewing on through. Finally, as the summer would wear on and it began to smell a little smoky in the air, like fall was knocking, the grapes came—the big, fat, juice-bursting scuppernongs, white and chokingly sweet, and the slightly tart black ones, as big as golf balls.

In my town they closed up Sunday school as well as regular school in June, which suited me just fine. About all I ever learned in Sunday school was how to shoot craps down in the basement, a pastime so deplorable that Mr. James Stebbins, the sandy-haired Englishman (a foreigner!) who tried to domesticate us young demons, eventually renovated our shocking morals by ringing in a pair of loaded dice and busting us all for the spring term of religious worship. He was as steely as a professional bookmaker about the IOU's, and he put all his ill-got gains into the collection plate. I remember I was just paid out, and was feeling pretty religious about it, when the Old Man cornered me one morning after breakfast.

It was one of those days when a boy figures he's got to pop if something doesn't happen to him—something big, something adventurous, something stupendous, like saving a maiden fair from the wild animals that have busted loose from the circus, or rushing into a burning building to rescue a child, or something. Anything. Making tar balls out of the bubbling asphalt pavement wasn't enough. Eating plums that were too green or trying out a sneaky slingshot on a catbird wasn't enough. It was one of those days you maybe remember, with the bobolinks balanced on the bending grasses in the breeze, and the Baltimore orioles scattering notes around like millionaires throwing coins, and the wild cherries black and sweating sweet on the big leafy tree with the Tarzan house built into it.

The Old Man stabbed me with his pipe stem and his eyes. "I been hearing about you," he said. "I been hearing a lot of things about you—about how you cut Sunday school every other Sunday, and about that dice game you young hellions started down in the basement at Saint James', and it seems to me you are doomed for perdition. I thought I had you straightened out in the school business, but now I reckon I got to teach you a little humility."

Here she comes, I said to myself. I'm goin' to get preached at, or made to do something I don't want to without knowing why I don't want to. The Old Man was awful shifty when he come down hard with the parables according to Himself.

"What are you goin' to do?" I asked him.

"Fishin'," he said cheerfully. "We're just goin' fishin'."

Now, you certainly don't punish a boy for irreverence by taking him fishing; so there has got to be a catch in this one somewhere, I thought. But I had learned from the Old Man to play pretty cosy; so all I said was, "What kind of fishin'?"

"Fresh-water," the Old Man said. "Maybe catch us a big ol' bass or so, or at least a mess of brim. We'll take the Liz and rent us a boat from a man I know on Big Crick. Wait till I go get the rods, and while I'm after them you go roll over some rotten logs and see if you can turn your undoubted talents to filling a tin can full of worms."

I ambled down to the cow lot, behind which there was a low, wet swamp where the pigs rooted and the quail came to drink, and turned over a few old punky logs and filled up a big paint can with fine fat worms, just as happy as worms to be wriggling around in the loose, wet dirt I put in the can. When I got back to the house, the Old Man had produced a couple of light split-bamboo rods and a couple of little reels that I never had seen before.

"Where'd they come from?" I asked the Old Man.

"Oh," he said, "I've had 'em around for a long time. There's a lot of things I got you don't know about. I ain't a man to take every whippersnapper I meet into my confidence. I got plenty of secrets I ain't talkin' about. These rods are one of my secrets. On this coast it's supposed to be sissy to fish fresh water —either sissy or downright po' barkerish." A po' barker is the kind of shiftless white trash who would be so trifling that he'd have to feed his family off perch and catfish.

I cranked the Liz, and we snorted off. I never went off in the old Liz without snickering a little bit. The Old Man said only a monkey was fit to drive one of the old T-models. "You need both hands on the wheel, both feet on the pedals, and a tail to keep the door shut," he said. But they never built a better car. It would go anywhere that one of those Army tanks would go, and with about the same amount of noise. It rode high off the ground and looked like an old lady with her skirts held up off the mud, but it never wore out.

We drove about fifteen miles and came up to Big Crick. It had some other name, I suppose, but Big Crick was what we called it. Actually, it was a little river that connected up somewhere with the Cape Fear River. There were a boathouse and a landing and a few skiffs pulled up alongside the landing. When we got there, it was about four o'clock in the afternoon.

The Old Man paid fifty cents for the rent of a boat. He just indicated the oars to me with a jerk of his head, and I started pulling upstream in the slow, brown, leaf-dyed waters, against a lazy current that made little ripples and bubbles and sucking sounds as it ran over and around little rocks and old green-lichened snags. While I rowed, the Old Man fussed with the fishing gear. I noticed that he put a split shot and a single hook on one leader, and tied a bright red-and-white wooden lure with some pork-rind streamers on the other.

We came around a bend of the Big Crick, and the Old Man told me to head her into the bank, where there were a lot of lily pads and weeds and, it looked like, some fairly deep pools. He handed me the rod with the single hook and the little sinker on it.

"Now," he said sternly, "we will fish. You will use some of those worms you dug up and catch us a mess of brim. I will see if I can't do something about a bass or so. When you've caught us a bait o' brim, switch the hook and try for the bass yourself. They won't be bitin' for another hour or so, anyhow, until the evening fly hatch rises.

"Now, then, son," the Old Man said, "we ain't goin' to talk any, because fishin' is a silent sport and a lot of conversation scares the fish and wrecks the mood. What I want you to do is set there and fish, and when the fish ain't bitin' I want you to listen and look and think. Think about heaven and hell and just how long is hereafter. Look around you and don't take nothing for granted. Look at everything you see and listen to everything you hear, just like you were brand-new come from another world, and think about all those things and how they got there. Now let's fish."

I threaded a big, juicy worm onto the hook and flipped the line over the side, and in less than a minute a big fat bream had seized onto it and I jerked him into the boat. They only ran about half a pound apiece, but they bit like they hadn't ever seen a worm and thought it was candy. The Old Man was potting away at lily pads or close aboard them and flicking his line along the shore under overhangs of old logs or rocks, and wasn't catching anything at all.

I pulled in about two dozen bream, and then switched to a plug and started to imitate the Old Man. I had a little trouble with the wrist, but not much, because I had been doing a lot of salt-water fishing, and I'd learned to throw a cast net, and boys don't have much trouble learning anything outside of book lessons. Nothing hit my hook either. It was just flip, reel in, poise, flip, and reel in some more, with the bait hitting the water with a *plonk* and the pork streamers making a wriggle in the water like a frog kicking his legs in a breast stroke.

Well, sir, when you can't talk, you got to think and look and listen, and all of a sudden I was the lonesomest boy in the world. You know anything about what it's like in a fresh-water swamp in the South when the sun is starting to drop and the noises begin? Or what it smells like and feels like as it cools off from the heat of the day? And what sort of things are all around you?

I got to looking at the water. It was clear and clean, but as brown as your hat from the leaf dye, and when you scooped up a handful it tasted a little like leaves smelled if you crumpled them in your hand. And it was full of all sorts of little things— bugs that hopped and popped, little crawlers that left a tiny wake behind them, like a mink swimming. Fish swirled and rose to snap at the first beginnings of the fly hatch. A big bull-frog gave a loud, croaking *ker-tunk!* and leaped into the water with a splash. Over on the other bank a water moccasin slithered down the greasy earth and slipped into the water without a sound.

It was so lonely in that swampy river that it made you want to cry. All the sad sounds in the world suddenly started. A dove set up that woeful *oo-hoo-oo-hoo-hoo* across the swamp, and another one, sadder still, began to answer him back. They sounded like two old widow women swapping miseries.

In the utter hush a million noises intruded. A bittern roared. A heron squawked. A kingfisher rattled. A deer snorted and barked. A bird screeched. A crow cawed. Somewhere deep in the swamp there was a growl and a scream as a wildcat skittled a rabbit. A squirrel chirred and was answered. Leaves rustled. Things fell off trees. Bushes stirred mysteriously with the pass-ing of unseen animals. Along the creek a piece a raccoon came down to drink, washing his little paws as daintily as a lady.

The sun sank lower, and the huge old live oaks, their Span-ish-moss beards swaying down to the water's edge, looked as ominous as monsters. The cypress knees made all sorts of strange shapes. Along the banks the ferns grew—the delicate maidenhair fern and broader-leafed ones I didn't know the names of—in an indescribable carpetry of cool greenness. Little silly flowers poked their button heads up among the ferns.

Away off somewhere a cowbell tinkled very sadly, and you could hear a rich Negro voice singing its way through the frightening, falling shadows of the intruding evening. He sounded scared, and he was scared, and he wouldn't get any less scared until he sighted his shack with the fire going under the big black iron kettle. Now the cicadas and the crickets and all the other loudly vocal bugs were beginning to sound their eventide notes, like an orchestra tuning for the overture.

In my brain I looked at all of it—the trees, the grass, the moss, the bugs, the birds, the ferns, the flowers, the setting sun, the rising hatch of flies. I felt the dark creeping and saw the first shining speck of star and heard the mounting noises in the swamp. I felt cold in my bones from the rising miasma of mist as the air cooled. I was so lost in what was going on, in the million slivers of vibrant life, that when a big fish hit I lost him out of sheer panic.

The bass bit beautifully, there just at dusk, and we caught ten or so between us—not very big; but a two-pound bigmouth on a whippy rod is quite an order. When it got black-dark, the fish eased off and I shoved the boat into the stream and let the current carry us down toward the landing. The Old Man took in the lines and put the plugs back in the tackle box, and I just sort of warded the scow off the snags. The Old Man lit his pipe and puffed peacefully. He said nothing, nothing at all.

It was main late when we hit the landing. The stars had crept out bright now, and a little wedge of moon was slipping sneaky-like up over the trees. The frogs, the bugs, the night birds, and the animals were making a din. I got to thinking about eternity, and how long something that never ended would be, and I got to thinking about how much trouble Somebody went to, to make things like cocoons that butterflies come out of, and seasons and rain and moss on trees, and frogs and fish and possums and coons and quail and flowers and ferns and water and moons and suns and stars and winds. And boys. Especially boys.

Once we got back in the Liz, the Old Man didn't say anything for a few miles. Then he spoke, without turning his head. "You ain't said much. What do you feel like?"

"I feel like I been to church. I feel like I got—that word you said."

"Humility?" the Old Man asked gently.

"Yessir," I said. "I feel awful little and unimportant, somehow, and a little bit scared."

"You're beginning to learn, boy," he said. "You're beginning to learn."

Summertime seemed to be almost equally compounded of music and baseball. The Old Man and I used to sneak off into the woods some nights, when we could get out of the house without an argument, and just follow the singing until we came onto a big revival meeting, white, or a big camp meeting, colored, or a most amazing exhibition when the Holiness people got took down with the Sperrit, rolled and writhed in the sandspurs, foamed at the mouth, sang to Glory, and spoke in the Unknown Tongues. My Great-Uncle Wade was a Holy Roller, and when the Sperrit got a firm grip on him, he was a sight to see. He got trancified, and walled his eyes, and spoke in the Tongues, and when he really got to rolling, he didn't seem to feel the sandspurs, which were nigh about as big as golfballs, with inch-long spikes.

The white revivals were a little depressing, because everybody including the preacher was full of sin and eager to admit it. People I knew well who hadn't had a bad thought or committed an evil deed in forty years used to go to the bench and confess to the most amazing breaches of the peace of state and soul. I always felt like they were bragging, so as not to be left out of things. One Sunday, though, we went to the Big Town and heard Billy Sunday produce a fire-and-brimstoner under a big tent, and I was powerful impressed, possibly because the Devil-hating Mr. Sunday had been a professional baseball player once. I didn't smoke for a week, not even corn silk or rabbit tobacco, for fear of hell-and-damnation. I even gave up baseball and fishing on Sunday for a little spell.

What I liked best—and so did the Old Man—were the colored folks' camp meetings. I reckon between us we knew every Negro in the country, old and young, male and female, ornery and exemplary. They would congregate in a clearing somewhere well out of town, with a thatched shelter over the big rough pine tables where the food was, and sometimes go on for days. The camp meetings had a lot of preaching and exhorting, and a lot of casting out of Satan, and a lot of mourning on the bench, and a lot of people reborn in the Lamb, but it was all much better-natured than the white folks' revivals. The colored folks seemed to be on a more intimate basis with the Lord. The backsliders were there to renew faith and acquire fresh hope, but the majority of the people who made up the congregation were there to have fun.

The smell of frying fish, and the spitting of the fish in the skillet, and the grease on hands and faces in the firelight, were part of it, as the watermelons and the lard cakes and the fried chicken and the rice pilaus were part of it. There was always some homespun corn whisky, and some home-stomped scuppernong wine too, which was as much a part of the festival as the music. I heard no music like that until I went to Africa a great many years later. When I first heard the Wakambas singing the working songs, and the lifting, toting songs, and the Waluingulus putting on a nocturnal meat-thanks concert in the bright of the moon, I could close my eyes and roll back thirty years to Brunswick County's camp meetings.

The singing would start out with a formal hymn, which would gradually syncopate into a chant, and would move easily from hymn to spiritual, with the African beat becoming more pronounced. The shuffling would become a stamping, hands would clap, and the first light stirrings would richen into a rolling sea of bodies, with the firelight flickering on grease-shining black faces. The voices of the women would separate into wailing minors from the deep rich basses and baritones of the men. Groups of singers would stray apart, answering and asking each other questions in song, blending in the refrain, pausing at the breath stops with deep-chested grunts from the men. (The old lion grunt is parcel to nearly all the African music I ever heard.) From time to time one of the women would let out a piercing, neck-hair-lifting scream, and throw herself on the confession bench, as the music took her and her sins welled up, to plead for purification. When Sister Mary had enjoyed her moment of full attention, Sister Kate would throw back her head and let out a screech, and in time all the good Sistren would have their prideful moment at the bench. Old Satan used to take a fearful beating.

The men very rarely were taken, but provided the constant chant. A good bass singer made the circuit of the meetings, and was nearly as popular as the preacher in terms of chocolate cake, fried chicken, and free access to the fruit jar. I remember the Old Man spotting a strange face in the crowd once, and asking the man where he came from, and why he was there. The man smiled, understanding our rather peculiar patriarchal attitude. "Ah comes from Onslow County. Ah come heah to drink whisky and sing bass," he replied in a voice that would have made Paul Robeson sound like a soprano. This fellow was very popular with the younger female set, and usually disappeared from view around midnight.

We never mixed into the festivities, of course, but sat at the edges, and were tolerated because we were the Cap'm and the Little Cap'm, and because my mammy, Aunt Laura, had been born a slave and wore a conjure bag until the day she died. We were kind of part of the family. From time to time somebody would fetch us a dipper of the scuppernong wine and a plate of fried chicken or some field peas with fatback. It was a mutually understood laissez-faire; the same shining black faces could be seen on the outskirts of the dancing when the white folks had their big square dances—interestedly watching the high jinks as the *bokra* (white people) leaped and cavorted and kicked their heels and sashayed in time to the fiddles. And I must say that a white-folks' Saturday night square dance, for action, might have made a Masai *ngoma* look tame, once the sweaty dancers got sufficiently lubricated on the white corn that burned a path down the gullet and landed with a fiery thump in the pit of the stomach. White music or black, summertime created a lot of vocal exercise, a power of banjo plinking and fiddle sawing.

The baseball was another thing entirely. The Old Man bought me a glove, a ball, a catcher's mitt, and a bat, which kind of gave me a corner on the two-o'-cat market. We pitched and caught interminably, under the shade of the big moss-bearded oaks in what was simply called "The Grove." We batted flies and rapped grounders on the one stretch of sidewalk in the town. This was perishing hard on the ball, which soon became scuffed, frayed its seams, and peeled its horsehide. The ball was then wrapped in bicycle tape, and landed in the glove with a leaden thump that like to have torn your hand off.

Walter Johnson was the big hero among the pitchers, and Babe Ruth was becoming so popular they named a candy bar after him. We, at least, promptly gave up O. Henry for Baby Ruth. Pictures of the stars came in cigarette and candy packages, just like the movie stars, and very brisk trading went on.

Saturday was the day of the big game between the town's pickup adult team and one of the surrounding hamlets. This game actually had as many as nine men on a side, and the catcher not only owned a "mast," we called it, but a belly protector and shin guards as well. It seems to me that a fellow named Fred Something played a fancy left-handed first base, and the two St. George boys, Donald and Bill, were the battery. They said that if Donald hadn't fooled around too much, and drunk a little too much corn, he could have pitched in the majors. I suppose there is always one man in every town who could have made the majors if he hadn't fooled around too much.

Saturday night in the summertime was when they swept the

small fry off the streets early, because the rival teams had a way of canceling hostilities by burying their noses in the same jug, and by midnight were apt to be burying blunt instruments in each other's skulls. The word would go out that Tom or Joe or Bill "was drinking"—they always used that phrase, "was drinking"—and sisters and mothers and aunts would hustle out like agitated setter dogs to retrieve their wayward kith and kinry. The fathers were known weaklings, and sometimes two members of the family would have to be fetched home; father and son wrapped in each other's arms and either fighting or singing lugubriously. We were not, as I recall, a breed of social sippers in that day and age. When a man got his face stuck into a fruit jar, he kept it there until paralysis set in.

The Old Man said that he approved of baseball because it was the only neat sport he knew of—three strikes, out; four balls, walk; fair and foul clearly marked; over the fence, a homer; just so far around the bases; and always the same distance from the pitcher's block to the plate. But he did not approve of the wassail-all which followed the games, and his heart nigh broke when the Black Sox scandals came to light. He reckoned among other things that there had been too much postgame drinking mixed up in it, and that was in some indirect way responsible for this breakdown of moral fiber in Chicago.

Yet there never was a man who liked a toddy better than the Old Man liked his. He just felt that if you were hunting, you were supposed to hunt, and a cockle-warmer came at the end, not in the middle of it. Same way about fishing, work, or baseball. He made an exception in camp meetings, recognizing that alcoholic incentive was part of the festivity.

There was a kind of unwritten rule in our town that nobody was supposed to have any fun on Sunday, but was to stay home, eat an enormous dinner, and spend the afternoon bored and half-drugged from the monumental midday meal. The Old Man took heavy exception to this. He said he had been clean through the Good Book, and while he admitted that it came out strong against working on the Sabbath, he couldn't see anything wrong in a man translating his day of rest any way it pleased him, so long as it didn't constitute a nuisance or offend other people's delicate sensibilities.

At this time there were very few privately owned automobiles, and one of the more barbarous customs was to pack the entire family into the Model T or the Locomobile and go for a grueling expedition called "the Sunday afternoon ride." For a youngster it was torture, packed in with the old folks and the musty smell of jet-beaded black funeral silk which constituted old ladies' Sunday uniform.

That's when we would slip quietly away after dinner and go fishing.

"The fish don't know if it's Sunday or Wednesday," the Old Man said. "It's all the same to a fish. So long as we are not catching fish for sale, which constitutes work, I reckon we are leaving the Sabbath intact according to formal rules. It certainly isn't any worse than racketing around in a car, or spending the afternoon playing this golf everybody's getting so crazy about, or just setting around the house trying to stay awake."

We never took very much trouble with Sunday fishing. If somebody else wanted the Liz, we just ambled down to the water, scooped up a mess of fiddler crabs, and sat quietly on the dock, waiting for the big sheepsheads to come out from their caverns around the rotted, barnacle-encrusted pilings. You caught more toadfish than sheepsheads, but occasionally there was a small blackfish to relieve the monotony. Now and again we shoved the skiff off the shingle and rowed half a mile or so to some holes we knew, close by an ancient wreck, stopping by the marsh on the way to net a few shrimp for bait. There was always a mess of croakers and the occasional weakfish to liven up the afternoon. Sometimes we just took the crab net and a piece of ancient meat and went crabbing off of one of the little piers. Or we'd rig up a light and a trident and pole the boat around after dark on low tide, stabbing the odd flounder. If the car wasn't working for somebody else, we might drive a few miles to one of the big fresh-water cricks and have a try at a few largemouthed bass when the evening cooled.

No, I reckon there wasn't very much to do in the summertime, but it got to be September before you knew it, with the big salt-water fish beginning to run, and the high, moonswollen tides to make the marsh-hen shooting easy on the first big norther. And then the tortures of school and shoes began, and before very long the frosts had crinkled the persimmons and the hound dogs started running the woods by night, with quail and Christmas just around the corner.

But I still can't hear that "Summertime" song without fetching up the Old Man, as large as life, despite all he said about summers belonging to boys and the old folks standing aside. I reckoned for most of his days the Old Man figured he was a kind of overgrown boy himself.

12

September Song—II

Even for a young ruffian like me, getting back to school in September was a little bit of fun for a few days. You saw a lot of people you hadn't seen for three months, and the football practice was starting. In class there would be one or two new pretty girls, who had moved in from some other town. There would be a couple of new boys, too, and it took a bit of time and a fist fight after school to squeeze 'em into the pattern.

This was a pretty good September. Through some sort of accident I skipped a grade and was now a senior in grammar school—practically grown, I thought. There was a very pretty blonde girl named Rose Ellen sitting next to me, and I fell in love the first day. This didn't mean much because I'd started falling in love in kindergarten and had two or three seizures every year from that point on. I carried a mess of books in those days.

I was kind of in love double that year, because we had a red-headed, freckle-faced young sprout of a teacher named Miss Carrie Mae Knight, who was a real humdinger. You hear a lot about juvenile delinquents these days, but I'm here to tell you that if every classroom had a Carrie Mae Knight in it there wouldn't be any trouble with kids.

You never saw such a woman as this Knight female. Mind you, she was teaching a class that had boys in it older than she was, because she was only nineteen, and some of those big country kids were easily twenty. They got in one grade and just stayed.

Miss Carrie Mae Knight could do nearly anything we did better than we could. She coached the football team. She scandalized the principal by putting on pants and showing a great big clunk named Clyde Something how to really take a tackle out of play, and she rattled his teeth when she hit him. She could play any position on the baseball team, and when she pitched she came in with a high hard one that bore no resemblance to the crooked-arm way that most girls throw.

She never sent any ratty notes to your folks about whatever deviltry you'd been up to, and she never squealed to the principal or shifted her disciplinary responsibilities, which we called "being sent to the office." Nobody ever got sent to the office, not even when some big oaf she was keeping after school made a grown-up grab at her. She killed her own snakes. She hit him a punch in the chin with a straight left and crossed with her right, and never had any more trouble. I seem to remember that she had been raised with five brothers, all red-headed.

Carrie Mae—we called her Carrie Mae outside the classroom —had a big following at the parties, when we played kissing games, like post office and spin-the-bottle. She seemed to know instinctively how to hang onto kids, boys and girls. She was taking flying lessons, and she used to give us a half-hour fill-in on her progress—in the middle of the study period.

She read to us a full hour every day. It was never kid stuff, either. She read a lot of Mark Twain and Kipling and contemporary stuff from the magazines. To the best of my memory, nobody ever made a paper airplane or threw a spitball when Carrie Mae was reading. She was one of those natural-born readers who could lift you out of your seat. She even read us Shakespeare and made it sound like a Wild West story, and I still get hungry when I remember the first time I ever heard her read Charles Lamb's dissertation on roast pig. I knew about cracklin'; I'd been raised on it.

Carrie Mae was the first real contact I made with the outside world of adults. Of course the Old Man and some of his shooting and fishing friends were sort of buddies of mine, and I didn't think of them so much as grown-ups. I had a lot of adult friends among the fishermen and the Negro field hands and suchlike, but teachers and people like them were all enemies, guilty until proved innocent.

What really sold me on Carrie Mae was the day the Old Man drove up to the school and asked for me about ten o'clock in the morning. Miss Knight went out to see what the old gentleman wanted, and then she came back and crooked a finger at me. I followed her out into the hall. The Old Man was in the lobby, twisting his hat in his hands.

"Your grandfather," Carrie Mae said, "has got a crisis. He has explained to me that this is the day the dove season opens and he just got a message from a friend of his that there's a big dove drive taking place, away off in the other end of Brunswick County. He says that he doesn't think the entire progress of education would be ruined if I excused you from the rest of the classes today to go along with him. He's also asked me to dinner to eat some of the doves. You better run along. I'll need about two hours' help with some papers tomorrow afternoon, and you can pay me back then."

That was as close as I ever came to kissing a teacher, until several years later, of course. I made my manners and roared down the hall like a train with all boilers lit. The Old Man sort of grinned.

"That's quite a filly," he said. "If I was about forty-odd year younger, I'd choose her up myself. She's reasonable. A reasonable redheaded woman is hard to come by. Let's us go shoot some doves."

The Old Man had the guns and little Mickey, a golden cocker that I haven't told you about yet. Mickey was of the old cocker breed—pretty near as big as a springer, and an all-round hunting dog. She had hair about the color of Miss Knight's, and she had a good flat head and a square muzzle like a dog, not like some of the popeyed, pointed-headed idiots they call cockers today. They've bred all the sense out of most cockers and made sissy dogs out of them, but there was a time when a good cocker would rassle a bear and hunt anything that flew, ran, or climbed.

We drove across the river on Mr. Oscar Durant's old ferryboat and pointed the Liz in the general direction of the Willets farm, a big corn, cotton, and tobacco holding. The roads were made of corrugated clay, and it took time. We had plenty of time to get there for the afternoon shooting unless the Liz decided to throw a shoe. As we bumped along, the Old Man was lecturing a little bit, as he generally did when we took on a new subject.

"Doves," the Old Man began, "are the easiest hard shootin' in the world. Or maybe it's the other way around. Maybe they're the toughest easy shootin' in the world. I'm telling you right now, you figger to miss more'n you hit, and it wouldn't surprise me none if you didn't hit any for your first box o' shells.

"A cranked-up dove that's been driven is as fast and tricky as any bird in the world. He'll swoop like a swallow, and he'll change his flight pattern just when you start to pull. He's got more feathers on him—loose ones—than a feather-tick mattress. When he's going away, you can shoot off his tail and pull a pound of fluff off him, and he'll still continue on his errand.

"In all the ballistic computations of mankind, ain't nobody ever figured a way to lead a dove too far if he's going past you in a high wind, after he's been chased from one corner of a field to another. When he's coming straight at you, you got to throw some shot up where he's going to be a second later, and that seems like it's near about a quarter-mile away, sometimes. If he's quarterin', you got double trouble. My blanket suggestion is just to point the gun about twenty feet ahead of him, pull the trigger, sweep the gun around, and pray. Mebbe something will drop."

We finally got to the farm, and there were twenty or twenty-five men standing around in the clean-swept sandy front yard under the chinaberry tree, smoking pipes and chewing tobacco and spitting meditatively at targets. They all had guns, mostly rusty-looking old pumps and a few wire-wrapped single-barrels. There was a general air of festivity and an odor of crushed grain that was not unfamiliar.

They all said a hearty Hello to the Old Man and tossed a few jokes at me, such as, "Are you sure it's safe to hunt in the same field with this feller, Ned?" Or "Can we trust him not to kill all the birds and leave a few for us? That looks like a mighty potent hawgleg he's carrying, don't it?" Then they would slap their blue-jeaned legs and guffaw. The opening day of the dove season was a kind of community party, like a house raising or a cane grinding or a quilting bee.

The Old Man laid a hand on my neck and said, "Don't you worry about this feller. He'll wipe all of your eyes when he gets the hang of it. I'm here now. What're we waiting for? Let's go shoot some doves."

It was about four o'clock in the afternoon when we started to trudge out to the stubble field, a huge cornfield that must have been a mile across and two miles long. I had two boxes of shells for the 16-gauge. The Old Man said I'd need 'em. The cocker spaniel trailed along behind us, as though she knew what she was doing.

We came to a far corner of the field, and the Old Man pointed to a big hickory tree with some old dogfennel bushes under it. "Sort of scrootch down here," he said. "I ain't shootin' much today. I'm going to help Henry drive. The dog'll stay with you. Just tell her to fetch, if so be it there's anything to fetch." And the Old Man laughed loud—"Haw-haw"—and stalked off to crisscross the field, driving up the doves.

All those grown men were strung out around the edges of the field, partly hidden by trees or clumps of bush. Half a dozen were driving, and pretty soon you could see the doves whistling up, aimless at first, but working up steam as they got higher and leveled off. Then the guns started to go off, boom-boom here, boom-boom there, and now and again you'd see a swiftly darting dove crumple in a puff of feathers and drop like a brick, or slant or flutter down in a long glide.

The late sun was bright on their rosy breasts when a few came my way, and I tried to remember about leading 'em enough, and hauled down. I made quite a lot of noise, but nothing dropped.

Evidently the shooting addled the doves, because as the guns spoke all round the field they crisscrossed back and forth, flying higher and faster, darting more, dipping more, swerving and looping more. I shot. And shot. And shot, until the barrels were hot. Mickey, the cocker, looked up at me with a slight frown.

I had two birds on the ground—both straightaway shots, with no leadoff involved—when I scrabbled for more shells. There weren't any more in the first box. I had shot twenty-five times and had two birds and maybe a couple of possibles that the dogs would pick up later.

Ten shells later I had four birds on the ground—one killed coming straight at me, the other quartering away. And then a little machine clicked in my head, and the lead-off angles worked themselves out. I was leading passing birds as much as twenty or twenty-five feet, and they were coming down like hailstones. I was nailing incoming birds, and they were falling at my feet. Old Mickey was spitting out feathers and cursing dog language, but she was cursing at overwork. When I fired the fiftieth shell, there were fourteen birds on the ground under the tree; and my muscle was black and blue and red from the kick.

I felt pretty pleased. I had knocked down ten doves out of the last fifteen shells, and some I had shot at twice.

I stuffed the birds in my old canvas hunting jacket, picked up the gun, and headed off across the field. It was getting a little nippy, and the sun was red in the face and headed for bed. I reckoned the persimmons would be ripe in another month or so —and then it wouldn't be too long before the quail season started.

The Old Man was sitting on the running board of a car— cars had running boards in those days—and holding forth on something or other. I walked into the yard and inside-outed my hunting coat. The birds tumbled out, and the Old Man looked smug at his cronies. The men nodded and smiled, and one of 'em said, "I wouldn't be surprised if he ain't set a record." He was kidding, of course, because nobody paid much attention to bags on doves in those days.

"Like I said," the Old Man remarked as we drove bumpily home, "it's the easiest hard shooting or the toughest easy shooting in the world. When you get it figured out, it's a cinch, but the figgerin' costs an awful lot of gunpowder before you'll admit that these things need all the leadoff you can crank into your head. The last ones come so easy you wonder how you missed the first ones—until next time, and then you wonder all over again.

"I must say, though," the Old Man said as we turned into home, "once you've got a dove on the ground, your troubles are over. You can breathe on 'em and the feathers will fall off. Suppose you go try to have 'em picked before suppertime."

Miss Carrie Mae Knight came over to the house for supper the next evening, and she ate three doves all by herself. She said she had never enjoyed any birds quite so much, because there were so few shot in them. I expect that Miss Carrie Mae Knight was righter than she knew.

I reckon the Old Man was about as queer as they come, a stickler for a whole lot of things that mightn't make much sense to other people. It was as if he had figured out a whole complete set of rules and regulations, according to his own ideas, which were good enough for him. You could do two things: you could play it his way, or you didn't play at all.

"I am an old boar coon," he told me one time. "I'm too old and sot in my ways to learn a mess of new teachin'. I have seen the elephant and heard the owl. I don't do nothin' I do except for a reason. The reason may not suit other people, but it suits me, because I have tried it all and made two mistakes for every mistake I didn't make. I am what you might call a monument to trial and error."

The Old Man had a lot of peculiar hates. He couldn't abide a loud talker, for one thing. He said a man that had to holler for emphasis was just echoing the wind that blew through the vacant space where his brains ought to be. He especially hated noise in the woods, particularly people that were always hollering at dogs. He said it not only confused the dog but confused him as well. It made him nervous.

He was a garrulous old man, and he loved to talk at length when talking had some point. But he purely despised idle chitter-chatter, people that just talked without having anything to say. And he hated to be interrupted. "The world," he used to say, "is full of fine fragmentary thoughts, killed at birth by the interruptions of damned fools."

The Old Man hated what he called uppity people, young and old alike. He had no time for a smart aleck. His friends were simple people that knew what they knew and kept their traps closed about things they didn't know. He hated discussions at the table, arguments, and problems and such. They interfered with his digestion. About the first thing I remember he ever said to me, when I was a very small boy, was that children should be seen and not heard at the table. This went for most adults too.

But he was a stickler for politeness. He claimed there was no excuse for impoliteness. He said that "sir" and "please" and "thank you, ma'am" were as cheap as dirt, and that ordinary good manners were a measure of the man, because only a dodlimbed fool was rude when he didn't have to be.

It was a long time ago, but I remember just as clear that one day when we had some trouble with what the Old Man called a Willie-off-the-pickle-boat. This Willie was one of those rich Yankees who had come into port with his ocean-going yacht. He had on a yachting cap and a double-breasted blue coat and white pants and pipe-clayed white shoes. There were another man and three women with him, and from the way they were carrying on in the stern sheets of that yacht they had been punishing the booze pretty frequent for some time. Between sunburn and whisky, the Willie-off-the-pickle-boat had a face like a beet, more purple than red.

I don't even know what the ruckus was about. I think it was something about the yacht being sloppily moored at a private pier that belonged to the Pilots' Association, and the yacht was beating up the pilot launch. The Old Man had some interest in the association, the pier, and the launch.

I believe he asked the Willie if he would kindly nurse his yacht around to another slip or sling his hook a little farther out so as to take up a little strain, or some such civil request. The Willie didn't take it kindly. He came bustling up on the pier, like he was about to pop, and started to holler and wave his arms. He said, playing it big for the womenfolk, that no old moss-backed yokel was going to tell him what to do with his yacht, and that if the Old Man didn't watch his step he'd buy the town, and so forth. The Old Man just stated his request over again, in a very mild voice, using "please" and "sir."

The Willie blew up. "Why, you old son of a bitch," using that Truman term which doesn't get you very far in an argument down South, "I've got a good mind to——"

Which was as far as he got, good mind or not. The Old Man. who was a good twenty to thirty years older, squared off and clouted him on the chin. The Willie staggered back and fell off the dock into the drink. His gold-braided hat went spinning downstream in the current. The Willie was about half coaled out, and he was flopping and spluttering in the water.

The Old Man hopped onto the pilot boat and grabbed a boat hook. He grappled the Willie in the seat of his flannel britches and hauled him aboard, choking and gasping like a big fish, and then being sick to his stomach. The Old Man never even looked at him.

He hopped back onto the dock and bowed to the women. "I wish to beg your pardon, ladies," he said. "I found the gentleman's language offensive in front of the ladies. Please accept my apologies." Then he turned to the other man. "And now, sir," he said, "*for the last time, move that boat. Please.*"

When we left the dock, the city slickers and the three women were moving the boat.

The Old Man muttered all the way home that he despised brawls, but there occasionally came a time and a place where politeness wasn't any good and you had to meet bad manners with worse manners.

"There ain't anything," he said, "that'll settle an argument as fast as a punch in the nose if you know you're right and the other feller knows he's wrong. But it sure is undignified."

The Old Man was strictly a shark on good manners in the woods. I have already told you how persnickety he was about cleaning up campsites and burying rubbish and washing down boats and keeping guns and gear clean and oiled. But he wouldn't hunt or fish with a meat hog or a rude man.

He used to shoot quail quite a lot with a man named Joe, a very pleasant fellow until you took him to the woods and let loose a couple of bird dogs. Then Joe changed coats and became a hog. He was one of those fast walkers, always right on the heels of the dog when it was working game. He was a fast shooter, too. A bird would get up, clearly in your quarter, and you would be taking your time to let the bird straighten out, and just as you were about to pull down, *pow!* Joe's gun would go off and the bird would fall, because Joe was a very fine shot.

I went along on a few hunts with Joe and the Old Man, not shooting, because the one thing the Old Man was adamant about was more than two guns loaded when you were hunting quail. Even not shooting, just watching Joe made me nervous as a fox in a forest fire. It made the dogs nervous too, because Joe was stepping on their tails all the time, and they didn't have a chance to work the birds properly. The dogs rushed the birds, and the birds flushed wild, and always there was Joe, right smack in the middle of the wild birds.

Even on steady points this Joe was a hog. Although they supposedly took turns on singles points, you'd never be surprised to see your bird drop before you shot, and Joe would say something like, "Well, I didn't think you were going to shoot," or, "I thought that palmetto bush had blocked off your bird."

The Old Man was deadly with his gun, but he never brought in more than half the birds Joe did. I noticed a lot of things. Every time they did get confused and both fired at the same bird, Joe would take the bird from the dog and put it in his pocket—even though it was the Old Man's turn. And when they got home, if Joe had fifteen and the Old Man had six, Joe would keep the fifteen, and there would be no mention of a divvy.

Finally the Old Man quit hunting with Joe. He said it took all the fun out of shooting. "Hunting ain't a competition," he said. "You ain't trying to win any prizes. Hunting is watching the dog work, and taking it easy, and shooting just enough, and walking slow, and enjoying the day. Damned if I figure to run any foot races at my age, not if I never fire off another shotgun. And if a man wants a bird more than I do, he can have him. But not in my steady company."

So the Old Man and I took to hunting regularly together, and we killed about as many birds as Joe did, but we killed them according to ordinary politeness and what the Old Man called protocol. We did it calm and easy. When the dogs would point a covey, I would stand to the left and the Old Man would take the right. If all the birds swung my way, he never shot. If they went his way, I let 'em go, and hoped a lay bird would jump up in front of me. Most of the time one did.

On single birds, we shot turn and turn about. If two birds got up when it was my turn, the Old Man never shot at all. He only shot if half a dozen jumped and one or two went away off to the right, 180 degrees from where I was pointing.

Quite a lot of birds got away from us, in one sense, but then quite a lot didn't. For one thing, knowing that you didn't have to compete with some itchy trigger behind you or on one side of you calmed you down. You'd let the bird fly and straighten out and kill him dead, rather than snap-shoot him and either miss him clean or blow him to pieces with the full charge.

And the difference it made in the dogs was unbelievable. The Old Man wasn't wrong when he said a nervous hunter can make even a good dog nervous, to where he starts crowding the bird and flushing him or running clean over a lay bird that he would have smelled if he'd been taking his time. I reckon we more than made up for the ones that got away with the ones we shot that we wouldn't even have suspected of being there if we'd been in a hurry.

After we'd put up a covey and shot into it and the dogs had retrieved, the Old Man would generally sit down under a tree, call in the dogs, and light his pipe. "Let's give 'em a little time," he'd say. "It'll take those singles ten minutes before they start to move around a bit and leave enough scent for the dogs to smell 'em out. A bird that's just hit the ground don't have hardly any smell at all. He has to move a little first."

Well, I learned something there, too. If you go crowding and stomping right into where you've seen the single light, you'll kick up bird after bird that the dogs have run smack over, especially if it's in thick grass. Lots of times the birds will get up again as a covey, or as two halves of a covey. Or if they've lit in sparse cover, they'll flush wild, whereas if you'd left 'em alone a little they'd have run for better cover and left a perfect scent for the dogs to follow, and you'd have gotten a stanch point and a good shot.

By just leaving them alone ten or fifteen minutes, when you did go to roust 'em out you'd have your dogs pointing a bird here, a bird there, two birds here, and each bird holding hard on the ground, even with the guns going off. The way the Old Man hunted singles, there was many a time we could have wiped out the covey, excepting that the Old Man didn't hold with shooting more than three or four birds apiece out of any one bunch.

I sat down one winter—we always kept strict account of the birds we brought in, and filed a report to the Game Department at the end of the year—and figured out an average bag for the pair of us. There was a fifteen-bird limit then, and we averaged twenty-one birds per hunting day for two guns. I missed a lot of birds, and I averaged eight birds per trip. That meant that, what with rain and snow and dry-nosed, sick dogs and just plain bad-luck days, we had to have a lot of days when we killed the limit, fifteen birds apiece.

But the important thing was that we had plenty of lovely time in between the actual shooting. So suppose it took us all afternoon to get a limit or a near limit? We had just that much more time in the woods, to see all the things a man can see in the woods if he's traipsing along slow and easy and taking his time. There's no fun going hunting at three o'clock if you're going to be back in the tin Liz at four-thirty, with the best part of the day still ahead of you.

In later years it seemed to me that this feller Joe missed all the important part of hunting, just from being in a hurry and greedy to see a little bundle of feathers fall. The Old Man said that hunting was not so much what you brought home in the bag as what you invested in it if you were satisfied to take a small return on your original investment.

"Otherwise," he said, "you might as well build yourself a

quail trap or take a couple dollars and buy a gross from one of these pot hunters. There just ain't enough meat on a bobwhite partridge to make it worth while to turn yourself into what that Willie-off-the-pickle-boat called me. I would rather come home any time with a few birds and a good day in the woods."

The Old Man was peculiar, all right. I wish there were more of his brand around these days. Maybe we'd have more birds.

13

Even School Can't Hurt October

It being Prohibition in those days, I had no way of knowing what brown October ale tasted like, but there were a passel of other things to recommend the month. I'm not referring to school, and wearing shoes again, because by October you'd got used to about six hours of torture and your feet had quit hurting. October meant a lot of things to me. It meant the oysters were prime again, and there was enough leaf off the trees so that you could see a squirrel. The big fish were beginning to run, and the first frosts had come, so that a fire felt fine in the evenings. And if October were here, why then it wasn't so long before the bird season opened, and once you had Thanksgiving settled you had Christmas practically made.

It was one of those nice bright Saturdays when it forgot to

rain. Speaking of rain, did you ever notice that for five school-days the sun always shone, but as soon as a boy got loose from learning and fixed his mouth to do something worth while with his time on a Saturday, it always poured rain?

Anyhow, this was one of those nice bright Saturdays, or promised to be, because the sun had just come up blood-red and was starting to turn gold, and the first mild frost was white and stiff on the browning grass, and there wasn't so much as a whisper of breeze to stir the trees. The Old Man had parked the Liz, and we were walking down a corduroy country road, heading for a big hickory grove we knew about. We were carrying a couple of .22 rifles and were accompanied by that fice dog, Jackie, the mongrel with the curled tail that swooped up in the air and came back to rest approximately between his shoulder blades. Jackie was dirty yellow and had a fox's face, and nobody could have accused him of having a hound's bugle, but there was one thing Jackie could do better than any other dog in the world. If there was a squirrel in a tree or rooting for nuts on the ground, Jackie would know about it, and tell you about it in a thin little voice that sounded like an angry woman quarreling.

"We'll just tie this masterpiece of bad breeding to a tree for a spell," the Old Man said. "All the squirrels are still in the trees, and we don't need no expert assistance until they come down on the ground. We will still-hunt 'em a spell. I reckon there's enough leaves off so we can see 'em."

We came into the hickory grove. It was as still as a cemetery.

"A great morning for squirrels," the Old Man whispered. "It's a waste of time to hunt them in the wind. They just don't move, and they don't feed much. Be quiet now, and let's walk soft and go sit under that big hickory yonder and see what happens. Ssshh."

We sat down, the Old Man on one side of the tree and me on the other. All over the grove you could hear the squirrels begin to talk. *Chirr* is about as close as you could come to the noise they make, but you can make about the same sound by sliding your tongue sideways across the top of your mouth. There was plenty of action going on this morning, I must say. You could hear them chirring all over the grove, and hear the click of their teeth on the nuts, and now and again you would hear a mild crash in the foliage as a big fellow traded trees and the branch he sailed off of would whip back.

I heard a chirr behind me on the ground, and a click, and I knew it was the Old Man talking squirrel. He was making the click with his safety. It sounded just like a squirrel bragging about the size of the nut he was tackling. Pretty soon there was a shaking in the branches of a tree just ahead of me, off to the right, and I sat still as a statue. Then there was some more shaking, and a head stuck out of a crotch. All I could see was head, but it was black-silver and it had to be a fox squirrel.

Bimebye I saw a tail flicker, and then the old fox slid round the trunk, flat-plastered to the bole. I let him come all the way round until his back was to me and he was peeping in the opposite direction. Then I raised the little .22 real slow, held high on his back between the shoulders, and squeezed her off. The long rifle hit with a thump, and Mr. Squirrel came down like a rock. He hit with a thud, kicked a couple of times, and quit. A soft-nosed .22 long rifle between the shoulders will make a man stop and think, let alone an old squirrel. From where this fellow lay, he looked as big as a tomcat. He was near solid black on top, with a lovely black-and-gray tail, and he was almost three times as big as a gray, or what we call a cat squirrel.

It wasn't long before I heard a rustling behind me, then a wait, and the Old Man's little gun spat. I heard a thump as something hit the deck, and judged the Old Man's gun eye was still working.

With the Old Man making his chittering noise, the squirrels came to that big hickory like they were cats and we had the catnip concession. First my gun would make its little *splat!*, followed by *tunk!* as the bullet hit, and *blump!* as the squirrel came tumbling down. There were mostly grays, but I acquired two more of the fox variety, one a lovely silver-gray and the other blacker than the first. The Old Man's gun was speaking pretty constant, too, and in less than an hour we had more than a dozen. Then I heard the Old Man creak to his feet and heard the rasp of a match as he fired up his pipe.

"Let's pick up and move on. We done wore out our welcome here. How many you got?" he asked.

"Seven," I told him. "Three foxes and four cats. How 'bout you?"

"I got eight," the Old Man said, "but only one fox. I missed another I coulda killed with a rock, if I had of had a rock instead of this cannon."

"I missed three," I explained. "I got fancy and tried to hit one jumping, and the other two I coulda caught with my hands. A squirrel looks like a mighty big target when he's flattened out or sitting up, don't he?"

We had a couple of towsacks with us, and I filled mine with my squirrels. Then I went around to where the Old Man had stacked his squirrels in a neat pile, and dumped 'em on top of mine. Fifteen squirrels in one sack is a powerful mess of squirrels. It was all I could do to heft the bag.

"Gimme," the Old Man said. "I'll just hang it up here in this low crotch, whilst you go let Jackie loose. It don't do to frustrate a dog, any more than you'd tease a young'un. He's been hearing the gun go off, and he's probably hung himself by now. We can still use a lot more squirrels. I promised a mess to half the neighborhood, and at last count Abner McCoy had at least fourteen head of young'uns to feed, and the boll weevils hit the cotton this year."

I grinned. The Old Man was powerful cute sometimes. Abner McCoy was as black as the ace of spades and he had a mouth as big as a scoop shovel. He farmed a lot of land next to the store, and he had more quail than anybody round. About a dozen fat squirrels would make a prime bait of meat for his family, and there would be enough heads left over for a proper squirrel-head stew. The squirrels would fix our hunting lease for another year.

There may have been a limit on squirrels in those days—I disremember—but we didn't hunt 'em much, and when we hunted we hunted serious.

So I rested my gun on my hat and trotted off to unleash Jackie, who was having a fit of nervous frustration and was foaming at the mouth. He nigh dragged me off my feet as we headed back to the grove.

"Turn him loose now," the Old Man said. "We'll go over yonder to that rise where all the scrubby oaks and chinquapins are. The survivors'll be on the ground. That's Jackie's business."

Jackie took off in the right direction, and presently we heard his squirrel-up-a-tree signal, a feverish yapping that would make you think he'd treed a panther or a bear, at least. He was standing under an oak—did I say standing? He was dancing an Irish reel and yipping his head off, with his sharp fox face pointing to heaven.

"You take that side," the Old Man said. "I'll take this. In a minute one of us will spot him."

Shooting treed squirrels is almost ridiculously simple. It is just a matter of knowing how to look for 'em. With two men to a tree, the squirrel, who is plastered to the trunk or squatting in a crotch or stretched full length on a branch, will move away from one side as soon as he is aware of the shooter on his side. That's when the guy on the other side shoots him.

Pretty soon I spotted a head sticking cautiously around the bole, and a gray body, stuck flat, eased around to my side. The little .22 talked some more, and down he came. Jackie raced over, picked him up by the back of the neck, gave him a sharp twist, and broke his neck. Then Jackie spat him out on the ground, barked a sharp bark of self-appreciation, and whipped off.

It went on like that until nearly eleven o'clock. I reckon Jackie must have netted us another two dozen squirrels, mostly cats, but at least six or seven more foxes. We filled the other bag, and it was so heavy that the Old Man ran a stick through a couple of holes in the hem, and we packed it out together.

When we got to Abner's, the Old Man dumped the first bag in Abner's clean, white-sanded front yard. Abner's vast, plumb-black face split in a grin as big and red as half a watermelon.

"Man, dat sure a bait o' skwull," Abner said. "What in de yudder crocusack?"

"More squirrels," the Old Man told him. "These fifteen are for you."

"Bossman, dat powerful neighborly. Us kin use some meat in dis house. Seem lak every day I count another young'un I didn't know us had, and de price o' sowbelly powerful high. Tell you what us best do," Abner said. "Dat too many skwull in de yudder sack for two people clean. I call my biggest chillun, and we set right down here and skin 'em now. You chillun! Come hope me and de Cap'm!"

Children of all sizes boiled from the little house.

"You, Woodrow Wilson, you go fotch de knives!" Abner ordered. "You, Hardin', you go tell Mama I say start de fiah and boil water in de hog-killin' pot. You just makes to sit in de shade, Cap'm, under dat chinkyberry tree, while de chillun fix de skwull. And if I ain't outa my station, Cap'm, maybe you like a little snort of somepin I found in de branch las' week, and de young Cap'm, maybe he like cool he th'oat with a little dipper scuppernong wine, yeddy?"

The Old Man said he couldn't think of a sounder idea. We sat in the shade, and Abner brought a half-gallon Mason jar full of white liquid, and a similar jar half-full of a darker liquid. The white liquid was sweet and cool from the well, and the brown liquid must have had plenty muscles in it, because the Old Man closed his eyes and his body contorted when he downed a dipperful. He wiped his mustaches with the back of his hand.

"How are the birds this year, Abner?" he asked.

"Never seen so many patridges in my life," Abner replied. "City man out here de yudder day, want pay me for huntin' rights, but I tell him I save my buhds for my white folks."

The Old Man looked at me and winked. It wasn't long before our two dozen squirrels, skinned, gutted, and washed, came pink and clean in the tow sack.

"I guess we better get on, Abner, and many thanks," the Old Man said. "Good-by."

Abner said good-by, and the chillun waved.

The Old Man drove slowly out of the yard. He turned and winked at me again. "There's more ways to kill a cat than to choke it to death on butter."

I reckon you all think I'm powerful concerned with food, because I'm always writing about it. I guess I've got to plead guilty, but it seems to me a boy lives mostly in his belly, and the Old Man said one time he didn't trust nobody that didn't like to eat so hearty that a nap was bounden necessary after Sunday dinner.

In those days we didn't have all the fancy outdoor barbecue rigs, with the host wearing a girl's apron and a chef's cap. Mostly what got cooked was cooked inside a house, on a slow-burning wood stove, by a slow-cooking colored lady who didn't want nobody messin' round her kitchen. The men didn't cook —least the men didn't cook public in town. But the sneaky spirit of the chef was always there, inside the hairiest of the roughnecks, and Christmas was a time of year when everybody who wasn't sweet as a peach (a Southport euphemism for being as drunk as a goat) was apt to be doing something in the woods or on the water. It was a kind of point of honor to go somewhere to spend a couple of days living off the land.

They still have them in my part of the South, but they've got a lot fancier now, and I'm talking about the old-fashioned oyster roasts. A roast was as much a part of the festive season as the Christmas tree, the holly berry, and the mistletoe. In these outdoor cooking sprees, the men mostly took over. The ladies had their hands floury enough from making the fruitcakes, and they just sort of sat back, patted a foot, and let the boys be boys.

The first thing the boys did was go out in a skiff and tong up a bait of oysters and clams. The oysters in that neck of the woods were mighty fine. They were big—big as a bar of laundry soap—gray, striated, and shading to white around their wrinkled edges. The clams were nearly as big as tennis balls, purple-black on the shell and a plum-yellow solid globe on the inside. They came up muddy from the cold gray water, and when you swished the tongs in the clean water they tumbled onto the deck of the boat shining bright as jewels.

The fruits of the sea were taken to a proper oyster shed, which meant a lean-to under which a rough wooden table perched on trestles; the chairs were anything from camp stools to packing boxes. Kerosene lamps provided the light—I forgot to say that no respectable oyster roast was held in the daytime. It was not considered polite to get drunk in daylight, and a good portion of our holidaymakers considered oysters and corn liquor inseparable.

Wet-down moss would do, but a really top-grade oyster chef smothered his oysters in freshly gathered kelp. The actual oven was a simple compromise on a modern barbecue apparatus, meaning that three sides of stone or concrete held a sheet of heavy tin or galvanized iron on top. A slow fire was built under the metal sheet, and the oysters, blanketed in seaweed, were allowed to steam until the hinges relaxed and you could slide an oyster knife between the shell lips without cutting the valve. The smell is still vivid to me, because the oyster roast was held close by salt marsh, the scent of marsh and myrtle and beach pine mingling with the steam from the roaster.

You were supposed to tee off with either clam chowder or terrapin stew; you never got both at the same event. If it was clam chowder, it was very simple. The chowder contained no milk or tomatoes. It had clam juice and clams and diced Irish potatoes and browned fatback and onions and salt and pepper, and it simmered into such a delicious symphony that you had to hold yourself back, remembering the oysters. One of the ladies generally bestirred herself to make the chowder, for the gentlemen were always very busy with the oysters and with the half-gallon fruit jars that contained a white beverage which was known simply as mule.

But the oysters were the main operation. The chowder just paved your stomach for the real debauch. I don't care how they eat oysters today; there's only one way. As the Old Man said sometimes, "I value your opinion, but not when I know better. And in this case I know better."

First you take a bushel of oysters, smoky steam writhing, from their bed in the kelp over the slow coals, and you introduce them to a small Negro boy who is standing on your right with an opening knife in his hand. In front of you, on the rough pine planking of the table, is a bowl of red-hot melted butter and a wide, empty plate—almost platter size. For a condiment there is a thin-necked jug of pepper vinegar, with the little curled-up red peppers, hot as Hades, still inside. There is a platter full of johnnycake, corndodgers, or even hushpuppies in front of you. For a beverage, you drink Bevo, a concoction that was supposed to taste like beer but wanting a little needle to gain authority.

At the signal "Go!" the colored boy starts to open oysters, and if you are a man of control and high purpose you will allow him to release a dozen before you start to dip them in the butter, season them with the pepper vinegar, and put them away, mopping up the "gravy" of oyster juice, butter, and marsh mud with the already greasy johnnycake, corn fritter, or hushpuppy. Somehow, the tiny bit of remaining mud gives a flavor that is incomparable to anything, unless you know exactly what a Carolina marsh smells like with the wind in your nose and the water oaks shivering before the wind. You then lick your fingers and look reprovingly at the little boy if he has not managed to liberate another dozen oysters during your complete concentration on the first twelve.

The Old Man used to say, "There ain't no such thing as *enough* oysters—it's just that the human stomach was never really designed to handle a decent bait of them." My best record was four dozen, each oyster as big as a candy bar.

It was possible, of course, for a man to open his own oysters, but you lost something of glamour in the process, for the small boy was as much a part of a roast as the odor of steaming seaweed, the smell of the sea and trees, and the scent of the roasting oysters as they reluctantly relaxed their valves under the steady pressure of the flame. You might as well have taken away the distant hoot of the owl and the hollow boom of the surf and the damp smell of the white beach sand, or the rustle of the sea oats that grew down on the dunes nearly to the water's edge.

There was another thing—two things, as a matter of fact. One was that a man opening his own oysters never had enough will power to unleash a dozen before diving into the butter. The other thing was that you robbed the little colored boys of a chance to bet their night's wages on which client could eat the most oysters. A man who was having his oysters shucked for him was duty-bound to founder himself, or it would cost his little assistant a mess of money, as much as fifty cents. The boys kept the shells as a tally. They rarely lost money backing my appetite.

There was a certain artistic elegance to this scene of gourmandizing—the firelight red on the already-flushed faces of the cooks, glistening off the white eyeballs and black faces of the little Negro boys, shining greasily on the lips and the fingers of the eaters, lighting up the rough shed with weird shadows, and making weirder shadows of the angular, wind-tortured trees. The road to the roast was always of gleaming crushed oyster shell, which seemed fitting, and there was a bone-white, high-piled stack of shells off to the side.

This was the coeducational outdoor aspect of the holiday time.

The more intimate and cruder cookery by the gentlemen came on the two- or three-day hunting trips. Some of the richer men, off after ducks or deer, took along a cook. At that time there was a profession amongst the Carolina colored folks that possibly no longer exists, more's the pity—that of "sporting cook." He would be a man of the approximate moral equal of his employers, which is to say he wouldn't work steady if there was an excuse in the world to run loose in the woods and listen to that fine man-talk. Generally he drank—intemperately, sporadically—and so was adjudged a poor risk as a house cook.

I knew several of these fellows, and the best of them all was a paroled murderer who worked occasionally for my family. The name has gone away, but he was wizard in the woods. He did some things with a few rocks and an iron grill, shoved some oak chips underneath, with hard hickory to flavor it, and the venison chops that came off the grill would make you cry. Venison is a hard meat to cook, and a lot of people spend a lot of time basting it with this and that, and undrying it with jellies and wines, but this fellow would just toss it onto the coals, haul it off, and slap it steaming on the plate, and you always burned your tongue because you couldn't wait. I used to go to bed, full as a tick, already thinking about breakfast next morning.

Breakfast would be something special in fried eggs—he always toted an iron skillet, because he said you couldn't fry anything so a dog would eat it in anything else but an iron spider—and usually some broiled deer liver, and slabs of fried buttered bread, and maybe, if everybody was hungry, a squirrel fricassee. He made hoecakes, which are nothing but hushpuppies—meal and water and salt cooked in ashes. You scrape off the ashes, and there is a noble one-bite piece of ecstasy, especially if you've got some redeye ham gravy or fatback-flavored potlicker to dip it in.

I have never liked any egg, in any form, in a restaurant, but a fried egg in the woods, sizzled in bacon fat until its white edges turn to fine Belgian lace, grading up to brown, is a noble thing. And if it is accompanied by fried sowbelly and busted into a plate of fine-ground hominy grits, and the whole mess flavored up with grease, there may be indigestion around the corner, but it is not worthy of worry.

A lot of people won't eat a possum because it looks like a rat, but our cook could take a possum and nestle it in sweet 'taters and little onions and a few carrots, and I've never eaten anything in Paris, France, that could touch it. It wasn't fat and it wasn't lean. It was a kind of blend of both.

Remembering back to eating in the woods, it seems to me that the main staple, apart from coffee and sugar and salt and stuff, was corn sirup or molasses. A can of beans slow-cooked with molasses and onions and strips of bacon quit being just pork and beans. We used the long sweetening for everything —to sweeten coffee, drown the hotcakes, help the beans. We even combined it with ketchup on the spaghetti.

There are worse things than a duck or a fish caked in clay and set to slow-cook until the clay cracks, and when you peel it off the feathers or scales come with it. There are worse things than a chunk of fresh-killed deer liver broiled on a green stick around a campfire. Nobody has yet found a way to commercialize creek water, with its taste of brown leaf dye, but certainly there is no comparable liquid for making coffee in a tin percolator in a nest of coals.

Of course you realize all this was a very long time ago, and memory tends to make a man salivate. Youth and a body unjaded by whisky and tobacco are part of it, and of course the excitement of being out of doors. The only thing I can't figure out is that when I do it today it still tastes as good as I remember it, and very possibly a little better.

The first real concept of conservation that crawled into my head was fed me gradually by the Old Man, without his ever saying anything much about it. It took a period of years to develop, but one day it came into bloom like an autumn rosebush. There are a lot of things mixed in with keeping your game supply up to standard; some things that even a millionaire can't buy, such as friendship and cooperation.

Like most boys, I was as bloodthirsty as a cannibal. I got my first air gun when I was just six years old, and the robins and the blue jays and the catbirds and the rain crows really took a pounding. I shot everything from English sparrows to the neighbor's cat. When we had nothing better to do, my Cousin Roy and I went out into the woods and played Indians and shot each other from ambush. Why somebody didn't lose an eye will always be a source of wonder to me.

A big, old, sassy mocker lived in the magnolia tree alongside our house, and he used to sing late at night in the moonlight. He would scatter those notes around like one of the fishermen on Saturday-night payoff. He was a pet of my grandmother's; so it was natural that when I took down the Daisy one day and removed him from the concert business, the Old Man took down my pants and applied a very limber lath to my behind. It was one of the few times I ever had a hand laid on me, and it made an impression.

"Hunting," the Old Man said when my noise had slacked off, "is the noblest sport yet devised by the hand of man. There were mighty hunters in the Bible, and all the caves where the cave men lived are full of carvings of assorted game the head of the house drug home. If you hunt to eat, or hunt for sport for something fine, something that will make you proud, and make you remember every single detail of the day you found him and shot him, that is good too.

"But if there's one thing I despise it's a killer, some blood-crazy idiot that just goes around bam-bamming at everything he sees. A man who takes pleasure in death just for death's sake is rotten somewhere inside, and you'll find him doing things later on in life that'll prove it. I realize all young'uns get that first phase when they want to carve up desks and bust windows and shoot mockingbirds, but I aim to see you grow out of it, or I'll have every last inch of hide off your rear end.

"I want you to go to bed tonight and stay awake thinking about the mockingbird that sung so pretty and your grandma loved, and then think of that little mess of dirty feathers even the cat didn't want. And then think a little bit about this nice air rifle that Santa Claus brought you to learn to shoot with, and wish you had it back again."

Whereupon the Old Man took the little Daisy and busted it over his knee, and threw it over into the bushes where he had thrown the carcass of the mockingbird. That was Lesson One.

I went quite a spell before I got my first shotgun, and when the Old Man took me out to learn to shoot quail he spent quite a time reading me the riot act about how many quail a man could shoot out of a covey and still have some quail left to shoot next year and the year after. Like most kids, my idea of what to do, once you got birds scattered pretty, had been to shoot as long as the dogs pointed.

That sank in pretty good, because those quail and the Old Man had been friends for a long time; because he trained dogs over 'em, and knew to a bird what came out of the spring clutches. I didn't want him busting up my 20-gauge like he did the Daisy. And since he was my pretty constant companion in the woods, I couldn't have cheated if I had wanted to.

We hunted for quite a few years before it dawned on me that we had exclusive shooting rights to nearly a whole county. We shot land that said "Strictly Posted." But we shot it with the owner's permission, and we always started out with a word with the farmer, black or white, in his back yard, and always had a long, cold drink of icy well water out of the tin dipper. And when we came in tired and reached the house, we went in to warm chapped hands by the farmer's fire. Then maybe the Old Man would have a glass of scuppernong wine, and I would have a little bit too, and a handful of cookies or a doughnut before we got in the Liz to drive home.

This applied to both white and black. The colored folks were generally landowners, not croppers, and they had a big pride of land. I do not know how many little clapboard or log shacks I have been inside, with a roaring pine-knot fire actually showing through the house, the yard full of pickaninnies and yellow fice dogs, with some old woman always doing something over an iron pot in the yard—scalding a hog, doing the clothes, but always doing. When we went inside to warm up, the house was always neat and clean, with the walls papered in colored pages from newspapers, calenders, or sometimes just newspapers. Outside, the white-sand yard was always swept clean.

I had my first taste of squirrel-head stew in one of those little colored-folks' houses, my first possum and sweet 'taters. I still love the taste of fatback fried hard, and stewed rabbit to me tastes sweeter than any of those fancy French dishes. I called the older folks "Aunt" and "Uncle," and the middle folks by their first names. They called the Old Man "Cap'm," and called me "Young Cap'm" or "Mister Bobby." There wasn't any special servility, because the Old Man was always laughing and joking, and they always made a lot of fun of me, all loaded down with canteen and Scout ax and a gun as long as I was.

Old Aunt Florence, grizzled and bent, would sometimes say, "Cap'm, strange city man come out here the other day with some buhd dogs, and he drive up and ask me if I got any buhds on my place, and I say, 'Nawsuh. Ain't seen a single buhd since dem big rains come last spring and drownded 'em all. Anyhow, dis place posted. We got too many hawgs loose in de woods.' I knowed you wouldn't like no strange passer-bys shootin' yo' buhds. I sont him off."

Aunt Florence's little farm was so surrounded by coveys of quail, on purely public property, that she practically had to build a fence to keep them out of the yard. But the only way to the big timber leaseholds and swamps was through her yard, and she could look pretty fierce, surrounded by dogs that yapped ferociously at strange white folks.

Or we would stop to pay a call on big Abner McCoy, who was six foot four and had all those young'uns. Abner would grin horribly over his gums and say, "Cap'm, stay 'way from that covey over by de Old Church. There a den o' foxes over there been eating up yo' buhds and my chickens, and I got traps set thicker'n pine needles. Wouldn't like none o' yo' dogs to get caught.

"But the other day I was cuttin' some kindlin' over by dat ol' graveyard, between de graveyard and de old sawdust pile, and I jumped de biggest covey of buhds I ever seen. Dese is new buhds. Must been usin' cross de road, where dat loggin' goin' on, and plain couldn't stand de commotion. So dey come live with us. Wait a minute, I finish dis chore, I come show you exactly."

We never wasted any time finding birds, whether we were hunting on Sheriff Knox's big farm or Aunt Mary Millette's, who did the washing. Either the birds were here or they were there. If they weren't here, they had to be there. And you found 'em from one year to the next. We had peafield birds and swamp birds and woods birds that roved a little to eat the pine mast, but usually centered around a certain scrub-oak grove or a sawdust pile or a copse of gallberry and dead branches.

What is more, we had the whole county—a big county—to hunt in, and only one large estate was off limits. The rest was private shooting for the Old Man and me. One day it suddenly struck me that no millionaire could own that much prime shooting, and there must be a reason for it.

Well, there were a lot of reasons for it. For one thing, country folks in those days had no interest in quail unless they caught a covey running down a corn row and could kill the whole kaboodle for a stew. Or maybe to trap a few when times were tough and bellies growling. So they never paid any attention to partridges—which is what we used to call the bobwhite—and never made any effort to help them survive or to keep people from just killing off whole coveys right and left. There were pot hunters in those days, dead-eyed gents with pump sawed-offs, who could wipe out a covey in a day if the birds scattered right in the broom sedge.

The Old Man was pretty devious, as always. Everybody in the county knew him. He was in a position to give credit at a feed-and-grain store he was connected with, and in the hard years a lot of people planted on credit, and fed their cows on credit, and got their laying mash on credit. The Old Man could be counted on for one dollar's or two dollars' worth of personal loans, and at Christmastime he always went around with the flivver full of oranges and red candy. He had what are known today as connections at the source.

Well, when he started to circulate the idea among his friends that he thought right high of those little speckled partridges that ran together in droves and called to each other so mournful at dusk, he got action. He would tell one farmer that it would be a nice idea if he planted just a few black-eye peas down by the swamp, or another if he would let some stock stand here or there after the harvest, or not plow that field of broom over to the west if he didn't really need the space that year.

He said he'd give two shotgun shells for every tame cat gone wild that anybody brought him the tail of, and the same for hawks and foxes and similar varmints. He said he'd kind of appreciate it if the folks would keep account about where they flushed the coveys oftenest, so he'd know where to go look for 'em.

In return he was a sort of game scout, rounding up lost hogs and strayed cattle, and he was a terror about fire in the piney woods. Any time he came across a coon or a possum he would shoot it out of the tree and fetch it along to the nearest family. He usually had a few tins of snuff or a plug of Apple tobacco in his hunting coat for the old folks.

Well, sir, the upshot was that we had the primest shooting land around, and we had it pretty much to ourselves, and we had friends all over the place who looked after our game and kept down the brush fires and planted a little extra for the birds to eat. We had fires to warm us and cold water to drink and whatever there was in the pot to eat if we were hungry.

A long time later I read about conservation, but it seems to me the Old Man had it taped a long time ago. The only thing was, he didn't believe in sharing the wealth with every Tom,

Dick, and Harry. Only his friends and me, because he could control us. The Old Man reckoned that those birds were *his* birds, and not for nonappreciative short-time murderers to shoot into extinction. The more I look around at the opportunities for good shooting today, the more I think he might have been right on all counts.

14

Everybody Took Sick but Me

I suppose everybody has one little particular chunk of time
he wishes he could get back and live all over again. The one
fine time I remember best and most lovingly was when
whooping cough hit the schools—all the schools. It was what
they called an epidemic.

The epidemic struck about two weeks before the Christmas
holidays started. First there was whooping cough, and then
there was measles, and everybody came down with them except a few of us lucky ones. The teachers had them too—including the principal. There wasn't a thing to do but shut up
shop and let the diseases run their course. By the time the race
was run, it would be so close to Christmas that there wasn't any

use in starting classes all over again, just for a few days. So they knocked off school for nearly a month.

I tried real hard to regret this unforeseen gap in my keen pursuit of such things as Latin and geometry, but it so happened I had enjoyed whooping cough and two kinds of measles, and I was salted. Maybe the other people were sick, but not me. I felt just fine.

The chances are I was grinning all over my face when I got home the day they announced the closing of the schools. The Old Man looked sharply up at me and asked, "What happened to start you grinning like a Chessy cat? Teacher break her leg?"

"No, sir," I said. "Better. They just closed down the schools until after New Year's. We got an epidemic or something. School's suspended. Hot diggety!"

"Look at you," the Old Man chided. "Happy as a dead pig in the sunshine. Here you are, going to grow up ignorant, and all you can do is grin. I'm ashamed of you."

"It's not my fault I already had whooping cough and the measles," I protested. "I didn't close the school. But as long as it's closed, I don't figure to cry myself to death. I think I'll just go and shoot some squirrels. You want to come?"

"Not me," the Old Man said. "This lumbago's got me. You're going to have to handle this misbegot holiday all by yourself. Just try to check in with me once in a while, so's I won't feel too left out of things."

The Old Man slid down in a chair and shoved his specs a little higher up on his nose and took to reading some book that must have weighed ten pounds. I changed my school clothes and went off to look for some squirrels. I didn't take the bird dogs along. I took old Mickey, the spaniel.

People today talk a lot about these German Weimaraners that'll hunt anything from rats to elephants, but I'll stack that Mickey up against any of them as a plain meat dog. She was a spayed golden cocker bitch, durn near as old as me and a whole lot fatter. She was a pure-T hunting fool.

Mickey was slow but she was certain. She would find a covey of quail as good as any professional quail dog. Although she wouldn't hold a point, she'd slow down enough to give you time to get up with her before she let out a yip and jumped.

She would run a possum at night or tree a coon. She was poison on rabbits, because, since she couldn't outrun 'em, she'd outthink 'em and run 'em past you. She loved to hunt squirrels, and she'd retrieve anything from a buck deer to a ground mole. She especially loved to go duck hunting, because the colder the water, the better she felt. One time I saw a big old bull mallard just about drown her.

I don't want to tell you any real big lies about Mick. She didn't run rabbits as good as a pedigreed beagle. She wasn't as dead on wounded ducks as a Chesapeake or a golden retriever. She didn't cover as much ground on quail as even a slow pointer, and she wasn't half the squirrel treer that little Jackie, the fice dog, was. But for most purposes she was the most all-purpose dog you ever saw.

As long as the Old Man was laid up I couldn't get too far away from base, because I wasn't old enough then to drive the Liz. And there weren't many quail around where we were living, so it was a waste of time to hunt much with the bird dogs. But there were a whole lot of little bits of game—a few quail, a few ducks, rabbits, squirrel, snipe. So for one solid month it was me and Mickey.

The cold had come, and there was a thin crust of ice on the ponds in the morning, not heavy enough to bear your weight, but enough to force the ducks into pools of free water. The leaves were off the trees, so that you could see the squirrels, and a lot of the underbrush had died, so that the rabbits were fairly easy. You could always find one in a brush pile. There were a few doves still in the fields. Shotgun shells cost a nickel apiece.

I reckon that this was the time when I picked up a very bad habit that has caused me a slew of complaints ever since. I wasn't then, and never will be, what is called a dedicated hunter, just burning to go and do one particular thing. I was more like a highly trained quail dog that has slipped his leash and is having a glorious time chasing rabbits. I liked to go out and just sort of mess around, with some No. 8's in the shotgun and a few 4's in my hip pocket and two buckshot shells in my shirt pocket just in case a deer should run up and start out to trample me.

One of the days I spent might have been typical of most of the days, and I will try to tell you how it was. I was out of the bed in the cold black night, with just a little glow in the old square stove in the living room. I dressed as close to it as I could get, and then went back into the kitchen and ate a cold sweet potato, a pickle, a glass of milk, and some leftover pound cake. I stuck a couple of apples and a bag of raisins in my hunting coat and didn't forget to grab a handful of matches on the way out.

In addition to the gun and the shells, I carried a small belt ax and a hunting knife and a light Army canteen. That was all I needed to be Dan'l Boone. Missis Mickey and I started out to conquer the country.

We'd go first, stumbling and half-frozen in the black morning, to a duck pond about half a mile away, and creep very quietly in the dark down to the water's edge and hide in some brush I'd stacked up to make a blind. When the first gray light came, there would be ducks on that pond—some butterballs and bluebills and a gray duck or a black mallard or so.

I knew what I was going to do as soon as there was enough faint light to see by. I was going to pop off the first barrel at a clump of them on the water and then bang at a flyer as they went away. Mostly I was good for about four more shots, because they'd circle the woods and come back again in small bunches. On a good morning I was a cinch to bag about four, five, six ducks, especially if I got a couple on the water.

This one morning I got only one on the water, and a wounded one fluttered up and I gave him the other barrel, just so I wouldn't have to go and hunt him in the woods. The ducks made the first return run, and I knocked down another and missed one going away. Then a fresh segment came in and I was lucky. I got one coming and one going. The first one I hit in the head. He went up about a hundred yards in the air like a skyrocket and came plummeting down as dead as a mackerel.

Well, that was a fine start, I said to Mick as she plunged into the icy water. One black mallard, two butterballs, a blue-bill, and a gray duck. We will now hang these ducks in a tree and go and investigate the squirrel situation. Mickey fetched the last duck and looked at me as she shook herself. *That's fine*, she said. *Man, that water's cold!*

We were just a few rods from a big stand of hardwood trees, hickory mostly, with a few wild pecans that had sprung up a long time ago when somebody was farming there. You could almost always pull a few squirrels out of it, because there were acorns and pine mast as well. We walked very slow and quiet, and you could hear the squirrels chittering and making that click-clack noise on the nuts, and once in a while that long, metallic chirring sound.

Mickey and I hunted very scientific. If the squirrels were on the ground, she'd chase them up a tree and raise the roof barking. The squirrels would watch her, and I would edge around the other side of the tree and shoot. One morning I saw a big black-and-gray fox squirrel go into a nest, and I shot into the nest and four fox squirrels fell out.

This morning we didn't have that kind of rich luck. There weren't any squirrels on the ground; so I told Mickey to hush and we sat quiet under a tree and called the squirrels, slipping the safety of the gun back and forth to sound like teeth on nuts, and making that *squirrrrr* noise with my tongue. A couple of fool squirrels came skipping through the trees to investigate the noise, and I collected the pair. We picked up one more by accident as we walked through the timber stand, heading for a big deserted peafield that usually had some quail in it.

Mickey lumbered off to where she figured the birds ought to be, and sure enough they were there. She shook her stubby tail and wiggled her rear end like she'd slipped a ratchet somewhere, and the birds got up wild ahead of her. I shot twice and downed one. I reloaded, and two lay birds got up, and I killed one and missed the other. The birds went into a wild-grape swamp that was so thick they weren't worth following; so we quartered the field, and I shot one dove that got up ahead of me.

We were doubling back around to pick up the ducks and go home for lunch when Mickey cocked her ears and jumped a big buck rabbit, and I added him to the bag. When she fetched him, he looked bigger than she was.

I pulled out my dollar watch, and it was only ten o'clock; so I decided to stop and light a fire and clean the game. There wouldn't be any lunch for another two hours anyhow. I took the belt ax, and hacked off some pine knots and a couple of chunks of dead log, and built me a blaze. I shucked the squirrels and the rabbit and opened them up and started on the ducks. I had already eaten the apples and the raisins and I was still hungry; so I took one of the quail and plucked him and stuck him on a green stick over the coals. He tasted a little burnt-feathery and a touch raw, but he filled enough corners so that I could make it to lunch without starving. Mickey ate the innards, she being a rather indelicate bitch.

When I got home, I washed the ducks and the one quail and the dove and the three squirrels and the rabbit, and cut them up and put them in the icebox. Then I washed my hands and went to lunch, which was black-eyed peas cooked with sow-belly and hard country ham and bright golden cornbread and milk and apple pie with cinnamon dusted on it. Then I took a little nap, after asking big fat Lil, the cook, to wake me up at 2:00 P.M., about the same time I'd generally be thinking of getting out of school. I reckon I smiled when I slept, because all I had to do that afternoon was what I'd done that morning, only in reverse order—rabbits first, then quail, doves, squirrels, ducks.

I performed this routine every day except Sunday for three weeks. Christmas Eve came, and the Old Man, better now of his lumbago, asked me what I thought I'd like to find under the tree the next morning.

I didn't stop to think before I spoke. "Nothing that I can think of," I said. "I've had my Christmas. Except maybe I need some shotgun shells. I'm about shot out."

The Old Man grinned. He'd been watching me every day, stumbling home dead beat with a backload of game. "I sure am glad that epidemic of yours is about played out or there'll be nothing else left in this neck of the woods to shoot. Remember what happened to the buffaloes."

Christmas morning dawned bright and clear, but I wasn't there in the house to see it. I was down by the duck pond, with Mickey shivering beside me. I had clean forgot to look under the Christmas tree.

15

The Goat and I

There was one spring when everything seemed nice; it came early and stayed put, so that you got out the baseball stuff a month ahead of schedule and started to think about fishing and summer vacation, all in one bundle. And in addition to fishing and vacation, I started to plague everybody for a pony. I had read nearly all of Mr. Zane Grey's cowboy stories, and I was horse-minded. The Old Man was pretty unimpressed with my Riders-of-the-Purple-Sage stage. He did not care for horses very much.

"A horse," he said, "is the dumbest animal I know, and he takes a power of looking after. He's got to be fed and watered and curried and combed. He's always knocking a fetlock on the stall or something, and you need the vet to come running every whipstitch. He has to be looked after like a baby, and I don't know if you've got enough concentration to look after an animal that big after the first interest in getting throwed off him has dwindled down.

"Also, you know," the Old Man said, "his stall has to be cleaned and his saddle polished and his blankets aired. He needs fresh straw, and he eats a mountain of hay and oats, and he has to be walked to get himself cooled out after you've run him hard. You got to watch his hoofs and take him to the blacksmith. You got a bicycle; what do you need with a horse?"

I muttered something about every boy ought to have a horse, just like every boy ought to have a dog. The Old Man snorted. He said that pretty soon I would be telling him that every boy ought to have an automobile, and that some day I would be arguing that every boy ought to have an airplane.

"Tell you what," he said. "A horse is too large an investment for an unproven ability. We will just sort of try you out on a goat. Anybody that will look after a goat and cart will be a likely candidate for a pony, because nothing is quite as ornery as a billy goat. I know where there's one for sale. He's a real handsome goat, if you like goats, and I'll knock you together a cart and make you some harness."

We went to a place called Foxtown, where the colored people lived, and we stopped at the home of Albert Grey, the big colored boy who worked in the yard and told me fascinating stories to avoid doing any more work than he had to. Albert's aunt owned a goat. The goat was for sale for five dollars.

He was a real good-looking goat, young, fawn-colored, with a black stripe down his back, neat black hoofs, and a white star on his forehead. His horns weren't mature yet and hadn't curved out, and he had a forehead that was rock-hard. He had the worst disposition of anything or anybody I ever met.

We dragged—and I mean drug—Billy home, and he was protesting every inch of the way. He didn't want to leave Foxtown. He was happy in Foxtown, living under the house and eating anything that crossed his view. He did not want to go and live with the white folks. But we dragged him, and penned him up in the cow lot. The first thing he did was charge the cow, to the intense surprise of the cow. It was a big old creamy-yellow Jersey, with big horns, but that pint-sized he-goat had her scared stiff in five minutes.

We left Billy glaring at us through the fence and went off to see about the cart. The Old Man brought the tools out, and we got a big packing box and converted it into the body. The Old Man found some wheels somewhere, and we mounted her on the wheels, stuck some shafts on her, and painted her red, and she was a very handsome cart. Then he got some leather thongs and some buckles from the hardware store and produced a fine harness. He even made me a small whip. "You'll need it," he said, kind of mean. "A goat takes a lot of explaining to."

The Old Man said that any boy fit to own a horse and ride the range would have to train the critter himself, because no cowpoke worth his salt would ride a horse somebody else had broken. The same, he said, applied to a goat. I would have to break Billy myself, so that Billy would respect me and be a one-man goat. In later years I began to suspect that there was a lot of evil humor in the Old Man.

Bright and early the next day I set out to break Billy to his proper role of beast of burden. I went down to the cow lot and jumped over the fence, and Billy charged me like a lion. He hit me square in the stomach with that knobby skull, and I went over, all the breath knocked out of me. Billy backed off, sort of roared, and came again, like a cannon ball. This time I got out of his way, ran him down, got a strangle hold on his neck, grabbed an off leg like I'd read the cow hands bulldozed a steer, and spilled him on his side. He lay there on the ground and hated me with his cold yellow eyes.

Well, sir, trying to put a halter and a harness on that durn goat was a sight to see. I know it was a sight to see because a few minutes later, when I was red-faced and sweating and as mad at the goat as the goat was mad at me, I heard a chuckle.

There was the Old Man, leaning on the fence and laughing so hard that the tears were streaming down his face and running into his mustache.

"I don't think you're going at this exactly right," he said, "but I'm danged if I can tell you what you're doing wrong, unless it's that you ain't got but two hands and need six. Wait a minute. I'll help you hook him up."

Somehow between us we rassled the ornery beast into the harness and then tried to lead him to the cart. He sat down on his behind and braced his back legs, and when we pulled on the reins his eyes popped and he started to choke, but he didn't follow. He wasn't a very big goat, and the Old Man finally picked him up in his arms and toted him to where the cart was. Then we tried to back him between the shafts.

I heard somewhere about the camel and the needle's eye, and the camel had a cinch to get through. Getting this goat backward into the shafts was like trying to thread a needle with a snake. He blatted and kicked and butted and wiggled, but we finally got him in and secured—we thought—with the little hames on his shoulders and the reins threaded. I got into the cart and cracked the tiny little whiplash and hollered, "Gee haw," or some such. The goat looked around at me with the purest, most undistilled hatred I have ever seen in any eyes, and promptly lay down.

We would drag him to his feet, and as soon as I got into the cart he would lie down again. And then he started to twist and turn, and before long the harness looked like a backlash on a fishing line. Billy looked pleased. The Old Man shrugged.

"I think that's enough for one day," he said. "We don't want to rush his training. Let's drag him back to the cow lot, and we'll have another shot at him tomorrow."

We had another shot at him tomorrow, and it was the same old thing. This was a goat who wouldn't gee, wouldn't haw, wouldn't lead, wouldn't be dragged, wouldn't get up when he was lying down, and wouldn't lie down if he happened to want to stand up. He wouldn't go through the gate in the cow lot, which had a low fence; so I just simply took to throwing him over the fence. I had heard about Milo of Crotona in school, and I reckoned by the time Billy was a full-grown goat I could still heave him over the fence. I wasn't sure where Crotona was, but if Milo could heft a bull, full-grown, by starting out with him as a calf, I wasn't going to be backed down by any damn billy goat.

We worked on that goat for three months, and he never gave an inch. We had to battle to get him in the harness and battle to get him out of it. We had to run him down and catch him to get him out of the cow lot, and we had to throw him back like a fish when we were done with him.

I was getting no mileage and no amusement out of this goat at all. Then one day I found out by accident that this goat was a true warrior. He loved to butt and to eat anything that was regarded as inedible, but he had another vice too. He loved to wrestle. He would rear up on his hind legs and charge, and when I grabbed him he would twist and turn and do his level best to throw me. Fighting was the only thing he took any interest in except food.

The wrestling wore a little thin after a while because if a boy wants to wrestle he might as well find another boy; and anyhow, my mother was beginning to complain about my smell. This was a complete billy goat, including smell.

I tried everything I knew in the way of kindness to gentle him, and all I got was that yellow goatish glare. It isn't any fun to live with something that hates you and won't work even a little bit for his board and keep; so finally we took Billy in the Liz and returned him to Foxtown. He let out a happy blat when he saw his old home, and promptly dived under the house when we turned him loose.

I must have looked pretty downcast, because the Old Man stopped at Cox's Store and bought me a soft drink and a nickel's worth of candy. When we went on home he said, "Don't feel too upset. There are some things—some dogs, some goats, some people—that ain't worth troubling over. You can feed 'em and gentle 'em and worry over 'em and coax 'em and try to teach 'em, but they'll stay obstinate right on, like that damn goat. After a while, when you see it ain't any use, the only thing is to give up. The thing is to know when to give up—not too early, not too late."

I didn't say anything.

"You still want a horse?" the Old Man asked very gently.

"Not this year," I said. "I'm plumb wore out with that cusséd goat. This year I'm going to concentrate on fishing. At least I can manage a rowboat."

"Now there you are showing signs of sense," the Old Man said. "No man can do everything well. A lot of men spread themselves out, trying this, having a dib and a dab at that, never finishing what they start, and always trying to look for something new when they've failed. A smart man knows when he has a few things he can do well, and he's wise to do 'em, especially when he's failed at something. This gives him time to collect his wits and calm his disappointments, and then he's fit to go off and try something new again. I think the bigmouths might be biting tonight, if you'd care to try 'em."

The bigmouths were biting, and pretty soon my hurt feelings and frustrations cooled off and I wasn't mad at the goat any more. But I will never forget that animal as long as I live. He put a scar on my self-confidence, and since then I have met a power of people like him. When I run up against a person or a situation that has all the earmarks of Billy, that is when I quit and go fishing. Up to now it hasn't failed to help.

16

The Pipes of Pan

The first promise of summer was always an exciting thing to a boy—the spring winds eased and the sun burned away the April rains, the green pushed softly up and all the smells began. Mornings before breakfast were delightfully cool and breezy, and bred a restless excitement that made you want to caper barefoot on the dew-wet grass.

The smells were something. Down by the creek the dogtooth violets pushed up through the moss. The heavy tuberosy smell of the yellow jasmine filled the countryside, and the dogwood trees were white and pink with delicate bloom. In the orchards the early peaches and plums were breaking into blossom, adding their scents to the wild ones. The first tame flowers were popping out into the warmth, competing with the wild violets and the Johnny-jump-ups. I used to think that heaven would smell like this—cool and moist and very delicately fragrant.

You took to the woods then, not as a hunter or a fisherman, but as a naturalist. The Old Man was very firm about that.

"You're a bloodthirsty savage," he said, "like all boys are bloodthirsty savages. But there's a heap more to it than killing. Seeing the whole world come alive again after a long winter's nap and a wild, wet spring is more fun, 'specially as you grow older, than all the shootin' and fishin' there is. And I never was able to explain it, but the critters seem to notice this too. You'll see how tame everything is this time of the year, when it's wilder'n a buck rabbit in the shootin' season."

Maybe it seems a little dull today, but we used to go berry picking, after the blackberries had turned from green to red to purple-black, glistening on their thorny vines, and found it exciting. There were so many things to see and hear in the spring when you took a pail and went out berrying, to come home tired, with a crick in your back and your fingers and lips dyed purple from the juicy berries.

There were birds around that I do not seem to see so often any more—brilliant bluebirds, which came early in the spring and went away later in the summer. There were lots and lots of the big, fierce-looking redheaded woodpeckers; lots of what we called yellowhammers, another species of peckerwood known as flicker; the big cuckoos we called rain crows; the carnivorous shrikes with the bandit's velvet masks across their cold robbers' eyes; and hordes of the big, brilliant, raucously screaming blue jays.

The wet, plowed fields were crowded with teams of killdeers and the dainty-walking titlarks, racing along like pacing horses. The bobolinks were beginning to sway on the ends of high weeds, the stalks bending under their negligible weight. Soon the Baltimore orioles would be along, filling the air with sounds like the clinking of coins. The big cardinals were patches of blood against the dark green of the pines and cedars, and the scarlet tanagers darted like air-borne snakes.

When I think of it now, I think of it in terms of sounds and smells rather than sights. The catbirds quarreled in the low bushes around the house, and the big, fat, sassy old mocker that lived in the magnolia mimicked the catbirds. The doves cooed sadly from a great distance, and the quail called from the brushy cover at the edge of the cultivation. They came marching boldly into the strawberry patches, not in coveys but in pairs, walking through the back yard as if they owned it.

The killdeers wheeled and dipped in clouds over the wet fields, the skies filled with the mournful *kill-dee, kill-dee,* and the meadowlarks sang in the fields, and out of the wet places came the wild, sweet song of the woodcock. The crows and the jays raised general hell with everything, including the spring, and you could hear the rain crows' hollow *tonk* from some hidden position in a tall pine, and the solid knock of the woodpeckers, and the sweet chirrup of the little bluebirds.

This was the time of the year when the boys rushed out of school to swim naked in the creek at recess, and when it seemed impossible not to cut classes. This was the time of the bellyache from eating berries that had not completely ripened, from experimenting with stone-hard green peaches; and this also was the time of the lavish use of castor oil and calomel. It was impossible to concentrate in school, for the drowsy hum of June was just over the hill. Hence this was the time that boys were kept after school for throwing spitballs and making paper airplanes and dipping pigtails into inkpots. Summer vacation was yearned for by the teachers even more eagerly than it was craved by the students. Marks dropped terribly, and discipline teetered on the ragged edge of anarchy.

The Old Man said he reckoned the whole world went a little crazy at this time of the year, and he told me if I listened real close I could hear the piping of some old pagan god named Pan, who was half billy goat, away off in the wood. I told the Old Man that if Pan was anything like *my* billy goat I would just as lief have nothing to do with him.

"Be that as it may," the Old Man said, "that wood back there is creeping with all sorts of forest gods and spirits right now, and if we went and set quiet I ain't so sure but what we might see some. Hear 'em, anyhow."

The forest he mentioned was located back of the cow lot, and it was bounded by a big field of sedge where my pet covey of quail lived, and by a gully in which my secret interlocking caves were built, and by a big pond in which the diedappers swam and dived, and by a big soybean field that was full of doves in the fall. The forest covered about six acres, and was composed of towering pines and twisty live oaks and dogwood trees. Its floor was clean and mostly free of brush, a slippery floor of pine needles and jaunty wild flowers.

The Old Man and I spent a lot of time back there. We had to remodel some of the caves, which meant we needed fresh pine saplings for the front and some fresh beams under the heavy sod roofs; so some woodcutting was in order. It takes a lot of work to keep a cave in good shape, especially when there are half a dozen connected by long tunnels. The reason we needed so many caves was that I was then chieftain of a robber band, and in watermelon season the robbers needed plenty of sudden sanctuary.

Sometimes, when we got tired of working on the caves, the Old Man and I would sit down under a tree and lean back against the bole. He would light his pipe and tell me all sorts of wild tales about the Druids, who lived in trees, and the first Britons, who dug enormous caves called dene holes in the Kentish countryside in England, and about the bad spirits that lived in the Black Forest in Germany, and about the old pagan gods like Pan, who, I gathered, was a pretty fast fellow with the girls.

The Old Man had been near about everywhere, and I guess he had read just about everything, because anything I remember today I remember from what he told me. I always got pretty high grades in geography, because if they asked what country Kent was a county of, like New Hanover or Brunswick County in my state, I could always say "England," on account of the dene holes. I understood what a dene hole was because the Old Man and I had just dug us one.

We saw a lot of interesting things, just sitting quiet or walking carefully. One time I saw a rain crow, one of those big cuckoos, chase a dove off a nest and settle down in it herself. I went back the next day and shinnied up the tree, and sure enough, there was one great big egg laid in the clutch of smaller dove's eggs.

We saw the squirrels fighting and chasing each other through the trees, and once I saw two squirrels breeding. The rabbits hopped around softly and unafraid of us. Once a deer and a fawn walked right up to us and stared for a long time, and then the old lady sort of nodded to junior and they went off, not running, not jumping, just sort of frisking, with junior kicking up his heels.

I never did get to see Pan or any of the other strange people that live in the woods, but I swear I heard noises that I couldn't hook up to bird or frog or animal or insect, and soft rustlings that proved to be nothing at all when I went to look, my skin goose-pimpled and my neck hair lifting like a worried dog's when he hears a sound he can't quite figger.

What I did get was the feeling that there were spirits who lived in trees, and that there was something very special about an ancient wood, and that there was some peculiar magic about the late spring that has been justified by the behavior of beasts and people down through the ages. (This I learned later from books.)

There had been some talk among the grown-ups at the time about sending me off to the mountains to a boys' camp, and I was hot for it until the spring got soft and sweet and started to beckon toward the summer, and the Old Man and I made our daily pilgrimages past the cow lot and into the secret woods. But in May I would begin to weaken on this camp thing, and by June the camps had lost a customer. I knew when I had it good, because the Old Man always used to say that a smart feller knew when he was well off and was a goldarned fool to change it for something he didn't know about.

Then, too, you understand, I was too busy to go to camp. The Old Man and I had a lot of projects together, apart from the baseball and the swimming with the other boys. We had to get the boat in shape for the summer's fishing, and there was a puppy litter about due. We wanted to do some work on the duck blind, of course, and there was this billy goat to discipline—I guess you remember we failed on that one. And then there was fishing, of course, salt-water for blackfish and speckled trout and croakers, and fresh-water for bass, and by the time we got done fishing it would be September and the tides would swell, and then there would be the marsh hens jumping creakily out of the flooded marshes.

When we finished with the marsh hens, the bluefish would be along; and when we got through with the bluefish and the puppy drum, then the quail season would be on us, and before you knew it, Christmas holidays had come and gone.

We were sitting quietly in the secret forest one day, waiting to hear some word from the Old Man's friend, Pan, when he stabbed his pipe at me and said, "I suppose you're going off to camp this summer and leave me alone and unprotected with all the grown-ups, eh?"

"I reckon not," I said.

"Why not? They got all sorts of things up there in the mountains. They got counselors, and a swimming lake, and archery, and woodworking, and basket making, and lectures, and all sorts of things. You'll get to live in a tent and paddle a canoe and——"

"I been in a tent and I got a boat and I got the Atlantic Ocean and the Cape Fear River to swim in," I told him. "I got you for a counselor. I ain't interested in basket making or archery, because I got a shotgun and a boat that needs fixin'. I just ain't got time to play with children. The duck blind's a mess."

"But here it is just spring, with a whole summmer ahead of you," the Old Man was teasing me.

"The way I figger, I'm through Christmas already," I said,

"and by that time it'll be puppy-training time and we're right back in the summer again."

"I expect you may be right," the Old Man admitted. "Time just seems to fly away for a boy. That, I s'pose, is why one day you wake up suddenly and you ain't a boy any longer. Anyhow, I'm glad you ain't going. It gets awful lonesome around here with all them grown-ups."

17

Life Among the Giants

"Did you ever wonder why I spend so much time and trouble and accumulated wisdom on you?" The Old Man paused to look at his pipe as if it were a strange contraption he'd never seen before. He convinced himself that it was a pipe, the same old scarred, crook-stemmed, thick-caked pipe which smelled like an incinerator and which he had owned about as long as he'd owned Grandma. Or possibly as long as Grandma had owned him, which was more likely.

Now, honest to John, what is a feller going to say to this question? *No, sir? Yes, sir?* I didn't say anything except a sort of mutter with a rise on the end of it, like a bigmouth coming up to see but not to bite. "Yumph?"

"You're gettin' smarter already," the Old Man told me. "I liked that 'Yumph' you just did. You didn't give nothing away, and kept yourself covered at both ends. Like poker. You know, poker is like fishin', or mebbe more like waitin' out a deer stand or a turkey blind. Did I ever tell you about poker?"

"Numph."

"Hmmmm," the Old Man said. "I would judge you had kings backed, and maybe my queens ain't good enough. You're gettin' real cagey in your old age, ain't you?"

"Mmmmph." I was noncommittal-like. I had stepped in those traps before.

"Why," the Old Man asked me, "would you suppose that a man of my advanced years and general accomplishments would waste so much time trying to beat a little knowledge and a few good manners into the head of an unlicked cub? Is this personal conceit on my part, or what? I dunno. Am I trying to leave a memorial behind me? You tell me."

"I don't know, sir." I reckoned I had taken that "Yumph, umph, mmmm" business about as far as it would travel.

"I like the answer," the old gentleman declared. "Damn rare thing these days, in the age of experts, where a feller'll set down and say he don't know something. It's a smart-aleck age, full of Willies-off-the-pickle-boat, people that'll just spar for time while they're trying to figger out a way to conceal inbred ignorance. You ever notice I talk grammatic about one fourth of the time, and vulgar the other? It's because a man has to be able to talk correctly before he can allow himself the privilege of vulgar speech. You ever get curious about it?"

"Yes, sir," I said. "I wonder, because they're always at you in school not to say ain't and not to drop your g's, and not use double negatives. I find it kind of hard to follow you sometimes."

"You like crackling?" the Old Man asked. I could tell this was going to be a hard day. Crackling is the seared skin of a young pig. It is as crisp and tasty as the things they give you at cocktail parties today, and has more nourishment. But it had no point in the conversation.

"Yes, sir. I sure do. I like chitterlings, too, and scuppernong wine, and ham hock, and collards. And candy." I was getting a little mad. If the old gentleman was going to throw these things at me, I figured I'd heave a couple back.

"Only reason I asked about crackling," the Old Man said, "was that I was rereading that thing of Charles Lamb's—what d'you call it, *Dissertation on a Roast Pig,* or some such, I forget—and I got so dodlimbed hungry I couldn't stand it. They make you read that in school yet?"

"Yes, sir." I was very heavy with those "sirs." Once in a while the Old Man went big literary on me, and "sir" was the only way out. We got mixed up with some old Englishman named Chaucer once, and Chaucer and I went round and round for what seemed like years, until I "sirred" my way out of it.

"Well, all I got to say is, any man who can make you hungry after he's been dead a hundred years is a hell of a writer," the Old Man declared. "Where was I? Oh, yes. What you gonna be when you grow up?"

"Confused," I started to say, and bit it off. The Old Man liked to handle the flippancy business himself. "I don't know, sir. Maybe an artist. Maybe a writer or a sailor. Something—I don't know."

"Well, that's handy, not to know what you want to be until the time comes to be it." The Old Man liked that one. "Until the time comes to be it," he repeated, and kind of licked his whiskers like a happy cat. "I'm pretty well pleased with you today."

"Yes, sir."

"You can overdo them 'sirs,' boy," he said. "You ain't fooling nobody with that mock humility. So I will tell you why I spend all this time and conversation in my failing years, when I could just as easy be setting and rocking instead of talking. The reason is that all I got of me to pass on is you, and I know a couple or three things I like. I know quite a lot of goods and quite a lot of bads, and as long as I ain't got any money I would like to leave a few of the good things behind. You want some more of this?"

"Yes, sir."

"Well, now," he continued, "a gentleman starts down at his boots and works up to his hat. A gentleman is, first of all, polite. A gentleman never talks down to nobody, or even to anybody that says 'anybody' instead of 'nobody.' A gentleman ain't greedy. A gentleman don't holler at anybody else's dogs. A gentleman pays his score as he goes. He don't take what he can't put back, and if he borrows he borrows from banks. He never troubles his friends with his troubles."

It looked as though we had disposed of what a gentleman was apt to be made of. I didn't say anything.

"What is a sportsman?" The Old Man wasn't even asking me this. He nodded his head, as if he was giving himself a vote of confidence. "A sportsman," he said to nobody, "is a gentleman first. But a sportsman, basically, is a man who kills what he needs, whether it's a fish or a bird or an animal, or what he wants for a special reason, but he never kills anything just to kill it. And he tries to preserve the very same thing that he kills a little bit of from time to time. The books call this conservation. It's the same reason we don't shoot that tame covey of quail down to less'n ten birds."

This I could understand. We trained the puppies on those birds, and the birds always stayed put.

"I never knew a bad man who was what I'd call a sportsman," he said. "I never knew a true sportsman who wasn't a gentleman. So if you are a gentleman and a sportsman, you can't be a bad man. Is that clear?"

It wasn't, but I said it was. It seemed to save an argument.

"I ain't going to live forever," the Old Man went on. "So I would like to think that I cut a few scars on your carcass that maybe you could remember me by, like the old beaver trappers blazed trees to mark their passage. This is why I'm such a windy old bore. But up to now you ain't shot anybody or busted into a store, and you haven't even been expelled from school. If they keep exposing you to education, you might even realize some day that man becomes immortal only in what he writes on paper, or hacks into rock, or slabbers onto a canvas, or pulls out of a piano. You know," he said, "I really am getting old. I ask your tolerance and forgiveness for the lecture. I reckon I've started talking to myself. What would you like to do?"

"You wouldn't think I'm silly, would you, if I showed you something you don't know about that I been doing lately?"

"I wouldn't think that anything you ever showed me was silly if it was something you wouldn't show just anybody," the Old Man said. "Lead on, Macduff, and damned be he . . ."

Well, I have to write this kind of quiet, because I embarrass easy. The Old Man and I walked over to a great big wild cherry tree, about a thousand yards from the house, and I showed him the steps nailed neat onto the tree, plenty wide enough for handholds and footholds at the same time. The steps went up about thirty feet or so. Then in a big crotch of this tree was a house.

I had been reading *The Swiss Family Robinson*, and I had been fascinated with the tree house they built, that they called "Falconhurst," and I had built me one, as I said. There was a curious four-way spread of branches in this cherry tree, and it was pretty easy to make a house in the spread. It was a good house, although hoisting up the planks with a primitive block and tackle had been difficult.

In this house there was near about everything that I didn't want anybody to be prying at. I'd found some clay down by the creek, good potter's earth, and I had made a very sad stab at being a sculptor. There was a bust of the Old Man I thought was right fair, but it had a tendency to crumble, and I didn't know the first thing about glazing clay. Then there were some awful drawings I had made with crayons of what I thought birds and dogs and deer ought to look like, and I had stuck them around the rough board walls of my Falconhurst. I had some pelts for carpets on the floor, some stiff-dried hides of rabbits and squirrels.

In this tree house I had a bed of pine tops lashed with rawhide over bendy branches. I even had a stove, which I had contrived out of some old junk iron from the local dump, and which nobody could have cooked anything worth eating on.

In this house there were spears which I had made and pointed with tin, and a hickory bow, and a quiver of arrows. There was a bookshelf, filled mostly with things like *Robin Hood* and Ernest Thompson Seton's *Rolf in the Woods* and *Two Little Savages* and quite a lot of *Tarzan* and *Buffalo Bill* and *Treasure Island*, and even Sir Walter Scott. There were some arrowheads I'd found and the usual junk a kid will hive up when nobody's looking—sea shells and secret stuff he wants to keep away from grown-ups who'll be apt to discount it as childish. I was taking a chance on the Old Man when I showed him my stuff. Really, I shouldn't have worried.

He climbed creakily all the way up the tree, sat down in a little makeshift chair I had built onto the planking of Falconhurst, and panted a little while he fumbled some tobacco into his pipe. Then he looked around at everything and asked me, one question at a time, about how I got the things, and why I got the things, and especially if I had ever read anything about sculpture, because he recognized himself in the rough-thumbed clay fright-mask I had made of him.

He took the books down off the shelf, reverently I thought, and he rubbed his hands over the badly tanned skins, and he tested the bounce of the bed. He looked at the stove, and hefted the bow and arrows and the spears, and clucked appreciatively when he noticed that the bowstring was rawhide and not cord. Then he looked at me as though expecting me to ask him something.

"I suppose it's kind of silly," I hesitated, and he answered with something I'm never apt to forget.

"I wish I had me a house like this," the Old Man said. "It's got everything in it that a sportsman and a gentleman needs to be happy in. And now I have answered that first question I was asking you, about why I spent the time and trouble on you."

A lot of people said a lot of nice things to me since, but nobody ever beat that last remark the Old Man made before he climbed down the tree.

There is a time in the life of every Lilliputian when the gigantic grown-ups around him are very important. This is the time when the boy is not so very far away from being a grown-up himself, and the grown-ups are not so far away from being boys. What I mean to say, a certain politeness is indicated. There is a time when it is very bad to patronize a boy, just because he isn't quite a man yet.

The Old Man was a couple of hundred years older than I, the way I figured it; so we didn't have any conflict there. I mean, he was old and seasoned before I was born; so I was willing to take him like you accept the old dog that's too tired and too creaky to hunt any more, and just wants to lie in front of the fire. The Old Man was past proving anything. He had it wrapped up.

I've been lucky all the time I can remember. I was surrounded by adults who were sensitive to what small boys needed in the way of companionship. Looking all the way back as far as I can look, I can't remember anybody who ever made me feel as small as I was.

This was a mighty little town in the South, a poor little town, which had one movie—it's still called the Amuzu—and one restaurant run by a Greek named Pete, and two drugstores, and two grocery stores, and one undertaker who was also the coroner and who had an interest in one of the grocery stores. It had a couple of boarding houses and something that could have been called a hotel if you stretched a point.

I want to stretch a point for a minute and tell you a little bit about the town. My cousin Kate Stewart ran a boarding house, and she had a colored man who worked as waiter and whose name was Allen Jinny. He was named Allen Jinny because his mother's name was Jinny, and there weren't a whole lot of extra surnames to go around the colored population.

Allen Jinny had a deplorable habit. He drank. When he got drunk, he was liable as not to spill some hot soup down the neck of a customer who was spending a whole hard fifty cents on Miss Kate's cuisine, which was excellent if it was eaten instead of being worn. One night Allen Jinny was weaving through the dining room at Miss Kate's place on the water front, and he tipped a scalding tureen of soup down a gentleman's best boiled shirt front, and the gentleman raised a considerable ruckus. Miss Kate decided she'd better have a word with Allen Jinny. She took him more or less by the ear and led him aside to tell him the ancient parable about what happened to the man who killed the goose that laid the golden eggs.

Miss Kate was a lengthy talker, and she sort of overpowered Allen Jinny with analogies and things. She considered herself as the classic goose, and Allen Jinny's livelihood as the golden eggs, and she allowed as how that unless Allen Jinny sobered up and quit spilling soup on people the goose was going to quit laying those golden eggs. This appeared to interest Allen Jinny strangely. He went back to the kitchen. The cook was waiting, because you can always sense a turmoil outside a kitchen.

"What Miss Kate done say you, boy?" the cook asked.

"I dunno presackly," Allen Jinny said. "Something 'bout some silly son of a bitch want to eat a goose, but I don't know who de hell gone pick it."

That's the way the town was. If you mentioned a goose, somebody had to pick it, parable or no parable. And so my goose got picked pretty good by some grown-up men—who at that time couldn't have been more than twentyish to my teenishness.

I've already told you about Tom and Pete, the boys who pogie-fished some and made bootleg licker and drank bootleg licker and poached a lot and always wore hip boots in the woods and made like they always thought I was as old as they were. But my special grown-up friends were my Cousin Tommy and my non-Cousin Doonie and my non-Cousin Reggie and Dick, my Cousin Margie's boy friend, whom she married later. There was my Cousin Bonner, who run the shrimp boat, and my non-Cousin Willie, who was a little bit deaf in the ears.

We had quite a lot of Scandinavians around at that time, and some Portygees, but the Squareneck I remember best was my

Uncle John Ericsen, who is still alive and looks better than I, which isn't hard, come to think of it. I remember there was a time when John and another Scandihoovian were mistily trying to get aboard a boat that was swinging away from the pier, and the other 'Hoovian said, "Yoomp, Yon, yoomp!"

And John said, "Yoomp? How de hell can ay yoomp ven ay got no place to stood?"

John speaks elegant English now, of course, because this was so very long ago.

There was Will Sellers Davis, and Uncle Walker Newton, and all the St. George boys, especially Bill, who played catch on the ball club, and Donald, who was brilliant, but of whom they used to say he drank a little. And then there was my Uncle Rob. Uncle Rob was married to my Aunt May, and Uncle Rob was what we called chronically peevish. That's to say, nothing suited him, except maybe me; and me and Rob, why, we always got along good. Uncle Rob looked like a Scotch terrier, which isn't surprising, seeing as how his last name was McKeithan, and he had no truck with frivol or fancy. He was a fact man. I will tell you what I mean.

One time Aunt May trapped him into going to church. There he saw another one of my female relations who would win few prizes for prettiness. Rob took one look at her and muttered.

"That's the *ugliest* damn woman I ever saw in my life," he said, and in church, too.

"*Shhhhh*, Rob," Aunt May said. "The poor thing can't help it if she's ugly."

"No, but ding-dong and double-goddammit," Rob said in his fretful falsetto, "she *could* stay home."

There was another time I remember when my best beloved uncle came in one Christmas Eve just a little, you'll pardon the expression, fried to the eyes. He fell into the Christmas tree, toppled it over, busted the decorations, and set fire to the drapes. We used candles in those days. Uncle Rob pulled himself up out of the mess, scraped some tinsel off one ear, and brushed some powdered glass from the smashed ornaments off his coat. He glared mistrustfully around him.

"God *damn* Santa Claus," he said, and staggered off to bed, summarily dismissing Christmas for all time.

I hung around these men and they treated me like a man, and I never learned any nastiness from any of them. Doonie Watts wasn't a gift, I suppose; he was a seafaring man and a bit rough, and so was Reggie Pinner, but he and Cousin Tommy and the rest took us young'uns to raise. Right.

Doonie would fight, and Tommy would fight, when the mood come strong when the moon was right and the moonshine was wrong; but when they had to do with me and my Cousin Roy and Harold and George Watson, they were the best governesses you'll ever think to see. If we cussed, we got walloped, hard. The men didn't even cuss around us much, just an old damn or hell once in a while, and if us kids talked dirty, bam!

We went to the woods and on the waters whenever school allowed a breakout, and there was always a self-appointed chaperone to teach us caution and care with guns, neatness with camps, fire prevention, and love and respect for wildlife. They taught us such things as how to smother a grounder, moving up on it, beating it by one jump. They taught us a few knacks of aiming guns, and not shooting robins, and why a boat must be kept clean and the oars taken away and the boat dragged up on the shingle and overturned to keep the rain from rotting her innards.

I won't name any names here, but some were drunks and some were loafers and some didn't shave or wash very often, but from a boy's-eye view they were the best men I ever knew. Some are dead today and some have reformed, but I've got more sweet memories of a tender taking-to-raise from those men than you could find in all the schools and churches and contrived ways to give a kid a little dignity.

Maybe we have lost this a little bit today. In the older times the town characters showed a little special wonderful tenderness to the kids. My ma and the Old Man never had a qualm when I was off in the woods with one of the roughnecks. They knew that roughneck wouldn't come home except to die, rather swiftly, if anything happened to Bobby or Roy—or Ted or Harold or Tom or George.

And there were all sorts of things on the side. For instance, I learned about Kipling and Chaucer from one of the roughnecks who had, at one time before the bottle bruised him, graduated with honors in three years from a rather famous university. But he also told me about the *barrio chino* in Barcelona, and what it was like on the *grosse Freiheit* in Hamburg, and how to bust a bottle to use it fast if you needed a busted bottle in a brawl. He had been to two colleges—one literary, the other practical. I s'pose he was the one made me run away, eventually, to sea—but it was my Cousin Victor Price who saw that nobody bothered me when I was ordinary-seamaning around the tough ports of North Europe. He was an executive in the line I was working for.

The Old Man, in his vast wisdom, never worried about what would happen to my moral character so long as I was under the care of one of the hairy townsmen. The Old Man said once, "A boy has got to grow up to be a man some day. You can delay the process, but you can't protect the boy from manhood forever. The best and easiest way is to expose the boy to people who are already men, good and bad, drunk and sober, lazy and industrious. It is really, after all, up to the boy, when all is said and done, and there are a lot of boys who never get to be men, and a lot of men who never quit being boys."

I'm not doing a very good job of this, I realize, but the tremendous love I had for all those people when I was a kid prevents me from doing a very good job of it. You've got to realize what it means to a boy to be treated as a man grown by men already grown. You've got to realize what it is like to be gently carried along by rough giants who have so much built-in decency that they fear to bruise the stalk which is an adolescent, shooting up and subject to heavy impression, subject to hurt, as you might mishandle a gawky plant.

I reckon that 65 per cent of the men who took me to raise couldn't be admitted to a club, a church, or a tea party. I reckon that most were unread, most were profane, most broke laws, most didn't work, most drank too much, and most had dirty fingernails. And I reckon if we filled the schools with them as instructors today, and gave them jobs as cops, and set them up as tutors and baby sitters and camp counselors, we wouldn't have so much of a problem of delinquency.

In my life as a grown man I have managed to stay out of jail, pay taxes, and live a life in which the values are pretty clearly drawn. This makes me lucky, maybe, but it is also a reflection on the positive contributions of the Toms and Petes and Doonies and Johns and Bills and Reggies and Bonners and Robs and, of course, the Old Man—all of whom, in their own fashion, took me to raise.

I got mixed up sentimentally serious with the Coast Guard at a very early age, because around where I come from the Coast Guard was an industry as well as a luxury and a necessity. We lived in a little town where the Cape Fear River emptied out into the ocean, and there were Coast Guard stations on a big island called Bald Head and also on a spit of land named Fort Caswell. There was a lighthouse on Bald Head, and there was a lightship a little farther offshore, because we had some shoals called Frying Pan that were powerful treacherous.

There is something about real functional Coast Guarders that is maybe a little different from other people. They are a special breed; you could maybe call them a race. They mostly all seem to come from down around Hatteras and Ocracoke—so much so that we used to call them "down-homers." They were nearly all named Midyette, except the ones who were named Willis or Pickett or Barnett or Robinson.

These men lived with windswept loneliness and they lived

with cold wet death. They were veterans of battle with what somebody later called the cruel sea. They lived on gale-raked islands and rode patrol on the silent beaches on horses and mules always looking seaward for signals of distress. I remember well that the father of a friend of mine, named Bill Styron, was struck by lightning while riding beach patrol at Hatteras. The bolt killed him but didn't kill the mule, which tells you something about mules.

When the wind came furious and whipped up a stranger's off-shore trouble, and a ship was fast aground or heading that way, when the lighthouse couldn't prevent it and the lightship off Frying Pan hadn't successfully done its job, friends of mine like Pete Midyette went into business. They had these double-bowed whaleboats, called surfboats, that nothing or nobody could capsize, and they shoved them through the mountainous black waves, straight off the beach into the cold, wet, enormous-waved nights to see what they could do about who was in seafaring trouble. To me they were greater heroes than anybody I ever met later, because they did their jobs when others would have run away to a snug bed and a fire. Quite a lot of them got drowned in a cold Atlantic Ocean, for very little money and practically no amusement at all, because those islands were bleak.

A boy named Dallas Pickett was a friend of mine when his old man was cap'n of the Bald Head station and an older friend of mine named Bill Willis was running Caswell. Bill was a pure down-homer, stringy and weatherbeaten and wrinkled, and in addition to his other duties he had to go out and knock off a rum-runner every now and then in the little cutter they gave him to chase rumrunners with. It didn't make no difference to me that they said Bill Tyce—that was his middle name, Tyce—never took on a booze boat until all his friends were fresh out of licker. The important thing was that he would sometimes take me with him when there was a rum boat to chase, and I learned a lot about fishing while we were chasing booze.

It was the same way with my friend Dallas Pickett's papa. He would let Dallas bring me and my Cousin Roy over for week ends to Bald Head, and we would stay in the big, bare, sandy-floored, stripped-for-action Coast Guard station. We would climb the watchtowers and make the beach patrol at night with the men, and we would go out in the heaving surfboats on practice beach launchings.

The Old Man encouraged these expeditions. He was a deep-water man himself, a sea captain and a licensed river pilot, and a fisherman too. In the off season he went to sea after menhaden, or pogies, the fat-backed fertilizer fish, in a creaky old boat called the *Vanessa*—and he liked me to know about water and what its chances of killing you were. Also he said he never knew a really bad waterman, and I could learn a lot by hanging around people that used the sea as a livelihood, always remembering it as an enemy.

In any case, I was over to Fort Caswell one time when Cap'n Willis, Bill Tyce, that is, broke out the rum chaser and said he heard there was a booze boat close at hand, and would I care to go help him chase the rumrunner. You understand the government boat was a rum chaser, and the quarry a rumrunner. This seemed to me to be an invitation worthy of acceptance, because I knew that on rum chasers there were machine guns and rifles, carefully cherished in scabbards of sheepskin with the clipped wool inside, well soaked in oil to prevent rust, and I knew the runners had the same armament, and once in a while when there was a disagreement between law and order and man's natural thirst, the guns came oily-wet out of the clipped-fleece scabbards and people started to shoot at each other. At my age, I hoped there would be a little shooting at each other and that possibly I could aid in some capacity in the shooting.

Well, we overhauled the runner off Frying Pan Shoals, and a sad little beat-up craft she was too. I have to report regretfully that there wasn't no shootin'. The Cap'n signaled her to heave to, and she plain hove to. She had a few cases of illegal booze from the Bahamas and a dirty, unshaven, scared crew of three, and so the Cap'n put a prize crew aboard her, and told the prize crew to take her in for the Customs to worry about and for the Federals to worry about. I think the prize crew was a man named Midyette, which is a safe bet, because the prize crew looked pretty thirsty.

Well, sir, with the business of law and order taken care of, no shots fired, we looked around. There the old chaser was right smack on the lip of Frying Pan. There are shoals, I swear, where a man who knows how to run a boat right can scoop up a handful of sand with his left hand and then jump over the side and drown himself on the starboard side, without changing course a half degree. What I mean, Frying Pan is tricky, and you may remember that tricky shoals breed fish.

Cap'n Bill announced that he hadn't had a mess of real fresh mackerel in a whole hell of a long time, and did anybody have any trolling gear aboard? The Coast Guard said yes, because in those days the Coast Guard was better prepared than the Boy Scouts ever thought of being. Cap'n Bill went for'ard and had a word with the Helm. The Helm knew his business. We started playing tag with Frying Pan Shoals. The Helm took the chaser so close to those shoals that you'd swear we'd smash aground if there was another knot in the breeze, but gentlemen, may I say, what fishing!

The gear consisted simply of hand lines and a couple of rods with reels older than Noah's original equipment. For lures we had quills run over the shank of the hook, or feathers, or a piece of sailcloth, or anything else that would create a ripple. You could of trailed a finger over the side and if there was a hook on the fingernail, you'd have caught a fish.

Now let me see if I can tell you what it was like. You had the white-gleaming shoals shimmering underneath a shining sun at about this time of the month, and you were a boy among men—a youth among warriors—and the sun and salt and breeze were fresh in your face. The water was the cleanest blue, clear, shading to green and finally to the white of shoal water, and in that roily water were fish.

They were maybe not the biggest fish a fellow ever caught,

but there were more of them than I can believe possible today. There were vast schools of blues—fat, greasy, jut-jawed blues— weighing up to maybe three pounds, and mean-frisky from the cold sea. There were gangs of Spanish mackerel, with a few bonito into the pot for variety, and even a horse mackerel or so. And they were hungry, eager for the hook.

I wouldn't say there was much sport in the actual catching of the fish, because all you did was throw out the line, let her trail a bit, and as soon as she was clear of the screw you had a customer on the other end. Then it was up to you to get the fish back into the vessel, whether you were hand-lining him or horsing him in on reels that wouldn't go either way, in or out, unless you fought 'em. And barked fingers.

The real sport was the job the man at the wheel was doing. He was playing the boat like it was a big salmon in tough swift water, on a four-ounce rod with a no-strain line. He didn't want to kill the fish, and to not kill the fish he had to slack his engines, and he had to fight those shoals with a knowledge of wind and water. I read some, later, about bullfighters. Never did any bull- fighter play a bull like this boy played that ship against those shoals. I swear, I yanked too hard one time and the fish flopped out on the beach. And we were deep-water trolling!

We filled that Coast Guard boat full of fish—brown-gray-green spotted mackerel, lean shimmering-steel blues with all the fat under the smooth submarine shape, and blunt-nosed bonito—and in a couple of hours we were headed home. I cannot remember the name of the man at the wheel, but he never touched a screw or a keel to those deadly shoals, and the ship frisked like a colt when he took her in to the last inch, and tossed her mane as she came away.

It was a tremendous thing to be a boy among men; and sitting in that rum chaser, sunburnt, sweaty, hot skin cooling from breeze, all full of righteous indignation that any bootleggers would even attempt to try to fool *my* Coast Guard, I was a young king amongst his faithful court.

It was *my* friend that drove the boat and kept her off the

shoals. It was *my* friend who was skipper, and who had kept the Atlantic seacoast free of the Demon Rum this day, while catching bluefish and mackerel besides. We were coming in triumphant after having saved America without firing a shot. The man at the wheel had headed the chaser home, and her prow knifed a clean line through the sparkling sun-kissed spray-tossed waters.

The things you see when you are going home triumphant are marvelous. I watched a gannet working on a red bank of menhaden. I saw the porpoise sounding and rising. The little ship bucked and pranced, full of rightful triumph. I was not even about to be seasick, because I was a man out with men, doing a man's job. Of course it is easily possible to say that a boy had no place, legally, on a rum-chasing expedition, and that a government boat that was coursing a bootlegger had no business to stop and go fishing, and that maybe the runner's cargo would most probably disappear, one way or another, before the righteous arm of the law could smash the bottles.

But there was one thing more: There was a boy's-eye view of men at work, but men with time to play, and men to make a boy feel a man. There was a Charlie Snow to ask you down to his house around Matamuskeet to teach you how to fool a goose. There was a Bill Barnett, a burly, red-faced man who was exec before Bill Tyce went off the station, who never made you feel a boy so long as you were with men, and who never expected you to act like a boy so long as you were with men.

These days I read about the delinquents and what causes delinquency, and I suppose you could say that a child as young as I was had no business combining rum chasing with fishing, that maybe I shouldn't have hung around the docks with people who cussed.

I don't know. Maybe my later character was imperfectly formed. But I tell you trolling for bluefish on the very frowning face of Frying Pan Shoals, after you've just knocked off a rum-runner, is a type of sport you aren't going to get out of comic books and television. And until a man has put his shoulder behind the sharp stern on a surfboat, to shove her in the black night through the shore-crashing seas, off the cold clean beach of Bald Head, with the gulls crying and a dying ship offshore—well. There are all sorts of ways to get to be a man, the Old Man used to say—and none of 'em easy.

The Old Man was fairly grumpy through the summer months, because the beaches were crowded with summer people and the bluefish knew it and stayed offshore. All our pet sloughs were full of swimmers, splashing and making noises, and if you tried surf-casting the inlets at night you had to pick your way through the neckers.

"Labor Day," the Old Man said, "is the best holiday of the year, because after it's over all the city people go home and leave the water to the professionals. A professional"—the Old Man grinned—"is the kind of damn fool who actually fishes when he goes fishin'. He don't turn it into a whisky party or an excuse to play poker, not that I'm low-ratin' either sport if taken in the correct perspective."

Some of the Old Man's feeling rubbed off on me. I could hardly wait for that first Tuesday in September, because the beach would be scrubbed clean of people by noon, the summer visitors having taken their hang-overs back to town for another year. Then and only then did the hardshells emerge—the year-rounders who were plank owners in the boardwalks. They were a grimy, grizzled, hard-bitten lot, including the few women who were admitted into the high society of surf casters. Then we owned the beach.

A beach suddenly flushed clean of strangers is a wonderfully lonesome place. All the boarding houses and summer cottages and hotels board up their windows against the first northers. The hot-dog stands close. The dance hall shuts up tight. The trolley service goes on winter schedule, and only the Greek keeps his general store open part time—I say part time, because most of the time the Greek is whipping the sloughs for the bluefish and sea trout and channel bass that come in close to feed off the minnows and sand fleas.

The weather knows it when the tourists leave. It invariably stayed fine for the long, noisy week end, but by Wednesday we generally had a gorgeous three-day norther started, and that norther was always the most exciting thing about the summer. An Atlantic beach in a norther is wild and exhilarating. The sky turns gray, and the wind drives the rain in angry gusts. The surf booms, and towering sheets of spume drive skyward as the waves smash onto the sands. Suddenly the tin stove earns its pay, and the driftwood in the fireplace burns blue and green. A sweat shirt and flannel pants feel wonderful, and there is a snugness to the little gray-weathered shingle cottage that is missing during the summer squalls.

For three days the wind screams and the water boils white, and then the best time of the year begins. The sun comes once again, warm and golden, and the skies are washed bright, but now the breeze is crisp and the air is full of wine. The water is not too cold to fish barefooted, but if you stumble and wet yourself all over, the goose-pimples form when the wind hits you. Give the waters a day to clear from the roily muddiness of the storm, and the fish swarm in to feed in the sloughs. The biggest fish haven't shown yet, and won't until late October, but the blues run to three pounds, and the puppy drum go up to fifteen, and there are always plenty of sea trout and Virginia mullet. All up and down the beach, toward the inlets, tiny, happy-lonely figures wade out and cast, walk backward and reel in as the rod curves and a bright sliver of fish flops through the shallows and onto the silvered sands.

That was a part of our September song. Another part was in the Sound, where the north wind raises the tides above the marsh grasses, and the mounting moon keeps the water high, until just the tips of the grasses show above the surface. That was when the Old Man's mouth cracked in a big grin and he took the shotguns from their cases and sent me under the house for the push pole and the paddles.

"Marsh-hen time," the Old Man said, and we dragged the old flat-bottomed skiff off the shingle, where she had been up-turned to keep her innards from rotting in the rain. We'd kick her across the channel with the little one-lung motor, and when we hit the grass we'd tilt the kicker and the Old Man would take the pole or—if the water was exceptionally high—paddle the skiff along like she was a canoe.

I don't suppose today that there is a great deal of sport in shooting the big rails we called marsh hens, but you'd be sur-prised how many you can miss. As the boat crept stealthily over the grasses, the big hens would spring creakily into flight, flop-ping low over the water and seeming slower than they actually were. The natural inclination was to shoot behind them, be-cause of the water-skimming lowness of their flights.

"Ain't but one man at a time supposed to shoot out of a boat," the Old Man said. "Otherwise you will be out with some blame fool some day and he will get excited and blow the back of your neck off. There's plenty of marsh hens to go round, and you can only eat so many."

So the Old Man would push or paddle and I would sit on the bow thwart. The hens would rise from under the boat with a cackle, and more often than not you'd have a chance to try for a stylish double. Then, after half a dozen birds were in the boat, I'd move aft and take over the propulsion, and the Old Man would creep gingerly forward and man the bow gun.

Poling after the hens was hard work; your boat was always getting stuck onto a mudbank, and there were still plenty of mosquitoes and other varmints clinging to the higher grasses. The sun smote down plenty hot, and your back ached like a tooth after hours of driving that skiff over what amounted to solid ground. But a boat full of the great, tawny rails, with their doe eyes and long legs and long, curved, mud-probing bills, made the blistered hands and sunburnt neck worth while.

There is no more fascinating place than a marsh anyhow. A marsh literally crackles and pops with life. Off yonder in a wide stretch of water, a thin ripply wake tells you a mink is swimming. An old blue heron looks grumpily at you and waits until the last minute before he flops away in swaybacked, ungainly flight. Over there a bittern booms like a tomtom, and the white herons sit silent and secure, because they know you won't shoot them.

Red-winged blackbirds love the marsh, and they swing like bobolinks from the barest ends of the swaying grass, hurling their joyful song into the air. The sky above the marsh is always full of crows, cawing angrily as they scavenge.

Along the edge of the mainland there was an enormous lightning-riven tree, where my private eagle always sat. The eagle, several times a year, was good for a fine show of aerobatics. There was a pair of fish hawks—ospreys—that haunted the area, and it used to delight me to watch them fish. You would see the male plummet down like dropped shot, smack the water with his outstretched talons, and struggle, wings flailing furiously, with a big bluefish nailed through the spine. As the hawk labored for altitude, Old Baldy would take off from his tree top and head for the stratosphere. When the hawk got enough height to level off and head for his nest with the flopping fish, the eagle, high above him, would fold his wings and come screaming down in a power dive. The hawk would make a few futile evasive motions, and then drop the fish. Usually the eagle, still screaming down, would flash by the hawk and sink his grapples in the falling fish before it hit the water. Then he would come out of his dive and leisurely flap back to his lightning-ruined perch. Then the hawk would go fishing again, and this time he would be allowed to keep his catch.

There were always 'gator holes to see, and occasionally you would see an old 'gator sunning himself on a greasy mudbank. The edges of the marsh were usually good for a coon or two, and the high hummocks close to shore were likely to yield you a brace of dark swamp rabbits. We 'most always took a couple of light rods and the cast net along, and when the water slacked

off and began to drop so you couldn't shove the skiff over the
grass, we'd take the net and seine a few shrimp and drop the
hook by one of the potholes we knew by heart. These deep
holes would give us a mess of croakers, blackfish, big sand
perch, and now and again a weakfish.

Or, again, when we spotted a big school of fairish mullets, the
Old Man swirled the cast net like a bullfighter's cape, hauled hard
on the draw cord, and dumped a half-bushel of leaping mullet
on the deck of the skiff. The big ones we kept for the skillet;
the little ones made wonderful baits for surf casting.

Around the edges of the sand bars there were always clams in
the mud—big purplish clams that came shining from the ooze.
They tasted wonderful in the raw, the hinges smashed with the
back of a fish knife, and eaten there on the spot. We always kept
oyster tongs in the boat, and added a bushel or so of the big,
briny ones to the mixed bag in the bottom. We'd roast these
later, covering them with seaweed, and when you dipped them
in melted butter there may have been better eating, but I
doubt it.

The trip was never complete until, on the back leg, we
chuffed under the bridge that spanned the channel and tied
up in the swirling dark water next a barnacle-crusted piling.
Here the huge, black, yellow-speckled stone crabs lived. Here
the sheepshead swam close to the old pilings, and if you knew
your business you could hook them in their silly little mouths
that spat out a shrimp unless you fixed the hook just right.

By the time we got back home and pulled the old scow up
on the shingle, it would take about three trips to the house to
completely unload her. By the time the fish got cleaned and
the marsh hens skinned and put in salt water to soak some of
the fish out, it was dang near dark and time to get out the surf
rods and fish the twilight into moonrise. It would be getting
cold on the beach around dark, and I usually fixed us up a
driftwood fire and set the oysters to roasting while we cast into
the surf.

By eight o'clock the Old Man and I had just about enough

for one day. That's when you ran a stringer through the fish, carried the steaming oysters up to the house, pulled off your wet pants, and shoved the coffeepot onto the stove. The broiled marsh hens followed the oysters, and once in a while we barbecued a fish or just settled for a cold crab salad.

A long time after all this happened I heard Walter Huston sing "September Song," and the old man seemed pretty high on one of my favorite months. But he was thinking about love, mostly, and love ain't but about one-fifth of what September's really like. My September song is still based mainly on the fact that all the tourists went home and left the beaches and the marshes to the Old Man, the eagle, and me.

18

November Was Always the Best

A lot of people figure November to be a middling sad kind of month, with the trees showing naked against the leaden skies late in the afternoon, and the grass all crisp and brown from frost, and the threat of winter turning your ears red in the morning, and the evening cold making your nose run. The year has only one more month to live, and that is sad too, to some people.

But November was the month I aimed my whole year at, for the very simple reason that the bird season opened round about Thanksgiving, and if you lived in my neck of the woods, "birds" didn't mean canaries or parrots or bluejays. Birds meant quail. The Old Man was with me all the way on that one, but he liked to fuzz it up with a little philosophy. Like most pipe smokers, he needed some extras to hang on it to make it dignified.

We were talking about the seasons one time, and the Old Man said that if he had to he could do without summer and all of spring except maybe May, and he would be just as happy to settle for October through January, and give the rest away. He said he would pick November as the best one, because it wasn't too hot, and wasn't too cold, and you could do practically anything in it better than any other time of the year, except maybe get sunburnt or fall in love.

"Although," he said, "there ain't nothing wrong with November, or any other month, for falling in love if the moon's right. But mainly the reason I like November best is that it reminds me of me."

He stopped and struck another kitchen match to his pipe.

"Look at me," he went on. "Here you see a monument to use. I'm too old to fall in love, but I ain't old enough to die. I'm too old to run, but I can outwalk you because I know how to pace myself. I know when to work and when to rest. I know what to eat and what sits heavy on my stomach. I know there ain't any point in trying to drink all the licker in the world, because they'll keep on making it. I know I'll never be rich, but I'll never be stone-poor, neither, and there ain't much I can buy with money that I ain't already got.

"A man don't start to learn until he's about forty; and when he hits fifty, he's learned all he's going to learn. After that he can sort of lay back and enjoy what he's learned, and maybe pass a little bit of it on. His appetites have thinned down, and he's done most of his suffering, and yet he's still got plenty of time to pleasure himself before he peters out entirely. That's why I like November. November is a man past fifty who reckons he'll live to be seventy or so, which is old enough for anybody —which means he'll make it through November and December, with a better-than-average chance of seeing New Year's. Do you see what I'm driving at?"

I said, "Yessir," because I didn't want him to explain it all over again, and because I was worrying about a young pointer puppy who was going to have his first chance at being a working dog, and I was worrying over whether those late rains hadn't drowned off the whole second clutch of quail, and I was worrying over my shooting eye, which had fallen off alarmingly the final two weeks of the last season.

"What's your idea of November?" he asked, his eyes half-closed.

I wanted to tell him that it was mostly the opening of the bird season, and the Thanksgiving holidays, the persimmons wrinkled and ripe on the trees, when the weather was real nice, and it was hog-killing time in the country, and the punkins looked yellow and jolly in the fields, and the sun set good and red, and a lot of other things; but I couldn't manage to squeeze it all out because I had no way with words.

"The bird season," I said.

The Old Man looked at me and sighed. "I reckon I ain't ever going to make no philosopher out of you. Let's us go look at the guns and figger out where we'll best go tomorrow, when she opens."

The day and night before the opening of bird season lasts longer than anything, including the week before Christmas holidays. Awful, horrible thoughts keep you awake, such as will it be raining, or what if the dogs get hot noses or the quail have all moved? And then the next morning dawns clear and bright with just the right breeze, and it is another ten years until afternoon. I used to beg and coax to start in the morning, but the Old Man was stone-set against it.

"There ain't no point to hunting in the morning. Not quail," he said. "They don't feed out until nine or ten o'clock, and later if it's cold, and maybe not at all if it's too hot or raining. And if they come out at all, they don't go far away from the branches, and they head back before you can get the dogs calmed down. You'll find you'll kill all of your quail in two hours—between three and five o'clock—with very few exceptions. All-day hunting just tires you and the dogs, and if you do get lucky and find birds in the morning you've got your limit and there ain't nothing to do in the afternoon. No, morning is the time for deer and ducks and turkeys, but the bobwhite's a late-sleeping bird."

So we would mess around all morning, and then have us a light lunch about noon. By two o'clock we'd be where we had headed, with the dogs shivering and nipping from excitement and slobbering at the mouth, and me wishing I could. We had a lot of places where we hunted, but we usually started her off at a place called Spring Hill, which we had a lucky feeling for, after trying for three or four coveys closer in, just to let the dogs wet down all the bushes and get the damfoolishness out of their systems.

It is difficult, very hard, to try to explain what a boy feels when he sees the dogs sweeping the browned peafields, or skirting the edges of the gallberry bays, or crisscrossing the fields of yellow withered corn shocks, running like race horses with their heads high and their tails whipping. And then that moment, after nearly a year, of the first dog striking the first scent, and the excitement communicating to the other dogs, and all hands crowding in on the act—the trailers trailing, the winders sniffing high, but slow now, and the final eggshell-creeping, the tails going feverishly and the bellies low to the ground, presaging a point.

Then the sudden freeze, then the slight uncertainty, then a minor change of course, and then the swift, dead-sure cock of head which says plainly the bird is here, boss, right under my nose, and now it's all up to you. The backstanders edge closer, especially the puppy, and the Old Man says sharply, "Whoa!" You walk past the backstanders and then up to the pointer, who is still stamped out of iron, like an animal on a lawn. And you walk past him and kick, but nothing happens.

At this moment a blood-pressure estimate would bust the machine that takes it. Your heart is so loud it sounds like a pile driver. There is something in your throat about the size of a football, and your lips are dry from the temperature you're running, which is maybe just under 110 degrees Fahrenheit.

You are looking straight ahead of the dog—never down at the ground—and you are carrying your shotgun slanted across your chest, the stock slightly cocked under your elbow. Nothing happens. The dog changes the position of his head and creeps forward another six yards, and you come up behind him when he freezes again. This time he's looking right down at his forefeet, and when you walk past him he jumps and the world blows up.

The world explodes, and a billion bits of it fly out in front of you, tiny brown bits with the thunder of Jove in each wing. They go in all directions—right, left, behind you, over your head, sometimes straight at you, sometimes straight up before they level. Then a miracle happens.

Out of these billion bits you choose one bit and fire, and if the bit explodes in a cloud of feathers you choose another bit and fire again, and if this bit also explodes you break your gun swiftly and load, figuring maybe there's a lay bird and you can turn to the Old Man with a grin, and when he says, "How many?" you can answer, "Three." More likely you'll answer, "One" or "None."

But the tension is over now, and you find you have broken out into a heavy sweat. If there's a crick nearby, you go and plunge your face in it, or at least you take a long drink from the water bottle. The dogs fetch, and there in your hand is the first bird of the year—the neat, speckled, cockaded little brown fellow with a white chin strap if he's a cock, a yellow necklace if she's hen. He weighs less than half a pound, but has just induced nervous prostration in a man, a boy, and two dogs.

This is when you first sniff the wonderful smell of gunpowder in an autumn wood, and notice that all save the evergreens have crumpled into red and golden and crinkly brown leaves, that the broom grass has gone sere and dusty yellow, and that the sparkleberries are ready to eat, the chinquapins ready to pick. The persimmon tree that always sits lonely at the edge of the cornfield is bare except for the wrinkled yellow balls that the possums love, soft and liver-brown-splotched now, and free of the alum that ties your tongue in knots and turns your mouth inside out.

The dogs are roving out ahead, and the Old Man says, "Well, we didn't do so bad for beginners. Anybody here notice where the singles went?"

"I thought about six went over there by that patch of scrub oak, just at the end of the broom," I say.

"Le's go have us a good look," the Old Man suggests. "The dogs seem to think you may be right. Old Frank has either found a friend or turned into a stump."

At the edge of the broom, with the scattered scrub oaks making a screen before the swamp, is old Frank, nailed to something. And over there, like a lemon-spotted statue, is Sandy, nailed to something else.

"You take this 'un, I'll take that 'un," the Old Man says. "We'll walk up together."

Two birds get up under my dog's nose, and I miss both clean, *blim-blam!* I hear the Old Man shoot once, and then the rest of the group explodes in my face, and me with the gun broke and both barrels empty. I load and another bird, a sneaker, gets up behind me, and I whirl and watch him drop off the end of my gun barrel.

"That's enough," the Old Man says. "We got three apiece. Le's go find another covey. There used to be one hell of a big one over the top of that rise that we never had no luck with last year. I was beginning to think they was bewitched when the season ended. Unless the cats and the foxes been at 'em, we could take the rest of the limit out of that 'un and not even make a dent in 'em."

The Old Man lights his pipe and I break an apple out of my pocket. I think I never really appreciated an apple until I ate it in the November woods, after the first covey of the first day of the year. We follow the dogs over the hill; and when we top the brow, there is the white dog stiff, the black dog backing, and the puppy sort of sitting back on his haunches, wondering what to do next.

This didn't happen every day, or even every year, but once in a while it happened like that, and I mean to say that the walk up to where the dogs were painted against the side of a hill was the longest, happiest journey I ever took in my life.

19

*You Separate the Men
from the Boys*

I don't know why they didn't take February right out of the calendar, instead of monkeying around with it and making leap years out of it, because it is the worst-weathered of all the months, being halfway between winter and spring, with all the bad habits of both. I mean cold and rain and a little snow and a lot of wind and just natural nasty.

The trouble with February is that January's gone and March is coming next, and March is the most useless month of all, since there is nothing you can do in March except sniffle and wish the wind would quit blowing. All the hunting's over and generally it's too early to fish. There's still a long way to go until school's out, and "There ain't any wonder," the Old Man said, "that they told Caesar to beware the Ides of March." I didn't ask the Old Man what an Ide was. I was afraid he'd tell me.

But we aren't talking about March. The subject is February, and there's one thing you can do in February better than any other time of the year. That is shoot quail. For a long time I didn't believe it, but the Old Man always insisted that February was the best quail month of all.

I remember one day it was drizzling that slow, cold, nasty, steady sizzle-sozzle that is so cold it burns like fire and turns your ears into ice blocks and makes your nose run steady. The sky was a dark putty, and you could see the icicles hanging on the window frames and on the roof of the porch. The Old Man was sitting in front of a fire that was drawing so strong that she whistled as the flames sucked up the chimney, and occasionally he would cut loose and spit in the fire. It sounded like a black-smith tempering a horseshoe. *Hisssss!*

The Old Man stuck out his foot and nudged a log that had al-most burned through. It dropped in a shower of red coal to the bottom of the hearth and shot fresh slashes of flame up through the topmost chunks. The Old Man looked at me.

"There is always one way to separate the men from the boys," he said. "That is to watch and see if a feller'll do a thing the hard way, when all the other fellers are sitting around grumbling and quarreling that it can't be done." He cut loose another amber stream at the fire and looked at me with his head cocked side-wise, like a smart old dog. "Most people quit doing things as soon as the wire edge has worn off and it ain't fashionable or comfor-table any more. That makes it the beauty part for a few individ-ualists. Soon as the clerks run to cover, the big people got the field to themselves."

I didn't say anything. I knew the old buzzard pretty well by now. He was as tricky as a pet coon. All I had to do was make one peep, and he'd have me hooked. It'd be something he wanted me to do that he didn't want to do himself. Such as going to the store in the rain for some new eating tobacco, or going out for more wood, or having to report on Shakespeare, or something.

"You take quail," the Old Man went on. "When the season

opens around Thanksgiving, every damfool and his brother is out in the woods, blam-blamming around and trampling all over each other. The birds are wild, and the dogs are nervous, and they crowd the birds and run over coveys they ought to sneak up on. The ground is dry, and the birds run instead of holding. There practically ain't no such thing as good single-bird shooting, because the bobwhites take off and land as a covey, instead of scattering.

"Then along comes Christmas and New Year's, and the part-time quail hunter is tired of bird shooting, and it's too cold and too rainy, and he has to clean his guns ever' time he comes in to keep the rust off; so he ties up the dogs and forgets hunting until next year. This leaves the woods free of the city slickers and the ribbon clerks and the fashionable shooters. By this time the birds are steadied down and the dogs have had a lot of practice, and they've steadied down too. The young birds have been shot over and have grown their heavy feathers, and the young dogs have figured out that if they find birds the man will shoot some and they will bring them to the man, and that everybody—the dogs, the man, and the birds—is in business together. It ain't a game any more, like running rabbits. It's men's work."

I gave up. He had me nailed. "I'll go get my gun," I said. "You can drive me out and sit by the stove in Cox's Store while I catch pneumonia. That is, if the dogs will go out in this weather."

"They'll go out," the Old Man told me. "The dogs are professionals. They ain't part-time sports like some people I know. Go get 'em, and you better wear those oilskin pants and the oilskin jacket. The woods'll be sopping."

Man, I reckon I'm never going to forget that particular day. I sure was glad I wasn't a fish, because those woods were wetter than a well, with the little droplets clinging onto the low bush, the gallberries, and the broom grass, and the trees dripping steady. There wasn't a steady rain. It just sort of seeped down, half drizzle and half fog. My hands on the gun barrels were so cold that my fingers practically stuck to the steel. Rain collected on the gun sight and ran down the little streamway between the barrels. The dogs looked as miserable as any wet dog always looks, sort of like a land-borne otter.

Rain is miserable anywhere, but I expect there's nothing quite so cheerless as a wet wood in February. The sawdust piles have been soaked stiff and hard and dark brown. The green of the trees all turns black in the wet, so that you don't get any color contrasts, and the plowed ground is a dirty, ugly gray. The few shocks of corn that still stand are spotted and shriveled, and the sad little heads of cotton hanging onto the dead stalks look like orphans lost in a big city. But the good Lord put feathers and fur on birds and animals to keep them dry and warm, and life goes right on. Except that the Old Man is right, as he nearly always is. Wet woods make birds a heap easier to find, because the birds don't move around very much, and you can spot exactly where they're apt to be. And a dog's nose works dandy in the wet, just as a car runs better on a rainy night, when you get richer combustion.

I hadn't been out of the Liz for five minutes when Sandy, the covey dog, disappeared into a little copse of pine saplings halfway between a peafield and a broom-grassed stretch that led to a big swamp. Old Frank, the single-bird expert, went to have a look and then came back to give me the word. He jerked his head in the direction of the pine trees, impatient as a traffic cop who wants a car to move on, and then he dived into the bush with his tail assembly shaking like a hula dancer.

Maybe I have mentioned that I don't shoot very well except when I'm by myself or with the Old Man, because I'm not self-conscious in front of him and don't have to worry about shooting too fast or competing for birds. But when I'm by myself it seems as if it's almost impossible to shoot bad, because you shoot in any direction—backward, sideways, or whatever—without worrying about blowing somebody's head off.

I knew what old Sandy would be doing when I stepped into the dark, dripping grove. He would have suggested to the birds that they move to the outer edge of the pine thicket, so that they would have a nice clear field of soggy broom grass to fly over on their way to the swamp. I was pretty well trained by now. The dogs had been working on me for a couple of years, and the Old Man said he was surprised, that sometimes I showed as much bird sense as a half-trained puppy, and there was hope that I might grow up to where the dogs needn't be ashamed of me.

Sandy had herded the covey to the edge of the thicket, sure enough, and old Frank had come up on his right flank, inside the thicket, and was protecting the right wing. All I had to do was show a little common intelligence and walk along the left wing, outside the thicket, and when I came abreast of Sandy's nose Frank would run in from the right and Sandy would charge straight ahead and the birds would flush, leaving both me and the birds in the open. Then all I had to do was shoot some.

It was an enormous great covey—about twenty or twenty-five birds in it. Either it was two shot-over coveys that had got together, or one that had been missed entirely; I reckoned it was the latter. When Frank roared in from the right and old Sandy broke point and jumped into the birds, they got up in a cloud and fanned perfectly past me, giving me the best shot there is—a three-quarter straightaway where you lead just a little and let the shot string out behind your chosen bird.

This was jackpot day. Lots of times I had killed two birds with one shot, which is always an accident. You pick one out and aim at him, and the shot string knocks off another. I held on one of the front-flying cocks and pulled, and the whole doggone sky fell down. I stood there with my mouth open, just watching the rest of the birds sideslip into the edge of the swamp, and didn't bother to shoot the left barrel.

The dogs started to fetch—even Sandy, who doesn't care much about it as a steady job, because he reckons any damfool dog can pick up a dead bird and fill his mouth full of loose feathers. But they were interested in this job, because by the time they finished collecting the enemy I had six birds in my coat with one shot. The answer, of course, was very simple. Just as I pulled on the cock bird some of his relatives executed a cavalry maneuver and did a flank on him, and I simply fired right down the line, raking the face of the flank.

Sandy brought the last bird and spat him out on the ground and looked over at old Frank and sort of winked. *Lookit the kid,* Sandy was saying. *By the time he gets home, he'll think he did it on purpose. This time next year it'll be twelve birds when he tells it.* Frank laughed and nodded agreement.

We hunted through the sopping woods, and everywhere a covey of birds was supposed to be, a covey of birds was. I couldn't miss anything that day. I had to use two barrels on one single, was all, and I got that extra barrel back again a little later. It was just one of those days when all the birds got up right, pasted flat within an inch of the dog's nose before they rose. The singles clung to the ground like limpets, and you literally had to kick them up. Birds fly slower when they're water-logged, and it was pretty near murder.

The extra barrel I got back, to make the score perfect for the day, was a present from Frank. I shot into the last covey and had fourteen birds in the coat with a double on the rise. Frank fetched both birds and then disappeared into the big, spooky black swamp into which the rest of the covey had flown.

A year ago I would have thought he was acting like an idiot, but, as I said, the dogs had trained me pretty good, and Frank, of all dogs, was no covey chaser. I reckoned that I had hit another bird and wounded him without knowing it, and that Frank had seen a leg drop, or something. I sat down on a stump and let the rain punish my face, and old Sandy sat down by me and shrugged his shoulders as an adult will when he cannot control a child. *If that damfool dog wants to go drown himself in that swamp on a wild-goose chase,* Sandy said with his shrug, *let him. Not for me, bud. There are too many birds around.*

Frank was gone for nearly half an hour. When he came back, he was wetter than a drowned rat, but he had a live bird in his mouth. He had evidently chased the runner for half a mile. I cracked the fugitive's neck and shoved him in my coat and went back to the store to collect the Old Man. He laughed out loud when we came into the bright warmth of Mr. Cox's potbellied stove. We must have been a sight—wet dogs, wet boy, wet coat full of bedraggled birds.

The Old Man is real clever. "How many shells?" he asked.

"Nine."

"How many birds?"

"Fifteen," I said, with pardonable pride.

"Don't tell me how it happened right now," the Old Man said. "I want to get you out of those wet clothes, and I reckon I'll need a little spot of nerve medicine to make me strong enough to listen to the bragging. But tell me one thing: was I right about February bird shooting?"

"Yessir," I said. "But then you ain't generally very wrong about anything in the woods."

"That," the Old Man declared, as we walked out into the rain and climbed into the Liz, "is a very sage observation from one so young, and I am highly flattered. If it'll make you feel any better, I made all my mistakes when I was young, which is the difference today between an old man and a boy. Youth is for making mistakes, and old age is for impressing the young with your knowledge. My Lord, it's an awful day, isn't it?"

"It's a beautiful day," I said.

20

March Is for Remembering

"March," the Old Man said, "is a fine month for remembering. I suppose that's because there is really nothing else you can do in it. Don't ever let anybody tell you that getting old happens in the autumn of your life. It happens in March."

The Old Man and I were sitting, just sitting, on a day you wouldn't want to give away to your worst enemy. The wind was blowing fit to split your teeth, so that your skin felt as if it was currycombed every time you walked out of doors. A few flowers had poked their heads up, and then a new frost nobody'd counted on arrived and the flowers ducked their heads right back again. It was just a touch too early for the geese to be flying north. Everything was finished—the quail season was over, and the fishing hadn't started, and in those days there wasn't any television.

I got up and started to pace, like a nervous cat when it's raining outside. The Old Man watched me walk a bit and then he sort of giggled under his mustache. He liked it right where he was. He didn't want to walk; he wasn't headed anywhere.

"Offhand," he said, "I would surmise there ain't nothing wrong with you that calomel can't cure. But if you'll settle down a minute, I'll read you a short sermon. It's this: Nobody ever got any younger, because if they had I would of heard of it, and maybe bought some. So what a man has got to do is take a little time off as he grows older, and devote the waste space to remembering the things he did that he maybe won't never do again. That's how you get your muscles back. It's also a fine preventative against the nervous indigestion. And when you get tired of thinking about all you've done, you can always use the time thinking about what you'd like to do in the future. You done anything lately you admired?"

I said, "Yessir, several things."

"Well, boy," the Old Man suggested, "suppose you sort of rehash 'em in your head and then tell me what it was like to do 'em. Just for instance," he said, "I bet you that you won't remember much of the little stuff. Suppose you start with those four geese you shot that day you came home full of the brags."

There had never been a day like the day I shot the four geese and came home full of the brags. I had had an accidental day with the fifteen quail on nine shots, but accidents don't count. Everybody touches perfection once; I touched it that day and knew I had it in my hand. But I hadn't tried to appraise it. I just knew I had it.

It happened like this: I was down in the east end of the state with some friends, down around Hatteras, and it was a fine big year for the old Canada honkers. By "fine" I mean nobody was shooting very many, because they would sit out there on the wide water until the shooting time was finished, and then they'd fly into the cornfields to feed. They must have been operating by stop watch, because you could hear 'em holler when the legal shooting was done, and then they'd come in to feed as tame as chickens.

Not having much else to do, I kept betting that some day they were going to get their time-check signals fouled, and some of those geese would flock in off the big water a bit early, and I would be there when they came. So I made me a nest in a ditch in the cornfield and waited 'em out with two shotguns, both 12's and both doubles. I didn't want to be undergunned when they did decide to arrive an hour early. I had both guns loaded with No. 1 bucks. In my youthful enthusiasm I reckoned that if No. 1's were big enough for a deer they were big enough for a goose, if you could hit a goose with 'em.

Every day I went and sat in my little hidey-hole in the corn shucks. Every day the geese came in just after the curfew. Every day I got up and went off with the two guns. The reason I didn't cheat was fairly simple. the Old Man said that if I ever had any trouble with the game wardens he was going to be on the side of the game wardens, and I could stay in jail and rot for all he cared. He said game laws were made on purpose, so you'd have some game to shoot next year.

There was that day I changed loads and shot a crow at a great distance because there weren't going to be any geese and I was bored. I shot him with an old thirty-incher double, full-choked, and he dropped like a stone at about sixty yards. There was another day I shot some doves, because the geese were still in a high V, talking, but not seriously, about dinner. But finally I learned the value of patience, and just sat there without shooting. I reckoned the geese would come some day, and they would be more apt to come if I didn't loose off at crows and doves.

It was late in the fall and the corn shucks were stained brown by frost, the crisp yellow leaves striped like streaks of nicotine. There were still a lot of yellow nubbin ears on the crazy-bending stalks, with the dried-out dark brown whiskers at the top of the ears and the husks split to show the seed inside. It was lone some, like it can get to be lonesome in a cornfield, because there is nothing I know of as shambly and dilapidated as an old cornfield. But there was still food a-plenty, and the honkers knew it. They wouldn't leave it until they finished it. And they hadn't even begun to finish it.

A late-autumn day is a wonderful thing, all by itself, because in hog-killing time the sun is bloody red from the wood smoke of a fire that's always going on somewhere. The ground gets gray and cold and hard in the late afternoon, and you find that your fingers stiffen from about three-thirty until you go home to the fire. All the lonesome sounds start earlier in the late fall: the scattered quail trying to call each other back into a covey; a cow lowing sad and hopeless away over yonder; even a crow's caw sounding wistful instead of ornery.

And then you have the goose sound. It isn't a gabble. It isn't really a honk. It just sounds like a goose, and it will never sound like anything else as the old gander lifts his gaggle off the lake or off the Sound and issues the correct instructions about where his herd is headed. A goose in the air is music. It is sad music when you know the goose is not apt to light, and beautiful music when he makes that big landing circle and stops his wings, holding them slanted in the cold, clean air, losing altitude and gliding down in a decreasing flight pattern until he drops his legs and bumps into a rocky landing.

The thing about a goose is he's a keen looker. He'll drop that snaky neck and shove his head down and check the terrain before he does anything at all about it. That is when you don't move an eyeball, not when a goose is looking. Yet he is stupid in one way. When I got a lot older, I shot blue geese in Louisiana, and they would even come in to a bad call, if they were young enough and had lost mama. They would also come in to a sheet of newspaper stuck on a stick or a dead cousin propped up on the ground.

But this one day I had in mind the geese left the water early. I held still in my cramped little hide-out in the ditch and looked at the three landing circles without getting nervous and without shooting too soon. I didn't move the barest part of a muscle, and when the old fifteen-pounder decided it was safe to land he said a word to the flock and they dropped in low.

I shot two coming. I dropped one gun and picked up the other and shot two going.

Possibly I never saw anything in my life like four geese, all seemingly dropping at once. They fell like shot-down aircraft and hit the deck with a thump like a bomb. Only one was wounded, the last one, and I shoved a fresh load into the gun I was holding and held the bead on his head, and he quit leaving the premises. The indignation in the sky was considerable. When the old gander came plummeting down and the other three fell out of the flock, there was a flat accusation of betrayal, and the survivors pushed on south, complaining bitterly as they flew.

I couldn't begin to describe the emotions. When you've got four dead Canada geese on the ground at once, you don't know which one to pick up first. I ran from one to the other like a nervous old lady, and then I decided I would just pick up the geese as I found them, starting with the first two that I shot coming, and winding up with the last one that I had to give the finisher to.

To me, a coat with ten quail in it is still a big event. But four Canada geese, four old ringnecks, is a feast, is a fortune, is a truckload of trophy. I cannot say how a small boy carried two big 12-bore shotguns and four mature honkers, but I managed. I think maybe I could have flown the load home with one hand.

To pluck a goose takes time, especially if you want the dry down to stuff a pillow with. To pluck four takes a lot of time, but somehow it was time I didn't mind spending. The old boss gander was tougher than whitleather, but I ate him happily. The others tasted not much better.

The guns, I thought, had a new dignity, because I had never met anybody who had killed four Canada geese in one salvo. I felt like a man who would never again shoot less than four Canada geese.

This is what I tried to tell the Old Man. "It was as if I had shot four elephants," I said. "I never had such a big day in all my life, with the exception of the one when we got the singles scattered that time and——"

The Old Man held up his hand, pushing it gently toward me. "No," he interrupted. "Don't remember any more today, or people will say you're a bore. You had enough remembering with the geese. You got to save some remembering for the next rainy day in March. But tell me one thing, what stood out the clearest about that day?"

"The day," I answered, before I thought. "All of it. There really wasn't anything bigger in it than all the little things in it. I felt lucky when I started it, sitting in the ditch in the cornfield, and I kind of knew that this was the one day for the geese to come in, and I knew I knew it. That was the only big thing. I knew it was going to be the right day for it."

"Well," the Old Man warned, "remember one thing. When you start remembering again, remember that there ain't anything in any one day any bigger than all the things that go to make up the day. This'll give you considerable comfort when you're as old as me. Do you understand what I'm driving at?"

"Yessir," I said, because this was getting too deep for me. "I sure do."

I sure didn't, actually. I just wanted to get off the platform. But now today I do. I remember very carefully, even a war, and there isn't any one event in any day I remember that was bigger than what I had for breakfast.

21

*You Got to Be Crazy
to Be a Duck Hunter*

The day was slaty, and the wind whipped the Sound into a froth. The clouds tumbled low and menacing, with a suspicion of snow to come. My ears seemed to catch fire when we came into the warmth of the house, and little droplets clung to my nose. My hands were wrinkled from cold water and as red as radishes. There was no feeling whatsoever in my feet, inside their muddy hip boots. I was never happier in my life.

"Just look at the pair of us," the Old Man said. "Froze stiff, probably going to die of the pneumonia, wet, muddy, and miserable, and both of us grinning at each other like Chessy cats. We're crazy as loons, but then you got to be a little crazy to be a duck hunter. Nobody in his right mind would get up before dawn to sit and freeze in a blind on the off chance that some old buck mallard full of fish will fly close enough to get missed."

We had had quite a day. The wind that tumbled the waters had broken up the enormous rafts of ducks—you know, the ones that sit so maddeningly in the middle of the bay on a bluebird day. The low ceiling had 'em well down within range, and the wind had also blown the water out of the little secret pools. As happens only once in a while, the ducks were hunting for a place to sit, and they came to the decoys like cats to catnip.

"There ain't nothing," the Old Man said, "as smart as a black mallard when the weather's with him. He can see from here to Japan, and he can spot a phony decoy from a mile high, which is generally where he's at. But you let that weather change and blow up a lot of wind, and mebbe a little snow, and there ain't nothing as stupid as a duck. That goes for geese too, and I reckon the old honker is generally smarter than the duck. You get the right weather, and you have to bat 'em out of the blind. How about that fellow today that lost his mama?"

The Old Man was talking about a two-thirds-grown Canada goose that had strayed off from the V, up there in the dirty gray sky, and was making pitiful sounds. The Old Man had snickered at it. "Some of them big fellows are tougher'n whitleather," he said, "but this little fellow will be real fine for your grandma's oven. See, now, how I call him down. I am going to make some noises like his mama."

He got out his goose call and began to talk like a goose's mama. I have no way of writing down the sounds, but you could see that lost goose stick his neck down as soon as the Old Man's wheedling call reached him. He dropped his flaps and came down out of the sky like a hawk after a fish. He came practically into the blind, and I took a whack at him and discovered I had done one of those things you do once in a blue moon—shot my gun dry and plumb forgot to load her. The goose took off, and the Old Man said, "Don't worry. Load her up and I'll call him back. Shoot him good this time, or we'll have him in the blind with us."

He set up a gabble again, and the goose turned and came

right back to the blind. This time I was loaded with 4's, and I delivered a mess right into his head and neck, and he came down like a rock.

"It's a mean trick," the Old Man said, "but you can always call a lost young goose with that mama noise. And they do eat better than the old ones."

The Old Man had shot behind live decoys in his time; it had been legal. You'd have a hen mallard tied to a stick that was stuck in the mud, and she had more conversation than a woman. She would stand on her tail and flutter her wings and talk sexy to the passing flocks, and they would turn on a dime and come in with their feet hanging out and wings cocked. There is no easier target than a fat mallard or pintail grabbing for water with his feet and his wings locked.

Well, the wind stirred the water to a devil's broth, the ducks poured in, and we filled our tickets. The mallards were the prettiest, of course, but it was the pins that the Old Man admired most. "The French duck is gaudy," he said, "with his yellow shoes and all those colors in his plumage and that big yellow shovel for a bill, but you can't trust him. He's a puddle duck, and if you don't give him enough grain he'll double-cross you and eat himself sick on fish, just like any old merganser. But not the pin. Look at the gentlemanly clothes he wears, while the mallard looks like a pool-hall sharpie. You'll never find a pintail eating fish. He'd starve first.

"I know you read a lot about the canvasback and how fine he is to eat, and how all the politicians in this neck of the woods won't eat anything but terrapin and canvasback at their big dinners, but the old can ain't got any more morals than a mallard about eating fish. The only big duck I can absolutely certify is the pintail. And amongst the little ducks, I never ate a fishy teal so far. As a matter of fact, when all is said and done, for the dinner plate you can't beat a teal.

"Ducks . . ." the Old Man said. "Now, take teal. They fly faster'n greased lightning, and on a teal in a tail wind you got to lead him thirty foot. But they will skitter in amongst the decoys right while you're blam-blamming at a bunch of other ducks, and swim around like they owned the pond. It don't make sense. Once you got a teal on the water, you practically can't scare him off it, 'less you shoot at him."

I mentioned casually that we seemed to waste an awful lot of ammunition shooting cripples, and that the few belts I had at teal, sitting, usually resulted in the teal's taking off to Mexico.

"I can't explain it all to you," the Old Man replied. "But you got to remember that a duck in the water is like an iceberg. About eight-tenths of him is under water, and water sheds shot like a tin roof. You practically got to hit him in the head to kill him, because his wings are folded and the wing feathers and the back feathers'll shed shot just like water. I've noticed that in all sorts of bird shooting it's a heap easier to shoot a flying bird than a sitting bird, all question of sportsmanship aside. A flying bird opens up his vulnerable parts, his softer-feathered parts, and he spreads his wings enough to give you a chance to bust one. Sitting, wings folded, he's damned near armor-plated.

"And there's one thing more: standing in a boat or a blind and aiming down at water does something to the shotgun pattern. Don't ask me what or how, because I dunno. But shotguns were made to shoot either up or straight out, not down. A smarter man than me could probably tell you. All you got to do to believe it, though, is to watch, on the next cripple, how irregular the pellets strike the water."

The Old Man and I were not steady permanent-blind boys. He was against it. Said the ducks got to associate the blind with noise and the sudden death of a relative, and would skirt it just enough to pass outside good range, unless it was such a dirty day that they completely lost their minds and became as crazy as duck hunters.

"The way to do it," he said, "is in a bateau. The Cajuns call it 'pirogue,' but bateau—which is French for 'boat,' my ignorant young friend—is a flat-bottomed skiff. You pole her out to where the wind and water seem right, and stick her in a bunch of reeds or rushes, and you cut yourself some *roseaux*, or *tules*—which is

French and Spanish, respectively, for 'reeds,' and build your blind around your boat. You always wear a khaki hat to match the reeds, and you keep your face down until you are ready to shoot, because anything but a teal or a bluebill will see your white face or bald head from as high up as he can fly, and all the decoys and calls in the world won't get him down—unless, like I said, the weather's so lousy they've quit caring. You peep through a little hole in the reeds, and you let them circle your blind twice, unless it's a very clear day, and on the second circle they'll decoy like cream.

"A man with patience will kill an awful lot of ducks, because when they drop those feet and lock those wings you get the first one automatic, and all you got to do is like the Cajun said—aim at the nose when the other half is climbing. A mallard looking for sky when he's just left the water is not really moving very fast, because he's fighting for altitude and his centrifugal force is all out of kilter."

I didn't ask the Old Man what centrifugal force was. Like I've said so many times, if you asked him he was apt to tell you, and it would take an hour or so, and everybody from Julius Caesar to Einstein would get mixed up in it.

The Old Man read me a lot of lectures about trash ducks and ducks that ought to be conserved. He wouldn't ever let me shoot a wood duck, because he said they were too pretty and too little, and besides, there weren't enough of them to go around. He never would shoot a gray duck or a spoonbill if anything else was flying, and when I complained that they looked like hen mallards at a distance he said I ought to sharpen up my eyesight or quit mingling with grown men. I took a crack at a swan once, and the Old Man took a crack at me. He said they weren't any good to eat and there were dodlimbed few of them around and what there was ought to be left in peace.

Come to think of it now, even in those days of practically non-existent game wardens, abundant game, and large limits, one thing stands out about the Old Man. He never willingly took more fish or game than we could eat or give away, and he never shot a gun—or allowed me to shoot a gun—just to hear it go off and kill something useless. He was absolutely firm about leaving a nucleus of game, whether it was quail or deer, and of never shooting females if the females were identifiable. This sex definition did not, of course, apply to quail or ducks, because unless it's mallards close at hand or a quail flying at you, there just isn't time enough to tell.

But it seems to me I've been rattling around all over the place, and what I really wanted to concentrate on was what the Old Man said first, which is that it takes a crazy man to be a duck hunter. As we stood in front of the fire, steaming out our wet clothes, after having risked death by drowning, exposure, and pneumonia, after having been up since black night, after having rowed and poled miles, after having frozen fingers setting out decoys and having frozen feet from inactivity—after having been uncomfortable constantly in the quest for a few pounds of bird meat that I didn't like to eat too terribly well, I concluded one thing: if you have to be crazy to hunt ducks, I do not wish to be sane.

22

X *Plus* Y *to the Second Power Equals Bluefish*

I think the subject came up because of some very bad marks on the report card, mostly having to do with algebra and Chaucer. Miss Hetty Struthers taught the algebra, and Miss Emma Martin taught the Chaucer, and I couldn't get anywhere with either one. My folks tore a small strip off me, and I was complaining bitterly to the Old Man one Sunday when we were going off to investigate the late run of bluefish.

"It don't make any sense to me," I grumbled. "What's the good of learning things like 'Whan that Aprille with its shoures sooty the droghte of Marche hath percéd to the rooty'? I can make more sense out of Geechee talk. At least when I ask a Geechee, 'Boy, where you get dem rope?' and he says, 'Man, I t'ief 'um off de dock,' I know what he's saying. I know he stole the rope."

"Well, everything's got some uses," the Old Man said mildly, tying a slipknot in a leader. "Maybe even Chaucer'll come in handy some day, although I must say I go along with you on this old English. We speak a lot of old English around here, such as 'holp' for help, and we call a bed a 'stid,' which I suppose is short for bedstead, and we say 'twig,' which I understand is Cockney for 'look.' "

"Yessir," I said, "but we're not pilgrims and we're not going to Canterbury, and we spell better than they spelled in those days, and I just don't see no sense in it, a-tall. How's it going to help me make a living?"

"Well, since time began," the Old Man said, "they have been jamming a lot of old stuff down young fellers because it is supposed to give 'em culture and make 'em think. What's your excuse for the 'D' in algebra?"

"Please, sir, you're not going to stand there and tell me that x plus y divided by z equals q? You taught me fractions by cutting up apples, and I understood that, especially when I ate the fractions. But this business of y to the third power is the cube root of p times 10 just don't rub off. What good is it?"

"I dunno," the Old Man admitted. "Maybe something will come of it, and maybe you ought to know something about it. You want to grow up stupid and work on a fish boat all your life?"

"*Yes*," I said stubbornly. "If it means Chaucer and algebra, I'd rather work on the *Vanessa* with Tom and Pete, and make liquor in the wintertime."

"*That* ain't any sort of an answer," the Old Man told me. "Mind, now, you're cutting that mullet too thick. You'll be going to college one of these days, and then you can study what you want to study, but first you got to get out of high school. And to get out of high school you got to make yourself do a lot of unpleasant things, which is how life works. It ain't all one way, you know. Hand me a sinker.

"Bear this in mind. Knowledge is an accumulation, like a pack rat hides things. Things you never knew you knew have a way of popping up later. You're supposed to fill your skull with a lot of things, against the day you might need one of them. And remember this, too: you can't pour a gallon of knowledge into a one-quart brain. The idea is to make the brain big enough and flexible enough to handle what it has to handle. I want to see some better marks next month, or we might just find ourselves not shooting any quail this fall. That ain't a threat. It's a suggestion. Let's go catch some fish."

We caught a lot of fish. The big blues had come in to feed in the sloughs, and so had the drum—the channel bass, that is— and there was a big run of enormous weakfish. We'd had a pretty good norther that had cut deep sloughs and firmed up the sand bar, and all you had to do was just give the rod a little flip, and the four-ounce pyramid sinker landed right in the mouth of something big and full of fight. I caught a thirty-pound drum that day, and the Old Man topped me with a forty-pounder. We quit when we were tired, and we had enough fish to fill up the back seat of the Liz. We went home dead beat, and for once the Old Man helped me gut and scale the fish. There were just too many for one boy.

We ate—not much, because I was tired; just some cornbread and milk and eggs and bacon and jelly—and I went to bed, but I couldn't sleep. Algebra and Chaucer kept chasing themselves round and round in my head, all mixed up with bluefish and channel bass and quail and camp making and horse riding and heaven and hell and how long is forever—one of those bad nights a kid'll have once in a blue moon.

About 2:00 A.M. I got up and dressed and called the dogs and went for a walk down by the river. The moon was nigh full, still sailing high and pretty in the sky, and all over town you could hear the dogs howl, like somebody was going to die and they knew all about it. I couldn't get one thing out of my mind: "You can't pour a gallon of knowledge into a one-quart brain," the Old Man had said. I wandered sad and lonely as a cloud—we'd had that one in English too—wondering if I was one of those people with a one-quart brain. One pint was more like it, I thought finally as we walked down to the wharf, and I sat and dangled my feet and watched the moon turn the water to milk.

Then I began to think of something else. I thought about how many things I already knew that the Old Man had taught me. These things skipped through my head helter-skelter. I knew how to train a puppy to be a good bird dog. I knew how to call a turkey or a duck. I knew how to row a boat and stand a deer. I knew about moon and tide and their effect on fish and game. I knew that a sea turtle wept huge tears when it laid its soft eggs in the sand. I knew how to hook a sheepshead with a sand fiddler. I knew how to make a camp and build a fire and skin a rabbit in one shuck. I knew how to cook in the woods and throw a cast net and lead a dove and grapple an oyster and draw a seine.

I suddenly decided I knew an awful lot about an awful lot of things, some of which I had been taught, some of which I had learned on my own. But mostly it seemed to me that what I knew—the odd pieces of information, like not calling the Aphrodite of Melos the Venus de Milo, and how the guano birds worked—all came out of the Old Man. It seemed to me that if they put the Old Man to work teaching school he could even make algebra easy. It also seemed to me that if a boy worked half as hard learning Chaucer as he worked hunting a coon, Chaucer would become a minor nuisance and could easily be got out of the way. Algebra wasn't any tougher than still-hunting a big buck deer, and probably had less mathematics to it. Whereupon I whistled up the dogs and went back to bed, and this time I slept.

Then a strange and wonderful thing happened to me in the schoolroom. I discovered reading. Real reading. I found out that Shakespeare had more muscles than Doonie Watts and was responsible for more rough characters than a water front. He knew more man-type jokes than the boys at Gus McNeill's filling station, and his language was frank enough to be of great interest to a boy.

I took on Shakespeare as I'd learned to build a turkey blind, and he was a cinch. I had more fun with Walter Scott than Ivanhoe ever did. I fell afoul of some naturalists like Ernest Thompson Seton, and some archaeologists, and some Gibbon, and I got so interested in Rome that I practically bought myself a toga. The Greeks and the Egyptians and the Phoenicians got to be personal friends. Robin Hood and *Treasure Island* and *Robinson Crusoe* were kid stuff now, although I must say that Mr. Defoe had a lot of know-how, and while Mr. Wyss' *Swiss Family Robinson* was a bunch of lies, mainly, it also had a lot of know-how in it. I mean about salting down fish and taming onagers and building tree houses and such as that.

The shock that I actually liked all this came one day when I was hunting with a friend of mine named E. G. Goodman, who was going to grow up to be a doctor like his dead daddy, even if his mamma, Mis' Eliza Goodman, had to beat him with a stick. The E. in his name stood for Erasmus or Erastus, I disremember which, but if you called him "Ras" you had to fight him.

G. and I had a real fine day at his farm. We hunted everything, like boys will—rabbits and squirrels and doves and quail. We were up before the dawn and bedded down early. We ate like starving Armenians and must have walked a hundred miles behind an old half-bred bulldog-plus-hound, who didn't seem to care what he chased.

That was the first day I really got into the texture of things. I mean, how big was a scuppernong grape, how much juice was inside it, what the moss on an old live oak looked like, the freckles on the leaves of an old cornstalk, the weight of a beefsteak tomato served with sugar and vinegar, the way a possum skin tacked to the weathered silver-gray boards of the smokehouse curled at the edges, the differing voice range of the bull hound when he was after a black swamp rabbit or was interested in a squirrel up a tree.

Inside the smokehouse the hams hung heavy and green-molded, hard-cured, and there was enough salt in the soil to assay at least 30 percent of the gross weight. The gourd dipper by the well was lumpy on its hard-dried yellow-green surface. The yard was clean-swept sand, like a beach, and the old house was stilted, like an old maid holding up her skirts when a mouse comes skittering into the room.

We hunted the swamp with one buckshot shell in the left-hand barrel, hoping to start a deer, and for the second time I truly knew about the solemnity of a swamp, green and cool and frightening, with the slow crick-colored brown from the leaf dye, the clusters of mistletoe high in the bare branches of the water oaks, the squirrels' nests brown and lonesome in the mizzen of the trees, and the high-cocked knees of the cypress. The mournful call of the dove came spooking, the last mournful cry of dove, plaintive whistle of scattered quail, the first wail of whippoorwill, and later the scary hoot of the elusive owl. Then the rise of moon and the devil shapes the trees made.

I had been living with this stuff all my life and had never completely noticed it before—never saw it, never smelled it, never heard it, never isolated it, never touched it. I had never thought of the curious fact that a drinking gourd was as rough as a file inside, or that magnolia blossoms turned brown if you touched them, or that the pomegranates that grew in Cousin Margie's front yard were composed only of hide and pulp and seeds.

I had given no real thought to the fact that the country at nightfall was so mournful that the Negroes whistled and sang to keep themselves company as they walked through the dark-ening woods, or that an iron caldron generally had three legs instead of four. The fact that smoke rose instead of falling had never touched my consciousness, or that frost was only frozen dew. I had eaten pork sausage and never noticed that the skin was mottled and generally made from intestines.

All this hit me that day at E. G. Goodman's farm, and in fairness I had to blame it on education. Without *The Decline and Fall*, without *Rolf in the Woods*, without Falstaff, without Lamb's roast pig (I had never even thought of what crackling really was, *mirabile dictu!*), without Chaucer and Macbeth and the crackling of prawns in a pot and that dreary dreamer, Hamlet—without these I would have passed through this fascinating life, accepting everything, seeing nothing.

The Old Man was old, but how much older was Cheops, whom I later came to know as Khufu. My house was old, but how much older Rome, how much older the Pyramids. "Rome wasn't built in a day" was a phrase we used as freely as "Sure as a gun's iron," and now I knew doggone well it wasn't built in a day. But I never did figure out how much higher it is than they hung Haman.

I have to admit I never made an "A" in algebra, but I passed it without cheating, and Miss Hetty said she never did see such a change in a boy. Miss Emma Martin was hard to convince that I wasn't cheating on Shakespeare, but I reared back and gave her a load of Chaucer one day and she had to hold still for the fact that I at least could memorize. Miss Claire Lathrop was flabbergasted when I turned up fairly sharp wih Julius Caesar in the Latin version, and she couldn't have known that the interest suddenly came via Shakespeare and the Old Man. I knew that all Gaul was divided into three parts, but I wanted the straight dope on why.

This is no advertisement for education, but I have to admit it had its points in teaching me what I was doing every day, with quite a lot of how and a little bit of why. Some of it came in real handy later, when I took up writing as a trade, but mostly it helped me heavy in the business of possum hunting and the anatomy of the large outdoors.

"Insanity," the Old Man observed, "seems to run in some families. It takes different forms. Some people bay the moon, and others think they are Napoleon. In my case, apart from being a duck hunter, I enjoy coon hunting. I even like possum hunting.

"Now, you just tell me," he went on, "why a man grown would admire to run around in the woods at night following a bunch of hollering hound dogs when he could be sound and warm in his bed. After a critter he don't really want. Insanity! Do you want to go coon hunting with me and the boys?"

"Yessir," I said. "I guess I've inherited it from you. When are we going?"

"Tonight. Tom and Pete and a couple other loose maniacs named Elwood and Corbett got some new hounds they went to try. Won't nothing much come of it except Corbett'll fight Tom and Pete'll be duty bound to take on Elwood—that's after they've got drunk—but if there's a coon or a possum or even a bear handy, we'll hear some music. In any case, we'll have some exercise."

I'd been around in the woods a lot at night, frog sticking and all, and early in the morning after deer and squirrel and turkey, but that is a kind of quiet operation. Coon hunting is a thing for bust-neck people who don't really care if they fall in holes and trip over briers and run against trees. Far as I know, a bone-bred coon hunter doesn't care whether he catches the coon or doesn't catch the coon. He just wants to hear the hounds make that music.

Even as a little feller I was always fascinated with woods at night. A wood in the daytime is a warm, friendly place, pierced with sunlight, splashed in the clearings with pools of light; but when she starts off to cool in the evening, she gets real spooky. Jungle isn't jungle in the daytime, but even a city park is jungle at night. The dogs know it, which is why they howl, and the colored folks know it, and even the sophisticated city folks draw the curtains and light up a fire.

To be in a forest by yourself at night is a large adventure in fear, but to be on a coon hunt with a lot of hairy men, most of whom have already been scarring their noses with the fruit jar, is another thing. People are stumbling around and falling and cussing and laughing, and all of a sudden the owl's hoot, the whippoorwill's wail, are no longer ghost noises but companionable accompaniments to the big spree.

The general idea of a coon hunt is you turn loose the dogs in a patch of likely cover, and then you run through the woods after the dogs. Maybe that is oversimplification, but it's about all I remember. On this particular night the dogs started a fox or so, treed a possum, and missed out completely on the coon. Another jumped a deer, and another took off after a rabbit, causing great disgust to his owner.

The possum I recall very well, because I was nominated to climb the old persimmon tree he was refugeeing in and to poke him out with a stick. The branch I was on busted, and the possum and I fell out of the tree at approximately the same time. We lost the coon in a swamp after he dang near murdered one of the dogs who was stupid enough to follow him into the creek. The deer went over to see friends in another county.

What I mind, mostly, is hearing the hounds on a night so clear and frosty sharp that the belling must have traveled miles; hearing the hounds crashing in the low gallberries and pine scrub, seeing the excited ring of hounds around a tree—from which the coon had departed—and the spectacle of a bunch of grown men acting so much like children that if they had been children other grown men would have tanned their britches.

I've got no real solution for what makes a man hunt coons at night unless he's crazy, like the Old Man said, but my mild idea today is that everybody, even a grown man, needs to get out of the house and cut up a little, just to ease his nerves. That's why the coon was created.

I don't know how many miles you travel on a coon-hunting night. The dogs circle, and you try to cut the circle, and you fall into the creek, and you lose people and lose dogs, and along about two or three in the morning everybody's had enough, including the dogs, the coon you didn't tree, and the deer that went over the hill. By some common accord everybody decides to quit. You know the hounds will come back, those you've lost, in a day or so. So you make for a headquarters, which would be Tom's place or Elwood's place, and you kick the sleepy fire into a blaze, and everybody lies around the kitchen floor while somebody else puts the coffee pot on the hob. Somebody else goes out to the smokehouse for a side of bacon, and somebody else disturbs a hen and brings in a gross of brown freckled eggs. Somebody else digs up another jar of hand-woven corn liquor, and somebody else gets out the guitar.

We sort of tended to the Elizabethan epoch where I was raised, and so all the songs you heard were old English folk songs that the hillbilly artists later made popular on the radio and juke boxes.

I don't know how or where the people learned the music. The Old Man, for instance, was a fiddler. First he carpentered his own fiddle, and then, seeing as how he had it made, he figgered he might as well learn to play it. Maybe he never played it very good, but he could squeeze as much emotion out of "Ol' Zip Coon" and "Pop Goes the Weasel" as anybody I ever heard.

Practically everybody played something. People that couldn't make anything more than a mark on a legal paper knew some odd things about harmony, whether they were playing a washboard, a jew's-harp, a banjo, or a mouth organ.

All the colored folks could play something or other too, if it was only the bones, and the singing you heard at the camp meetings and revivals, the old spirituals, had a beat that they're still struggling to put a finger on today. I can still get me a set of goose-pimples out of remembering what "Go Down, Moses" used to sound like when about a hundred colored voices took hold of it.

Seemed like nearly everything you did had some music in it. The dogs made music in the chase—rabbits, deer, coon—and it was sweet music. When the big, sweaty deck-hands were hauling seine in the pogie fleet, they used a chant with a "huh!" to mark the haul, a chant that I heard a lot of years later in the middle of Tanganyika. The chain gangs had their special songs, and the Cap'm in charge of the convict camps used to put on regular free concerts after the bad boys quit pounding on the railroad ties. The roustabouts around the turpentine camps had their song-and-dance specialists too, and altogether—rich and poor, black and white, chained and unchained—we made some mighty mellow music.

The square dances on Saturday nights were a throwback all the way to Sir Walter Raleigh. The music hadn't changed, and the intricacy of the figures hadn't changed much either. The best set caller in the county was a little, prune-faced, sawed-off fellow named Dan Ward. When he hit that part about "ladies in the middle, gents to the wall, take a chew tobacco, and balance all!" he used to leap half his height straight off the floor, kick his heels, and leer in a positively marvelous fashion.

I kind of got off the subject of coon hunting, but so did the coon that night. What I was generally aiming at, though, was the fact that so many good things were mixed up in whatever you did, whether it was a coon hunt, a ball game, a fish fry, or a camp meeting.

Whatever you did, there was music in it, and good food in it, and science and knowledge of a special sort; and there was always the fun of the firelight, and lazy rest when you were plumb beat. There was a slug of mule at the end of the day for the men grown, and maybe a sip of scuppernong wine for the boys. There seemed to be some sort of point to everything, a beginning, a middle, and an end.

The Old Man used to say that the best part of hunting and fishing was the thinking about going and the talking about it after you got back. You just had to have the actual middle as a basis of conversation and to put some meat in the pot. "Everybody," he said, "should be allowed to brag some about what he did good that day, and to cover up shameless on what he did wrong."

Lying around on the bleached white-pine floor of a country

kitchen, with the thin fat-pine walls literally vibrating with the heat of the roaring fire, the smell of eggs and bacon mingled with coffee and corn whisky, I heard all the stories that had become legend to the vicinity. All the past coon hunts were recounted. All the lies about hounds and bird dogs were retold, including the one about the setter who was so stanch on point that she got lost one day and was found a year later. There had been a change in the weather, and she froze to death. Her skeleton was found, still pointing at the skeletons of a covey of quail.

I heard Corbett tell all about the time he was "working for the state," a euphemism for a stretch in jail for bootlegging. I heard about the First World War. Crime and punishment, war and peace, came hand in hand with a coon hunt and a skillet of bacon and eggs.

It was bright light when the party broke up and we headed home, with one scarred dog and a possum to show for the evening's work. Sure enough, Corbett had got into an altercation with Elwood, and, being as how they were brothers, Tom and Pete had to show their sympathy by starting a private quarrel over who owned a cast net or a shotgun or something. Corbett swung at Elwood and missed and fell in the fire, and we had to haul him out. Pete and Tom took their argument out on the porch, and Pete dived at Tom and fell off the porch and just stayed where he was. Tom thought he looked lonesome; so he went and lay down by him, and a hound came up and lay down with the pair.

The Old Man shook his head and sniffed the bright morning breeze. "I'm telling you again," he said. "Insanity runs its own peculiar way. Coon hunting is a very strong symptom. In a way it reminds me of what life's like. You work and you fall down and you eat and you fight, and when it's all over you feel awful foolish. Because, generally, you ain't even got a coon to show for all the commotion."

23

The Women Drive You to the Poolrooms

It was one of those miserable spring days, with the wind whipping down in gusts and fetching the rain along with it, and nothing much to do. Too hot for a fire, and too cold not to have a fire. The rain rattled on the windowpanes, and the glass shivered when the spurts of wind struck.

The Old Man and I were just sittin', scratchin', and fidgetin'. Everywhere we'd light, in a minute Miss Lottie, my grandma, would be right behind us with a dust rag or a broom. If we sat on a chair, she'd come up on us and start to bustle around, like women will, and we'd know she was set on shifting the chair to some place else where it wouldn't look any better, but would give her some satisfaction. She kept hustling us from one stand to another until finally the Old Man sighed and said,

"Let's go down to Thompson's poolroom. At least there ain't any women in it. I am against poolrooms on principle, but there are times where there ain't any other place for a fellow to get away from his womenfolks."

About this time Miss Lottie came at us with the carpet sweeper, and we got up and walked the three blocks to the poolroom and sat down on one of the high-legged stools and drank a Coke and listened to the click of the balls and watched the players as they bent over the cool green baize of the tables in sometimes impossible positions as they shoved a bit of body English into the shots. Thompson's poolroom was full that day. "Evidently," the Old Man said, "all the local ladies have come down with the nervous wet-weather furniture-moving disease."

He pulled at his ragged mustache and lit up his pipe. Watching one of the players nudge the eight ball into a side pocket, he spoke more or less to himself.

"Women are the most curious of all the animal critters in the world. I have made a lifelong study of women, under all climatic conditions, and I reckon there ain't a varmint loose in the woods or water that takes as much figgerin' with no real answer. You can train a no-'count dog, or fool a fish, or outguess a fox, or outsmart a coon, or make a buck deer run your way, but there is no real past performance that you can use against a woman to cut her off at the draw. Just about the time you got her figgered she whips out a fresh bag of tricks, and you got to start all over again.

"Now, you take a poolroom," he said. "There ain't anything really sinister about a poolroom. I don't shoot pool, but the poolroom is where I come when I got a new dog to show off or some fresh exploit I want to brag about, because I know I'll find a lot of men to listen to what I got to say or see what I got to show. In a small place like this, a poolroom ain't a den of iniquity. It's the only refuge in town where a man ain't tormented by his womenfolks.

"Pool," the Old Man went on, "ain't nothing but heavy-ball

tennis, using a stick instead of a catgut fly swatter. When I was in England once, I looked and saw the high muckety-mucks playing pool in a couple of clubs I wangled my way into, except the Limeys call it snooker. But in our curious thinking, tennis is a ladylike sport and pool is bad. That's because the ladies can't get into the pool halls to bedevil their men, and the ladies resent it."

I watched Dooney Watts do a highly illegal jump shot. The cue ball leapfrogged over a blocking ball, picked up its target, and nudged it into a corner pocket.

"Pretty," the Old Man said. "Illegal, but pretty. Tells you what sort of a man Dooney is. That sign saying 'No jump or massé shots allowed' don't mean no more to Dooney than if it said 'Posted' or 'Hunting Strictly Forbidden.' Dooney ain't what you'd call a natural-born law abider. What was I saying? Oh, yes, I remember. Women.

"There ain't but one law you can use against 'em," the Old Man continued. "That's what I call the law of negative acceptance, or the power of reverse-English suggestion. You got to operate on the basic idea that they are two steps ahead of you, and then take a step back'ards and throw them off stride.

"Women are natural-born perverse. Anything a man takes delight in which they don't understand, and can't share, makes 'em mad. They keep trying to kiss their elbows and turn into boys, and when they can't be boys they don't like it; so they declare war on the boys at a very early age, and win the final victory when they trap themselves a wild boy and turn him into a house pet. Or try to.

"Boys like to cuss and chew tobacco and drink a little liquor and shoot pool and play poker and smoke cigars and go huntin' and fishin'. These generally ain't supposed to be sports the girls can share in; so the girls resent 'em.

"It ain't like any of these things was bad, if taken in moderation. I never knew no man to come to harm in the woods or in the water, or in a poolroom for that matter, if the man was a good man to start with. You have noticed that I smoke and take a little nip now and then, but no jailhouse ever knew me, and I pay what I owe and speak civilly to the preacher. You can overdo anything, including sweet charity and mashed potatoes, and turn a good thing into a bad thing.

"But the women automatically think it's bad if they got no part in it. An English fellow, name of Chesterton, once wrote a line that went something like this: 'There are three things in this world women don't understand: liberty, equality, fraternity.' I reckon that may be a little tough on the girls on the equality side, but on liberty and fraternity they ain't got a whisper of understanding."

One of the boys, maybe it was Bill St. George, did a three-cushion bank shot that nudged a ball out of a difficult lie and into the leather webbing of the pocket.

"That's how you handle 'em," the Old Man said. "Bank shots. Aim for about three extra cushions and they're so busy following the cue ball they don't see the main ball drop. They lose interest on the second cushion." The Old Man was pretty windy this day, and full of his subject.

I piped up, "I don't follow you. What do you mean, lose interest on the second cushion?"

"Come on home and I'll show you how it works. I taught you to shoot and make a camp and catch a fish and train a dog. I may as well complete your education with women."

The rain had stopped when we went out, and the wind was dying. The Old Man sniffed the air and grinned under his mustache. "She's going to be a good day tomorrow. What'd you most like to do?"

"I dunno," I said. "How do you figure bass'll be biting?"

"Fair," the Old Man reckoned. "Think we ought to go fishing? It's a week end."

"Yessir," I answered. "And we haven't done anything about fixing up the shack on Corncake. That'd be fun. I reckon she's in a mess, after the last blow."

"We'll see," the Old Man said. "We'll see how the land lays."

We went on into the house, and Miss Lottie fixed us with a wifely eye. "Where've you all been?" she asked.

"Down to the poolroom. You seemed awful busy, and we didn't want to disturb you."

"Taking that boy into the poolroom with all those loafers!" she said, and went on for about five minutes about how no good could come to anybody that hung around pool halls associating with riffraff, et cetera. The Old Man let her carry on till she was blowing like a winded horse. He never said a word, just let her have her head.

When she quit, he said, "Excuse me," and went out in the back yard and crawled under the house and got his cast net. He came back to the living room, spread it out on the floor, and sat down cross-legged and took a sail needle and started to mend it. He winked at me and whispered, "Go get the fishing rods. They need looking over."

I went and got the rods and broke 'em down and started cleaning the reels on a big spread of newspaper. Miss Lottie came in again, hopping mad when she saw all the truck over her fresh-swept rug. "What's all that mess you've got there? On my rugs!"

"Just the cast net and some fish poles, Lottie," the Old Man said, sweet as pie. "While we're at it, boy, you better go get the guns. This wet weather ain't helping them any."

"Yessir," I said and got up.

The old lady let out a screech. "You don't clean any guns on my clean carpet!" She was red and flustered. "Oil all over my ——"

"But, Lottie," the Old Man protested, "it's too wet to work outside, and since I took all them trunks up to the attic it——"

"I don't know who's the worst, you or the boy," she said. "Seems to me all you do is clutter up the house when I've cleaned it. Why don't you take the boy and go somewheres?"

"The poolroom?" The Old Man's eyes were wide and innocent.

"I don't care where you go!" Miss Lottie hollered. "Just get that much off my rugs!"

"Of course." The Old Man winked at me sideways. "There's so many no-'count people hanging around poolrooms that——"

"If you had any sense, you'd take the boy and go over to Corncake and fix that house you're always talking about," Miss Lottie told him. "You can make all the mess you want to over there, and at least be out from underfoot while I get on with my cleaning."

I started to say something, but the Old Man hushed me up with a wave of his hand.

"You know as well as I do, Lottie," he said, "it'll be cold and wet on Corncake, and there ain't any provisions in the house and we're apt to catch our death of cold and——"

"Oh, shush," she said. "You're a grown man, and you spend half your time either soaked to the skin or parboiled in the sun. There's plenty of driftwood under the house, or ought to be, and you can take some things to eat with you. You're always talking about how good you cook. Go some place and prove it."

"I don't know . . ." The Old Man shook his head. "My rheumatism has been pretty bad lately. I think we'd best just stay here. Come on, son. If your grandmother doesn't want us in the parlor, we can go to the dining room."

"You set foot in my dining room, and I'll—— You stay right here!" She rushed off toward the kitchen.

"Just set quiet and make a motion with that oily rag," the Old Man said. "She'll be back in a minute."

She was, too. She came back, bent over, carrying a big basket with both hands. "There's half a ham in here," she puffed. "There's three dozen eggs and some beans and bread and coffee. There's an apple pie and some oranges and bananas and part of a pound cake. Now, take that truck off my rug and go some place and play cowboys for a couple of days."

"I reckon we've been run off, son," the Old Man said.

"Gather up that gear and throw it in the Liz. Maybe we'll both get drowned; then she'll be sorry."

"Small loss," Miss Lottie snapped.

The Old Man sighed and went out the door. I was just getting into the Liz when Miss Lottie called me back to the door. She had a paper bag in her hands. It was hard inside and gurgled.

"He forgot his nerve tonic," she said. "If I was you, I'd try the bass first, before you go to the house. I think they might be biting." And she shot me a wink. "Stay out of the poolrooms."

When I handed the Old Man his nerve tonic, he sighed. "You see what I mean? There ain't no way to fool 'em. What'd she say?"

"She said go fishing first."

"Then we'll go fishing," the Old Man said. "But it would have saved us a lot of time if she'd come right out and said she had a hankering for fish."

24

Thar She Blows

In the old days the pogie-fishing industry was about as exciting a way to make a living as a fellow could run across. My first sharp awareness of the immensity of the sea, and with it the world, was when the Old Man decided I was big enough to pull a little weight on a pogie boat. A pogie is a very greasy, fat fish whose proper name is menhaden and which is used for fertilizer and fish meal and what not. You can do anything with a pogie but eat it, and I suppose if you were hungry enough to choke it down it wouldn't kill you.

Pogie fishing was big industry in my town. Between pogies and shrimp and the pilot business, we managed to eat. The Old Man had a pogie boat called the *Vanessa*. I suppose she wasn't the biggest ship that ever went to sea, but to me she was bigger than the *Queen Mary*. She was big enough to carry what seemed a million miles of seine, a flock of purse boats, a skipper, a mate, a winchman, a slew of strong backs, which were mostly colored—and a small boy.

The pogies went in shoals and they were followed by clouds of birds—gannets and gulls and such. They showed brassy in the sun, and you could see the big fish—the sharks and dolphin and mackerel—cutting into the bait, and the birds swooping and dipping down to grab a fish in their talons or beak.

My job was aloft in the crow's-nest. I was the lookout, the fearless fellow high above the decks. All alone up there in the boundless sky, I scanned the boundless sea, looking for an undulating shoal of fat-backed menhaden, to be seined and hauled silvery kicking aboard, then taken to Charlie Gause's refining factory and rendered into an awful smell that meant sowbelly and beans and long sweetening in the colored folks' houses and another installment on the flivver in the driveway of the white folks' houses.

"This is big business," the Old Man said. "You ain't just a kid wedged into the crow's-nest of a fishing boat. You are the economic difference in a lot of people's lives. You belong to see a shoal of pogue before the other lookouts in the other ships see 'em, so we can get to 'em first, or there may be no Christmas next year. See if you can't pretend you're Cap'n Ahab with your eye peeled for Moby Dick. After all, a good haul of pogies weighs as much as a whale, and is worth about the same amount of money."

One thing about the Old Man was that he always had a sort of play-toy approach to everything. A boy looking for a bad-smelling fish that is headed for a fertilizer factory is one thing, and pretty dull doings. But a boy with a title of Cap'n who is hunting a great white whale is quite another kettle of conditions. Man, when I perched up there high in the sky, with my eyes skinned for the fish, I was about as close to being lord of the universe as you're apt to get.

I'd spot a shoal of pogies and holler down, "Bridge ahoy!"

when I could just as easy have said, "Hey, Grandpa!" And I'd say, "Fish! Bearing two points off the starboard bow!" or some such formality, when I suppose all the time the Old Man had seen the fish before I'd sung out, and was just waiting on me out of politeness.

We'd cut off in the general direction of the fish, and the purse boats would swing over the side from their davits, and the great seine would be set from the bobbing boats. The enormous, shining, sweaty black deck-hands would heave and haul and grunt, and the fish would come with a surge into the hold of the ship when the donkey engine hauled the catch aboard, flapping and kicking, a treasure trove of marine organisms.

"Let's see what we got this time," the Old Man would say, and give over the wheel to Tom or Pete or somebody else.

That was the thrill, because you never knew what you'd be hauling out of the sea along with the pogies. There would always be sharks—hammerheads and shovelnoses—and once in a while a big one. Now and again a tarpon would find its way that far north, and there were always scatterings of the fine edible fish—mackerel and blues and dolphin. I had a new job then. With my feet shoved into rubber boots, I was down in the hold to plow through the surprise package and sort out the good fish, which the crew divided and sold fresh to the stores when we got back to port. I was allowed to keep my share of the money, and no questions asked about what I spent it on.

They were bright and golden days of sun and sea spray, the salt gritty on your lips, and your nose burning as the sun graved salt into your skin. There were so many things to watch: the way the birds worked the fish, the dorsals of the sharks slicing the water, the dolphins running a match race with the bow of the ship, the porpoises, jocular and friendly, cutting caracoles as they played around the boat, big clownish show-offs happy to have company.

There was always weather to watch—watching it breed and handling it according to whether she was squall, or storm, or dirty-mean with hurricane tendency. I had a small suit of oil-skins and a sou'wester and boots, and I loved it when the sky turned gray and dirty and the clouds lowered and the seas began to pile, sending great sheets of spray over the forecastle-head, even up to the bridge. There's always something wonderful about storm at sea, especially if you can trust the skipper to get you safely back to a fire and a clean bed.

The smells aboard a ship are special—oil and tar and clean hemp and canvas and salt, grease and fuel and paint. I first made the acquaintance of sujimuji on the *Vanessa*. It is a virulent lye concoction for the swabbing down of paintwork, and it burns holes in your hide. A lot of years later, when I went to sea in the merchant marine, I needed very few lessons concerning forecastlehead lookouts and the application of suji to paint.

The Old Man said that, as I was a common deck-hand (except when I was Cap'n Ahab looking for Moby Dick) I certainly couldn't expect to eat with the skipper—himself. He said a skipper had a certain amount of dignity, which must be preserved at all costs, even to eating by himself. So I messed with Tom and Pete, who constituted mate and bos'un. Seems to me we ate very high on the hog. Or maybe it was just hunger, because fried salt pork, grits, eggs, salt ham, canned salmon, and fried fish, with coffee and sea biscuits, molasses for sweetening, and maybe an apple, were about all we had to eat. I learned a long time later that if an army travels on its belly, the Navy lives off coffee. "Coffee time" has more significance in seagoing talk than "Damn the torpedoes!"

Best of all I can recall, none of the men, black or white, ever made me feel like a boy, or out of place, or a nuisance, or anything like that. They taught me things, but they were what a boy ought to know, such as not dumping a bucket of swill over the windward taffrail, and how to steer a bucking ship in a heavy sea, taking up two or three turns of slack in the wheel according to which way the wind and currents were driving you.

I got to where I could come hand over hand down the guy

line from crow's-nest to deck—or slide it if I had gloves. When the Navy got me years later, one thing I didn't have to learn was the difference between a clove hitch and a bowline, a square knot and a granny. Tom, or maybe Pete, taught me how to make a Turk's-head, handle a heaving line, and splice a spring line. I could run a winch and cast off or tie up without busting up the vessel or the dock.

All this may not sound as if it would ever come in handy, but there was one dirty night, a few years later, when the skipper, the mate, the cadet, and yours truly warped a full-sized freighter out of a dock in Hamburg and up the river to Bremerhaven when the crew and other officers were all drunk, and I was all by myself on the poop, handling two stern spring lines and two winches and saying profanely reverent thanks to the old *Vanessa* and its cooperative crew.

What I can remember best is the ghostly cold of a predawn sailing, the clammy dew on the tarpaulins—dew stiff-bristled on the hempen lines, cold-freckled on the deck, smeared across the glass of the bridge. I can remember the crash of sea against ship, the tremor all the way along her as she took a big one, the way anything that wasn't battened down took a walk when the seas were on the beam, and the crashing in the galley and the cursing of the cook and the smell of coffee grounds frying when the coffee pot up-ended on the galley stove.

I remember the bone-crushing fatigue at the end of the day, when you came bravely into port with your full-up flags flying, and the sun going down red, and the night chill coming on again. And the way the dock pitched when you tied up and your sea-limber legs hit firm planking again, and still continued to roll and pitch with the motion of the sea.

I saw an albatross before I read *The Ancient Mariner*, and what is more, I knew a boat that was named after one. I knew about the hunter home from the hills, and the sailor home from the sea.

The Old Man said one day, when I was taking a trick at the wheel, "I spent most of my life on the water, and so did your

Uncle Jack and your Uncle Tommie and your Uncle Walker and all the other ones ahead of us, and it looks iike we got a straight succession to blue water in you."

There was a time, somewhere east of Oran, during the late unpleasantness called World War II, when I remembered what he said, and wished we'd had a few more soldiers in the family.

25

Graveyards Are More Fun Than Sunday School

"It seems to me," the Old Man said one summer Sunday morning, "that it's about time you started teaching me something. This has been a one-sided operation for too long a time. What do you know that I don't?"

"Is there anything you don't know?" I countered.

"Don't be rude," the Old Man chided. "I was being serious."

"So was I," I told him. "Everything I know, you taught me."

"I wouldn't say that at all," the Old Man said. "An old codger can learn an awful lot of things from a kid. Except you're coming on for not being a kid any more. Seems to me you grow a foot a week."

"I seem to be mighty hungry all the time," I admitted, laughing. "Somehow or other, I never get enough to eat. You suppose I got a tapeworm?"

"Wouldn't think it likely. You couldn't eat enough for both of you. Stop fooling around and tell me something. Out of all the stuff I've rubbed off on you, what stuck the most?"

"Serious?"

"Serious."

"You'll laugh."

"I won't laugh. When did I ever? Out of place, I mean."

"All right, sir. Politeness."

"Politeness?"

"Yessir. And I bet you don't even know this about yourself. Everything we ever did together was mainly based on politeness."

The Old Man whistled. "Well, damn me," he said, and lit his pipe. "Proceed to inform me."

"I don't want to sound like Sunday school, but——"

"You couldn't ever sound like Sunday school," he interrupted. "You haven't spent that much time in it. I'll tell you one thing I've learned about boys before you continue. A boy who says he cut Sunday school to visit a graveyard because of its archeological importance is either going to be a chronic liar or a man of great vision. Proceed."

"It was a nice day, and I kind of like graveyards," I said. "Better than Sunday school. They're more cheerful. But if you still want to listen, what I was going to say is this:

"You taught me never to holler at another man's dog. You taught me never to hog a shot at a bird. You taught me that there isn't anybody who doesn't feel like he's a person too. I'm specially thinking about the colored people, like Aunt Florence Hendricks and Albert Grey and Mary Millett and Abner McCoy —all the people that let us shoot their quail and kind of look after us when we're in their neighborhood. I ain't speaking about 'yessir,' and 'please,' and 'thank you, ma'am,' and taking off hats and bowing and scraping, and children-will-be-seen-and-not-heard-at-the-table sort of things. But what I mean is I never saw you mean to anybody, including fice dogs, even including that Willie-off-the-pickle-boat you hit in the chin and knocked off the dock that day."

"That was a kind of special day," the Old Man murmured sheepishly. "A man hadn't ought to let his temper rule him. But I'd knock him off the same dock again, beggin' your pardon, and knock him further."

"You remember the time you whipped me for not fighting Wendell Newton?"

"That I do," the Old Man said. "I warmed your tail for fair, and I'd do that again too. Because you got up and beat the tar out of Wendell Newton, and have been fast friends since, with no worries about whether you're a coward or not. A lath on the tail has a certain importance in its place and time. Everything has its importance in its place and in its time. Including cussing. Sometimes you cuss and sometimes you don't. Sometimes you fight and sometimes you don't. You got to know when to pick your spots."

"How do you know when to pick your spots?"

"I dunno. I reckon you got your finger on it—politeness. When politeness gets infringed on, somebody's wrong, you or the other guy, and it calls for a fight, whether you're using words or fists."

"You'd be embarrassed," I admitted, "if I told you all the things you taught me. It'd get to sound like a lecture."

"Don't tell me," the Old Man said. "Just think about them, if they make you comfortable. I'm sorry I brought the whole thing up. The one thing I wanted to make out of you, apart from you not blowing your foot off with a shotgun, was a non-noble character. Our nation is afflicted with nobility, everybody wanting to reform somebody else.

"I take a little nip from time to time against the agues and aches, but your grandma thinks it's sinful, even though she'll take a little nip herself if she figures she's sick enough. But when I do it for fun, it's wrong, automatic. There ain't really a reason why anything that's fun ought to be wrong, but women are queer critters. I reckon you couldn't hardly call 'em human, but in the end they're necessary, or we wouldn't be here. But this is a distraction. What I had in mind was a simple injunction: don't be noble. It's wrecking the country."

"What's noble?" I asked.

"Well, it used to mean other things," the Old Man said. "It meant a man of gentle birth, which is to say gentleman, which is to say somebody whose papa had enough money so's he didn't have to soil his hands with toil. It was a part political, a part heredity, and a lot of who had what, such as more pigs than the next lad in the bog. Then it got degraded down to a mental level, with people thinking they were better than other people, due to having more pigs. Then they get a stern look on their faces and an urge to reform people who ain't as noble as they are, and bimeby somebody shoots 'em—somebody who ain't noble, I mean—and it all comes down to pigs. Do you follow me?"

"No. I ain't that noble."

"I see," he went on, "that you have picked up two deplorable habits from me—the use of the word 'ain't' and occasional flights of sheerest honesty. This will make you no friends, either, but will probably keep you from getting shot because of undue nobility. Are you tired of this?"

"Yessir," I said. "To be downright honest, you left me somewhere about halfway between Knox's Farm and Shallotte. About Lockwood's Folly, I'd say."

"Now there's a man I would of liked to of knowed—Lockwood," the Old Man mused. "I use the 'liked to of knowed' advisedly. Here is a man with a home on a crick and an urge to see the ocean in his own boat. So he spends years building the boat, and the boat is so fine and big he can't get it under the bridge on the crick, and it draws too much water anyhow; so he becomes immortal. They named the crick Lockwood's Folly. Such," he sighed, "is the material of which fame is constructed."

"How did we get started on this?" I asked.

"I don't really know," the Old Man replied. "I think I asked you an academic question, and got very little in the way of an answer. Something about politeness or some such. You wouldn't care to sneak into the attic, taking pains not to be seen by your grandmother, and get our fishing tackle, would you?"

"Yessir."

"That's what I like," the Old Man said. "A nice, polite boy who says 'yessir' to his elders. So many other boys would have said, 'No, sir. I want to go to Sunday school.'"

"It *is* Sunday, you know," I reminded him.

"If we play our cards right," the Old Man said, "we can get back in time for dinner, and tell Miss Lottie we went to church. Being noble, despite my warnings, has a certain amount of practical value, especially on Sunday morning when the fish are biting." He winked. "If we get caught, we can always tell her we went to the graveyard to study the archeological significance of early North Carolina tombs."

26

Christmas Always Comes Too Soon, Which Is Ungruntling

The Old Man squinted at the sunny summer day, the washed sky lightly fleeced with cloud. He filled his pipe and lit it with great care. Then he puffed it into strong coal and pointed the stem at me.

"I don't care very much for you today," he said.

"What have I done bad now?"

"Nothing," the Old Man answered. "But you will. And that's got nothing whatsoever to do with the reason I'm not particularly fond of you today."

The Old Man raised me to be polite; so I was polite. "Why?" I asked.

"Because you're a boy," the Old Man said. "And I am an old man. And there are days when an old man looks at a boy and realizes what it is like to be a boy. And that makes the old man mad, because he can't ever be a boy any more."

Privately I reckoned that this was as useless a piece of confab as the Old Man ever unloaded. I didn't say anything at all.

"It's envy, of course," the Old Man said. "Just pure jealousy slightly complicated with rheumatism, sciatica, and the knowledge that all roads point only to the grave. I apologize for bringing up the subject. But I would like to leave you with one thought: Don't look forward to next Christmas. You'll just be six months older, and you can't get those six months back. And try to train yourself to milk the most out of any experience you're having at the moment, whether it's being kept after school or having the measles. Most of the things you do, you do only once, the right way, including whooping cough. I'll see you around."

The Old Man stuck his pipe in his mouth and stumped off. He was seldom if ever surly, but he was plainly what he called "ungruntled" today. He hadn't been really well for a long time, and I guess being sick was riding his nerves pretty hard.

All of a sudden I felt mighty miserable. You know how it is when you get used to a person—you can't see them change—and I was so used to the Old Man it never occurred to me that he was getting older all the time, and feebler, and maybe a little bit crankier. But now I watched him walking down the street, and he walked slower, and his feet sort of dragged, and his shoulders hunched more, and the thought suddenly struck me: He's getting *old* and so am I. It had never occurred to me, in a life where I waited for school to close, or Christmas to come, or the bird season to open, that I was merely marking time between one date and another, and wasting the hours in between. It never occurred to me that as the Old Man got older, so did I. All of a sudden the sun wasn't quite so bright, the sky was not so lovingly lined with soft cloud.

The Old Man used to say that most people looked but never saw anything. "Most people go through life," he told me once, "stone-blind with their eyes wide open. Anything from a chinch bug to a clam is interesting if you will really look at it and think about it." I was now beginning to understand what he meant.

I dived under the house and got the oars. I went to the attic and collected the cast net and a light fishing rod and the tackle box. I shouldered the lot and headed for the river. It never occurred to me that everything I did was dictated by something the old gent had told me. "Son," he would say, "when your heart is sick and you got some thinking to do, there ain't no substitute for a boat and a fish pole. Water eases the mind, soothes the eyes, calms the nerves, and you can always eat the fish."

I got into the boat and rowed out across the channel, the sun sparkling off the jolly little wind-tossed wavelets, and the smell of salt water and steaming marsh strong in my nose.

I don't know if you've ever been lucky enough to smell a salt mud marsh on a fresh summer's day, but this here Chanel No. 5 I read about can't smell near as good as just plain channel with the wind blowing off the marshes, fetching the smell of mud with a little bit of the cedars and cypress that line a sound mixed up in sun and grass and plain old mud full of sand-fiddler holes, oyster beds, and rotting clams. I never thought too much about a marsh, but it's really the richest piece of real estate in the world.

The life you don't see that goes on in a marsh is fantastic. There are little dark brown—almost black—marsh rabbits frisking about, and if you plod through the mud to a high hummock and turn a fice dog loose he will run any amount of rabbits past you. The quiet mink is hunting, stealthy as a serpent, and only once in a while you may see him swimming, making a tiny bow wave and leaving a neat and ripply wake behind him.

What I loved to hear was the bongo booming of the bitterns you never saw, and the cawing of the crows, and the occasional shrill scream of a lesser hawk as it swooped low and graceful over the tips of grass, looking, always looking, for something to swoop on and seize. The yellow-green of the marsh was spotted with great white herons, blue herons, and a rather droopy-looking heron we called a "cranky." The brilliant red epaulets of the blackbirds looked like rubies scattered in the grasses.

In the clear ponds the summer ducks paddled and dived, and the tiny didappers went under for unbelievable lengths of time. A long time ago I had given up shooting grebes and mergansers. They weren't any good to eat and no fun to shoot, and anyhow I'd rather watch them.

The sandpipers walked high-stilted along the edges of the sand bars, full of jerky dignity, and two oyster birds flew low along the water, big-billed and curious.

Just off the sand bars, in the mud, I drove an oar into the bottom and tethered my boat to it. Then I took the cast net and waded around until I saw a school of shrimp making little pops of water; two casts got me four or five dozen baits. A school of mullet was jumping—rather big ones, ten, twelve inches long—and the cast net took care of supper, even if I had no luck with the rod.

It was the time of year for soft crab, and I found half a dozen with my feet. A boy with nimble toes will always stumble over a clam or so, and by the time I got ready to unleash the boat, I had it pretty well stocked with crabs and kicking shrimp and mullet and big, blue-purple, white-lipped clams.

Don't let anybody kid you about a fishing hole. You can throw a bait all day long in ordinary water and get nothing but exercise, but if you know a deep sinkhole or an old wreck or some barnacled pilings, according to what you're looking for in the way of fish, you've got it fixed when you first drop your line. I rowed the little skiff to a hole I knew that was as certain a source of supply as a deep freezer, which had not at that time been invented. This hole was populous with blackfish and perch and an occasional trout—nothing grand, maybe, but powerful nice for the pan. I fished as happy as a boxful of birds for two hours, and filled the crocus sack I kept tied over the stern of the little boat. A half-pound of fish on a tiny rod seemed as big as a marlin in those days, and a two-pound weakfish was a whale.

In the boat's locker I always kept a frying pan, some cornmeal, salt, pepper, and vinegar. Driftwood was no problem on a sand bar, and I had myself a North Carolina approximation of a shore dinner when the fish quit biting and my stomach started to growl. There is nothing really wrong with soft-shell crabs, fresh clams, and fish that don't stop kicking until they feel the flame, not if you are a boy and starving and all by yourself in a boundless burning sweep of sand and marsh and sky and water.

When I washed the skillet clean with sand and salt water, wiped the grease off my hands and face, stomped out the fire, and got back into the boat, the tide was running strongly out, and shoving the skiff along was a job for a whole set of galley slaves. The sun was hitting like it always hits around three or four, hotter than the noonday sun, and by the time I got back to the shingle I was pouring sweat.

It was a simple enough matter to drag the boat up on the shingle and then walk down to the pier for a fast jump into the water. When I collected what was left of the fish and clams and crabs and shouldered the oars and the rowlocks and the cast net, I was just about barely able to make it to the house.

The Old Man was sitting on the porch, smoking his pipe and rocking gently in his favorite chair. He looked like he felt better. He looked younger. "What you been doing?" he asked unnecessarily.

"I went out in the boat," I said. "I went fishing."

"See anything interesting you want to tell me about?" he asked.

"Nothing very much," I said. "It was just the same old thing, marsh, water, fish, birds—same old thing."

"I am not being rude when I call you a little liar," the Old Man said. "It is a term of respect, not to say endearment. I apologize for this morning all over again, and I am no longer jealous of you because I am not a boy. Go wash the mud off you and come to supper. We're having steak, as I figgered you've had a bait of fish for one day."

The Old Man smiled. "I really wouldn't want to be a boy again," he said. "It's too much work."

27

Terrapin Stew Costs Ten Bucks
a Quart

"Things," the Old Man said, "certainly ain't like they used to be. It's the penalty we pay for getting wise. About the time a man decides what he likes or don't like, either he can't find it, can't afford it, or can't handle it. I can sum it all up with the diamondback terrapin."

"Yessir," I said politely. It was September, and we were just setting around waiting for the moon to full so the tides would rise and give us some marsh-hen shooting. There isn't much else to shoot in September but doves, marsh hen, and the odd squirrel, but the leaves are too thick on the squirrel trees, and it's a little bit too hot to shoot doves.

"All the wisdom of the world is centered in the diamond·

back," the Old Man said. "If you ain't too busy, I will proceed to elucidate."

"I ain't too busy," I said. "School hasn't even started yet, and there's too many snakes in the woods to train the puppies. Pray do proceed," I said, and snickered. I had got a wayward *ain't* mixed up with some of the Old Man's occasional high-flung phrases.

"Well, even today, as poor as everybody is, with the depression and all, a terrapin stew costs you ten dollars a quart. In a hotel it'll cost you three-fifty a plate if you can get it at all. This means that I couldn't buy it, even if I could eat it. And I can't eat it, because it's too rich, for one thing, and another reason is that you have to make it with a decent sherry wine. With this goldanged Prohibition, you can't get any decent sherry wine. And if you could buy it, the doctors say it would be bad for my blood pressure or something. So between scarcity, poverty, Prohibition, and the gout, I am not a candidate for any terrapin stew. It shows you the futility of living too long."

The Old Man heaved a sigh.

"Boy, you know you're getting old when you start saying, 'Things ain't like they used to be.' But you're right, every time. Because things *ain't* like they used to be. There was a time when I was younger a Nigra never came out of a marsh without half a bushel of terrapin he'd dug out of holes, and he'd be happy to sell them for a nickel apiece—cows, that is. They are bigger than the bulls. Cows run about seven inches, and it takes them nine years to mature. Bulls never run more than about five inches across the belly shell, so the colored people would sell them for three cents. Now they get from three to five dollars for a grown terrapin, just because they got fished out in the nineties. Every rich politician that ever threw a dinner had to have terrapin as a staple."

The Old Man sighed again.

"I used to go up to Maryland to visit your Uncle Howard, when he had a lot of money and was consorting with governors and breeding horses. Seems like we never had but one type of dinner. After the early whisky they brought you Chincoteague oysters as big as a wharf rat. Then they laid on the terrapin stew. Then they fed you breasts of canvasback duck with stripes of red ham, and from there you went to the brandy and the cigars. I say canvasbacks, because you could buy a brace of four-pounders for two bits. It would have been an insult to feed a guest anything but cans, unless mebbe once in a while pintail. But now you're hard put to find a canvasback. The meat gunners shot 'em out because they were so popular."

"How did they shoot them?" I asked. "I mean how would you shoot them to sell for the pot?" I was always more interested in techniques than in the Old Man's philosophy. But I got pretty philosophic myself. I knew I couldn't have the one without holding still for the other.

"Well, they used punt guns, for one thing. They would take a flat-bottomed boat and secure a smoothbore cannon to her bows. They would load the cannon to the gunnels with anything you could imagine, from nails to stones to bullets. Then they would wait for a big freeze-up, so the ducks were rafted in little pools in the marsh, surrounded by paper-thin ice. They would go out at night, poling through the ice, and come up on a pool which would be jammed with ducks. They'd let fly with the punt gun, and the punt would jump, and there would be two score or more of dead ducks in the pool.

"Then, of course, they'd bait blinds, and then use hens to call in the high-flyers. The hen would stand on her tail and let out a chuckle-chuckle, and the men ducks would come down in swarms, and the pot hunters would loose off with 10-bores. Ducks used to be a lot stupider in those days, because there were more of them and fewer people were shootin' at 'em. Wild-fowl was standard on any two-bit hotel menu. But we ate better in and around Baltimore than any place else I was ever at. It was a big part German, and Germans take a powerful fancy to their vittles."

"How did you cook the terrapins?"

"There was a lot of ways, but I still like the Maryland way

best. Saying you got two mature terrapins—and can afford them —you would get a pint, more or less, of meat. You pop in a pound of butter and a couple pints of Jersey cream, throw in a big slug of sherry and some seasoning, bring her to a boil—and, son, that is a stew that makes my gouty foot hurt just to think of it. They talk about turtle soup and stuff. Nobody ever touched terrapin for flavor and substance."

"How did you find them in the old days?" I asked. "Could I maybe find some now?"

"Not here, I reckon. They seem to have gone away. But away back yonder they had little feisty dogs they called terrapin hounds. They used to get them in the winter, because terrapins burrow in the mud and hibernate just like a bear sleeps away the cold months in a cave. They leave a little air hole in the mud, and dogs could spot it. This ain't surprising if you remember how many times you've seen a good bird dog false-point on a horse-turd terrapin or a snake. They got a definite musty smell. Then the darkies would dig 'em out and sell them. When I was a boy, in the slave days, seems to me I recollect they fed terrapin to the slaves because there is some sort of superstition that terrapins encourage breeding. Whether's anything to it, I couldn't say."

Being what used to be popularly known as a greedygut, I saw I had the Old Man going on food, and wished to keep him on the skillet and out of philosophy.

"Tell me some more about the olden days," I said. "What else was easy to eat that you can't get much of now?"

"Well, I never ate any buffalo hump, because that was before my time, and I got a hunch it was overrated. Also we never had too many buffalo in these parts. But I reckon you would have to go a far piece to beat quail on toast for breakfast, just the breasts of course, and a broiled soft-shell crab ain't exactly obnoxious. Today you can't buy quail except illegal. In the old times they didn't shoot them. They trapped them, and you weren't always digesting a No. 8 shot.

"I never ate any plover's eggs or hummingbird tongues, or anything fancy like that, but if you cook a rabbit right, it's hard to beat for tasty provender. I like 'em both better than venison, no matter how much wine and butter you shove into the saddle. To me the best venison is fresh-killed, with the chops and the liver broiled over hickory coals, when you're tired and hungry and just getting warm in front of the fire, after a couple of taps at the jug. Somehow venison in a hotel seems a little bit wicked. A deer don't belong in a hotel, dead or alive, but it was a poor hotel that couldn't give you the whole list of wild stuff, including bear steaks."

"What else?"

"Well, I suppose you know I fancy a little piece of whisky once in a while. Before that *man* Volstead put his act in, a man could buy a decent bottle of whisky for about a dollar, and if he drank in a saloon, he could get himself a shot of bonded stuff in quiet, refined surroundings, without any women in the bar, for ten cents. Not like this white poison they age with brown sugar and sell in fruit jars. A decent red whisky was a comfort to a man instead of an enemy. And the beer come honest out of a bung on a keg that the beer had got friendly with. It cost a nickel, and the free lunch was unlimited."

"I never heard of free lunch," I said. "What was it all about?"

"Free lunch was an invention of the angels, thought up by honest bartenders to encourage the purchase of beer and to prevent drunkenness in the clients, so they could buy more beer without making a nuisance out of themselves. When I was a younker a man with two nickels could feed like a king. The bartender was a little suspicious if you dug into the grub on the strength of one beer, but when you bellied up and ordered the second, you were a guest of the house and could eat your head off."

"What did they give you?"

The Old Man smiled wistfully, then blissfully licked his lips.

"Everything," he said. "There would be a big glass crock of pickled pig's feet, and a wooden pair of scissors to fish them out of the brine with. There would be a bowl of hard-boiled eggs, naturally, and another bowl of raw onions. Some barkeeps fancied hot roast beef, others liked cold tongue or cold beef, but they all competed to see who set out the best free lunch. There was usually a big loaf of salami, a bowl of mulligan, and nearly anything the Germans liked—sardines, herring, and all sorts of cheeses. A man drinking whisky could run the course. A man drinking beer had to pace himself a little, so the beer could keep up with the vittles.

"When Prohibition come, and they started making this needle beer and inventing whisky in the barn and sending people blind with the staggers, the country died. Whisky, legal, might come back some day, but I vow there won't be any more free lunch to go with it. Things won't ever be like they used to be."

"What went wrong with it all?" I asked.

"They shot off the buffalo, and they meat-hunted the game. They slaughtered the wildfowl, and they give the vote to the women. The women stirred up a ruckus about their menfolks spending too much time in the saloons, and so they got Prohibition and handmade corn whisky and what they call 'speak-easies' in the cities, where you can drink gin that was made out of embalming fluid and go blind for twice the price. They invented the automobile and the airy-o-plane and speeded everything up. They got mixed up in other people's wars and got to betting on the stock market and altogether they're in a hell of a mess. And *no* free lunch."

"Any cure for it?"

"Not much," the Old Man said. "People ain't like they used to be, either. A bunch of smart alecks, running around in circles like beheaded chickens, dancing the Charleston, and raising hell in general. They tell me some fellows won't dance with a girl without she takes her corsets off."

"I wouldn't know about that," I said. "But I do know I'm hungry, and that moon tells me tomorrow's high tide, and we'll be up early. Let's go down to Pete's and get a hamburger or something."

The Old Man spat.

"A *hamburger*," he said, as if it was a cuss word. "A *hamburger*, at my age. Like I said, things ain't like they used to be. But I suppose from some standpoints, they never were."

"I ain't been feeling so good lately," the Old Man said to me one day. "I think I need a change of air. I think I need to go to Baltimore for a physical check-up at Johns Hopkins. At my age a feller can't be too mindful of his health. And anyhow, Howard writes that the pheasant season is going to open next week. If you was to play your cards right I might talk your ma into forgiving you a week of school and take you with me. We can drive her easy in a day."

I had been driving the car for quite a spell now, although I wasn't old enough for a license, and nothing could have pleased me better than the idea of (1) missing a week of school, (2) shooting some pheasants, and (3) seeing some fresh real estate. The Old Man was always talking about Maryland, and he made it sound like the Promised Land. His friend, Mister Howard, had this big horse farm up in the Blue Ridge foothills, and from all I could gather from the tall talk, the pheasants and quail just about beat you to death when you got off the back porch.

The Old Man made some hocus-pocus with my ma, and somebody called school and got me paroled for a week, and we set off on my first big safari. You'd of thought we were going to Africa, instead of just Baltimore. We had a lunch packed, and the guns stowed, and road maps, and all sorts of clutter. I was strong for taking our dogs, but the Old Man, he said no, Howard had more dogs than he knew what to do with, and ours would just add to the confusion.

We set bravely off in the Liz, hoping she'd hold together, but glad we had a car of her virgin determination, because good roads were scarce in those days, and that Virginia red clay as you approach Fredericksburg and Richmond was a caution. Fortunately it was dry enough, but it rained on the way back, and it was as greasy as lard and twice as slippery.

It was a handsome piece of country then, with very few roadside advertisements to wreck the beauty of the rolling green hills, dark forests, and mile after mile of golden farmland. After you got out of Washington, heading toward Baltimore, it got prettier and prettier as it got hillier. Thinking back, Maryland looked more like a classic slice of English countryside than a classic slice of English countryside actually looks today. It was horsy country, and nearly every big holding had literally miles of white rail fences, with neat paddocks and immaculate barns and outhouses. The houses didn't just sit up naked in a flat piece of land, like they did in Carolina, but were kind of folded into the hills, and peeped through from thick trees. The miles of rolling pasture were either golden with wheat or brilliant, golf-course green—dotted here and there by golden or black-and-white cattle or grazing red horses.

Maryland was one of our very earliest "civilized" states, I suppose, and the English who followed the Calverts had plenty of time—and not too many angry Injuns—to make it into a graceful replica of what they remembered back home in England. And to a kid accustomed to live-oak and cyprus swamps, and clean-swept sand for front yards, and low, marshy mosquito-and-sandspur country, this was a picture-book adventure.

We stopped in Baltimore long enough for the Old Man to make his hospital arrangements, and then we went to some restaurant he seemed to know pretty well. He fished his greasy old wallet out of his pocket, thumbed through some bills, and nodded.

"You remember what I told you about terrapin stew and canvasback duck?" he said. "Well, it'll nigh break us, but I aim to have us a bait. Might be the last I'll have. It ain't on the menu, but if I know anything about this place, they'll have a duck or so on ice and some cooters in a barrel hid out in the yard."

He called the gray-haired Negro waiter, and whispered something, and I could see a bill pass and a flash of white teeth.

"Yassuh, *boss*," he said, and went flat-footed away. The Old Man grinned.

"I dearly love money," he said. "It'll get you so many pleasant things, and you don't have to rely on friendship. I took one look at that waiter and just naturally assumed that although that such-and-so of a Volstead run that Prohibition abomination through, they hadn't quit making red licker in Maryland. The grass here is just too good and the water too fine to pay any attention to the likes of Volstead. You're getting on to be a big boy, and I want you started off right on this grog business. What you are going to have is a proper Maryland old-fashioned, made with proper Maryland rye. We are going to have some sherry in the stew, and we will drink a glass of Burgundy with the duck. Thank God for Lord Baltimore. He could have been a red-nosed Puritan that thinks boiled salt cod is a banquet and rum punch fit to be a table wine."

The waiter shuffled back, grinning.

"Heah yo' *tea*, boss," he said, and put down two fat square glasses with a reddish liquid in them. "We always serves *tea* in glasses heah, boss," he said. "They tells me it is the fashion in Europe." The Old Man winked and the waiter guffawed. Then the Old Man picked up his glass, sniffed, smiled, raised it in a toast, and said to me: "Drink yo' *tea*, boss," mimicking the waiter. "But sip it, don't slug it down like an ignorant tarheel from Brunswick County."

I sipped slowly on my first legal drink of illegal whisky. I had tried our local home-stomped scuppernong wine, and our local home-brew, and our local moonshine, but it was nothing like this mellow, charred-keg rye, with just a touch of bitters, a cherry, some sugar, and a slice of orange over the ice. I grinned and smacked my lips. The Old Man looked stern.

"You hold in your hand," he said, "man's best friend and worst enemy, depending on how you use him. He's been a firm friend of mine for over fifty years, but I never saw too much of him. Any friendship goes sour if you overdo it."

The waiter brought the terrapin stew, so hot it bubbled in the dish, and I won't even try to describe what can be done with butter, terrapin eggs, sherry, Jersey cream, and clear terrapin meat. Then the waiter brought in a brace of canvasback. "These powerful unusual *chicken*, boss," he said. He fetched a bottle of what I can only describe as another kind of tea, except this was red in color, and might have been described as having been made from grapes. I was in a state of complete contentment when we finished the coffee and headed in the direction of Ellicott City. The Old Man was driving, and it seemed to me that the Liz rambled a little.

I was sound asleep when we arrived at Mister Howard's place, and they just slung me into bed. I was lost for a minute when I woke up with vestiges of my first hang-over. I washed my face in the basin and put on some clothes and found my way downstairs. The Old Man and Mister Howard were already working on breakfast. They looked almost like twins as they shoved eggs and bacon past the same kinds of ragged mustaches. Mister Howard stood up and shook hands and laughed.

"You sure have come on since that last camping trip we made," he said. "Ned says you were pretty far gone in drink when you arrived last night. I thought it was for the young folks to put the old folks to bed, not the other way round."

"I was tired," I said defensively. "It was a long day."

"Well, have some breakfast," Mister Howard said, "and I'll show you around the place. And I wouldn't be surprised, if we had the foresight to take a dog or so and a gun, we might manage to produce a pheasant for you."

I gobbled some food and went to look at the house. Dimly remembered, it was the kind of house which was too good for women, if you know what I mean. Mister Howard came from an Irish aristocracy which thought horses and guns were more important than anything else in the world. The rooms were huge and filled with horse prints and hunting scenes, plus a few family portraits. The women were all pretty and the gentlemen all looked very well fed.

The sideboards and glass cases were filled with stuffed birds, everything from pheasants to orioles to quail to turkeys. The walls were dotted with foxes' masks and brushes, because this was prime fox-hunting country. There were portraits of horses and cows and bulls receiving blue ribbons, because Mister Howard's blooded stock committed suicide if it failed to hit a blue.

Everywhere you looked there was riding tackle—saddles and boots, surcingles, crops, spurs. The leather gear was old and mellow, as mellow as the hand-waxed floors. There was a wonderful smell of good pipe tobacco, saddle wax, and oily guns, and an even better smell of ancient leather-bound books, which were shoved by the hundreds into cases which covered whole walls.

There were guns everywhere—Revolutionary muskets, dueling pistols, modern rifles and shotguns, hung on the walls in brackets or standing in corners or lying in red-plush-lined cases in the halls. I remember that next to some of the guns and china figurines there were great flat silver bowls full of flowers, red and yellow roses mostly. The chairs, except for the polished mahogany of the dining room suite, were all of leather, deep, rump-sprung, broad-armed easy chairs and vast divans, some maroon, some deep forest green, some honest black.

Everything in that house had been lovingly used for generations—the heavy, worn silver table service, the old Wedgwood plates, the boots, the saddles, the guns, and the books—especially the books. There wasn't a book on the wall, whether it had to do with stock registration or the novels of Ouida, *Black Beauty* or the complete set of Dickens, that hadn't been rubbed smooth by handling.

In the center of each room was a fireplace a tall man could walk into, with enormous wrought-iron dog-irons and fireboxes and hobs to hold great kettles. Every bed I ever saw upstairs was a four-poster big enough for four people, and there was a fireplace in every room, including the bathroom. The tub, I recall, was an enormous thing, with the ceramic set into a huge walnut coffin sort of arrangement. The accompanying sanitary utensil was similarly set into walnut, with a removable bottom, such as today are expensively used to make liquor cabinets.

Outside, there seemed to be six acres of flowers, even though it was autumn. The green meadows rolled as far as the eye could see, until they hit the haze of the Blue Ridge. Streams cut through the pasture and paddocks, twisting silver threads among the green of the clovered paddocks, and accented, from time to time, by copses of trees.

The barns were a jolly hunting-coat red, and every fence was a glistening white, as clean as a dogtooth. There seemed to be about two acres of fowlyard alone, cut into littler paddocks, one for chickens, one for turkeys, one for ducks, another for pheasant, another for guinea fowl. Big black-and-white Holsteins and Jerseys the color of their own cream were in the milch-cow paddocks. The saddle stock was also confined, sixteen-hands-high Irish jumpers, but afar, in the vaster areas, barrel-bellied mares nudged their high-stilted colts, and yearlings gamboled like lambs. The breeding studs were in loose boxes with small yards, and the beef cattle, white-faced Herefords, roamed to the horizon.

Everywhere you looked there was a dog run. Hounds of all shapes and descriptions—bassets, beagles, Walkers. Spaniels, mostly springers but for a gross or so of golden cockers. Labradors—for this was duck country, down to the Eastern Sho'—and pointers and setters in legions. They set up a clamor fit to wake the dead as we passed, Mister Howard beating his riding boots with his crop.

The sky was a clear, sparkling blue, with a hint of cloud, and the morning frost had melted under the friendly sun. A small breeze stirred the trees. A quail called, and there was the harsh squawk of a pheasant. A horse whinnied, a cow lowed, and the dogs barked. Mister Howard pointed to a big black Gordon setter, and then to a husky black-and-white springer. "We'll just take Mac and Sue," he said. "Mac's the Gordon, of course. Between them, they invented pheasants. Get your gun and we'll put some meat in the pot. That is, of course, if you haven't lost interest in hunting?"

I declared firmly that the interest was undamaged, and I made a private reservation to have a house and property like that some day. Of course I never did, and never will, but in a way it's as well. For I can remember the house, and no pipes ever burst in my remembered house, no bank ever forecloses a mortgage, nobody ever dies, and no stranger buys the books and guns and saddles and beasts at a knockdown auction.

I still have clear title to the sight of the two old men, as we followed Mac and Sue over an undulating pasture toward a patch of bush where there would just naturally have to be a big, fat, sassy green-headed pheasant with my name on his tail.

28

But Not on Opening Day

Now you know your first big cock pheasant is a sight to see. There maybe ain't nothing as dramatic, whether it's an elephant or a polar bear. A cock pheasant is like a mallard duck. Maybe the pintail or the canvasback is better to eat, but there is nothing in the flying department as wonderfully gaudy as a cock pheasant or a he-mallard. Well, *maybe* a peacock, but we have so few peacocks around our neck of the woods.

You take a big cock pheasant, and you shoot him, you got a real bird in your hand. He'll weigh about four pounds, and he has this lovely long tail, and he has a ring on his neck, and he is colored green and red and brown and white, and he even has ears you can see. He is not so much dinner as trophy, but when he is cooked correctly, he is not so much trophy as dinner, if you see what I mean.

Mister Howard, he said to me after we quit looking around his farm in Maryland, "You don't want to make any mistakes about pheasants, boy. He looks like he is two yards long, and he looks mighty slow. But when you subtract his neck and his tail you are shooting at a pretty small target. He flies faster than a bobwhite, or so I'm told, and he sheds shot like a duck. I'd lead him pretty far and then double it. No man ever killed a cock pheasant by shooting it in the tail. All you get that way is feathers."

I can skip telling you about the first pheasant, since he is still alive, so far as I know. Mac, the Gordon setter, rounded him up for me in a patch of bush. He had a bell on his neck—Mac, I mean—and we heard it stop tinkling when he went into some scraggy sumach. Then he came out and kind of beckoned with his head.

"Got a bird," Mister Howard said. "You stand over there, and I'll put Sue on the flank and send Mac into the bush to flush him. If he tries to run, Sue'll nail him." Sue was a big springer who had a kind of casual air of saying, *What do we need a gun for, when we got me and Mac?*

The Old Man nodded at Mister Howard and winked when the Gordon setter dived back into the bush. I reckon the old boy knew what was going to happen.

There was an outraged squawk inside the brambles, a rapid beating of wings, and something—it might have been a bird or possibly the Graf Zeppelin—erupted in my general direction. It seemed to be less than a hundred yards long, and I could swear it was not actually breathing fire. Otherwise I never saw such a production in my life.

I shot at this thing twice, and it went away with very little damage, although one tail feather got dislodged, very possibly due to the imminence of the moulting season, or something.

Mister Howard looked at me while I was breaking the gun to recharge it.

"I told you," he said. "They ain't really that big. You just figure that you're shooting a teal, and we might eat tonight. Lead it. *Lead* it."

We walked across a meadow, were snubbed by several cows, and Sue, the springer, wagged her tail assembly and then fell on her belly. Mac, the Gordon, took a wide cast and came up in front of her, about fifty yards away.

"Now watch this," Mister Howard said. "You just stand behind Sue. I'll call Mac in, and he'll drive that bird right into Susie's nose. A pheasant ain't dumb. With Mac behind him and Sue in front of him and us here with weapons, he'll fly. But he'll fly slanchwise. To your left. And *lead* him. Three times his length, anyhow."

Mac came mincing in, putting his feet in front of him pad by pad. I looked at the ground ahead of me, wanting to see the pheasant before he flew.

"You *know* better than that," the Old Man said. "I *taught* you better than that. You look at the air where the bird's going to be when he jumps. What kind of raisin' will Howard think you've had?"

It was indeed a sight I never wish to forget. Mac came in so close that he was nearly rubbing noses with Sue. Somewhere in between a big green-headed cock pheasant jumped, squawked, and took off, like Mister Howard said, to the left. I hauled the gun ahead of him and squeezed off, and down he came like an aircraft, almost in flames. Sue went over and picked him up gently, fetched him to Mister Howard, reared with her front paws on his coat, and dropped the bird into his hand.

"Nice shooting," Mister Howard said. "You led that one, didn't you?"

"Yessir," I said. "May I touch him, please?"

"I forgot," Mister Howard said to the Old Man, handing me the pheasant. "I forgot how big a first pheasant is to a boy. It's kind of like an early squirrel. He is a little bit larger than a later lion."

If Christmas came on the Fourth of July and it also happened to be your birthday, you might have some idea of what a first pheasant is like on a clear, crisp Maryland day, with the hills behind, and the tender-green meadows reaching out to black-green blotches of trees, and nothing very much to do but watch a couple of expert dogs work over the noblest Oriental stranger we have in our midst, while two mellowed old gentlemen do not interfere with a boy's passionate effort. They were not shooting; they had been there before. It took me another thirty years to find out how much fun you have *not* shooting if there is somebody else around who wants to shoot it more than you do.

On this day I wanted to shoot it more than they did, and they knew it, and I think possibly the dogs knew it. They were working for me like I was a corporation or something. It was a conspiracy, the two Old Men and the dogs working to teach me the pheasant business.

One thing happened I want to tell you about. I winged a bird, and it flew into the side of a hill. There was a hole, like a little cave, in the side of the hill. The big Gordon, Mac, tiptoed gently on a narrow ledge until he got to where he could see inside the hole in the hill. He dabbed tentatively with his paw and found it dangerously awkward. He then walked backward, gingerly, until he achieved wider ground. Then he raced over the top of the hill until he came to the ledge on the other side of the hole.

This was a broader ledge. He walked now with assurance. He came up to the hole, and he clawed in it with his right forefoot, and he brushed the bird out of the hole. The bird was still very much alive.

Mac took the bird in his mouth and backed carefully down the ledge until it widened into a safe position. Then Mac released the pheasant, which tumbled down the hill. Mac slid down the hill on his backside, the bird scrambling along beside him. They reached the base of the hill together. Mac pounced on the bird, cracked its neck with one bite, picked it up gently, and fetched it to Mister Howard. Mac—believe me, it's true—

shrugged his shoulders, as if to say, "For heaven's sake, from now on, kill 'em clean and save me some trouble. I'm afraid of heights, and this kind of work constitutes overtime."

We had quite a day. I hit some and I missed some, until we had accumulated six cocks. Six cock pheasants are a pleasant load for a boy to sweat back to the handsomest house in Maryland. The Old Man carried my gun. I insisted on carrying the birds. When my back began to creak I wondered how it was possible to miss something so big. I have been wondering about this for several years now. It's still possible.

There have been times since when days were especially special, when the sun was bright, the breeze fresh, and the dogs and the birds motivated by a general desire to please. But I cannot confuse those days with the sort of tender, happy sadness that I garnered from the Old Man and his final pheasant hunt, with a child he had raised from a pup, in the company of his best, most trusted friend.

I suppose I had the usual insensitivity of the child to possible tragedy, but it seems to me now that the Old Man knew that he had eaten his last terrapin stew and his final canvasback, and had seen his ultimate pheasant. This may sound silly, but you could kind of see it in his mustache, which appeared a bit wilty.

We went back, three grown men together, with the pheasants. I cleaned them and felt it a pity to remove so much beauty from a bird. I felt almost like a cannibal when Mister Howard said, "Damn this business of hanging them until they're rotten, we'll eat a couple tonight. They'll be a little tough, but jelly and wine and bacon strips can do a power of good to ease up the toughness."

The fire was lit and blazing chirpily in the stone fireplace when we returned. There was a tray of drinks on the table, and the Old Man showed no hesitancy in offering me a sherry. It was Bristol Cream. I had two. I was reaching for the decanter for No. 3 when the Old Man said, gently, "Let's not overdo it, son. You can't get to be a man in a day."

It was an enchanted week we spent, before we went back to Baltimore and Johns Hopkins, to find out what the Old Man knew all along was wrong with him. We got the doctors' reports and drove home. The old man was silent for most of the way.

When we got to a place called Jackie's Creek, where we had seen turkeys and shot quail, the Old Man said, "Stop the car. I want to look at it."

When we got to a place called Allen's Creek, and Moore's Creek, he said the same thing. We stopped and we looked. The Old Man nodded his head, and said, for no reason at all that I could think of, "I'm satisfied. Nobody owes me nothin'."

We pulled up in front of the live oaks that clustered round the house. The Old Man looked at the magnolia where the mockingbird had lived, and smiled.

"It'll last," he said. "It's a very durable tree."

We accepted congratulations freely for a safe return trip, and then the Old Man said, "Let's take a little walk and let the womenfolk get over their excitement. I got a thing or two to tell you."

We strolled down the street toward the Cedar Bench, next to the pilot office, where I used to steal the cream crackers and drink the hot tea with the sickly sweet condensed milk. We sat on the Cedar Bench, uncomfortably, because it was intricately carved with everybody's jackknifed initials.

"I ain't got to tell *you* that I am going to die," the Old Man said. "*You* would know it. You've had the best of me, and you're on your own from now on. You'll go to college next year, and you'll be a man, with all a man's problems, and there won't be no Old Man around to steer you. I raised you as best I could and now *you're* the Old Man, because I'm tired, and I think I'll leave."

My eyes blurted into tears, and I said all the things young people say in the presence of death.

"Leave it. *leave* it," the Old Man said. "Like I always told you, if there was a way to beat it, I would have heard about it. It'll even happen to *you*, unlikely as it seems."

"But *how, when, why?*" I said, for lack of anything better.

The Old Man lit his pipe very carefully and grinned under his ragged mustache.

"I promise you," he said, "on my word of honor, I won't die on the opening day of the bird season."

He kept his promise.